The Path of Minor Planets

Also by Andrew Sean Greer

How It Was for Me

The Path of Minor Planets

Andrew Sean Greer

Picador USA • New York

Picador® is a U.S. registered trademark and is used by St. Martin's Press under license from Pan Books Limited.

www.picadorusa.com

Library of Congress Cataloging-in-Publication Data

Greer, Andrew Sean.
    The path of minor planets : a novel / Andrew Sean Greer.—1st ed.
      p. cm.
    ISBN 0-312-27556-0
    1. Astronomers—Fiction. 2. Friendship—Fiction. 3. Comets—Fiction. I. Title.

PS3557.R3987 P38 2001
813'.54—dc21

2001041818

First Edition: October 2001

10 9 8 7 6 5 4 3 2 1

For David

Acknowledgments

This is not a book about science. Nonetheless, the scientific elements required research, and I am especially indebted to David Levy's *The Quest for Comets* and *Observing Comets, Asteroids, Meteors, and the Zodiacal Light* (with Stephen J. Edberg); *Comet* by Carl Sagan and Ann Druyan; Patrick Moore's editions of the *Yearbook of Astronomy*; and *The Stars Are Not Enough* by Joseph C. Hermanowicz. I also spoke with scientists and their children, including Meriko Blink and my own parents, Drs. William and Sandra Greer, both trained in science but not in astronomy. I apologize if I have occasionally tinkered with the universe to suit my story.

Although numerous friends advised on the title, David Gilbert created it, and J. Robert Lennon, Alicia Paulson, Allyson Goldin, Marissa Pagano, Sandra Greer, William Greer, and Ruth Fassinger all offered careful and patients edits. Almost a third of this book was written during a summer residency at the Millay Colony for the Arts in New York, and I am grateful for that time.

My editor, Josh Kendall, pushed for this book and spent long nights working on the manuscript with me. I'm also indebted to Frances Coady at Picador USA, as well as everyone at Burnes & Clegg.

Most important, I'm grateful to Bill Clegg, not only for his tireless reading of this novel in its many forms, but for his unwavering support and friendship.

If we knew what we needed if we even knew
The stars would look to us to guide them.

W. S. Merwin

1965

near perihelion

Comets are vile stars. Every time they appear in the south, something happens to wipe out the old and establish the new.

—Li Ch'un Feng, A.D. 602–677

The sky always kept its word.

That's how she had seen things since she was a little girl. Shouts might ring inside the house and teachers in school might grade unfairly, jealous of her knowledge, but if little Denise leaned out her window, begging the San Francisco fog to clear from the cliffs, she might catch Jupiter's approach, or pluck a meteor from the night's thick hide. So she spent her nights like this, staring from her window even when the fog lay heavy across the sky and made her shiver; she still knew the stars were behind it, as always, something to count on. And as she grew up, and came to know the world a little more, she grew more and more reliant on the night sky. In high school, in college, as the other girls giggled and saw movies and went on dates, Denise instead appeared late at night at the Palomar telescope, talking to the bewildered scientists, insisting on taking a look. She often got one. You would not exactly have called it girlhood—she mooned and daydreamed through the fifties like any teenybopper, but Einstein and handsome Oppenheimer were the posters on her walls, and when she went to sleep she traveled past the Horsehead Nebula in search of quasars. She was an odd child, and became an odd young woman as she grew. Her heart had little room for anyone; it was too crammed with stars. For a long time, she took their distant heat for love.

But now, on the deck of this ferry on the South China Sea, Denise understood that what she had felt was nothing like love. At twenty-five, she had finally felt the real thing and, as often happens the first time, she had chosen badly, fallen too heavily, and lost him. His name was Carlos. It was over within six months, but the affair had burrowed much deeper than she'd first suspected. When had an astronomical mistake ever felt like this? Denise, acting out the adolescence all the other girls had long since passed through, began to skip her graduate classes, miss her meals, spending days in bed in bitter agony. It became so bad that her mother, one sunny afternoon, arrived at Denise's apartment in a green cloak and fedora, her gold hat pin glittering, bearing soft words and, hidden in her alligator purse, an airline ticket. She comforted her daughter, but when Denise saw the ticket brought out at her weakest moment, she understood two things: first, that her mother was paying her to forget Carlos, buying amnesia the way a sly tip gets a good table in a restaurant. And second, she knew she would accept.

It was a ticket to an event hosted by her professor, Dr. Swift, the famous discoverer of a comet. This year, 1965, was the year in which his comet had returned, beautifully, just as he had predicted, and to celebrate he was taking a group of colleagues and graduate students to the island where he had made his discovery. The excuse, for grant reasons, was to observe the meteor shower which, Swift also predicted, would be brightened this March by the arrival of his comet. It was already understood that these annual light shows occurred because Earth passed through the comet's path, but Swift wanted to know if the recent passage of that parent body would replenish the meteors, causing a spectacular display. He wanted fireworks to follow his comet, and he had chosen the darkest corner of the world from which to view them. The celebrity of the day—Comet Swift—lay in the eastern sky just now, hidden by sunlight, a streaming Chinese kite. It would come again in 1977, 1989, and so on.

They were on their way to that island now, on an old wooden

ferry from the mainland, braving the noonday sun that beat down on their heads like a mallet. All of the grad students—whether they luckily had been part of Swift's grant, won their own awards, or scraped together money for the trip—were huddled in the violet shade of the boat's canopy, hiding from the sun and laughing. Denise looked at them, gathered chatting together, and wondered if they had gone through what she'd felt. They were scientists, as well, passionate, arrogant. Had they grown up as stunted as she had, unable to cope when love at last approached? Or had they pruned their hearts like bonsai trees? How had they managed it?

Denise was managing by getting a little drunk. She was not used to drinking, but she'd brought a flask of bourbon along and it helped dull her mind a little. She was not what people expected of young women in 1965; her mind whirred on without her willing it. It covered every object with figures, trajectories, velocities, barnacling the world's underside with calculations. It made her brilliant, the best student on the boat, obsessive, wearing sunglasses all the time to protect her night vision, but she felt this kind of madness also spoiled life a little. She wished, at times, that she had been born with a duller mind. This blundered love affair, for instance; her brain tugged at it relentlessly, a dog with a rag.

That is how Denise, twenty-five and nearly beautiful, came to sit on a coil of ropes, her face mottled with specks of light that fell from rips in the canopy; how she came to be drunk by the time they were halfway across the water.

"Isn't this great?" she asked her friend Eli. She grinned, leaned out into the hot sun with her camera, and took a furtive picture of him writing in his book. The young man scowled, and tried to grab the camera, but she easily escaped. She had brought this to annoy him, along with an atomizer of water that she sprayed at him and his wife until Eli had to confiscate it. Ten minutes from now, he would have her camera as well.

"I don't know what's come over me, really," Denise told him merrily.

"I'd guess a fifth of bourbon. . . ."

Denise squinted under her white hat; the sun flashed like foil in the sky. She said, "Well, and who could blame me? I think I have license to drink."

"Give me a sip," he said quietly while his wife looked away. He gulped the bourbon happily, looking up at Denise. Gulls were cackling around them.

Faces are rooms, and Denise thought of her own as clean, rich, but carelessly arrayed. You might have said that, like furniture, all her best features were inheritances from her mother's French family. You could tell at a glance, though, that while women before her might have been beautiful, she hadn't any idea about how to use her looks. On her, they were fine but ordinary; she knew this, and accepted it. Denise felt she was a boarder in her own face; she leased its loveliness. What Denise had instead, of course, was her mind, and in her face you could in any moment see a thought sitting there in a chair, or in a corner, cross-legged on the tattered rug.

Denise laughed at Eli glugging her bourbon. "That's enough," she told him, grabbing the flask back and dropping it in her purse.

"Do I have to confiscate everything you have?"

She grinned and looked at him. Eli had changed so much even in the two years she'd known him: hair cut close, his goatee gone. When she first met him, in the hallway of the grad student offices, he'd seemed so long-haired and wild. His wife had smoothed him down, a young married man, like a cool bed in the morning.

"Make sure Kathy doesn't fall over," she told him and his head turned quickly to see his wife, a mysterious, bookish woman with glasses, long black hair and a slouch. She was leaning far over the railing, dropping bread into the water.

"Kathy!" he yelled, and the woman lifted her head without expression. She was too distant to hear correctly.

Denise said, "Ask her if she wants a drink."

Eli watched his wife resuming her bread-toss, and the lit quarter of his face, that crescent, was bright with fear. In a moment, he turned back, and the shadow covered his expression. "She doesn't want a drink."

"I'll ask her."

"You know they're going to take that booze away when we get there."

She raised the half-empty flask and laughed. "I'm well aware!"

The canopy cracked in the wind, changing their view of the sea and the hot lavender sky. There was no island on the horizon now, either before them or behind.

"Spray me with the water," she told him, and he took out the atomizer and did. She yelped and he smirked as the Muslim guards turned and watched.

Denise would look back, days later, on this scene when she felt dizzy, dry as tinder, sick with the waves and the way she'd let her mother buy her heart. She would look back so differently on it all—the scene on the boat would seem idyllic, sweet and bright with sun. Before the night was over, something was going to happen that would subtly change things for each of these scientists, for her and Kathy and Eli. She would think, years later, how funny it is that you can't know which moment will matter, what to pay attention to, how to pull yourself out of the muck of *now*. How could they have worried about anything except what they knew: old loves, bright stars, all that? We strain to hear the future, she would later think; we are deaf to it.

"Spray me again."

Eli did, methodically, as if he were watering a lawn, and Denise thought he looked so old, so middle-aged, as if he should be stroking a beard and smoking a pipe. Calm, serious and wise. Yet he was her age; he was twenty-five. Would he never act young at all? Or would it overcome him in a later decade, rush at him in a ball of abandon and regret? She watched him put the atomizer back in his pocket.

"Happy?" he asked.

"Hardly," she answered.

It was at this point that Eli stole her camera. She yelped, noticed the looks from the guards, and held her hand over her mouth. Kathy appeared above her, eyes large through the glasses, a cryptic smile on her pursed lips.

"Denise," Kathy said. "It's solved. I have a new man for you."

Eli's wife, quiet and small, was nonetheless intimidating. How mighty her hidden thoughts and passions were. Like some rare and intelligent species, Kathy would not be domesticated. She often disappeared for hours at dinner parties to sit on a rainy porch, read a book or go through the hostess's medicine cabinet in search of unusual drugs. Eli seemed not to notice any of this. Denise adored his wife, but was slightly scared of her, of what she might think of her own spoiled, indulgent life and mind; but Kathy, wearily misanthropic toward most of the other grad students, was kind and attentive to Denise. She called her late at night with ideas, plans for art shows they could see together, political events they could go to. Kathy treated her like a favorite, but it still surprised Denise to find that Kathy had thought of her at all.

"I don't want a man," Denise told Kathy, unsure of herself. She knew that her chest was so wide open that any man could walk inside, anyone who seemed a little kind. Her voice seemed angry, frightened.

"Well, I only said I *had* one. You don't have to take him."

Eli, looking suspicious, asked, "Who is it?"

Kathy said, "It's Adam—I don't remember his last name."

He laughed. "Oh that's rich, Kath. He's out of his mind."

"Perfect for me," Denise said. She watched Eli tilt his head to one side, raising his thick eyebrows. Sometimes, Denise thought, he could be handsome. His dark, shadowed eyes under a thick brow, the shining bone of his nose, his boy's mouth always open in thought—Denise admitted to herself she'd had a little crush on him when they first met, in that hallway, when he threw his ideas at her with such passion. That was before she'd learned he was married, and now the crush had become a harmless trinket to carry; obvious, impossible. She knew how his wife loved him. Denise was in their house once, washing cordial glasses in the sink, and she saw Kathy standing, staring at a photograph of her own wedding day—yellow daisies and bare feet and a stern rabbi to contradict the mood—and Denise imagined Eli's younger, beautiful face approaching the woman like a ghost.

The Spivaks were a funny couple. Together, they were aggressive and fun; but when you got either of them alone, in a coffee shop, or in the corner of yet another dreadful department cocktail party where sullen and attractive undergrads served tiny ham sandwiches, each would always talk about the other one. Secretively, adoringly, as if they were truly the constant subject of one another's thoughts. Kathy and Eli still acted so adolescently crushed that Denise sometimes wondered if they'd had sex yet. *Now she's mooning over him!* Denise thought that afternoon when Kathy stared at her wedding photo, wearing a loopy grin as she twisted her pearls. *But she's got him! She married him!* In the lab, astronomers analyzed a star's light to find its composition; here, with the Spivaks' marriage cast before her in a spectrum, Denise read only bars of gold.

The Spivaks had taken in unmarried Denise without the words of pity other couples tried. The gentile couples, Denise could not help thinking. She hadn't ever met Jews before, and she tried to say nothing, to ask no particular questions when they first sat in that dining room full (it seemed to Denise in memory) of various many-armed candelabra, inscribed velvet cases, leadless silver pencils, scroll boxes and urns. The room shone blindingly—how did bookish, intellectual Kathy find time to polish all these religious dishes? Was there a miracle Hebrew product that gentiles knew nothing about? She asked nothing; she acted as if she knew all about it, were practically Jewish herself, and found ways to have a common religious talk without promoting any difference—*those Mormons, weren't they a kick?* The Spivaks had taken in the single girl, and she was grateful. The single blond California girl, arguing politics at a dinner she didn't know was Shabbat, sitting in front of a scroll she didn't know was Eli's family's Torah. Maybe they were as relieved as Denise—they had only the stars to talk about.

"I'm convinced," Kathy announced again out of nowhere. "That your Professor Swift is wearing a false beard."

"You know, Kath," Eli said, not missing a beat, "I think you've really hit on something."

Birds were flying overhead, crying, and the three could see those shadows cast on the canopy above them, turning and joining and fading as they rose. "See you later," Kathy said without a smile, and made her clumsy way over coils of rope, out of the canopy's shade and into the sun. Eli watched seriously, reminding Denise of the way a young father might watch his child. Kathy and Eli had no children.

How had they done it, with all those stars in the way? Had he compromised his astronomical first love for this second one? Or had Kathy paid somehow in the end, slept alone while he was at the telescopes? Denise would have to start over, learn from them, forget what Carlos had taught her. Her mother had paid, after all, a great deal for her to forget.

"What are you reading?" she asked Eli, who had dipped his nose back into his book. The cover had a painting of a sad man in a white coat, and a busty woman in a yellow sweater haughtily turning away. "Is that a *romance*?"

He looked up, distracted, then turned the book over to look at its cover. "What? No. Oh, I see. No, it's *The Search*. You've never read it? It's about chemists."

"Like the hot number on the cover?"

He smiled, but seemed annoyed. "No, she's not a chemist."

"I bet she isn't."

Eli opened the book again and looked very much at ease, as if this page were the pleasant view from a window. "It's sort of a love story," he said vaguely, then looked at her sharply. "And you can't borrow it, because I'm making Kathy read it. The minds of scientists. It's required reading in our marriage."

That look—her girlish crush rose up again inside her, made her blush. Denise asked, "What does she make you read?"

He squinted in distaste. "Virginia Woolf," he said, turning back to his book and walking away down the deck, leaving Denise alone under the canopy. Love stories about scientists—only Eli could find a book like that. A man in a lab coat, a dame in a sweater; a simple version of a complex story. Here she was, for instance, the dame in the lab coat, standing in the hot still air, the sun white as a salt lick, left with only her mother's command to forget, like a naval order in a sealed envelope, to be opened once at sea. She would forget; she counted on it. But please, she thought, not yet.

Denise had hardly noticed Carlos the first time she met him. It was at a grad student party, and her mind was on her mathematics.

When the host, Jorgeson, introduced her to the tall, handsome man, she dismissed him: affable and rectangular, balding with a military cut, always in a tie and always grinning. To her, Carlos seemed thoroughly fifties, thoroughly married and dull. And being married was the final strike against him. Carlos was taken, and practical Denise simply wiped him from her mind.

Later, however, in the lab, studying data with Eli, Jorgeson and others, someone mentioned Carlos and his wife, the shrill pointless woman, their loveless life together. Her labmates painted steady, devout Carlos as sympathetic, disintegrating, desperate and pleading, available for some woman to save. They hadn't meant to do this, to hook Denise. But that information was a thistle snagging her thoughts: not important, not part of some greater idea, but lasting because suddenly this dull man became a problem some woman could solve. Later, when she ran into Carlos in the market on Telegraph Avenue, she seemed to be meeting a different person. *I know your secret,* she thought to herself as he talked about weather and student protest; *you're trapped and lonely.*

This time, she noticed his small clear eyes, the clean-shaven underbite, the oddly miniature ears sticking out from his buzzed black hair. Normally, she would disregard a man so clean and regular, but now she knew the truth. She imagined this was an act—the polite, kind man, the good husband. She imagined he was tormented by this life, this conventionality, which in the mid-sixties already looked flimsy. On the spot she gave him an entire hidden life; like a caricaturist on a boardwalk, she dashed off a sketch for Carlos to hold in front of himself. They arranged to meet next afternoon to exchange some books they'd talked about. He had taken her number on the inside of a gum wrapper.

"If you could change one thing about me, what would it be?" Carlos asked as she was turning away with a polite smile.

"What?"

"The way I look," he said, standing tall and looking himself up and down. "What would you do to make me better-looking? I wanted to ask a woman."

There were a thousand things she would have changed before, at those parties—the hair he was losing, the stiff posture, his thin lips, and she wouldn't have minded telling him—but suddenly she saw nothing that she would alter. Make him better-looking? He had already changed, during their petty conversation, from a man of separate qualities to judge and dismiss, a stranger understood in pieces, into Carlos. A whole man, this grinning Carlos, too familiar to take apart now. Here was Carlos, all of one piece. Here he was.

"I'd make your eyes more blue," she said.

"More blue," he repeated, looking at her, then spreading his arms to show her his body in that dark suit. "But the rest is okay?"

"It's fine."

His fingers landed on her shoulder, then flew off again as he backed away, saying, "More blue, that's good. Thank you. See you tomorrow." He waved, carrying his bag of oranges, and walked into the crowd. She remained, unsure as to what had just happened.

Carlos would do this—seem so normal, hopeless, bland to the point where he bored Denise and she resolved to end things—and then, at the last moment, he would say something that made her realize he was smarter than she was. She was young; she could not resist it. That face she had never noticed before became beautiful— the eyes, nose and mouth, all his features stayed with her, coins held in her hand. She felt powerful, could feel his beauty clinking in her fist as she thought about him, even before he took her to bed, while they were having their sly and innuendo-filled afternoons of coffee and matinees. In time she seduced him away from his wife, from his frozen longing, and that gave her an even greater power. She would see that same smile each time he bent his head to enter her apartment, that wave and grin, that scar on his chest, and it would be beautiful every time. Love was so new to her that seeing him asleep or talking on the phone amazed her, never bored her. What else could fascinate but never change? The sky?

But very soon, it did change. She grew too attached, or her virgin charms wore off, and he began to make excuses and then made her believe that ending things was her idea. She realized very quickly that any other girl her age would have known better. How stupid, how obvious.

"What are you telling people?" Carlos had asked her after it was all over. They were sipping lemonade in a coffee shop in the city, in North Beach, where no one they knew would find them. At that moment she felt the whole weight of their six months together; but of course, later, in her memory, all that would remain would be that meeting in the market, one perfect afternoon on the cliffs with wine—and this, the end.

"I'm telling them you went insane," she said.

He squinted, sipped his drink. "Well, Denise . . ."

"I'm saying it's a problem you're having," she said, knowing just as she spoke each word that it sounded desperate and would never win him back. "You're in therapy, you're on some kind of new medication for it."

He listened without saying a word, smiled, squinted and told her he had to go. It was wonderful seeing her again, and he wanted her to think of him as a friend.

No one ever understood, though, that it had never really been about him. She'd loved Carlos, but always knew she would have loved any man who bothered to seduce her. Why had it come so late? Had she never been worth it before? Denise felt angry and terrified, jealous of other people's lives—their youths spent making love in old cars and graveyards, passing notes and receiving scented letters, working up the nerve to touch a shivering body, to whisper lies to get what you wanted. What could her youth have been? Dances, coy looks, unwanted advances? Instead of stars? No wonder she clung so tenaciously to the memory of Carlos, hoping for a word from him, hoping he would still come back. She was confused and full of hate; somehow she felt it was her last chance; she saw people around her, and thought the life you got by twenty-five was what you would be stuck with.

So, paid to forget, she spent her time hoarding her memories. Here, on the boat, she had even found a way to hear about him. One of Carlos's friends was on board, the ugly grad student who had introduced her at the party, and she felt her gut tightening. She needed to talk to him, learn about her old lover. She knew it was ridiculous, and she tried to think about her thesis, gently leading her mind away from Carlos the way you might coax a jumper down from a high building. But her mind wasn't interested. It forced her to watch this ugly student, the glow of Carlos he had about him, and she planned her approach. God, she would never forget; mother had wasted her money.

"Don't let Kathy fool you," Eli said to her. It surprised Denise; he had been walking along the deck, writing quietly in the margin of his novel, and now here he was, staring at her, his glasses gleaming in the hot sun. He had sweated through his white shirt at the breastbone, and a translucent diamond formed there, showing the hair on his chest.

"What?"

"This guy she wants you to meet. Don't go for it." They did this often, Eli and Kathy: seemed to work against each other when, in the end, Denise believed, they were really two arms of the same creature, pushing her toward a single future they had both planned for her. Perhaps this was marriage? Eli peered down at her, but she could not see his eyes in the glare of his lenses. "A writer or something," he said. "But sort of . . . I don't know. . . . Not like us."

What did they want her to be? Alone? Was that it—they were happiest when she was utterly alone?

"Not like us?" she asked. "Are we somehow special?"

He brushed the crumbs of her words aside. "Oh, he's just conventional. He's nice, he's nice. But he voted for Nixon. He memorizes jokes. That kind of thing."

"See," she said, struggling to raise herself and feeling dizzy in the crowd of murmuring people, in the pounding waves and salt air. "See, now I'm intrigued."

"Suit yourself," he said, folding his arms and looking old again, grown-up and convincingly wise. "I wash my hands of this whole thing."

"Do you think Kathy is okay?" she asked him.

Eli squinted to understand her. "What, do you . . . oh, oh you mean over there?" He turned his head to see the dark form of his wife at the other end of the boat, tying a scarf around her head. Sun caught half her back in a bright curve. "Kathy?" he said. "She's fine.

Look, that girl loves her." Indeed, Denise could see a little girl, their professor's daughter, Lydia, tugging at the woman's skirt until Kathy looked down and started talking.

"She's so great," Denise said simply. The canopy flapped above them.

He wiped sweat from his forehead. "Yeah."

"Once again it's all BADgrads and her." This was a nickname the students had—Berkeley Astronomy Department graduate students— as if they were a gang, ready to rumble.

"There's Jorgeson's girlfriend. . . ." He pointed her out, still looking away at the frothing wake of their boat. He was talking about a thin, timid Chinese girl who had come with the ugly student.

Denise leaned over to whisper happily: "Mail-order."

"Who told you that?"

She smiled. "Kathy."

Eli laughed and shook his head in that fatherly way, saying, "Don't listen to everything she tells you." Then he looked at her, smiling, his small eyes inscrutably examining her face while he kept the smile intact. She immediately recognized a mind in action, and it made her tense her shoulders, focus her mind on the details of his body. The half laugh he gave now, the hands brought together in his lap. What was he thinking? Sometimes she saw people as intellectual problems; if she paid attention, she might solve them. In a lower voice, Eli asked her, "So what does she tell you?"

Denise said nothing. Clearly, Eli believed his wife had whispered some secret to Denise at one of those barbecues, or out shopping, but what could he mean? Kathy told Denise nothing, nothing at all, and it surprised her to think that Eli knew his wife so poorly. Kathy never fidgeted with secrets; if she had them, she kept them sealed tight, waterproof. She was the kind of woman, Denise found, whose lock could not be picked—you might catch her gazing wistfully out to sea and, believing she was pondering some old love or regret, you'd carefully ask what was on her mind. "Thinking about a book," she might say, smiling a little, or "I think I'll roast a chicken tonight." There was no confession brooding there. Didn't Eli know this? Or was there something wrong with their marriage? Denise was so young, so caught up in her own mission to forget, that she had never considered that her friends might not be happy. It was an awful thought. She laughed with confusion.

"I've had too much to drink!" Denise said, fanning herself with her hat.

Eli smiled, giving up. "You think it's a good idea to be drunk so early?" he asked.

"Yes. I do."

"Good," he told her. "So do I."

He quickly pulled the camera out of his bag and took a picture of her sweating there, fanning herself. She squealed. Then someone shouted "Land ho!" and all faces on the boat turned to see the island. Denise could hear tiny Lydia calling out, "I don't see it!" and everybody shushing her, but Denise could see it: a dark, green animal shape on the horizon. Why was she here?

The boat turned, and the sun crept through a rip in the canopy and lit her upturned hand so that the light, the foreign light in this place, was a warm lemon in her palm. She knew her sadness was a foolish one, but it was real, and despite her mother's wishes, she could not forget. She had to feel that again, to feel alive before her youth was over; if not Carlos, then some other man. She remembered herself in love, and that memory glowed with a blue flame behind her thoughts. But now she was unhappy—now, on the boat, with Eli, with the island appearing before them, and the light sitting in her hand. Just as Eli touched his face—this was the worst here, for some reason—this, *now*. She turned her bright palm. It passed, the light, onto the water.

And everyone was shouting as they saw the island. They had no wish to know the future.

If you flew from Singapore to the main island, Raya, and from Raya by propeller plane so that you approached the island of Bukit from above, you would say it looked like a rabbit: the mountainous haunch of the volcano, the tea-plantation uplands where the sultan had his palace, the paler forelimbs reaching down to the shore, terraced with rice paddies; then the flat plane of the head and, of course, beachy spit of ears drawn back in fear. It would seem almost ridiculous to you; it would define the island in your eyes, the shape like a rabbit, the shivering blink there in the jungle, the nearby archipelago of wolves. The native people had never considered their island in this way. They had never seen their island from the sky. They had never seen a rabbit.

Their lives were very different from the Americans'. How could an island girl, equally brokenhearted as Denise, passing the woman as she left the boat, how could she understand her? They each stared at the other—the girl in a red sarong and headscarf, the tall beige-colored woman in khaki and pale blue—and could not comprehend that other life.

The only one among the Americans who knew this place was Dr. Manday, who had left to go to school in California twenty years before and had never returned. He stood next to Professor Swift, wiping the sweat from his broad mustache, chattering to the bearded man about his island, the sultan, the customs. He told him that the old sultans had never accepted the Gregorian calendar—the decision by Pope Gregory in 1584 to recalibrate the calendars by ten days—so that the island was always ten days behind the rest of the world. Actually, he told them, the error had grown to thirteen days. All the students were listening as Manday spread his hands across his chest, across the dark sweat heart there. "It's thirteen days ago here. Not March twentieth: March seventh. A little joke, yes?"

But it was more than that for all of them. It allowed them, as they trudged across the hot beach, men in sarongs carrying their bags, it allowed them to feel less of a shock—this was old soil, in the past. Everything strange or uncomfortable was due to that, to Manday's little joke about time, and they could feel, oddly, at ease believing (knowing it was ridiculous) that the modern world would arrive in thirteen days and change things, that they weren't trapped here, that life wasn't really like this.

"Look," Eli whispered to Kathy and Denise as they walked toward the shade of a tree. He pointed to a man sitting beside a brightly painted fishing boat, smoking a cigarette and looking at them. "Manday said some of the men tell time with cigarettes."

"Like a sundial?" Kathy asked.

"Like I'd say to you, 'I'll be back in two cigarettes,' and you'd smoke them, ten minutes would pass and I'd be back. Like that."

Denise shaded her face with a hand, beginning to be hung over now, feeling her mind becoming iridescent and confused. "Oh my God."

Denise, Eli, Kathy, Jorgeson—all of them might have gone a little mad if they hadn't been given Manday's little joke. They were allowed to feel like aliens, like different creatures, like visitors from the future.

It was a familiar feeling, scientifically. They could look into the heavens like any human and see a swarm of lights receding from the earth, but their minds would spoil the wonder with mathematics. They knew, for instance, how distant each point was—in blackest space, and in time. The light from the closest stars had originated only years before, but images of the most distant objects arrived millions of years old. Yet each star sat equally on the dark palm of night. Orion's belt had three stars of equal brilliance; yet Swift could point there for his daughter and tell the girl (baffling her) that the rightmost light showed that star two thousand years ago, but the center showed light thousands of years older—a visual paradox, a time machine. What could the daughter say to that? *What do I care, what does it matter, I can cover them both with my thumb. . . .*

They could feel proud, the students and the professors stepping across the fiery sand. They could feel in command of light and time above them, of the rabbit-shaped green clump of land before them, of each staring woman passing with fruit in a basket upon her head. Yet at home they were lost. They could travel thousands of miles and be in command, but at home, where they should have seen the world so clearly, they were blind—one eye to the lens each midnight—and already part of the past. It was 1965 in Berkeley; they were each twenty-five or twenty-six, yet they were born too soon to be young anymore. They remembered the end of the war, the atom bomb, the music of victory and Daddy coming home; they had parents born in the teens, the twenties; they remembered beatniks; they could conjure up an image of an old TV, a gray blob in a radio cabinet; they had worn hats on the street as young men, coats and ties in college (Denise had worn white gloves each day). Just a week before, in Berkeley, they had sipped tea in the lounge at Campbell Hall at 3:30—they did this, every day, tea at Campbell. They were young, in their prime, yet they had been born too soon.

The truly young had just arrived at Berkeley—first as naive undergraduates, still in their bouffants and skirts for the first few months, then falling into dingy shirts and jeans when the work began; there they were, thousands of them, swelling the lists. Loud and joyous, they were already outnumbering and outshouting the older students like Denise, Eli, and Jorgeson. These new students knew the death count in Vietnam, knew what it meant to have the Black Muslim headquarters in San Francisco burned, knew every detail of the Reeb beating in Alabama. They began their marching, their sign-painting and anger, their senseless carefree parties, too, out in the sunshine. But it should not have been the eighteen-year-olds' time. It belonged to the scientists—the BADgrads—this time had been promised to them, promised by their parents and teachers, as their time to shine and take over the reins of America. It was their moment, now, as older plants folded and left a thinner shadow, to rise and flourish above. Their eyes were on their comets and fireballs, though—they read poetry aloud in bed and didn't hear—they didn't notice their moment being stolen. America was being shaken by their students while they slept. By the time this comet came around again and shed its meteor shower, they would realize their time had never come at all.

So they seemed a little innocent, a little more kind, walking toward the jungle and their huts, pointing at the man smoking a cigarette beside his brightly painted catamaran, at the pounded tin dome of the mosque, at the girls hiding their faces under their hands, dropping nuts for a frenzied monkey on the ground. The wind caught the palms and turned them, wheels in the sky, and a veil of dust rose between them and their boat. A cloud hovered magic carpet–like over the stunted volcano—on its hillside, you could see gleams of white from houses, bones buried in the lush green jungle. The women approached, smiling, their sarongs red and gold, their fingernails long and pointed, and they began to dance, smiling, jerking their arms, tossing rice in welcome. Each of the Americans shivered; thought, *I've lost my way*; then turned and caught someone else's eye. *Look at us,* they all thought in relief, *we're wonderful, look at us.* And they saw Dr. Manday halfway down the beach, holding a woman with a thin light-blue cloth over her head, a stout woman who touched his mouth, his cheeks, whispering. Manday laughed and whispered back, pointing up to the sky.

They all saw her head turn, owl-like, as she gazed at the bright sheet of sky, her mouth slack and expectant, her long black hair brushing his cheek. Through the cloth, you could see two golden combs in her hair, glinting. Manday was telling her about the comet. She was looking for it near the sun. They all saw that she did not understand, and they all saw him insisting. He took her arm, talking in her language but not in words she could understand—*perihelion, aphelion, coma*—and she kept her face to the sky, nodding and seeing nothing and looking afraid. She was his wife, they would all later learn, whom he had not seen in eight years, wearing gold combs in her hair for him.

Oh look at us, they thought, standing on that bird-haunted beach before the dancing women, *look how wonderful we are.*

Eli was quiet in his chair that night. A few meteors had already streamed across the sky, the earth passing through that cometary dust, and people had called out "Time!" to mark those few teeth pulled from the night's dark mouth. Too early for the real shower—only midnight—but Eli was still searching the sky; every moment, his eye would flicker on its own. He had learned, over the years, to ignore the imaginary flashes in his brain and pick out the real ones.

They had found their huts and unpacked in the humid afternoon air. They had eaten lunch under a palm-leaf roof on the beach itself, and Swift had told long astronomical stories and jokes as Kathy and Eli held hands and tried to spoon the thin soup into their mouths. Denise had been quiet, staring at her food, sad or hung over or both. Later, they all returned to their huts and slept deeply in preparation for a night of watching the sky, each turning in the hot air, feeling a fever coming on. Around them, the jungle had rustled and made noises they had never heard before. Then it was dinner, and up the long stairs from the beach to the sultan's broad overlook, where the chairs had been arranged. They took their stations. Eli and Denise, the best eyes, were put facing south, and Kathy was put facing north with some other wives. The Spivaks had kissed and parted. A few of the children, including Swift's daughter Lydia, fell asleep out on the open stone, and others played catch with a baseball, which went over the edge of the wall and had to be retrieved from the beach far below. It was midnight. Darkness lapped against the overlook wall, the night's tide coming in.

Eli could smell the sea coming over the white walls, the slight leafy death of it, something like flowers from the jungle below, and something sour as well. Above them all, a bowl of sky with nothing in the way but the low wall and a small gold dome that hid the staircase. They had traveled far for this diamond-clear view. Dr. Manday had taken out a notepad on which to record the meteors, and he walked among them all with an old man in gold brocade— the sultan himself, who murmured and scratched his slippers against the rock, talking about the repairs he would make to the overlook's wall, which had been damaged during the war. There was no wind. People were whispering. Denise had chattered for a while, but seemed to be asleep beside Eli now, her headache beginning to fade. Eli listened for his wife's voice across the parapet. There was no sound but the whispering, the sea, the flutter of bats' wings. He stared at the sky, then over to the wall, where he saw that a gecko had crawled onto the whitewashed surface. Eli could hear it faintly croaking, a quasar in the night; he stared and wondered if they were all wrong about him.

He was lucky to be brilliant—his father had been so brilliant, a lawyer in Seattle, and everyone had watched Eli to see how this egg would hatch. Would he be ordinary and forgettable and safe in blue-collar Washington? Afterward, as an older boy, he had found a copy of *Action Comics* and felt just like that, like a death-kissed superhero with the parents peering over the crib to see if he might be human or extraordinary, if they should bother sewing capes. But he passed this test—his mother came home one day when he was three to see the letters *ELI* written in crayon on the wall. Had they really held a party for that? As if it were a true passage into genius, like the sailors passing the equator and pouring milk joyfully over one another. He had sweated after that, to live up to their prophecy.

But they were wrong. He had so easily conquered the scientific math, of course, shone so brightly as a student that even Swift remembered his name soon after Eli became a BADgrad—and wasn't he one of the two fellows picked for this trip? Hadn't he, finally, been tapped? But Denise, silently, was more brilliant. No one could see it but him. She had taken her preliminaries a semester early, and now was ready for her qualifying. Was anybody watching? Didn't they see her there, with no praise, no support or notice, calmly jerking her slide rule through its motions until she had the answer before the rest of them? She didn't raise her hand or speak, but she was first. Didn't they see her?

Eli, on the other hand, was fading. He felt it fading, his brilliance, at twenty-five, like an aging actress feeling her once beautiful face. And somehow, in Eli's mind, as he stared at the pale wall and tried to see the tiny lizard crouching there, croaking, the equation was simple and true: If Denise was brilliant, then he was not, and they were wrong. QED.

He turned toward his station again, and there above him was the constellation he had described to Kathy the other night: Centaurus. High in the southern sky, hidden from their usual vantage in California, it spread out hugely above him, the body of the creature drawn from the star Menkent and east toward the Southern Cross, where the imagined human head looked down. But there was nothing there, no meteors anymore—an empty vessel held before them all, or a magician's hat which might (a childhood hope if anything) produce a rabbit all in fiery shards tonight. This he could see with his eyes. It was so clear here, and it was still so new to him that he could make out for the first time the stars of the Southern Hemisphere: the Southern Cross, Menkent, that open star cluster NGC 3532 just to the east of where the meteors would fall—wasn't it amazing! All his life some curtain had been held up at the horizon, and here it lifted, as in a carnival tent, to reveal this museum of oddities—southern stars unknown to the ancients, named after objects in the sixteenth-century world: clocks, telescopes, air pumps.

But you could not describe these things to Kathy. You could try; you could name the stars and draw their lines on scraps of paper; show where, deep in the constellation, a spiral galaxy brooded. But in her folded arms, her tired stare, you would know it didn't leap and form in her head; that even if she tried to pluck an image from his scribblings, hanging like a grape among the vines of math, it would not keep. Her mind was a poor place for his kind of wonder; after a while, the joy of it grew bad, turned to nothing. He had wanted, when he married Kathy, to take her up and show her what obsessed him as a boy, the hours he had stolen to bike in darkness to an observatory, the passion for it in college (all gone, of course, or changed). His mind was overfilling, like a library crammed with volumes to the ceiling, stacks on the tables, pages dusty on the floor; he had wanted to attach her to his library and fill that, too, with charts and names and nebulae. It was a foolish way to treat people, Eli knew, standing staring naked-eyed at the constellations (nothing yet in Centaurus, no sparks from its hoofs), and he felt very sorry.

Still, he wanted her closer. He had met Kathy at Harvard, through a friend who was a mathematician, at a party full of chemists. She had been a chemist then, bright and self-sufficient and promising, wearing a white dress with daisies and a frayed strap, sipping a rum drink through a straw, her hair in a shining ponytail. (He would always think of her that way, with her face stretched from the straw to the elastic in her hair, as she glanced up at him and raised her eyebrows.) He had stood near her, and, as he remembered it, she moved over on her chair so he could sit beside her. They dated in what seemed, now, like such an old-fashioned adventure: huddling in drive-ins on too-cold evenings, eating at odd foreign restaurants and laughing when misordered food arrived. And at first they didn't go very far—it seemed impossible, just two years ago!—and she giggled and said they were all-American Jews now, and she should get a circle pin like a WASP and dye her hair. Kathy was dating two other men as well (a premed and, of all things, a math professor), but she ended things with them. She changed her major, without a word to him, to English. A friend lent them a house in Provincetown that winter, in their senior year, and, to his surprise, Kathy let him take off her clothes. They had sex there on the couch, breathing clouds of cold air. Eli fell hopelessly for her. She became his wife.

But she was never his; she was always a little apart, a little unhappy. She treated chemistry like a childish fad of hers, a rag doll she was embarrassed to hear about, and tossed the topic into a corner. She cooked and cleaned for him. She somehow knew her role as an academic's wife and charmed his professors, his colleagues, and took poor waxy Denise under her arm. Kathy was clever, sometimes too bright for the men at the table, but she also didn't mind their talking shop. She only minded that in Eli; the stars were not part of the deal; she wasn't a woman in mythology, Kathy told him, marrying the sky. And there were times he heard her in the shower, weeping. It seemed so calculated, to time your sadness for the shower, to hide tears in water and camouflage red eyes with the steam and heat. He would have held her. He looked at her after a shower, smiling, beautiful, a towel wrapped around her, searching in the medicine cabinet—where was that piece caught inside her, cutting her, where was it?

But he dared not ask, nor mention any of his guesses about her mind. He knew, from experience, that he'd be wrong. He would just guess his own worries. He thought, for instance, that she cried about wanting a child; but his rational mind knew that this was off, somehow. Eli was the one who wanted a child. Kathy was the one who changed the subject, at dinner, or in bed, or looking at a baby in a carriage.

Whenever he saw her staring at the wall in bed at night, not at her book but at the wall, he patted her arm and said, "What's the matter? It's all right, things are great," and then began to list off everything wonderful in their life. She looked peaceful, listening. It *was* wonderful! The house here in the city, their friends, the food and fun they had despite their poverty, the freedom of this time in history, his own career. He held her, loving her—it was wonderful.

"I'll give you a hint," she said one night as he held her and she felt stiff in his arms. It was in their small bedroom, almost a closet, high above the street near the campus. There was a picture of baby Eli and his brothers hung on the wall, yellow and old. The curtain was a green bedsheet, and they lay in a bed too big for the room. There was a tone in Kathy's voice that he sometimes hated. He couldn't imitate it, or tell you what it was until he heard it, but there it was. It usually came when she didn't want to have sex. This time, however, she said, "When I look sad, don't tell me things are great, that I shouldn't be sad."

"But." He tried not to feel angry. He was so patient, so good, didn't she see it?

She thrust out her lower lip, as if pitying him; he hated that, too. She wore her hair in a flip that stroked the pillow, and her glasses magnified her eyes and made her face seem pinched just above her nose. "Don't even worry about why I'm sad, or what I tell you. Just say, 'That must be hard.' "

"Kathy, you'll know it's a line. I want to help you. . . ."

"Trust me. Just say, 'That must be hard,' like that." She leaned back on the pillow, her face so pale. Outside, sirens blasted through the dirty streets. They were both silent. "You can say it now," she whispered with a little smile. "I'm feeling sorry for myself."

"That must be hard," he told her, baffled, almost horrified that she would give him a trick to work on her.

But for some reason it appeased her. Something in her unhooked and relaxed. "It is," she told him, resting her book on her chest and closing her eyes.

He'd held her moist hand and wondered why she loved him.

Eli was a few distant yards from her now, gazing at Centaurus above the Southern Cross. Something moved in the blackness—a bat—there were bats crossing the sky and he couldn't see them, just the way they blocked some stars in a jagged pattern. Instinctively he leaned his head down, and then saw others doing it as well. Denise awoke and let out a little scream of terror. Where was Swift? Farther toward the golden dome, his daughter asleep at his feet, a pale bundle. Eli set his eye to the sky again, and Centaurus leaped toward him like a tiger. In its teeth was everything the men and wives could not see, not if they had the keenest eyes—that irregular galaxy spotting the centaur's hide, the globular cluster—and there were objects too faint even for normal telescopes, objects Eli knew were there from his late nights up in the mountains of San Jose, above the clouds: two spiral galaxies turning in the centaur, bright and spending gamma rays like drunken sailors. It was true, what he told Kathy, all of it—that life was wonderful, every precious particle of it.

He would buy her a present. He had already written a note in the margins of his novel, hoping that she would come across it late one night while he was at the telescope. He imagined her in bed, yawning, dutifully reading along until she noticed the tiny message beside the words. Then she might understand what he somehow could not tell her. But more. He would bring something tomorrow while she slept off this night—not a photograph of a fireball, nothing as selfish as that—one of those golden combs. Like the combs in Mrs. Manday's hair. He would try to talk to the island woman where she sat with a look of girlish concern beside her husband. Kathy was beautiful— the pink-tinted smile, her lost sleepy look in the morning when she was weak and funny, her sharp stare across a room of people which meant she was bored and missed him, the times when he could read her mind, those few times—she was beautiful. If only she asked him questions about the sky, told him her secrets. He strained to see her in her chair but she was turned away. He would tell her. He would bring her combs. That was why she loved him.

"Do me a favor," Denise said, appearing close with her hair falling between them, smelling too rich and flowery. She had clearly slept off the bourbon; she looked determined as she often did under the stars. Off at the far end of the overlook, one of the students was signaling and approaching. Eli looked at Denise, and saw a piece of sunburned skin on her nose, curling from her like smoke. He recognized, too, some new tension in her face, some new tone in her voice.

"Do me a favor when Jorgeson comes over here." She was talking about the graduate student, a gangly Midwesterner with horn-rimmed glasses, the one with the mail-order bride. "Find out about Carlos."

Eli sat struck for a moment by this shift, almost angry. He watched Jorgeson waving his arms. Eli had been relaxed and fine a moment before, and now here was Denise, reminding him of her ridiculous love affair, her fling with that crew-cutted Chicano rich boy, that married Republican cad. Eli looked at his poor friend and thought *Don't be so sad,* and not from sympathy, not because he knew what it might be like to have moods like this one, dropping like spiders inside her. It was a command, a wish made because he couldn't deal with sad women, especially one who wasn't his wife. He almost couldn't stand their sudden, crystal grief. Professor Swift had predicted that the comet, tonight, would bring with it a meteor shower. So why not make such wishes? Thousands of stars were already poised, ready to fall.

"What?" Eli asked, feigning ignorance. The Swede was listening to a colleague, stopped maybe fifteen yards away.

"He's his friend. Find out."

"Find out what?"

Denise didn't answer, sniffing the vegetable air.

Eli remembered when she'd met this Carlos. A garden party at Jorgeson's house, and Denise in a green frilly dress, talking to some handsome, military-stiff man, cocking her grinning head to one side in a girlish way that was utterly unlike her, some remnant of the upper-class coquetry she'd been taught in San Francisco. Eli could tell the man was a swindler. When he heard this Carlos had a wife, sitting inside the house, he assumed the meeting had been harmless. Carlos left, Denise came over and listened to one of Eli's astronomy jokes, joined Kathy in a few drinks, and all was as it had been. It was months before Denise admitted she was seeing him—and then only through Kathy, who told the story plainly, as if it were a natural course of events and not a painful mistake. Brainy Denise had been seduced by married Carlos, had believed a promise from a man who could make no promises. And, Kathy told her husband, their blond friend was in love.

It had been infuriating to watch. Denise came to dinner far less often, rarely made it to the movie dates they all had together, and in general began to treat the Spivaks like a phase she had passed through, an old routine she wanted to forget. She was still friendly at school, but he could never catch her for coffee after class because of her complex schedule with Carlos, one that involved grabbing his lunch hours and breaks and free weekend moments, tiling her life with these shards of love.

When it had ended, a few weeks ago, Denise had returned. The prodigal friend. Kathy had listened to the whole tale, gone over the words Carlos had spoken, sat with Denise late at night in the living room with brandy and read these phrases like entrails, telling a fortune. As if this Carlos were a deity, hiding his heart in this tangle of clichés! Eli kept quiet; he knew the phrases, the phone calls and visits meant nothing. There was no code to break; there was no lock to pick; there was no anagram of love within this fool's farewell.

He listened to her plea that night and stared at her sunburned scrap of skin. He seemed as if he wanted to reach out and take it from her, such was the look in his eyes. Perhaps he thought it was rare to own a piece of someone's skin, taken from a memorable first day on this island, on this trip where she might have a chance to forget a bad romance and take the course he'd planned for her. Because he did have a course for her; he felt he made good choices for other people, but from experience he'd learned not to tell them. He had kept his silence, but here was at last a way to touch and change her.

"I need a favor, too," he said.

She gritted her teeth, staring at him, then said, "Oh Eli, just do this for me."

He was quiet and watched the boys throwing a ball, the background of stars behind them. Eli knew he couldn't ever win by talking; she was too stubborn and selfish, and he had lost too many scientific battles with her to bother now with a real one. He couldn't argue with her, but he could wait her out, let Denise fill the silence with arguments far better than he could come up with. He'd learned the trick of her. So he sat and let his pupils dilate in the darkness while he felt her beside him, looking, thinking too hard.

Denise folded her arms across her breasts. She asked softly, "What is it?"

"First, after this, let's not talk about Carlos anymore." Her face folded in subtle rage, but he knew she'd forgive him. He was always hard on her in a way no one else dared to be; that's why she cared for him.

"Eli. . . ."

"And also," he said quickly, and she was quiet. He thought for a moment about how to put it, then he said, "I hoped you could . . . I want you to ask Kathy something."

She closed her eyes and the sunburnt skin fluttered on her nose as a cool wind came. The breeze lifted her hair slightly from her face. Eyes still closed, she said, "You don't just want me to ask. You want me to report on what she says."

He said nothing. There was a breeze that took the edge off the hot night, and you could hear the soft noise of people leaning in their plastic chairs, relaxing, taking it in.

Denise asked, "Is this a trade? That you'll talk to Jorgeson if I talk to Kathy?"

Eli murmured something, nodding, and looked toward the tall Swede. Jorgeson was close now, looking ridiculous and shouting something. A few yards away. A choice had to be made.

"What am I asking her?"

He quietly told her to ask if his wife was pregnant.

She sat back and placed her fingers to her forehead, as if her headache were returning. He knew she was watching Jorgeson's approach, timing her decision.

Eli wanted to be patient with her, but it was difficult—she seemed so much younger than he was, so frustratingly fragile for someone so brilliant. He looked at her face, how it cracked—shouldn't she be hard as a diamond? Weren't people either weak or strong, he wondered, not both at once, not unpredictably both? This was the flaw— he hated finding it—the flaw, as if she were a vase he was examining in a shop, cinnabar with two handles, discovering the flaw that would widen with time, crack and destroy the shape. He had found it now, a hint of it; you can't return a friend at this point, but what do you do? You wait; you try to see if they will fix themselves before they grow too old to notice. Eli turned away as the Swede approached, as Denise considered the deal, and he let his doubts enter again.

He had his own flaw, of course. The great sign of this decline had come half a year before when, after collecting a preliminary set of data, Eli had let Swift sign him up to give a presentation at a professional meeting in Berkeley. A presentation—it was an honor. But he was not ready. Eli had taken the data so carefully over three nights at Palomar, but he found himself in Campbell Hall at four o'clock in the morning, unshowered and feeling crazy, unable to resolve his data into the answer that he knew was true. It was not even important; it was not even the purpose of his research, and yet it had to fit for him to move on. Eli stood up and walked down the polished halls, listening to his steps, peering into all the darkened offices until he came again to his own with its one fly-specked light. He was alone. What had happened to those years of surefooted reason? When he could bend gravities with a mechanical pencil? Now, when the other BADgrads slept, he scrabbled at the simplest set of data and could not get a hold. And it wasn't even that he didn't understand. No, he knew exactly where his paper should go. It simply would not go there. Standing outside his office, listening to the buzz of the hall's fluorescent lights, Eli imagined the rows of scientists, coughing impatiently as he described his inability to bring this simple research to conclusion. "Thank you," they would each say, "but not entirely persuasive." Those would be the exact words.

So he trimmed. That was the expression they used back then, the scientists who spoke of such things; he sat back at his desk with a clean sheet of paper and trimmed the data of its upsetting spurs. He left a roughness to the shape, but now the numbers fell more or less as he predicted. He sped through his conclusion and moved on. The presentation came and went with no surprise, the scientists applauded him, and Swift, impressed, had offered Eli part of his grant to come here to this island. No, he would never tell anyone. This was how you overcame your flaws, he believed; with tricks like this one, which he wanted to teach Denise, about letting yourself forget.

The bats were back again, catching insects drawn in by their feeble lights. He looked to Denise for her answer. Just then, that small piece of skin broke off in a gust of wind, and he watched it fall slowly through the air and into the darkness of the jungle.

"All right," Denise said finally, facing away with a smile. "Hello there, Jorgeson." The deal was struck.

The blond Swede stood above them, chattering in his antisocial charmless way, and Eli began to lead the conversation toward Carlos. He kept glancing to Denise, seeing the vague smile on her face as she listened. Eli could see only her pale, thankless profile now as she waited for some morsel of information to pounce on. As he pulled her Carlos from the weeds of this conversation, he noticed how his words made her face shift—and not just in expectation of her lover's name, but at what Eli himself said. She was coaxing him on with small gestures: her eyes, a smile, a stiffening of her features. She was leading him. All this time, Eli had thought he'd tricked her into doing what he wanted her to do, leading the life he planned for her, but that wasn't what had happened at all. He was doing what she wanted—the very sentence falling from his mouth came only as she'd planned it. There was no one like this woman, no one.

Eli said loudly, "So, Lars, tell me about your friend Carlos. . . ."

Three days later, nothing but the accident would matter.

You could have walked down the aisle of their plane, headed through the dawn toward Hawaii, toward California, and seen the difference in their faces. Every window shade but one was pulled down to create an artificial darkness in the uncrowded cabin, glowing in places because light came in through the crevices nonetheless, jungle vines breaking into the room. The one open shade belonged to Dr. Hayam Manday, who sat with his chin on his hand, watching the dawn without his glasses, alone. The rest of them—the students, wives, professors, children—were hours into a fitful sleep: faces crumpled against pillows and bulkheads, bodies spread uncomfortably across a row, hands grasping at thin blankets to cover a shoulder.

Many, though, like Manday, were awake; they sat wide-eyed in the darkness, their wives or children sleeping against their sides. They thought of a scene on the overlook, or another scene from their lives which now seemed different. An accident had happened. Not all of them had seen it, but none could forget the brief cry from the wall. None could forget they had witnessed a death.

Any group but this one would have blamed it on the comet; that's what the locals did. They had stood near the body on the beach, then pointed east to where Comet Swift still shone its chill arrow in the sky, and the shadow doctors proclaimed that the comet had scattered misfortune on the island, left it behind for them to breathe like dust from an ox-drawn cart. This was not ignorance; the shadow doctors belonged to a centuries-old tradition of comets and their ill augers, from the ancient Chinese and their dying emperors to the latest return of Halley's Comet in 1910, when Americans panicked in the streets, afraid that the comet's tail would poison the earth with cyanide. Any group but this one would have believed it: that comets were vile stars.

But, worse for them, the scientists blamed themselves. They had come to the island to draw a net across the sky and trawl it for meteors, and, like fishermen, they planned with care each part of the project, where each person sat and how they looked at the sky. They were scientists, and could turn life into a laboratory setting, control every aspect so that it pointed toward an answer. They could bend even nature to their bidding. Yet they had failed. Something had gone undone, and they had lost a life. A crowd of artists, of dancers, of poets could never have blamed themselves for terrible chance, but these scientists thought they held chance firmly in their grip. Like trainers, they bent their heads happily between its open jaws. But it was as Eli had always feared: They had been wrong about themselves all along. Someone had died. A child, no less.

Some of the wives and children had gone home days earlier, unwilling to sit for more nights under the comet's watchful eye. Kathy had been among them, her eyes darkly circled, waving from the boat at sunset, as the ones who stayed behind, the young astronomers, pretended to be stronger than those leaving. None of them doubted this was a lie. The remaining days were spent sleeping and reporting back to California; the wide-awake nights of meteor-watching became silent now except for the hesitant cries of "Time!" and it was hard for anyone not to glance over to where a piece of wood lay propped against the wall, covering the part that had crumbled.

The plane flew on silently. Professor Swift, three seats behind Manday, was wide awake as well. He sat in an empty row, smoking a pipe, turning the pages of journals under his crisp reading light. The light caught the gray in his beard and turned it tinsel. He was not known to sleep well, and students heard rumors that he had, in fact, become nocturnal in order to function under the telescope, forcing the department to schedule his classes to coincide with dawn or sunset. The professor seemed to be working, jotting notes; but in fact he turned the pages only to signal time passing. He was not reading them, and the notes were part of a letter to his wife. He would see her the moment he walked across the tarmac, only hours from now, but he wrote her a letter nonetheless. There was no way to express this out loud.

A woman woke and moaned. Her husband whispered to her, patted her arm, and she fell asleep again, her brow creased in worry. Manday sat by his open window, growing golden from the dawn over Hawaii. A stewardess in a cap and miniskirt came down the aisle, touching a seat in every row as if she could heal them by her passage. She showed a little girl to the bathroom, then returned the way she had come until someone asked for water. She left briskly and did not return. Passengers lit cigarettes, smoke trailing into the cabin, giving the air a thin blue haze. A man stumbled from another bathroom, ill, and fell, sighing, into a seat that was not his.

Denise sat in the middle of the plane, sleeping at times, hopelessly awake at others. She lay under her blanket for a long time, eyes open and glistening. Then she pushed the blanket from her and noiselessly left her seat, padding down the aisle to the very last row, where Eli sat, leaning against a carpeted wall with his hands together in his lap. His glasses were off so that he could sleep, but he wasn't sleeping;

he was staring ahead. Kathy was far away. Denise moved into the seat next to him and pulled the blanket across them both. He looked . over silently and touched her head.

Manday pulled his shade against the golden bars and closed his eyes. Swift turned off his reading light. The underwater darkness was complete. People settled into their places with whispers and sighs, and even the stewardesses dozed off up front, near first class, sideways in a row with their white boots up on the seats. There was no one in the rear of the plane to hear the few quiet words floating in the last row. There was no one to see Denise talking in Eli's ear as he sat staring ahead of him. Or when she touched his chin and turned his head toward her, when she kissed him with a hand spread out on his chest. If someone had seen the two friends, eyes closed, almost asleep in grief, kissing and holding each other in the last row, would they even have said a word? After all, for them, nothing on that flight, nothing from the moment of the accident until their arrival in California, was real.

But three days earlier, on the first night of the storm, they all lay innocently under the stars. Kathy sat in her station, far from her husband, bored and confused by all these shouts of "Time!" sprouting in the air. Around her, young scientists were rising from their chairs, pointing, grinning excitedly and then they would yell "Time! Time!" And though Kathy knew it couldn't be anything as literary or religious as she imagined, still she amused herself with the idea that she was caught in a starry revival tent. That these precocious introverts had seen some vision and were witnessing, shaking like Quakers in a meetinghouse. She knew it wasn't true, but she also knew that eventually someone would explain it to her—these people were forever explaining—and she enjoyed her own version for a few minutes. Eli, Denise, the others, handling snakes. It made all their passion seem ridiculous.

Suddenly, a little girl went running across the parapet. It was Lydia, Swift's daughter, a five-year-old who had a kind of wild, baby animal look beneath her pigtails, running close to the wall. Kathy was surprised to feel her stomach clench, and she shouted. The girl stopped, and Kathy shouted again. She coaxed her away from the wall. Lydia was looking for a monkey that had long since been taken inside. The girl refused to believe it was gone. Kathy asked about the shouts of "Time!"

"They're seeing meteors" was how Lydia explained it, looking doubtful that this was a real question.

"I don't see them," Kathy said, looking up. Nothing but that foreign spread of stars. "Are you sure?"

"Well, you have to look very hard. My dad tries to show me, my sister can see them. You really have to keep looking in the same place and sort of make a wish for them."

"I thought it was the other way around."

This idea was too confusing for poor Lydia and she stood silently, letting her doll's feet drag the stone. Her hand went to her mouth, and Kathy watched her slowly chewing something. Her nails? Nervous habits in such a young girl? Or had she found something to eat?

"Did you see where Riki went?" Lydia asked again, hopefully. This was the monkey's name.

"I think he said something about baking a cake."

"Monkeys can't bake cakes!" Lydia said, grinning, something in her eyes saying she believed quite the opposite.

"Oh yes they can," Kathy told her, deadpan. "Just not very good ones."

Two American boys, a redhead and a fat kid, ran by, coaxing a local boy to join their game of catch. He failed to catch a baseball and it went flying, once more, over the edge of the parapet into the darkness and down to the beach fifty feet below. Parents were shushing them but they would not listen, producing another ball and tossing it again.

"Do you have him?" Lydia asked, meaning the monkey.

Kathy ignored the question. "But why do they yell 'Time'?"

Lydia sniffed and brushed loose curls out of her eyes. "I don't know. So Mr. Manday can write it down. Didn't they tell you?"

"I don't think I was listening."

"You should really listen."

"You're right."

"Sometimes," Lydia said quite seriously, leaning forward, "I'm a princess." Then she went away.

Kathy was more astonished by this little girl than by anything happening above her. The stars were forever falling, the sky turned nightly; but how often did you find a subtle strangeness in an ordinary girl? It was a precious thing to see. Most of the people who knew her would have called Kathy a misanthrope, but they misunderstood her. She adored people, loved being with them and talking to them, but she didn't like any of the obvious things about them. She hated joke-tellers, "charming" people, beauty or grace in any form, raconteurs or wits or geniuses. What Kathy loved were the hidden, tiny madnesses in ordinary people.

At a party, for instance, she often found herself confronted with grinning, clever couples. The man could always talk wittily about the president, and the wife could whisper cunningly about the hostess. This kind of stable marriage, this vaudeville act, bored Kathy to tears. She had come up with clever ways to separate the spouses and then pry past their dull exteriors until she discovered an obsession, an old regret, or a long-abiding fury that quickly subsided in an embarrassed murmur. It wasn't that she wanted to humiliate these people. Really, Kathy just wanted to like them a little more. She wanted to discover how they, too, were human. And when she told you that she liked someone, what she really meant was that she'd glimpsed some unexpected oddity within them, and loved them for it. It was why she liked Denise, for instance—that ordinary rich girl who revealed her craziness so easily, almost happily, at the first scratch of a nail. It was also what had drawn her to Eli.

Eli had at first, like all people, seemed unnecessary. Another Jewish boy at a chemistry party, another dark-browed and selfish intellectual for her mother to adore. After being introduced to him, Kathy had quickly escaped to a corner where she could sit by herself, but he had persistently found her and the safe corner became a trap; they were walled in by laughing scientists and girlfriends, and Kathy was forced to sit beside this dull man on the plush red love seat, listening to him chat about his life and prospects. Kathy pretended to listen, sipping her gin, looking at Eli's face; noticing how he had tried to slick his curls back; thinking how, in his narrow tie and dark suit, he looked like a child dressed up for a wedding.

She wasn't pretty or clever, and she knew it. Kathy was plain, odd and aloof and, as she understood it, men wanted nothing to do with such a creature. Her mother had often yelled at her to stop reading, fix her hair, sit in the parlor when boys came around so they might see her. Her mother tried to teach her a secret way to bake a pie, thinking this kind of talent might give Kathy's ashen skin a buttery glow, but cooking had merely made the girl interested in chemistry. Once, before a school dance, her mother took Kathy downtown to look at dresses, promising her a book if she would go into Sears, if she would at least point out something she liked. Kathy dreamed of her book—*The Waves*, by Virginia Woolf—and, impatient for the feel of its cover, gestured toward a white dress with daisies all across the bodice, knowing her mother couldn't afford it. One morning a week later, Kathy awoke to see a shabby copy of that dress hanging on the door. Her mother had stayed up nights to make it. She had sewn it all from scraps and memory and a sharp, desperate hope. Kathy wore the dress that night as Eli tried to charm her, not out of sentiment or vanity. It was the only nice dress she had. Her only thought was how to escape this nice, dull boy, until she began to listen to his babbling monologue about comets and realized he was out of his mind.

"Wait," she said, searching his face. "Did you say they were like little girls?"

Noticing her interest, he perked up, began to move his hands, elaborating. "Like little girls in their dark rooms, combing their long hair, it's really the image of the hair, and we are, the astronomers, we're sort of peeking in on them."

"Like voyeurs? Watching little girls?"

"Well, I . . ."

She considered this, looking at a picture on the wall. "There's something so sinister about that image. . . ."

He looked confused, a little angry, and another curl came loose over his forehead. "I . . . I didn't mean it *that* way!"

"Oh," Kathy said, facing him again, clearly disappointed. "You didn't?"

But she'd sighted something odd about him, despite all his attempts to cover it. Every time she saw him, it became more clear that he was deeply strange and utterly wrong about himself: He was convinced he thought rationally and carefully, but in fact Kathy could see how he was ruled by contradictory passions, old beliefs, religious superstitions, cowardly prejudices of all kinds. She saw how his thoughts flew recklessly, never landing, and it excited her. Hour by hour, he became more fascinating to her.

"You look like a married man," she told him one night in Provincetown, months after the party, when he had arranged for them to spend the night together. Until then, because of her indecision, they had never done anything more than kiss. How long would he seem wonderful to her? Would she reach some final strangeness and watch his personality wither back to normal? Kathy knew what this night meant; she could see how nervous Eli was, that his mind was full of countless ideas about how this night might go, for the better, for the worse, depending on her.

"Married? Me?" He held up his ringless hand, confused. They were sitting on the couch, in front of a fire, two feet apart. "You think I'm lying to you? You think I'm married and . . ."

"I didn't say you *were* one, I said you *looked like* one, which you do."

Kathy watched his desperate stare, his long face half in shadow, his eyes shining, and she saw how in love he was. He had told her the history of his heart, the girls he'd dated, how a beauty last year had toyed with him cruelly and left him childishly moping. Kathy saw in his look how that pain had been wiped away. He thought only of her. Amazing. In the darkness, it lit every inch of his face.

"I always wanted to look married," he told her.

"It becomes you," she had said as she stood up in the firelight and began to unbutton her blouse. She could hear him catch his breath.

On the overlook, Kathy watched her husband, a few years older, looking more like a married man than before as he and Denise whispered in the red glow of their flashlights. She watched another student approach, talk with them, then walk away. Denise glanced across the broad, dark stone and caught Kathy's eye. They must have been talking about her. What would they have said? That she was as odd as ever, Kathy assumed. That's what people had always said. She saw Denise look away, then back again. How could they be so similar, her husband and this WASP girl? Whispering like spies across the parapet—how had these friends found each other across the crowded plain of youth? Kathy had never done it. She had never found an ally. She had only held on to Eli, first because he fascinated her, then because she loved him, but never because he was like her. Nobody was. Turning away, she dismissed the thought as pathetic and terribly vain.

The cries of "Time!" were coming thickly now. She raised her head to see if she could catch a meteor, but the cries kept coming and she saw nothing. A bad fisherman. She longed for a book, but this was not allowed. What did they all see up there that kept them riveted past the hours for sleep? What had made her husband bike up a mountain as a boy? What had drawn Denise away from her comfort, her wealth, her family? Nothing seemed to change up in the darkness. Nothing made a sound. Kathy felt like a skeptic in a haunted house. These necks craned upward, these tense smiles of suspense—a creak on the stairs, the chandelier moving eerily—then the gasps around her while Kathy couldn't see a thing.

What would it be like to have one single passion? The question worried her. She looked over at her husband, who sat alone now in his chair, head to the stars. He loved her. But he loved the dead sky a little more.

"Time!" she shouted loudly.

The only one who looked her way was Professor Manday, who nodded and scribbled in his notebook. So now she was part of their record. It would appear in a journal, that stray mark, that lie. They were so easy to fool, these true believers, taking any sign to be from their specific god.

"Time!" she cried again, grinning.

She tried to feel good, solitary, strong—the way she had in college, the way she had before she'd married Eli, before she'd chosen him, before she'd fallen in love and found herself puttering and sulking when he was away. He didn't know, he couldn't understand her, he was nothing like her, but over the years she had come to need him. Kathy felt powerless. Why had it come upon her so unexpectedly, even after marriage, when she was sure she'd be safe? Why love him now? But there was nothing she could do. It was all right, anyway. She turned back, saw him tilted toward the sky. And once again, as always, a horse began to run in her heart.

She heard a woman say beside her, "It feels like we're at war."

It was Denise, sitting in a chair, her face pale and prominent. She went on: "War. You know . . . castle ramparts, the tense beachhead, the palm trees. The rockets' red glare. . . ." She smiled and Kathy wondered who had put her up to this.

"Who are we at war with?" Kathy asked. "I forgot. . . ."

"Spain."

"Oh that's right," she said, holding herself against the breeze. "Spain."

"How are you doing?"

She looked over and examined Denise carefully. "Oh, I'm fine."

Denise smiled, brushed an invisible hair from her face. She looked weary, maybe hungover, or tired from the pressure to forget. She said, "You seem a little off tonight. Is it being around all those stupid wives this afternoon? All the cocktail queens? Or something else?"

"You saw Carlos last week, right?"

Kathy saw Denise stiffen, and thought she might shake off the question, insist on probing Kathy's own mood; but in the end Denise relented, saying, "That's right. We had lemonade, if you can believe it. In his friend's restaurant, and it had a lousy jukebox."

"Did you say anything mean?"

"No."

"I remember I used to say mean things. It doesn't help, though."

The way Denise looked at her suggested that she couldn't imagine this: Kathy heartbroken, Kathy being cruel. As if she'd found Eli so easily, as a gift, perhaps, or by saving up on green stamps. "Of course not," Denise said.

"I used to think you could win them back."

Denise didn't say anything for a moment. Then she grinned. "It's stupid, isn't it? Here I am, a grown woman. It's just so stupid of me. And I just heard," she said, talking slowly now because she hadn't yet spoken these words, "Jorgeson said Carlos bought a new house with his wife. So it's clear he's not leaving her."

"He was never going to leave her, Denise."

"You know," Denise said, smiling ironically and clucking her tongue, "I could never quite believe that."

Kathy looked at her friend, beautiful in the night air but truly nothing like she seemed, somehow more like a child driving a beautiful car. She had no idea of how the world went. Kathy spoke the truth that came into her mind: "You have to stop loving him."

"Oh, I don't love him," Denise said, shaking her head.

Kathy paused a moment and shouts came all around them, those calling out the falling stars and those of boys in a baseball game. Kathy felt a little angry, cheated. "You don't?"

Denise leaned her head against her palm. "I must have, at some point, but I think it's not about that. You know, I can't even picture more than his face."

"I don't understand."

"It isn't love." Denise grinned and looked away, saying, "It's something else."

Kathy, confused at her friend's obscure heart, tried to be incisive. "Maybe no one else ever had the last word before."

Denise turned and looked at her, perhaps a little hurt. "No," she said. Kathy wanted to retract her words, but Denise had clearly forgotten them already. She looked upward and merely repeated, "It's something else. I have to get the feeling back. I can't explain."

Kathy loved something about this woman, although she couldn't have said what. Her neuroses were so common, and it could anger anyone to watch her wasting herself on men, dressing in so matronly a way in her gloves and pearls, hiding her brilliance inside that ridiculous hairdo just to be admired. Yet Kathy loved her, perhaps because she was loyal, or because she was inscrutable like this, valuable and odd.

Denise gestured and said, "Look, the sultan wants to see the comet."

The monarch stood regally, as Professor Swift tried to adjust the royal telescope nearby, which was old and full of brass dials and screws. He fiddled with it for a while, peering through the eyepiece now and then, and finally turned to the sultan and announced that the thing was rusted firmly in one position. The local boy was called over from his baseball game to help.

"Are you pregnant, Kathy?"

Kathy laughed, not looking at her but picking at her dress.

Denise stammered, her fingers tapping nervously, "I . . . I just . . . you seem . . ."

"You can go back and tell Eli I'm just anxious tonight. It'll pass."

"I only . . ."

"No, I'm not. It's okay."

Her friend smiled. "Okay."

The two women moved closer, shivering slightly as the night grew colder, feeling the lightless hulk of the island behind them. Around them were the scuttling students, the redhead tossing a baseball, the boy working on the telescope, the girl propped on a lambskin, the waves and the stars.

Denise spoke again. "You don't want one, do you?"

Kathy said nothing, and did not move. She felt Denise's gaze burning the side of her face, and it made her smile, but she didn't feel the need to explain. Denise had this habit of saying everything she was thinking at the moment she was thinking it, unable to wait. Here, in the cool, quiet air, the words were wasted. Kathy thought it funny that she had often heard Denise complain about this very same trait in her mother yet didn't see it in herself. Kathy smiled at her odd friend, pleased and annoyed.

"They're doing that all wrong," Denise said finally, standing up and pointing to the men and the boy at the telescope. She dusted off her pants and said quietly, "I'll be back later." Then she was gone.

Bats were crossing invisibly again. Kathy ducked; everyone on the overlook was ducking, so used to a sky that couldn't touch them. Bats—hidden children spoiling the view, blind, careless, knocking down the lamps, the pictures, the portents.

Kathy looked back to see her husband, only to find that both chairs were empty at the post; Denise was walking back across the stone, and Eli had disappeared somewhere in the red-spotted darkness. Where was he? It panicked her. Then she saw him: He was approaching Manday's wife, pointing to her golden combs. What was he doing over there? He squatted beside the woman's chair and began to talk. She heard a boy shouting happily in English, but she ignored it. Later, she would recall that he had shouted "Catch! Catch!"

Another call of "Time!" Kathy looked up and saw not a meteor, but the comet up there in Centaurus. She admired comets, creatures that didn't race violently through the sky but quietly and coldly burned above without burning out, returning; they were things to count on. She looked down and saw Lydia lying on her lambskin. She thought of what her husband had said on the night she had met him. Comets, girls with long pale braids. Careless girls. Girls with heads full of thoughts, full of details from the tiring day. Girls walking slowly toward their vanities, undressing, blind to the thousands watching them from below. She felt they were in danger.

At the time, she hardly noticed their positions: Denise walking back to her seat, stopping and pointing; Eli squatting near Manday's wife; Kathy herself craning her neck to look at Lydia. A perfect triangle. It meant nothing; yet, looking back, this triangle on the sultan's parapet would seem like such a crucial sign to miss. Such a clear image. That was when it happened.

She would remember this moment all wrong. She would place Denise's shout one second before the accident itself, nearly in time, and she would make it into a warning shout and not what it was: a call of annoyance, a shout that they were doing things wrong. In memory, she would wreathe the scene with worry. But there was no worry. There was no time for it. The baseball went flying from a boy's freckled hand, through the dark meteor-spangled air toward the telescope—so low that Swift or Manday or even the sultan could have caught it if they had been looking—into the awkward palm of the grinning island boy. No one could have reacted yet—it was just a thrown ball—but someone watching might have noticed how wrong the next moment looked: the curled position of the boy's arm, his jagged stance on the ladder, his other arm flying up to balance in the air. That was the moment to yell; not before, where she would place Denise's warning shout. For some reason, though, she needed to remember it that way.

Everyone turned at the boy's cry, but it was just a fall from a short ladder. Eli would describe it later as a yelp, a crack of worry but not of terror, which somehow would seem wrong but true. The boy's arm was tangled in the telescope, and he began to pull it with him. The only one who took action was Swift: He held the telescope upright so that the boy fell free of it. He fell, his arm unloosed, and this made his body turn so that he landed with his full weight against the wall of the overlook; and the wall, a bad repair from the war, crumbled beneath him. There was no cry this time. It was too quick to catch—the interval between the boy hitting the wall and his disappearance over the cliff.

The first silence was of curiosity. Where had he gone? Surely . . . surely . . . and then the second silence came in a white burning flash. Kathy still craning her neck, Denise still pointing, Swift still holding the telescope from danger. This silence was the moment when their eyes revealed to their minds, like terrified messengers, what had to be true.

The scene released its catch. Swift threw the telescope aside and leaned over the wrecked hole in the wall, shouting with the sultan, acting as if there were something they could do. Those already standing raced to the edge, followed close behind by those, like Eli, who had left their seats. Some did not run, but grabbed their children or wives and held them close. The baseball-playing boys were embraced immediately and coaxed away from the edge by parents who shouted, trying not to sound too frightened, trying not to think about what had surely happened. It still had not quite happened; they had not fully realized that the boy was dead, bones broken on the rocks of the beach below, near a fan of seaweed, where each wave unfolded its luminous edge onto the sand.

The students moved all at once to the wall, but randomly, like molecules of water panicking at the boiling point. They ran around each other, toward the open edge, drawn to the horror. Denise and Kathy, together at the beginning, split around the huddled parents and children, and this might have made a difference, in the end. Together at the wall, or apart. Kathy stopped to hold frozen, crying Lydia, taking her in her arms. Eli came with the Mandays and headed straight for the wall. It was only chance that put him next to Denise. Kathy stood in the middle of the overlook, hushing Lydia, kissing her cheek. Everyone was yelling until they heard voices from below.

When the shouts floated up from the beach, those on the overlook understood. Denise and Eli stood together at the wall, looking down on a village darkened by the sultan's edict, one small lantern recently lit and showing a scene too complex to understand: rocks and drift-wood and, somewhere in the rubble, a small, thin body. Denise took Eli's hand and felt it shaking; she looked up at his eyes in shock. Kathy held the little girl. Island voices shouted in a foreign language. A high girl's voice, which they later learned was a grown woman's, began to wail somewhere in the darkness. They understood before the sultan faced Swift and whispered a translation; before the solemn, bearded professor turned toward them all like a giant and told them what had happened. If only Manday's time machine were true! If only each of them could have gone back thirteen days, they would have chosen to remain in their old lives: Swift writing a letter; Lydia hearing her mother's bedtime story; Eli writing out his thesis pro-posal; Kathy washing dishes and listening to the Beatles; Denise wait-ing in a café for her old lover, shaking her head at the waitress, *nothing yet*, as she read through the jukebox choices. Each of them would have chosen those petty worries over this one, but how could they have known? We are deaf to what our lives will bring us.

It began here, when they were young. Denise held on to Eli's hand and he whispered to her. Kathy, far away, stared at the crumbled wall. It was born of this moment. They stood on the overlook, silent, watching, listening to the men and women shouting and crying below. The meteor storm was reaching its peak above them, sending sparks of light across the stars, shattering the dark bowl of the sky as if a god had dropped it. Only the children raised their heads to see.

1971

near aphelion

It is always hard to realize that these numbers and equations we play with at our desks have something to do with the real world.

—Steven Weinberg

Her father would not let her chop the vegetables.

"But I'm *sooo* good at it, and *sooo* careful," she complained, pulling up a bar stool and resting her chin on the countertop.

He refused, wiped the blade of his heavy knife, and began slicing a moon-white onion, letting the rings fall silently to the board.

"Oh, come on," Lydia said to her father, and then flailed her arms out, crying: "Oh, just drop it!" She was trying out a new way of talking now, similar to her friend Kim's voice—so many sighs and *ohs* and weary eye-rolling expressions—but she hadn't got it right yet, and could see it wasn't working now. He glanced up at her and she was a little afraid she'd offended him, somehow; acted too teen-agerly for a girl of eleven, like a tourist saying the wrong words from a phrasebook. But he waved her away with the knife—he was un-concerned, and unmoved. Usually, when she wanted something, Lydia returned to childhood and her early successes at manipula-tion—that artificial smile she was flashing now, the giggle with a finger at her lip, the curtsy. But the tricks tended to cloy these days, and they rarely worked on him anymore. Yet, despite this Kim lan-guage, she had not come up with new stuff. It made her furious and confused, and she walked away looking for something to destroy in retribution.

Swift continued to work away at his onion, turning the rings ninety degrees so he could chop from a new angle. Everything had to be done in a particular way—you wouldn't have guessed this about him if you'd caught him drunk and boisterous at a party, spraying rum into his beard, telling stories of Richard Feynman and those mathematical jokes—and even he wouldn't have recognized or admitted it. He would have said that it was easy and obvious how to cut an onion: the best way. You might have said this was a sign of his genius, the outward show of his facility with stars and numbers, but the same obsession in a lesser man could just as easily have been taken as desperation. Because Swift was also desperate, moving on to his red peppers, half-listening for his daughter as she stomped around the house. He was afraid, despite all his efforts, that he had grown suddenly old.

It was 1971, and for so many professors like Swift, it was hard to read the newspapers and believe that this was the world they'd known. Bombs were everywhere: on airliners, campuses, even in the rest room of the Capitol. Science jobs were at an all-time low; Nixon had cut aerospace funding drastically, and then, inevitably, an Apollo mission had gone horribly wrong and the scientists themselves were blamed. Universities had closed down to protests after the invasion of Cambodia, and many of the male astronomy undergraduates, in a panic over the draft, had abandoned science and left for Canada and Denmark. Young professors led their students in protest; older ones shook their heads at empty classrooms. Science, the savior of the world a decade before, had become some kind of enemy, so how could men like Swift feel they belonged? He tried; he lectured against the war in his classroom, smoked pot with his students, bought trippy records they recommended and listened to them over and over until he found something to enjoy. He tried to feel some sympathy for the young.

Lydia was already outside. She knew very little of what was in the newspapers. She had stolen a handful of crackers from the table, and here she stood outside in a mist of crumbs. They were on their farm in Sonoma, north of the city—once her parents' place, and now just her father's; a weekend at the apple orchard in mid-March. Usually it was still cold at this time of year, officially winter, prone to fog and night chills that sent the spiders indoors to torment them, but nothing was for sure in northern California, and the late afternoon air was unseasonably warm and bright, birds wrestling in the budded trees, the weeds and grass of the field she stood in glowing greenly, smelling deeply of themselves.

They were there too early. They had never come to the farm in March before, but when her father suggested it, she had grown so excited that she puzzled even herself. She had friends in Berkeley, a birthday party to go to (Kim would be there), but there was something so secret and true about the farm, something so old in her that she could hardly resist it: the half-a-year of waiting, then that sudden reward that she was never able to predict (though it came every year, without fail) that first weekend when her parents, filled with relief, would pack food and coffee and drive off with Lydia and her older sister. There was the mysteriously long route across a bridge, the familiar water tower in white, then the old unchanged and cobwebbed homestead where her mother had always crept off happily with a book and her father paced restlessly through the fields in an old fishing hat, leaving her alone with her sullen sister and a dark barn full of attics, coops, sharp mysteries. March—they were there too early; it threw her off. But she didn't question it. Perhaps some wonderful thing had happened to her here when she was young, so young she had forgotten it—a gold earring found in the dry straw, or a nest of chicks—something lost and invisible that drew her here without the *ohs* and sighs and feigned boredom.

This month was the aphelion of Comet Swift—its point farthest from Earth. Her father had told her this the week before, in explanation of their early trip, pulling a pink piece of construction paper from her art table and drawing ellipses across it in dark ink, lovingly sketching the comet with its old-man's beard. He talked about the attraction of Jupiter, the Oort Cloud, the effect of the solar wind. Spirals and lines covered the pink paper. He made sure Lydia understood the science of it, and she nodded as if she did, and then

Swift folded the paper, squatted down beside her and asked the strangest thing: "Do you remember the boy who fell?"

Lydia did not know what to say. It was a terrible crime to say you didn't know something in her family, in that house crowded with books and maps. Could you say you didn't remember? "Sort of," she said carefully.

"At Bukit? At the perihelion?"

It was another word she knew she was supposed to understand, so she didn't hesitate to smile and nod. So he smiled, too, relieved, and began to talk with her about it. He gave her the details that she'd lost in the confusion of youth—the rusted telescope, the broken wall, the baseball moving against the sky—but instead of bringing back her own memories in a rush, she regarded this as another of her father's amazing stories, from a long time ago. And though he put Lydia in the story, placed her on a mat in the middle of the overlook, playing with a monkey, she believed this was, again, his old device. She was always in his stories. Lydia knew she wasn't there that night—how could she have been? Nothing so terrible could happen except in the distant past of fathers. No one died these days.

Swift did not always know the right thing to say; he told her things adults should never share with children. He talked about the crazy, wailing women on the island and the money he'd had to give to the sultan. He talked about his own doubts, about how he felt, for a long time, as if it were his fault—he had moved the telescope out of the way, just at the wrong moment, pulled the boy's only support from underneath him. He no longer believed this, he told her, smiling through his beard. He'd meant to save the boy; that was all that mattered. He had tried. Lydia sat very still on her bed, afraid that if she moved, she might crack the mood and lose this odd confessional, lose the intensity of her father's memory. So often he ignored his younger daughter, caught up in his stars, and here he was squatting before her, talking as if he was sharing a secret with her. She loved him desperately.

He told her the story, he said, getting up at last, because people might talk about it at the party. He wanted to make sure she knew. Lydia nodded, acting as if it were nothing, but the image remained in her mind long after he left the room: *A boy fell from a cliff, through palm trees, onto a darkened beach.*

What she considered now, however, was not the boy at all; it was the people who might mention him. The scientists. Lydia didn't like them; they were too strange, too unlike her or any of her friends' parents. They talked about the oddest things, and their fascination with Lydia was beginning to seem suspicious to her, because they didn't seem to recognize who she was. She felt this meant they didn't recognize her star appeal, the beautiful and lazy way she reached for a pear (something Kim had taught her), the sexual batting of her eyelids and (of course) the clear brilliance of her mind. She was an Indian princess in disguise among the common people, and they should take note. But really it was just that they didn't treat her like a child; they talked to her like an adult or, rather, as if they were children, too, as if she were no different; and yet, still, secretly, she pined for that distinction. She loved the way other adults, like Kim's parents, fawned over her, brought presents, deferred to her as if she might save the world. None of that happened with her father's friends. Instead, these scientists and grad students might spend an hour in her room playing with her camera while she sat on the bed picking at her jeans, arms crossed and furious. Didn't they know who she was?

Lydia ran across the field toward the barn. She had decided she would spend the whole evening there, in the loft with her magazines and diary, spying on the adults. Grass broke at her ankles, wet from an earlier rain, and flecked water into the air. Her socks were getting wet, and green, but she was careless. She hardly ever noticed anything except the object of her focus; somehow, the absentmindedness passed over the professor and grew in his daughter. Blue moths were floating over the field—she didn't notice them—and, caught in her wake, they flew like tissue into the sky, which was as blue as they were. She hated being eleven. It killed Lydia that she wasn't twelve; she despised being eleven; it was so young. It seemed to her that she'd been cursed with childhood forever, that no one else in the world had ever been so young for so long.

So there she was, climbing up the splintered crosspieces of her ladder, wet straw clinging to her hair as the bats slept high in the rafters; there she was getting higher but, to her mind, no older. And there was her father, cutting lamb into cubes, humming some new song through his gray beard, some tune he'd heard on the radio, trying to be relevant and oh-so-seventies. Yet he could hardly go to bed without another year passing him by. The girl with straw-littered hair, a mere slug in time, and her portly father moving like a greyhound through it.

The doorbell rang. Someone had arrived too early.

Above, out away from the little farm built on its quarter-lot of an orchard, the apple blossoms only green teeth on the branches—above, into space, past the Moon and Mars and the asteroids, somewhere out near Jupiter—the comet sailed on its bent orbit. Just a fist of ice and dust now, a few kilometers across, nothing propelling it but momentum and these giant gravities, no heat here to give it a tail or any brightness. Dark and asleep. It was nearing its farthest distance from them—its aphelion, its half-birthday—oblivious, of course, to the party being thrown in its honor.

"Manday!" Swift yelled in the doorway and it was indeed Dr. Manday, holding a bottle of wine like a baby. His skin was drier and paler than it had been years ago, and he was as stout as Swift now, though a decade or so younger. Perhaps it was his timidity that aged him faster, and his old friend had always cursed him for that, demanded that he listen to rock music and wear blue jeans instead of the stiff collars and slacks of an old man. Manday couldn't bear it; it was hard enough for him to be an American. The loudness and frankness of being American, the utter selfishness and greed and great compassion of it, the whole opera whose stage he stepped onto—it was hard enough acting his role without having to be young, or brave, or handsome as well. Did he have to leap into the very fire?

"Best wishes to your comet," Dr. Manday said and waited in the doorway.

Swift made no gesture for him to enter, but stood there in his apron, that frightening knife clenched in one fist. He was looking past Manday into the sky, burning blue as flame, and perhaps to what might be hidden out there, impossible to see; perhaps wondering whether either of them would live to see it again. These were troubled times. A cloud moved away from the sun and warm light made its way to them, first to Swift, then to Manday, as they both stood in awkward contemplation of this invisible object and its course. It seemed to Manday that Swift had forgotten him, or could see through him, and that he simply didn't matter. Even standing in the doorway with a bottle of red table wine, he didn't matter. The bearded man finally took the bottle and patted his shoulder.

"Let's hope the old boy's fine," he said.

Manday stepped into the house; he was careful about crossing thresholds here. Americans were so territorial. "The old boy?"

Swift brandished the gleaming blade as they walked through the mud room and into the kitchen. "1953 Two," he said. "The old vile star." He always used the numerical name for it, being too humble or aware to call it Comet Swift.

"You think it's gone?" This made no sense to Manday; there was no way to calculate such a thing. The comet, with no tail now, could not be seen or even sensed on Earth.

"Well, that's always the fun part, isn't it?" Swift said, violently pulling open drawers in search of a corkscrew (he always had to relearn this house, his mistress). "You remember Van Meehern, poor guy. He was my best friend, you know. I remember we were so young when he got his comet. He was . . . oh, it was called 1948 Three, so how old was I? Thirty-five or something, truly young, truly young. Beautiful comet, brand-new from the Oort Cloud, just bright and amazing." Swift seemed to be talking wistfully about a woman as he opened the wine bottle between his legs. "We were at Palomar at the next calculated return, just a few years later—oh, it was exciting! Were you ever young, Manday?"

Manday hadn't expected a question. He was just holding a wineglass, waiting for it to be filled, and then here he was, being asked if he had ever been young. It felt like a punch—him, young, no he hadn't ever been young. He had been a different person. How could he ever explain it to this man?

But Swift didn't wait for any reply: "We had signed up nights for a week, and we were there with some grad students, up all night with coffee, talking, looking at the sky to see that signature glimmer. Five nights passed before we realized it wasn't coming back, and then another night before Van Meehern ran outside and just looked up at the sky. Damn cold. Never trust a woman or a comet, Manday."

"Was it Jupiter?" Manday asked, although he knew this story, and knew Swift's old expression. He knew what was missing from the story, too: the real grief of Dr. Van Meehern that night, something they all had felt at four in the morning when the lenses showed nothing, a strange sadness over empty numbers; forgetting, in that cold air, the people whom they loved or ought to love.

Swift poured wine happily, never mentioning that embarrassing sight of his friend under the dark sky, weeping. "Who knows? Did it break up, or was it too big? Did it shoot out into space? It's lost. So, as for 1953 Two, who knows?"

"Here is to 1953 Two," Manday proposed, lifting his glass. They toasted, old friends, and talked in very specific, mathematical terms about the stars and clouds of dust, a nonsense topic they could float in harmlessly.

The doorbell rang again, rhythmically—*shave-and-a-hair-cut*—someone funny must have arrived. Grad students.

Up in the loft of the barn, Lydia was missing her sister and, specifically, missing the pot they had smoked together over Christmas on Alice's last break from boarding school. Part of her parents' fight over custody had ended in Alice, a thin, gloomy, guitar-playing girl who wrote verse plays in a flowered notebook, being sent off to a boarding school near Mendocino. This was a perfect, King Solomon–like solution to the adults' wrangling, but baffled both sixteen-year-old Alice and her sister. But Alice hadn't really changed—she had grown harder, of course, picking up the sixties' remaining scent of rebellion and breaking out of Mendocino anytime she could, but really she was as dreamy and distant as before. The last time Lydia saw her sister, just a few months before, the older girl had dispensed with her former sororal cruelties and lit up a joint for them to smoke together in their room after dinner. It had been a bizarre evening. Their parents had insisted on having Christmas together despite their obvious animosity, so the two girls had sneaked off to their room and, with the low rumble of voices below, leaned out of the open window, coughing, laughing (Lydia was not really stoned but thought she was), and then used a purple magic marker to draw smiley faces on their jeans.

Lydia had a wooden stash box up here in the barn, but it was empty inside. She was still enough of a child to play at things, just as she'd baked plastic muffins in a cardboard box, now she was pretending to smoke her invisible joint out the cracked window of the loft, the bats adjusting their dark wings above her. She should have loved the freedom of suddenly being the only child, alone with her father, having escaped from the city this weekend to wander the farm without the threat of her sister making her eat green strawberries from the mud. But of course that's not what she felt. She was eleven; she longed for change but was afraid when it arrived, and this year without her mother or her sister was stretching on and on like an endless rehearsal.

The dusty air above her seemed like the smoke from her invisible joint, and she posed on her stomach in the hayloft, legs crossing, scissoring behind her, head leaning on a hand and inhaling her pretend adulthood. Lydia wasn't a quiet or contemplative girl, but was the kind who had to be entertained constantly, either by an adult, another child, or by herself or nature. She wasn't meditative and bookish and could barely make it through a teen magazine without tossing it out the window and bursting through the parlor, singing something, "Raindrops Keep Falling on My Head," anything. To the frustration of her father.

So she was active even while lying quietly in the loft. She could see her father through the window of the kitchen, and three long-haired graduate students in T-shirts (one of them seemed vaguely cool to her, in a peasant skirt and braids, but the others were worthless), all of them holding covered dishes or spelt bread or something. They were always polite and ill-gendered, the men too wispy and effete, the women loud and almost mustached. It made Lydia glad she wasn't there among them—there would be the usual bizarrities of conversation that upset her, the insistent phrase "let me show you something" that always preceded a grainy photograph of Mars. She could see the whole of the house, its craggy shape partly restored, the field dark with old rain and hazy with light, the sky diamond-bright just now, and all the plain broad world below it.

And here was some man, some stranger coming toward her, struggling through the weeds. He was tall, with curls of long coppery hair, and moved so oddly in the grass, working his hands and fingers to part the tall garlic flowers, the stalks of seeds, but keeping his body stiff and upright away as if he were made of glass, as if the slightest pressure from a blade of grass would shatter his chest. She watched how he went, avoiding nests of wild roses and gopher holes—he seemed to have an extraordinary eye—banking like a river, meandering so wide across the field until it seemed as though he planned to cover every inch of it before he reached her.

He stopped, raised an arm of his plaid shirt to show it covered with burrs. She tried not to laugh. There was something about this man, though, that made even Lydia pause and think. Something un-laughable, really. He was so different from the other people at the party. Maybe it was because he didn't look desperate or scared while hip-deep in this swamp of thistles; he merely looked out of place, determined, fixed on crossing. Just as Lydia herself might look. And that was it: He was ordinary. Here was that rare thing in her father's crowd: an ordinary man.

Soon he was in the barn, and his easy breaths made it clear he'd forgotten all about the weeds. "Tycho!" he yelled, hands around his mouth in a cone. "Tycho!" Lydia kept silent above (as silent as she could, though one foot kept nervously tapping against the straw). He was calling for her dog.

In the granular darkness of the barn, his hair had lost its metallic shimmer and looked dull, brown, with the vague swirl of a bald spot. He was young, though—just thirty this month, newly a father, with the glow that only a young man would have at being a father—amazed, glad at his own life, that he has come to this. He had never enjoyed the instability of youth, the hidden parts of love, and was relieved to have arrived here: a son, a wife, a house. They gave him a contentment he would not relinquish easily. Lydia saw none of this—she saw an adult calling foolishly into an empty corner, hay dust settling on his head. In a moment, she leaned over the loft and shouted "Boo!" so that the man fell back against a post, facing her astonished, hands limp. Above them, alive things shifted. And then the retriever came bounding in, barking because he was missing something here, and pounced carelessly on the man, who rolled him over on the ground and scratched him.

"There you are!" the man yelled in a childish voice. "I got you!"

"Who are you?" Lydia was leaning fully over the loft now, aware of the danger, aware of how she might seem dangerous to this new person.

He didn't look up, but kept petting the dog, as if she weren't noticeable, as if she weren't amazing and frightening up there in the loft, as if he were through with her. "Who wants to know?"

"That's my dog, and he doesn't like you to scratch his ears."

He paused for a moment. "Does he bite?" he asked. Tycho whined.

She tossed straw down and watched it float in the air, hoping it would reach him, land on his shoulders; but it took off under her, out of her sight. "Oh, come on," she said, then asked, "What's your name?"

"Adam. What's yours?"

"Alice," she told him plainly.

He smirked and stood up, letting the dog lick at his fingers. He said, "Well . . . *Lydia* . . . they sent me to get your dog."

She was furious; she'd tried this trick before, and it had worked. Now she was embarrassed and felt like scooting to the back of the loft. "Why?" she asked. "I wanted him in here with me."

Adam was poking through a box of tools now, pulling out rusty objects, not looking at her again, and it made her more furious. He said, "Your dad wanted him to do some tricks for us, so he sent me up to get him. Is that your hideout?"

"Oh, come on, I'm eleven. I don't have a hideout," she said, pulling out her Kim voice. "It's a barn."

"Sorry. What are you hiding up there, though?"

She struck a formal pose, hands on her knees, rolling her eyes. She had found a new tack here. "Are you one of my dad's students?" she asked regally, looking away from him. "I *adore* students."

"I'm not a student. I don't know anything about astronomy. I'm Dr. Lanham's husband."

"You're Denise's husband."

"That's right. You know her?"

It was funny—she didn't, though she had of course just now said her name. It was something Lydia would learn, later, that everyone she'd met before she was fifteen would diminish in her memory into just three aspects. Manday, whom she knew so well and talked with often at the university, would become just a funny man with a birthday cake; a wad of blue cotton candy beneath a Ferris wheel; a dark, fat body in a swimsuit near the ocean. The rest would all disappear. Denise was the same—a necklace, a book, a friendly black cat—and that was all. Adam she would remember better; but this conversation in the shifting light of the barn—these words that he would recall so clearly—would be lost to Lydia.

"She's been to my house before, I think," she said, not really sure who they were talking about, although she knew the name. A blond woman?

He told her that his wife had been a student once, back when Lydia was a little girl, back even before he knew her. Now Denise worked for the government, doing experiments that had to do with the sky, publishing papers when she could. These were boring, adult details, and she wasn't listening to them at all.

"You got a kid?"

"A son."

"How old is he?" she asked.

"Just a year," he told her, and she felt disappointed; she liked the weird toy quality of babies, but she'd hoped there would be another girl her age at this party, instead of the usual crowd of dull, stunned-looking five-year-olds. Somehow she imagined that a young man could have a child of twelve or thirteen for her to talk to.

They talked for a while in the barn while the other party went on in the house, where there was all the laughing and nervous nonsense while everyone downed their first drink hastily, hoping it would catch and create its effect as soon as possible. Torches were being lit in the yard as the light grew dim, as clouds covered the sun and caused a chill wind to blow across the field, picking up the stray stalks and flowers Adam had broken, scattering them into the road. The two only talked a little while, and she thought he found her interesting, intelligent and fascinating in her vantage in the loft. She mentioned her dance class.

"What do you do?" she carelessly asked him at one point, leaning on her knees, feeling very adult and clever.

He merely laughed, saying, "You don't care what I do, you're eleven," and it was very true and made her angry and embarrassed. That's when he took the dog, said, "Don't take any wooden nickels!" and walked off through the cool twilight toward the house.

Lydia sat stunned by her own stupidity; to act so falsely just to impress him, without even thinking. Who was that who had spoken? Her, really? Sometimes, in conversation, it seemed as if she had no control over her own words, as if she were reaping the words that someone else had planted. It happened around friends when she was trying to be clever, and around adults when she didn't know what they wanted her to say. Who was it talking? It made her nervous; everyone else seemed, like Dr. Lanham's husband, so easy, so quick and confident with words. It was not that way with her. Perhaps she was what her father always secretly feared: not very bright.

It would be the Swifts' catastrophe if it were true; the curse would stay for generations. There was no worse insult, late at night around the fire, than to call a friend or colleague "stupid." To the family, sitting shocked while sipping their chocolates or brandies (when they were all still together), it wounded the ear, sounded as cruel as "kike" or "nigger." Someone had to correct the family member and whisper, *That's terrible, they aren't stupid, they're just slow.* And why was it so terrible? Call someone dull or preening or ugly, and everybody laughed, nodded, agreed. But call them dumb, and you had claimed they lacked the only quality that mattered in the world: intelligence. In the Swift household, it showed everywhere: the family Scrabble contests, the math quizzes on their breakfast napkins, the long botanical nature walks (her mother's doing) where every minute some new branch was bent for identification, the *New York Review of Books* stacked in the bathroom as the only reading material. This wasn't pressure; to the Swifts, this was fun. You fought at dinner over nothings. You lay in the sun and bothered everybody else by reading your book of poetry aloud. You stood in bookstores and cooed like a child over a first hardcover edition of Will and Ariel Durant. It was normal, essential to be intelligent. To the Swifts, it was the primary quality of being human.

But what if she weren't? What if Lydia preferred to lie on Kim's carpet and sigh over teenage movie magazines? What if it turned out that, at eleven, the age when Lydia's mother had bred a new variety of fern in her basement vivarium, what mattered most in the world to Lydia was her pair of carefully patched and decorated jeans? What if her bad grades in school weren't, as her parents believed, a sign of her boredom with classroom trivia, a rebellion against the academic zoo, but rather just herself—little rusty-haired Lydia—sitting at her desk and staring at the mimeographed quiz, knowing only answers three and seven? What would that mean? Surely the hot earth would split open and swallow them all.

So she had a whole smart act that she had perfected. Part of it, unfortunately, involved never admitting ignorance or asking any questions, so she could carry on whole conversations with those dull, moley graduate students as they talked (unaware, of course, of what would interest a child) about solar absorption, cometary ejection and ion tails, never knowing that this little girl did not understand a word. Manday was particularly dense about this, and regaled her for sunny hours as Lydia replayed hit radio songs in her head. But she could not let on; she could not ask about a word or, worse, act bored or stunned by knowledge. Instead, she wore her fascinated smart face at all times, gleaming like a paste tiara, and no one watched her closely enough to see the difference.

From the high peeling window of the barn, she could see Adam and Tycho making their way across the field toward the farmhouse, the man wandering in his careful way around the thorns, bladelessly machete-ing the weeds, sidestepping the hazards he imagined, some plaid and curly-haired explorer on safari, while the dog leaped freely forward, looking back, waiting, gnawing on something near the ground, then rushing out toward the lights and flames and insects of the patio where a barbecue was already smoking. Someone laughed loudly, already drunk—her father? Lydia hid her diary again under a red wool blanket (where her old brown doll also lay, torn and armless, a strand of scarlet thread dangling from its empty mouth) and set her foot on the first dry rail of the ladder, feeling, as she leaned back, the weight of her descent.

Denise, from where she sat on the patio with her son burbling into her arm, could see her husband coming toward her from the barn. He had finally found the dog. It always surprised her how he could appear from nowhere and delight her—a calm, pedestrian delight, just a thought of *Oh, it's him!*, like passing a theater showing a favorite movie. There he was, somehow finding the struggle in an otherwise simple field of grass, the dog clearly frustrated with him, his hair (she loved his hair the most) in some kind of golden tussle with the wind. She felt he deserved a gnarled stick and a backpack to go with his ruddy expression. She felt he deserved a high alp. Then she was irked, for a moment, by the thought that he would never be this way: a stick, and alp, a high terrifying view. But of course she'd known that when she married him.

Adam waved. Denise tried to wave back, dealing with the gelatinous bundle of her son who jerked his arms around and stared, stared, always stared at the world. She could tell, though no one else could, how much her son looked like her, in the eyes, the color of his face. Something of her would continue now. She waved.

But these worries—her husband and her child—were only two of the many things that concerned Denise at that moment. There was, for instance, her worry over Manday, who seemed to be drinking a great deal of wine this evening and had come up to her already and jokingly demanded her passport, insisting on verification until she showed him a cocktail napkin and he stamped it and moved on.

There was that worry. Then there was Swift, who seemed to be angry with her, although you could never tell, especially ever since his divorce; Denise knew, though, that she had to overcome this because she needed several professional favors of him. Then there was this grad student sitting in front of her now on a stool, wearing braids, a peasant skirt and an intense expression that Denise took for youthful political conviction (she seemed to be talking about Africa)—the conversation had to be kept up at least with "ohs" and "uhs" and an occasional statement of militant agreement. And then, finally, there was Denise's main concern of the evening: to get invited to a Passover seder.

Each year at this time, she would realize how quickly it was approaching, and the idea of being invited overtook her. It had something to do with a change in her when she was younger, the change that came with her move from her parents' house in northern San Francisco to that tiny apartment in Berkeley, to that two-burner electric stove and root drawer, the tattered curtains, the warped boards near the windows. A move into a crowd of people unlike anyone she'd met—opinionated and outspoken people, sometimes charming foreigners, sometimes silent intellectuals—and each year a few (who she hadn't even known were Jewish) would invite her to these seders as if it were completely normal, even boring—*You don't have to come, the wine is awful.* But Denise did come, and found it confusing and enervating. So oddly devout for a crowd of atheists (the songs and prayers in Hebrew, all the praise of God) and so unexpectedly volatile for a religious event (a rabbi and an astrophysics student arguing about the hardening of Pharaoh's heart, then about Israel, then about the Blacks). Something exciting, Denise felt, was going on, something important, and when had anything important ever happened in her church, or at her parents' table? What really altered Denise in those first years in Berkeley was something atmospheric and profound across the bay (the protests, the red-hot anger in the air, the dizzy riots and freedoms), but she would never remember it that way. Denise would point to the tattered curtains, the warped boards and those evenings spent waiting impatiently for the brisket to arrive, listening to her new friends shake their heads in disagreement over Johnson, King, the deaths of the Egyptians' sons.

It had all ended, though, when her friends moved on to postgraduate work elsewhere, when she met and married Adam and they were left (as the young never expect to be) alone with each other, two WASPs in a yellow house near Santa Cruz. March became a wasteland—nothing but drear, pastelly Easter with her mother in that ridiculous hat.

The problem was, of course, that Denise couldn't throw a seder herself. (Did you "throw" one?) They were both gentile, and she could come up with no justifiable reason for having one at their house, so she gave it up. It was like when she was a child and stared at the tall glass cabinet in the living room, the upper level of which was filled with porcelain birds. She had to wait for some adult to open it; otherwise, she could only stare. But Denise missed the seders too much—the politics, the fervor, the insipid wine—and her new plan this year was to get invited even if she had to crash the congregation of B'nai Israel. Mentally, she had a list of Jewish colleagues and graduate students who were possibilities. She was feeling them out, one by one. The young student of Swift's before her now—Denise wasn't sure.

This obsession was, perhaps, a detail. One of many in a life which had not turned out the way she had expected. Denise always thought that life would build upon itself, that people would multiply, events would crowd for time, that life at thirty would seem like twice of twenty. She thought it might overgrow itself like a garden. But it wasn't turning out this way. Your twenties choked with flowering vines; your thirties thinned to only what you tended. People disappeared, and events, and opportunity.

Her career, for instance, was not what everyone had expected. She had published with Swift upon graduation, but she had also published on her own, laboring alone with the equipment, writing alone, putting no one's name on the papers except her own. She did this pragmatically, because an older female astronomer had advised her once never to publish with a man; everyone would assume he had done all the work. Her solo publishing lent her distinction; it also raised eyebrows on search committees. Her graduating colleagues (Eli, Jorgeson, the rest) were being given postdoctoral positions across the country, and some even had faculty positions, but Denise was left in interviews calmly trying to explain that it truly had been her work alone. She was offered nothing. The best in her class, the field wide open with Sputnik money, dozens of interviews, and she was offered nothing. So she married Adam and, eventually, took a government position in Santa Cruz. It was a humbling choice. Few people did research there, or even published; it was nothing like the brilliant industry of grad school, but felt instead like a kind of occupational heat death. Only hard work could bring you out, and she worked hard. Denise was also the only woman there, and her supervisor often showed her lab to visiting scientists as a curiosity: *We are proud to have one of the few female astronomers with us, Dr. Lanham. Denise, are you free for a moment?* Denise complained about this habit to Adam, calling it "feeding time." It reminded her of how the male BADgrads had all visited her office when she'd first arrived at Berkeley, a "field trip" to see the female student. She had assumed it would all change once she published. Nothing changed.

But she was in a wonderful mood tonight, Dr. Denise Lanham with a baby on her lap. This woman amused her, she amused herself, and there was her husband clambering ridiculously through the grass. She had a child, a glass of wine, a breeze. It was all right. Life was wonderful, every particle of it.

"And what does your husband do?" the young student wanted to know, which was a surprise because she had talked only about herself for twenty minutes now, as if it were a strict exercise in sticking to a topic.

Denise adjusted her son in her lap. "He's a writer," she said. She looked up to the sky, dimming now, the purple shredded clouds moving in the wind, wool caught on a barbed-wire fence. Her first thought was: We won't see the meteors tonight. Her second: It's getting too cold for Josh.

"What kind of writer?"

"He writes fiction. Novels."

The woman brought out a stick of gum and began to chew it, her expression deepening, and Denise thought to herself, *They're so serious, this generation, they say they're so fun and free, but look how dark and serious they are.* The woman asked, "What kind of fiction? Science fiction?"

People always asked that question at astronomical parties; it was all anybody ever read. "No," Denise said, adjusting her son and watching her husband appear from the weeds in a scattering of seeds. "No, like novels that take place a long time ago." She was groping here, always finding it difficult to describe these things her husband made. "Historical novels, I guess."

The student nodded, the pink gum appearing in her mouth every few seconds, a bright spot in the darkness. "Have I seen them?" she asked.

"No, they're not published," Denise said.

She hated saying that. The face on the student now, the puzzled face of science staring at art—she hated it. They were so literal: A scientist without papers is a charlatan, and a writer without books is a fake. Always this puzzled face—as if Adam were one of those madmen scribbling letters to astronomy departments (Denise had read dozens), claiming to have found a message hidden in a nebula. It was an act of faith to call him a writer, the kind of faith a wife should have, must have. And yet, Denise's anger came because, partly, she didn't quite have it. She had read his failed novels and hadn't understood or liked them; they seemed static and a little dull. *I'm wrong, though, of course,* she thought to herself. Surely she had made the right choice. Surely he, too, was a genius.

Adam was moving from group to group like a bee pollinating a field of clover, picking up a drink along the way (a martini, which seemed very unlike him). As he reached a group, he would lean his head forward and nuzzle it between two people so he could address someone, and then, fairly quickly, he would take off for the next. Sweat was showing just under his hairline, glimmering in the torchlight. There was the smell of smoke everywhere. Denise knew what he was doing—he was bumming cigarettes. He had supposedly quit, but the calendar was a checkerboard of quitting and resuming the habit. Denise smiled because it was all right with her; she had never tried to have any control over him; and anyway, he was younger than she was by two years and deserved more time to make mistakes, time to wean himself of the habits of his youth. She had to give him things like that. But still it made her husband seem, sweating in that light, a little dwarfish and pathetic, dipping into crowds begging for a cigarette, pointlessly stooping so his wife wouldn't notice—a boy cheating badly at cards.

Denise got back to the point: "So, are you looking forward to next week?"

"What's next week?" the woman asked.

"You know," Denise said, stroking her son's head and thinking it was odd how he could suspend a bubble on his lip for ten minutes, in defiance of known physics. "You know, the holidays." She was fishing for Passover now, hoping she wouldn't get Easter.

But the student, straightening the part in her hair with two fingers, laughed and brushed the entire topic aside. "Oh that, oh no—oh, I don't do Western congregational religions anymore. I'm into meditation." She said this almost as a challenge.

"TM?" Denise asked wearily, but the conversation was on automatic now as the student went on happily about the wonders of a trance state, and alpha waves and all the pseudoscience Denise was used to hearing from young people these days. Here was something Denise did not understand, not at all, this need for religion. She felt pure, this way, needing nothing but light through a lens to explain her world. She understood this was snobbery; she could not resist it. In any case, the girl, Jewish or not, was not inviting Denise to any seder.

Adam had found a cigarette and seemed happy. That was good. He was talking to a spouse with old-fashioned peroxide hair (like something from a billboard), smoking, looking handsome, and the woman was laughing. Good. Denise would grant him all kind of pardons tonight if he'd look happy for her.

"And in London," the student was saying now, taking the gum from her mouth, "I hear there's an amazing swami. Kathy was talking about him at the conference, if you can believe it."

"Kathy who?"

"Spivak, Eli's wife."

Denise tensed. How strange: Here was this young woman with pink gum in her mouth, talking nonsense, and then out of nowhere here was Eli. How unexpected. Who knew conversations could be as haunted as old houses?

She had not seen or talked to Eli in years. That summer after the comet's return, a cold green summer faintly echoing with that cry they'd heard, the boy's cry from the overlook, Eli had abruptly transferred his studies to a lab in England, and within a month was on a plane with Kathy through the fog of San Francisco. Denise remembered their breakfast in the airport lounge, stiff scrambled eggs and coffee sipped loudly through the silence. Eli would not look at her, and Kathy kept an inscrutable smile on her face, somehow thrilled by all the mess and frenzy of this unexpected change, this flight from San Francisco. But it was a good-natured leaving. Kathy had waved to her from the tarmac, brown suede gloves in her hand, that green-apple-colored kerchief wrapped so tightly around her head, and Eli had not looked back but moved resolutely through the rain, hat-first. It was these two, of course, who had invited Denise to all the seders. And here she had forgotten it.

Denise remembered Kathy's smile, her wave in the mist of the airport. Had Kathy known? Surely not; she would have said something. She would have found a way out of having that awkward breakfast. What had he told her? What excuse could he possibly have provided for doing the unthinkable—switching not just advisers or courses of study but *programs,* slowing his Ph.D. process by two years—and all to move to England, across the world? Denise could imagine no scene in their bright dining room that might end with Kathy patting his hand and agreeing. She could only see a wife bewildered by her husband's insanity. Because of course he couldn't tell her the real reason for his flight: his sudden and strained love affair with Denise.

It had surprised them both, standing there on the overlook six years before, looking down at that broken body. Broken, twisted, with his legs curled in one direction and his head facing the wrong way, flattened and bloody on a rock. Arms out, hands in loose fists among the seaweed. People were running around and screaming below, but they kept at a distance because a snake was in the rocks, apparently, stiffly terrified beside the body. Denise could not see the snake, only the body lit by torches and the women's faces streaked with tears as they were held back. Her hand crept along the wall until it touched another's—Eli's. He grabbed her hand and held it tight, and she looked up into his eyes. In each pupil, a little torch flickered. She read there: *I understand, Denise, I'm the only one who understands.*

Kathy left on a boat the next day, waving to them in the hot, pale air, and when the boat was far enough away, Eli told Denise to meet him down the beach in a few hours. He walked away; she was confused. Suddenly, she couldn't stand being alone there in the hot sun. Her studies could not console her, nor her books; and even the image of her old lover Carlos's lips, which she used to love so dearly, meant nothing now. *It's not enough, it's not enough.* So she did as Eli said. That afternoon, while the other astronomers slept, she made her way down the jungle path to the beach, where she found him waiting in the shade of a frangipani, nervous, as serious as death. They made love in an old stone hut on a spit, sun flowing through the keyhole in a chesspiece of light, only because it seemed the most natural thing to do. Life was in crisis, somehow; this was the shelter. She simply did as Eli said. They kept their eyes closed when they were together—kissing, lying beside each other—which made the time so different from their afternoons arguing at the college, standing in the shining hallways with cups of coffee, staring at each other, shouting. Eyes closed; this was a secret they kept even from themselves. In the hut, on the plane. And when Denise arrived back home, when her mother greeted her at the terminal with a bouquet of white roses, she was able to tell the woman that it had worked. The trick, the deal: Denise had forgotten all about Carlos, her old lover. Her mother was so pleased.

Denise very quickly brought it to an end. Not consciously, not intentionally; but somehow she found ways in their long hours together in class, under the telescope, to avoid moments alone with him. They had not spoken, on the island, like lovers—they'd made no admissions, no promises or confessions to each other; it was simply that they understood, they were the only ones who understood. And now Denise acted almost practically, living around the secret, the way a family in a war-torn land might live around a hole in the floor. Of course she could see the pain in Eli's face, but it began to anger her, how obvious he was. She would come to dinner at the Spivaks, and every time Kathy left the room he would turn quickly to face her, staring, those eyes wide and full of meaning—but meaning what? That they had shared a little portion of death, of love? What was there to discuss?

One night, months after the boy's death, he finally caught her alone. She heard a knock on the door and it was Eli in a trench coat, hair glistening with fog, whispering that he'd come over to talk. He had driven across Berkeley, late at night, to talk with her. He cleared his throat and she knew he had been practicing this in the car, that he had left Kathy alone with some excuse and practiced a speech in the car all this way. Denise had practiced nothing; she had stuffed the whole event—the broken body, the frangipani, the chesspiece of light—behind her sweaters in the closet. If she let him speak now, so prepared, he might convince her. So she interrupted him with a hand in the air.

"We don't need to have this conversation," she said.

"Listen, I want to say I'm sorry. I was so confused. . . ."

She held the door halfway closed, talking in the narrow space. "I'm not, don't worry."

Eli shuddered, cold, "Denise, you were in shock. I don't know. . . . I know I shouldn't have done that. But I wanted to tell you. . . ."

So this was the beginning of his speech. Apology, and then some rare admission. "We don't need to have this conversation," she repeated, feeling she had struck upon a phrase that might save her. Then she added: "I can't afford it."

He got almost angry, whispering, "Listen to me, listen to me. . . ."

She shook her head without looking at him. "I'm the expert on this one. I'm the expert on married men. Go home, please," she said. "Please." Eli didn't move, but stood there silently, as if he knew this was his great chance, that this was the only time they would speak of this while they were young, and so he stood there. She understood, as he must have, that it was just a crisis on an island, that they would not fall in love, that they would be fine; still some perfect combination of words might alter them both, open them to a terrible adventure. She could see his mind already searching for those words, tossing its net, catching them one by one. She could not let it happen; she could not bear it. So she talked through the moment. She killed it: "We don't need to have this conversation. I'm fine. We'll be fine. I'll see you in the morning."

Then Denise closed the door on him, turned off the light, walked to her kitchen to sit down at the table and put her hand over her mouth. She heard a car start up and drive away. *Two torches flickering in his pupils.* She sat there for a long time, hot and stiff in that placid light, before the sobs broke through her fingers.

The image that came to Denise's mind, however, six years later at Swift's party, was not Eli filled with longing in her doorway, or his checkered hat in the airport fog, or even some moment of him sunburnt and smiling on the island, lying on the beach with sand stuck to his naked body as he held her hand. He did not come to her that way. The moment the student mentioned his name, the man she saw was Eli as he had been when she first met him. It was after the male grad students had visited her on that awful "field trip" of theirs, after they had stood gazing awkwardly at her, shaking her hand, and left in a group full of nervous laughter. It was after they were gone, when she stood up to close the door, worried and upset, that Eli suddenly appeared in the hallway. "Are you Denise?" he asked, grinning. "The comet girl?" He gave her a few quick words of advice about Swift, then invited her to dinner with his new wife, who sat waiting out in the car. Slouched against the door frame, hands moving as his ideas flew everywhere, face goateed, hair long and curly and voice full of passion. A young Eli, anxious, exciting—a person who no longer, of course, existed.

Eli in the hallway. Eli standing on this slate patio, young and curly-haired, breathing chill air. How strange. She thought of him as a dead person.

"How are they?"

The student pulled herself into a batik bundle on the chair. "I didn't see Eli, but Kathy was fine. She's working for a publishing house over there, pretty cool stuff. It was a book conference I'm talking about here. I went with a guy I was dating," she said, giving a cryptic smile.

"Kathy's in British publishing now?" Denise pictured old Kathy in her pinched ponytail, laughing in the kitchen over frying potatoes. She tried to place a new life on the woman, like a paper dress folded over a doll—the professional sweater, the manuscript, the blue pen—but it kept refusing to fit.

"Oh yeah," the student was saying, looking around toward Swift, who turned his sweet-smelling kabobs with a flourish. "She's doing great. Good overseas job, no kids."

"A real woman of the seventies."

The student laughed. "I don't know about *that*. . . ." she said, grinning, and Denise got the impression that women like Kathy were too old to represent this decade.

"And what about Eli?" Denise asked, although she had to turn away because her son was fidgeting, awake and anxious. She had a sense that he was hungry.

The woman looked confused. "Job at Tech. You know they're moving back here, don't you?"

But then the baby began to cry, loudly, and Denise cooed and tended to him. His face was red and sorrowful, wadded in anguish, the tiny fists beating the air, and something in his cry resounded in her. As if she had a taut wire running from her skull right down her spine, and he had plucked it. She stroked his face and talked low, whispering *Look at you, look at you, look at you.* Denise brought out her breast into the cold air for him to feed at. She did not notice the graduate student sitting quietly, fascinated, then gathering her drink and leaving. She did not see her husband, his cigarette extinguished, watching her. Or Dr. Manday, leaning against a tree in the darkness, doing the same. They were all gone, and Kathy was gone, and Eli, who had so suddenly flourished in her mind like a flower taken for dead, was gone. Her son was here. If you asked, she would tell you that this was the great change in her life. She would say she was a different person now, a mother. All old grief was in the past.

Except—those evenings when she would sit in the darkness of their living room, in an old rocking chair, listening to her husband upstairs washing her son. Then she would think, *There's time.* Time yet for another life, after this one. At forty, at fifty. *Little torches flickering in his pupils.* Then, ashamed, she would hide the image in that room where no one else would ever find it.

Denise was whispering to her son: *Look at you, you're wonderful.* It was as if she had a lapel-full of old medals, her old hopes for herself, tarnished things. It was as if she were unclasping them one by one from the past, wiping them clean, pinning them bloodlessly onto the future—onto him.

The last twilight flickered and moved west, and, with the growing chill of the air, people moved inside to eat. Swift handed off his tongs to other husbands and men who stood in threes around the grill, drinking and shivering and laughing. Inside, they were balancing paper plates on their laps, eating the greasy shish kebabs with food other people had brought: three-bean salad, pasta, a Julia Child recipe for quiche. Swift told some of his stories about science in the Sputnik years, about his Communist parents and his own fear of being discovered, and people sat and listened because it seemed, in his words, so long ago they needn't fear it anymore. There was so much new to fear. Adam was sitting with the baby, smoking another cigarette in the living room, listening to the long, dull travails of some bald astronomer. Denise was off with the women in the kitchen, mixing drinks. Lydia sat on the floor with a girl of five or six, explaining, with growing frustration, about sex. Time passed, falling like the darkness in veils around their feet. The bats left the barn and wandered drunkenly in search of insects. The coals in the grill died and turned to ash.

Out near the orbit of Jupiter, the comet, which had been moving more and more slowly each hour, measured in yards now, now feet, inched to a cold point in space and held still for a moment. Every other object in the universe seemed to continue its task, spinning or dying or blasting fire into the void, but this lattice of ice held still. It had not been in this place since 12.2 years ago, and (though no one on Earth knew this) it was not an old comet; had only come around twenty times since it was first caught in orbit. To human eyes, it would seem to catch its breath. Distant rocks were falling toward the sun's gravity well; far away, a bright blue star was being born within a cloud. The moment passed, the aphelion, and slowly the rock began to move back toward Saturn, gaining speed each instant, already growing warmer for the time, six years from now, when it would race through the inner solar system, a white tail burning behind it. It moved, the dead thing, coldly toward them.

The wind changed in northern California, bringing warm air up to Sonoma, surrounding the farm, brushing the field's long hair. The guests, done with eating and (the older ones) feeling slightly guilty about what they ate and how much, broke from their clusters and reassembled in groups of two or three, wandering into the gardens and the abandoned tennis court, walking quietly and softly and talking more honestly now under a bright moon which, with the hour and the warm air, had appeared. With it had come all of the stars.

Dr. Manday sat on a low stone wall, searching for his cigar. A moment before it had been in his hand. A moment before he had been so happy, full of red wine, talking to the little girl and puffing at his cigar, and now they were all gone—his glass was missing, the girl was gone, his hand felt light and empty. Had he missed something? Had he jumped forward ten minutes and lost them all? He turned right and then left, peering in the dark bushes for where he might have dropped his smoke, but, strange for an astronomer, he could see nothing glowing down there. He could smell it—the earthy chocolate odor of it—but where could it be?

It was resting a foot away on the wall where he had put it just the moment before. The end was burning away, turning the tobacco into collars of white ash; in a minute or two, it would burn enough to topple into the very bushes Manday was searching. That had not yet occurred.

But the girl was back, and with her, the wine. Life was wonderful again.

"Here you go. Is this okay?" she was asking, offering the full glass with both hands.

He received it like a chalice, saying, "You are a joy. You are a terrible joy." He must have asked her to refill it. As he watched, the liquid tilted inside and left dark elliptic rings that turned to droplets, running down in lines—a subtle and beautiful effect. "A joy."

Lydia stood with her hands behind her, turning back and forth, a slight tree in the wind. You would think that she'd be bored with such a man, of her father's generation and a foreigner to boot, but she wasn't. Perhaps he was, at least, familiar and, in an awful way, perhaps she'd also learned that Manday was harmless, had seen people treat him kindly, dotingly, more like a pet than a man. That must have satisfied her somehow, and she stood talking to him more at ease than at any other time this night:

"My dad wants me to do a dance. I don't want to do it."

His fingers searched the stone wall busily. "What dance is this?"

"It's something I'm doing in school for the Easter assembly, but it's so stupid, and he's always wanting me to do things at these parties." She began to pick a white string falling from a rivet in her jeans.

"Did you ever notice your father carries around a little book in his back pocket?"

"Yeah," Lydia said, and she almost told Manday about the time she'd found it, paged through and thought it awfully boring; but she knew such a confession never paid off with adults, even when they acted like your friends.

"I was telling a girl about it this evening," Manday told her, raising a finger in the moonlight. He was held by two lights, actually, by the moon and by a torch ten feet away scattering a yellow glow—it made him two-sided, shadowy, glowing diamond-blue on his fat left cheek, and saffron on his right. He leaned toward her, round and appealing on the wall, his gray-streaked mustache bristling with his words, and asked her if she'd ever looked into her father's book.

"No."

Manday peered off through the trees to be sure Swift was still distant—there he was, the old white man, bumbling his arrogant way into a circle of twenty-three-year-olds, trying to get them to sing with him. Denise was there in the group, Dr. Manday noticed, smiling with a baby in her arms. Manday watched Swift thundering around the group, and it seemed, in the torchlight, as if his beard were on fire; one could almost smell it.

"It is an address book," Manday said quietly, leaning with a grin toward Lydia. He had two shadowed crescents of skin under his eyes, and they grew darker as he leaned forward. "It has the alphabetical pages, but he doesn't write addresses in it. It's his little book for ideas. Your father is a brilliant man, of course. He writes down his ideas, like he might write about the moon tonight, up there, at three-quarters, and how it is moving by degrees. He would write that under *M* for Moon. Now see that star out there above the trees? The little green one?"

Lydia looked up, seeing the still light, questioning her own intelligence. "Is it a star?" she asked nervously.

"No, you're very smart," Manday told her, touching her head. "No—it's Venus. He writes about Venus under *V*. It's a wonderful book. And as for all of us, all his friends at this party, when he has an idea about us, or wants to remember to call us . . . he puts us under *P*." Manday sat up, hands folded, gold and blue. "For People."

But Lydia did not understand this was the end to his story; she knew all this about her father's book, and she really did not think it was so odd. *She* did not go under *P*. She felt embarrassed for the dark old man, that he had failed at a story, and she tried to distract him: "What are your sons' names?" She was fascinated by his children, whom she had never met.

"*P* for all the people in his life. We get such a . . . a sliver of his mind."

"Your sons, Dr. Manday."

"Oh?" he asked, because he had started searching again for his cigar. If he'd told her, she could have pointed to where she'd seen him place it five minutes before, where it sat ashing toward the tipping point. Instead, he kept dizzily feeling around the stones, saying, "Oh? My sons? Sami and Ali. Sami is twenty, and Ali is just a little older than you. Maybe you'll get married to him."

She laughed uncomfortably, looked off to where that graduate student with the cool braided hair was walking toward them, her skirt a white undulating triangle against the garden darkness. People were moving in and out of trees, in slow couples, ghostly in the jazz coming from the warm bright house.

"He's handsome. Now about this dance? Will you do the dance for me?"

"No. It's stupid."

"Well," Manday said, sipping his wine and forgetting the topic entirely. "Well . . ." He had begun to think about his sons, Sami and Ali. He had not seen them in three years, and so he was not always thinking of them. He had lived without them for so long, only coming home after his job was secure here in the States and he had money, seeing Sami grown eight years in the meantime, from a little boy of six afraid of crabs of all kinds, spiders, anything with many legs, to a young man in a gold sarong, fourteen, stern and trying on a mustache, learning to build boats. The next time, a few years later, Sami had a house and a wife and was already a boat builder near the volcano, with a child of his own whom Manday had not yet seen. The scientist did not feel sad about missing Sami's growth; he had seen some of his childhood, and shown him how to swim, where to find the Southern Cross in the sky and how it pointed to the Pole, and tricked the boy into speaking English until he grew old enough to revolt, terrified, running to mother and swearing in her language never to utter fire again. The truth was that, as a boy, Sami had been wonderful and full of unexpected whims, and that, as a man, he was dull and dark from the sun, with his shy plump wife, his concrete hut, with his refusal to raise his head to where Manday pointed out the prospects of the night sky. "Father," he would say in a growl, leaning his long neck to look down on Manday, "I have to see my family now, come with me." The truth was that, as a man, Manday did not like him.

It was Ali who cracked a little vein in Manday's heart, because Ali (nine when his father last saw him, seven before that) was going to be lovable. No doubt—he was quiet and curious about the world, and you knew, watching him, the round-faced boy with sticking-up hair, or talking to him, that he shared only a hundredth of the thoughts going through his head. You knew, when he looked at a stream, that he planned, in his little-boy mind, a dam across it, a wheel powered by it, a bank to divert its waters into his own hut. Manday recognized the widening eyes (which the boy had not yet learned to hide) and it destroyed him that he would not be there to save Ali. If he had been there, Ali might have been like him, off to college in the States, one of the very few to leave. But Ali was not going to leave; Manday's wife was there to squeeze him till he stopped breathing those wishes. However, Manday was not always thinking of his sons.

There—the cigar formed one new wreath of ash and toppled into the dark leaves.

"You're Lydia, right?" It was the student with the braids, the one with mystical ideas, who chewed pink gum and, somehow, knew Kathy Spivak. Manday was almost blinded by the whiteness of her dress, covered on top by a wool shawl but bright and full of wind below. She leaned down and kissed Lydia on the forehead, not noticing the girl struggling. "Your father sent me, it's time for the dance recital," she said.

Manday knew this student; not as young as the others, and so full of experiences and real stories about the world besides the stars. She had written a book of poetry and had it published as a chapbook out in Berkeley; in fact, it sat beside his bed (it was called *Cool Agony*), bent where he had made it to page twenty. He also knew that she had been seeing Swift secretly for months now, perhaps longer; he had caught them in a coffee shop in Oakland, holding hands. Manday felt, at last, looking at her, how very drunk he was tonight.

Lydia put her hands on her hips, trying to look strident: "The dance is stupid." She simply could not let them know she cared.

The student saw this, taking her arm. "Listen," she said. "Listen, if you do this dance for your father, I'll give you a little present later." Lydia whispered something to her, and she nodded. Without a word to Manday, the girl was off through the trees, toward the patio. A decade from now, of this round man on the wall, she would remember only cake, blue cotton candy and a brown man at a lake.

The student smiled at Manday. She was not beautiful, but she was confident and fairly young, sun lines curving from her eyes ahead of her years. She had a dusty kind of skin, and rather large nostrils, but she seemed so sure of her beauty that you became convinced of it. He wanted her to ask him what he was reading; Americans were always asking you that. He would have said, "I'm reading you, it's you."

"You coming to see her, Dr. Manday?" she asked instead. Her focus went off behind him to some people who must have been walking by. The shawl fell and she readjusted it, straining her neck to see whoever it was.

Manday felt, with each blink, that he was flipping through time, missing every other second so that he had to piece together what she was asking him, what she was doing with her neck. His arm stiffened on the wall and he stopped himself from tipping over. Then he felt suddenly warm and pleasant.

"What is it about us fat, old men that you like?" he asked her.

All the little actions of her body ceased.

"Swift and me—is it our position on campus? Or is he actually sexy? Wouldn't that be lovely, if beautiful girls started undressing for old astronomers. . . ."

"Dr. Manday," she said, pale and still. "You're a little drunk. I'm going to get someone to help you." The student turned away from him, into the sulfur glow of the torch.

"I'm reading you," he said.

She looked back, her face pulled tight. "What?"

"It's you, I'm reading you." Half of him blue, half gold, like a foreign god. "*I have two hearts, one in each breast,*" he said, quoting her with his shaky hand outstretched, only half-realizing that what he was thinking had come out of his mouth, that he was telling her all this and it was permanent and real. Yet he went on: "I will kiss you better than him. The old goat. Come back here with me. I will kiss you better."

She was gone behind a tree.

Manday sat on the wall for what seemed like a long time. He was realizing, so slowly, that he had actually told the student that he wanted to kiss her. He was still thinking he could change things, but the moment was long gone. The branch that she had thrust aside to leave had snapped back, tottered in the air, releasing leaves, and was already still again. He had stamped and sealed the moment, tossed it in the mailbox, and there was no scrambling at time's metal door now, retrieving what had happened. Manday was drunk and a fool; that now was clear even to him.

But there across the patio he could see the white abstract form of the student moving across the yard toward a group of people—God, it was going to be worse! There was Denise, in green with her baby in her arms, chattering to the crowd while her husband stood in silence, hiding a cigarette behind his back. The student was approaching; soon they would all lean in and listen, then turn and see him toppling from the wall. It was too much to bear; he had to leave. He tried; he couldn't move a muscle; he lost his train of winey thought. All he could focus on was Denise's husband, taking his turn to talk while his wife stood by smiling pleasantly but with a look of anguish in her eyes. Manday could guess what was happening there; he had felt that way before. Her husband was talking about her, giving the crowd his own amusing story of her life. A cocktail party version of that scientist's hard life. Bowdlerized, that was the word, a bowdlerized version of a spouse's life, told to tittering strangers, with all the terror taken out. The tense smile and the look on the young woman as if she might snatch the conversation from their very lips, take it back—Manday was sure of what was happening. His friends had done it to him many times.

He managed to stand up, losing his wineglass in the shrubs at last, and made his way across a lawn to escape their sight. He was opposite the tennis court now and could see Swift, smoking a pipe, holding a small box before one of their colleagues, obviously in deep consultation. Above them all, to the east, Cassiopeia was spreading her tortured, glittering arms. Manday watched Swift and the scientist for a moment, seeing their nodding heads, and then turned behind a hedge to escape them, too. They had always treated him like an old man, all of them. Even when he was young, in his thirties, they had spoken easy English to him, petted his hand, kept difficult news from him as if he were a doddering grayheaded fool. The dark man, the Indian, handsome and vibrant in his way, but never to them. An old man. And here he was, actually grown old, and still the secrets were kept from him—why had Swift, his best friend, never turned to him with a box? He padded through the shadow of the hedge, came into an open field, and was alone again. Cypresses leaned back and forth, and the grass rippled colorlessly. The moon floated above him, a glowing jellyfish, a man-o'-war, and its long threads of light touched and stung him all along his face. His life was so unlike theirs.

The course of Manday's life was altered by the sultan. Manday had grown up with a wealthy merchant father and two sisters; he did so well in school that he was soon working for his father, figuring all the calculations for the business with an abacus and his scrap paper. It became widely known that he was brilliant with numbers, and when he was a teenager, the sultan called him to the palace at night to show him the stars from his rooftop. There was a brass telescope there that the sultan had bought long ago in England, when he went to university, and the old sultan pointed out the constellations, the planets, opened books on their orbits and ephemera, hoping he could catch the boy's imagination in these numbers. He did, and young Manday came up to the palace on moonless nights to check his calculations against the movement of the heavens; it amazed him that numbers could burn and gutter like candles. The sultan was bored and lonely, having been sent away to England for his education only to return full of ideas and languages and no one else to speak them with. Though Manday never knew it, the sultan was trying to make the boy into someone he could talk to. He was waiting for the young man to grow up, become another man to sit in a cane chair and speak with about the universe. In 1938, when Manday was eighteen, the sultan arranged for him to go to England to the same university (where he was a year behind the sultan's own son, who was interested in nothing academic)—and this was how the sultan ruined his own plans, offering this treasure of foreign numbers, poisoning this skinny boy against his own island.

When Manday came back in 1942, the world was at war. Nothing was the same about his island for Manday, and in March 1943, the Japanese landed on Bukit. There was little resistance, and the sultan was allowed to remain, but young, outraged intellectuals such as Manday and two political philosophers were imprisoned on a spit of land at the north end of the island. Manday stayed there for a full year, in a cell where the salt air blew in hot and stale, the harsh sun coming through the keyhole outlined like a chesspiece. He had, though, a wide view of the night sky where, with a telescope sent by the sultan, the twenty-three-year-old Manday watched the meteor shower of the Leonids and the forty-eighth return of Comet Encke and used a nail to scratch his calculations on the cinder walls. He would never tell his American friends what had happened in that prison.

After the war, he had no choice but to fall into his old life at his father's store. The island had to be rebuilt, and the sultan had grown old and weak during the humiliation of his island's capture; he could not sit out at night, nor bear any visits from a young man with a college education and no life he could attach it to. So Manday worked selling rice and tea from the island's north and south sides, trying to make a living in that hard time after the war. He met a girl through his family, married her, and watched his first son Sami growing. He lived as though he had forgotten that whole other life he'd planned.

In 1948, however, the old sultan died, and it felt, to Manday, as if some ancient temple had crumbled in an earthquake. There was no replacing that time or those chances; somehow, the young man had always thought he would lift his life back onto that road, but here was the only man who had seen it in him, and he was dead. The new sultan, the man's brother, had no interest in the stars. Manday began to ignore his family, his business. He took long walks up the side of the volcano with his six-inch brass telescope, desperate and lonely. Then, just months after the sultan died, Manday saw a fuzzy glow in the sky and was able, through the use of an old sky chart, to determine that it was a new comet. He telegrammed his discovery to England, to one of his old professors, who forwarded it to Berkeley. The note Manday received back was a terrible blow: "The new comet you refer to was discovered one month ago in Australia by Harrington." It went on to inform him, however, that his calculations had been valuable in determining the period. In 1949, this note got him into a U.S. graduate school in astronomy, and he never truly lived on Bukit again.

And here he stood, old man Manday, dizzy from his wine and stumbling into a clearing in the moonlight to escape his friends. Twenty years later, and he had discovered no comet. His students drew low lottery numbers in the draft and left their papers on their desks to go to Vietnam; two had died there. People on the street still looked at Manday in a way that made him want to run up to them and shake them, as if they were the locked gates to a kingdom, as if they understood at all what lay between them and this man. No one knew about his life, his island, his wife, the prison. *Were you ever young?* Swift had asked him. Someone had been, a skinny boy on a rooftop had been young. But not Manday, not ever.

He opened his eyes to find himself inside the house, walking up the stairs, being supported by a woman—Denise, it was Denise in her green blouse.

"No," he said softly, not understanding how he had come here. "No I have to talk to that girl."

She was struggling with him, helping him to walk, taking him toward one of the bedrooms. "No, Dr. Manday, you just get some sleep," she was saying and he could smell her hair—apples and something; smoke, apples, something.

"I am all right," he told her, falling into the bed. What had happened to everything? He was in a bed, his shoes being taken off, and a child's mobile swung above him like a mad set of planets. He had been wanting to talk to Swift; he had something to tell him; he had to get up.

"Just get to sleep, Dr. Manday," she told him forcefully, pushing him back into bed, pulling a blanket over him. She looked so calm and good, and yet he'd seen her just moments before (or how long ago was it?) standing in that crowd of people, letting her husband hack up her life and present it cleanly on a plate with toothpicks.

"Denise," Manday said. He was sweaty, and the crescents under his eyes were shiny and dark again. Only moonlight came through the window now, and Denise drew the curtain against its brightness. If they had cared to consider it, they would have realized that they were alone for the first time in their lives.

"Yes?" she said, close to him again. *I don't know this room,* he was thinking, nearly panicked under the blanket, looking at the mobile turning in the darkness, the pale poster of an animal, the books, toys, gingham curtains blocking the moon. *Nothing's familiar here, nothing at all, and is this woman good?*

A new hope marched through his mind. He said, "Beautiful Denise."

The sound of her son's wail came through the door from downstairs, and she turned her head, touched her wooden necklace, and looked back at Manday with a smile. "Yes?"

"Come in bed with me."

Trees shifted outside the window, and the shadows moved like gentle hands upon the two of them in the room, rearranging their faces and positions. He became calm and quiet, pleading, making her palm sweaty with his, touching her arm with his fingers to persuade her. *Come in bed with me.* And she changed, her face broadening in sorrow, slipping her arm from his touch and reaching out with a tissue to dab his forehead. Kissing him on the cheek, whispering something in his ear that he would forget by morning; he closed his eyes and smiled. The shadows rearranged the room again and she stepped quietly out.

He lay there, bloated and exhausted, crazed, his thoughts deformed as they trod through his brain. Colors seemed to flash around the room. He turned his head to the pillow, smelling Lydia, and cried until he slept.

What would remain: a birthday cake, blue cotton candy, a lake in June.

Lydia, in the pleasant slow-motion haze of marijuana, was trying to remember her dance. As she turned, she could see the adults arranged before her, against the bushes, all at different heights, slumped in metal chairs, lying side by side in the hammock, standing with a hand on a spouse's shoulder, all watching intently and smiling. All those spectacles, jewelry, scotch glasses flickering as they moved; all those pipes, cigarettes, joints and cigars fuming into the air and making all the light (from the torches, the setting moon, the bright farmhouse with its glass doors) diffuse around their bodies, a phosphorescent vapor or a lit veil. They shifted and whispered to one another. They touched each other and kissed. They watched poor Lydia crouched on the floor, rising as a growing flower to the tune of "Good Morning Starshine."

The girl had found the pot just ten minutes before. Someone had left a paper-clipped roach in an ashtray, and Lydia was able to pinch it and sneak into the bushes. She found a disposable lighter and puffed away, delighted, terrified, lonely. She thought of what she would tell Kim about tonight, the wonderful shocked look on her pink face, a boy in her class who would be impressed, and she thought about her sister, Alice. Lydia had only smoked pot with Alice, and she associated the stupefying sensation with those times up in their room, giggling, their roles at last undone. She was amazed that doing this alone, it was even better. In the cold waxy leaves of an azalea nearing its prime, listening for a telltale footstep or crunch of leaves, hearing all the laughter and outdated music from the patio, it seemed better. When you do some things alone, you give up worrying whether you've done them right. She sucked on the few strands of smoke, closed her eyes, felt like she wasn't stupid after all.

The pot was making the "Starshine" dance difficult, however. Lydia found her mind wandering as she rose from the floor, became a bird, soared in a figure eight around the stage. She kept floating into kinds of memory, and then thudding into the present, where she discovered herself twinkling her hands before a crowd of her father's friends—were they laughing at her? Was she doing this right? Then her mind would exit again, thinking about her sister and her mother in the kitchen, kneading dough for raisin bread and singing along to the radio, the pale yellow daisy pattern of the curtains rising with a breeze into the middle of the room. And there she was, doing a dance move that her teacher called "planting flowers," tossing her hands out toward the adults, because there they were in crisp detail— Denise grinning with her baby, looking down at him and making him clap his hands, her husband smirking, other students singing along themselves, swaying back and forth, the student with the braids applying lipstick and her father laughing, patting the woman's knee, turning to say something to an older colleague. There they were, all the judges of her young life in their box—and here she was, Lydia, called to testify at last; and she could not help it, turning in her planetary circles, could not help spinning hopelessly out of control to the words: *Gliddy glop gloopy, niddy naddy noopy, la la la lo lo. . . .*

This was her life with her father: Mornings of boxed cereal and milk, evenings of radio news heard through a speaker in the kitchen, dumplings boiling on the stove, her father railing at every comment from above, and weekends spent in parks doing unparklike things: discussing (on his side, mostly) a two-dimensional world, discovering the fastest position for the slide, getting hot dogs from a vendor and putting on spots of mustard, ketchup, relish, onions just to taste the independent flavor of each. And parties like this, with all these people whom he called his friends but who were not his friends, not in the way Lydia had friends, people who held no secrets with him, who had shared nothing terrible together, parties of nuclear fission jokes where Lydia was always called upon to perform. She had to be brilliant in conversation, worldly in appetite, and, above all, as talented as they were. Faculty brat—of course that was what she would later call this early life. How could she complain? She had, after all, chosen it.

At the custody hearings a year before, the judge had granted both daughters to her mother. Lydia and her sister had hugged her dad, crying, afraid, and gone to live with her mother in that new apartment in the city where at night they barred the windows and ignored the sounds of shattering glass in the streets. But it was going to be okay, Lydia told herself (barely eleven), because her mother had told her that new lives were always hard, but always worth it. There would be more of the good times—the raisin bread and lifting curtain—even without Dad, just us girls, just us. Lydia's sister (typically) disappeared into her room most of that first month and their mother's speech had turned out to be a lie. There was a man who came over, took her away so that the girls were left alone. The man would call and in a minute Mother would be ready to go, smiling, pulling an orange scarf around her head as she went out the door. The girls could sense a change, though, and in winter Lydia found her mother out on the balcony in the freezing cold, dressed in only a bathrobe, holding an unlit cigarette and a martini. Ice frosted the glass. The woman's face was streaked with red, veined like her own botanical drawings, and even Lydia's persistent tugs on her sleeve could not get her to move. That was the end. There was never going to be a new life for the girls—there was only room for one now.

Her father took over the court process to bring them both back to him, but it was long and complicated, and they had to live in the house with their frozen mother, who would crack open in anger at times, at other times despairingly waking them both in the middle of the night, holding them, whispering things they wished she had not said. It was clear, though—both girls wanted to leave. The worst part about leaving, however, was that they had to testify in court against their mother. Lydia remembered sitting in the chair and the judge asking questions, trying to be kind, trying to mask the cruelty of it all: "Tell us, Lydia, if you want to, about that night you found your mother on the balcony."

And the poor girl had to tell it all. She lied; she changed details to make her mother seem warmer and caring, not drunk, not crazy, but living a good life that was eaten (with an image of shiny termites) by small, terrible details: a phone call, a broken vase, a cigarette burned to the fingers. But Lydia gave them the scent on which they could hunt her mother down. There her mother was, of course, sitting there the whole time in a light blue suit and white gloves, very much the way she must have dressed on her honeymoon, her face kind and understanding, and Lydia remembered (strangest of all) how, as she spoke, she examined her mother's face, and saw each wrinkle as a notch her body had made: each smile, each raised eyebrow, each summertime squint at the sun. Her mother's face was an index that Lydia, as she tried to ignore her own testifying voice, could finger through at last. She was looking for a particular expression, given many years before, and Lydia paged through each wrinkle of the woman's forehead until—the greatest surprise of all—her mother gave it to her right there in the courtroom: a creased sigh of relief.

Life with her father, this was the life she had chosen. Spinning like a planet before a crowd of astronomers, their glasses shimmering, their eyes blinking in calculation of her orbit, the smoke, the beards, these men and women, standing here, in a universe unlike the normal world—they were smarter, colder, unskilled at small talk or people, the kind of nerds Lydia's friends would beat up in school these days. You would see children like this coming into classes with bloody noses, smiling oddly, mumbling to themselves. Spinning before them—how had she chosen this?

When her dance was over, all the women ran up onto the patio and hugged Lydia, toppling the poor girl because they were far more stoned than she was. The student with braids was passing around her lipstick, and the women were kissing the girl all over, leaving bright marks on her legs, her neck, and Lydia was surprised and frightened by this sensation. The geekish, manly women, the skinny science-fiction geniuses whom she laughed at and wanted to impress—they were kissing her. Her wide eyes searched for her father as she rolled in this pile of women, and there he was, proud hands-on-hips near the edge of the slate patio, drunk, approving. Didn't he see what was happening? Was it too Greek to be believed, that they were eating her alive?

"I would like to propose a toast!" her father shouted, and his voice sprayed into the cluster of lipsticked women and dispersed them, leaving Lydia alone on the slate patio, breathless, giggling, quite alive.

"This toast may sound grand," he said, "but forgive me." He was standing taller than them all, raising a mug of beer that had long ago lost its frost (though three more sat in the freezer), and seemed a little bit surprised that everyone had turned so quickly to listen, leaving his daughter and her dance behind. He was used to others listening—he was a professor, a commander of attention, an old ham— still, it left him silent for a second as Lydia, covered in kisses, watched. His daughter loved him, how he was larger than any other man in sight, left a silhouette against any sky, how he never twitched or fidgeted like other adults, how he was bold with her mother, how at night sometimes he whispered his scientific German to her while she was on the edge of sleep. She loved how with a word he could draw everybody in, Jupiter-like.

"I would like to propose a toast to comet 1953 Two!" There were *Hear! Hears!* and little claps from the drunken adults. "I know that sounds self-serving, but she's the birthday girl tonight and by god we'll toast her."

There was a shuffling and clinking sound as people moved to get their glasses, or, discovering they had lost or drained theirs, hustled to find more. Denise was proposing to share her husband's glass of wine, and Lydia was on all fours now, struggling across the patio for her Coke. Glass and plastic were lifted into the air as people laughed, someone yelped as she was pinched, and some other young man's voice cried out "Let's hear it!"

Swift stood still, smiling under his grizzled beard, arm raised in the pose of an old statue. He looked up, and there was Mars directly overhead, beaming pinkly from the constellation Virgo. The other planets were scattered across the sky as well, invisible to the eye, but on the southern horizon the constellation Centaurus could barely be seen, and Swift had a hope just then that they might see a meteor or two at that moment, because it was rare to glimpse the constellation this far north, and it was the night of meteor showers, of remnants from the comet he was now openly adoring. Swift looked up at the sky; it looked back down; they were old friends.

"To comet 1953 Two," he began.

"Comet Swift!" someone shouted.

He pointed with his other hand. "Now don't get me started on that one!" It was some old joke within the department, a false joke about his modesty. "To comet 1953 Two, on the evening of your aphelion . . . somewhere"—he motioned toward the universe with his glass—"*out there.*" People laughed. "At least we *hope* it's near your aphelion, because if my calculations are wrong again, the Nobel for 1977 is definitely out."

More laughter.

"But we wish you the best of luck on your coldest day. May you not be approaching Jupiter too closely." More calls of *Hear! Hear!* from the crowd. "May you not run out of gases and come back too faint to see. May your coma be bright, and your orbit predictable, and may we meet again around this time six years from now. Lydia will be eighteen by then, Denise will be—how old will you be, Denise?"

"Twenty!" came her joking voice from the crowd.

He bellowed a laugh. "If only it worked that way, dear. Well, sixty-four, I'll be sixty-four when you see me next. I'll be old and ugly, so be kind. We'll see you then!"

Dr. Swift raised his glass and everybody followed. Some just drank, and others, insisting on touching each glass with theirs, walked around the bundle of people clinking and talking, making the superstitious round. Swift drained his glass and lifted it again before he turned around. Perhaps he was worrying that he had said something tonight he would regret, something he didn't remember now. It tugged at his brain, as if he'd left his oven on—he had said something terrible, earlier when he had been more drunk, and to whom had he said it? Had he grown this old? Perhaps he was going through his list of people, mentally checking off their names. Perhaps, also, there was much more on his mind tonight. He had a young woman pour him more wine and he moved off out of the light.

Lydia lifted the needle, removed the record from the player and slipped it back into its cover (accidently ripping the sleeve), watching them all dispersing. Some shift had occurred in the evening, and people revealed more of who they were—some couples were no longer walking but leaning against walls, standing in the darkness under trees, the younger ones, nervous and whispering and, most of them, fretfully in love. Others seemed too tired to move, caught with whomever else was sitting in a deck chair nearby. The moon had set, and so others, more active, were at the rooftop telescope, visually searching the darker regions of the sky for comets. They were the comet hunters, the obsessives who could not leave a clear, moonless night unwatched or they would lie in bed, restless, regretting a night on which they had surely missed the find of the century. Swift's toast, various loves below, their children—these were forgotten once the moon had set, and so the comet hunters could move the telescope across the heavens in an attempt to catch the fuzzy evidence of some cold star approaching. Denise, propping her sleeping baby in her lap. . . . Dr. Manday, invisible, asleep, dreaming of a prison window. . . . Lydia watched them all.

It was all too much, and too far from what she had wanted coming here, days before, on some ancient wish for a gold earring in the straw, a nest of birds with a sky-blue hemisphere of shell. Lydia had to struggle between what was easy to dismiss in these adults and what she longed for. They were ugly, arrogant, constantly wrong on politics, ignorant of fashion or life outside an observatory dome; pretentious, selfish, prone to laughing at their own awful jokes; and yet she stood below them, holding her record album, observing them and—this infuriated her most—longing to be just like them.

Why *just like them*? Look at them. Look at the woman with the braids, disappearing just now into a dark path, walking quickly, the white skirt folding over itself—look at her confidence despite her plainness. When had Lydia ever seen this in a woman before? Her own mother, beautiful, talented, sitting at her desk drawing a leaf in pen and ink—she used to turn and stare at the mirror, whispering, taunting her own image. Her sister, glum, growing fat, was becoming a great caterpillar in jeans and a trail of smoke. Yet here was this intelligent woman—here they all were: the skinny astrophysicist with a vague mustache, the fat blonde gamma-ray photographer laughing with her hand on a man's knee—they were going to be all right. They had all the outward signs of failure, what Lydia's friend Kim called the "mark of the dork," yet you could never break them, or tree them like a cat. Talking, laughing, even singing to a crowd, they were still recluses; they lived privately in their minds where you could never reach them. They were brilliant. It was all around—brilliance— if you could only see it with the naked eye. Lydia had to leave.

She would go to the barn. She would tempt Tycho to come in with her, and they would spend the night there together on a bale of hay. It would be a world away from all this.

On her way out to the field, she had to work her way through some clusters of people, and the first was immersed in quiet conversation (the marijuana being passed around again as a young grad student strummed a guitar) with Denise at its center. She was relaxed, touching her son with just one hand as he lay sleeping, leaning her head against the pillow of the chair and looking up at the sky as she talked. Lydia envied her. She listened.

"Oh, I grew up with all the Easter trimmings—the hats, the grass in the baskets, the chocolate egg hunts and the dyeing—but it's kind of a dumb event, don't you think? Mostly seems like a holiday about interior decorating. What I miss are the seders I used to be invited to. Don't you miss those?"

A woman in the crowd: "Well, we're having one this year. . . ."

"Really? See, that's wonderful. Lucky—at least you eat your eggs in salt water. I'm stuck with pink dye."

"Well . . . I mean, would you like to come?"

"Oh no—I couldn't."

Lydia could not have imagined that once, years before, Denise's mother had given her money to forget, or that now Denise paid her own wages. She could not see a woman who had striven to forget the boy who'd fallen from the cliff. Or the man whose hand she held. All Lydia could see was a woman who was happy now, with a husband, a son, a career. There was no glimmer that once a man Denise might have loved stood wet with fog in her doorway, his face tense as a fist, holding something dear that she refused to consider. That once she'd closed a door and picked another way to live. Denise laughed and held her son close to her.

Lydia passed by, staring, the pot still dull in her mind. To her, people were just what they seemed to be right now—Kim, hilarious now and popular, would be thrown over for another friend within a year's time, and there would be no nostalgia or wringing of hands over it. Kim would no longer suit her; Lydia did not weigh old times, or forgive moods or family problems or bad talks on the phone. She was in the present moment only, and the present felt very different for her, very unlike that of these languid scientists with their wine-glasses and smoke. For them, the present was a hinge between the past and future, but for her it was a wide, clear plain in which to act. No wonder she misunderstood their happiness.

She stumbled across the man who had come into the barn. She remembered his name was Adam, but he seemed so different. Here he was merely Denise's husband, a scientist's spouse, bored and a little drunk. He swayed his head side to side as he talked, weary, closing his eyes at moments while his lips kept moving, and one hand stayed in the air before him, pointing and pointing at his ideas. An ordinary man. He wore a fisherman's cap now (the wind had been driving him crazy) and it made his face sharp as a gem.

"How you doing, sport?" he asked. The man next to him, in a tie, put on a patient smile.

"Nothing," she replied.

Adam shook his head. "What? I said *how*, not *what*. You did a great dance back there, you're real talented."

The mustached man nodded, holding his cordial against his chest, saying, "Absolutely wonderful, dear," then adding quietly, "and such an interesting song."

"That song's cool, and so are all your kisses," Adam said, leaning down and pointing to the lipstick on her neck. "I can dig it, can you dig it?" He held out a palm.

"I can dig it, man," she said and slapped his hand, laughing. He was with her now.

The man with the cordial spoke again: "Lydia, I've just discovered that your friend here is a fiction writer and a rogue, isn't that what you said?"

Adam laughed, saying, "Oh, it's true. I tell people things to make them do what I want. That's what fiction is, making your readers feel a certain way. But it slips into life a little. . . ." But he was away from

Lydia again, far away in a conversation he had done dozens of times over the years, falling into an old clever act that did not include her.

She waited to see if the conversation would come back to her— "people are so willing to believe you"—but it did not, and though a few women came along and touched her shoulder, smiling at her, she was alone again. She did not understand Adam any more than she did his wife. She did not understand any of them. They seemed happy, brilliant, witty, experiencing all the bits of life that she desperately wanted, and she envied them their age; yet compared to them, it took almost nothing to make her happy. A pair of jeans. A new album. A call from Kim with news about a boy from school. These things would delight her beyond the adults' comprehension, beyond their own memory of themselves. What did it take to make them happy? If hers was simple sugar, theirs was a recipe so complex it was almost not worth making. One could really live without it. And here was Lydia, more thrilled by the pot than anybody, it seemed, had ever been. But it was not, as she thought, because she was superficial, or (that terrible fear) a little vain and stupid. It was because, even so close to puberty, she was merely a child.

She waited at his side, and when Adam finally patted her head and smiled at her, she moved out of the group and off the stone of the patio, onto the dark blue grass. As she stalked away, somehow furious, somehow not caring, the world became quieter, starlit of course (were there any comets to be caught tonight, up on the roof?), and if you watched the black shapes of the cypresses against the lighter sky, you could imagine they were weeds washing back and forth in a dark tide. Jupiter had just risen, a bright light to the southeast—you could imagine, if you were Lydia, that there was a great deep-sea fish out over the horizon, and here it laid its trap with the luminous tip of its tongue: Jupiter. She looked out at the cypresses and the planet and could almost imagine the thing, jaw open, letting the dark water move the fringe on its back, waiting, shaking, trying to keep its tongue still for her. It was, perhaps, how her mother might have seen it.

Off to the left she heard some rustling, and in a moment she saw that, under an unbloomed dogwood, two grad students were making out. Not sex, not white limbs working in the darkness, but two young people in their warm clothes, lying together in the grass. She might have just missed some wonderful scene where he pulled a flower from a vine and showed it to her, and she took it from him, tore the petals from it nervously, and they sat in the grass, talking nonsense. Lydia might have just missed the pauses, the looking-away, the tattered flower tossed into the weeds, the quick breath as they caught each other's eyes and thought, *It's going to happen, it's happening.* The relief of falling to the grass with someone you had never kissed before.

Lydia could only watch the slow frenzy of their mouths, their careful hands, and hear the quick solemn breaths. She was hidden behind a tree. The boy, she saw, was one of her father's students, a quiet man in a plaid shirt, someone you would never notice. The girl she had seen for the first time tonight: long dark hair, a woolen cowl-neck sweater, eyeshadow that didn't suit her—that was all Lydia could make out. How long had they known each other before this happened? Just hours, or months now? There was no way for Lydia to put them into a story, into any of the sorts of stories that interested her. There was nothing romantic about the two of them or their faces mashed together or the little noises they made. Lydia stood behind her tree and watched for a while, smiling to herself at what they said when they came up for air—"Oh Susan, you're so beautiful"—and feeling very distant, foreign, buried under the earth. Yes, she was buried up to her nose. Lydia watched for almost fifteen minutes, scratching her jeans, until the young man took the woman's hand and led her away to who knows what fate. Lydia was left to watch the patch of matted grass they'd left behind; it shone, wet with light, each pressed blade slowly uncoiling. She missed the life she'd had at ten.

There was a light in the barn. That crossed glow in the window—had it been there all this time? No, it must have come on as she had stood watching the empty grass. Something wet was on her fingers, and she jumped, frightened, only to find it was Tycho, idiotically adoring her, panting, padding on ahead of her to the barn.

There were faint shouts behind her, but she didn't turn. The men on the rooftop had caught a few shooting stars passing above the trees. A few early fireflies on the horizon, but nothing (unless you were drunk) worth shouting over.

Lydia did not turn; it was not the time to be looking up. She watched the grass unspringing from the shape of bodies, and walked on. She watched her own feet walking, wet and dark, and Tycho's blob of movement far ahead of her, shaking back and forth and dipping into shadows and out again. There was no thought in her mind of *I remember being with my sister here,* or *I remember my mother standing in just this spot,* but instead she had a pleasant sensation looking at a wild rosebush on which a few of the yellow heads had shattered, leaving petals bright on the dirt. She knew she liked the bush, and this whole part of the farm, but she dropped the feeling before it had time to form—that this plant had come from their old house in Oakland, the only thing salvaged from that life before Berkeley, that her mother had worried over it on the car ride and kept repeating that transportation is the worst killer of rosebushes in the world. There was also a beloved hamster buried under some part of its root system; but, without a marker, only Tycho seemed able to find it now, sniffing endlessly before Lydia clicked her tongue and he ran off and disappeared.

She was talking to the woods now, quietly, proudly gesturing. She was pretending to be a superhero of some kind, hands on her hips, head high, peering boldly into the leaves. *I am not what I appear to be!* she whispered to the dogwoods. *I am not Lydia Swift, the dancing girl, at all. . . . I am in disguise!* She came around the corner, raising her arms: *Behold!*

The light in the barn had been lit by her father. He was there with the student she had seen earlier, the one with the white dress, the braids, the confidence that she must have stolen from a prettier girl. They were sitting on an old bale of hay, the gray strands crushed under their weight, splintering, and the light came from a hurricane lamp her father had hung on a nail over them. They sat on the bale, together, holding hands. Lydia moved back into a shadow.

The student was speaking: "I can't, you know I can't."

Lit from above, Lydia's father seemed more strikingly bald and worn. Every crease under his eye became prominent, and he seemed badly sewn, bulging at all seams although, in the light, he also seemed to be smiling. It was a trick of the light—it was the shadows around his eyes, and how his beard hid his mouth—but he seemed happy. His beard had strands that shone when he moved, so that it seemed like a net of something silver, coins, something bright. He gripped the woman's hand with his left, not with fingers meshed but with them coupled, like two cars of a train, and his right palm lay open before her. Clearly the student had, just the moment before, taken a small black box from that palm, opened it, then closed it again. She held the box against her chest.

"Don't decide now," he was saying in his low voice, seeming to smile. "It's too late to think, dear. Tell me in the morning, or whenever you feel right."

But she was already giving the box back to him, and Lydia thought for once she looked beautiful in this light, her bright face cut off in shadow. The woman was already saying, "You're such a brilliant, wonderful man. . . ."

He would not let go of her hand as she stood. Lydia watched him rising with her from the bale, and a dozen strands of hay floated upward into the lamplight, then fell out of sight in the dark barn. Lydia was behind that darkness, keeping still, holding the edge of the barn with two hands, taking it all in without a word.

Her father was trying to give the box back, laughing, making jokes about comets and women. He seemed desperate, and he even said that to the woman before she kissed him on the cheek. He stopped his babbling, stopped laughing, paused to stare at her and quietly said, "Then think of me as desperate, Jenny." These words made the woman stop, as if she were considering him seriously for the first time, once he had run out of argument and clever ammunition, once he'd tried all his memorized poems, his loving touches on her arm. Here was the famous Professor Swift, and she could have had him down on his knees in this rotting barn if she had wanted. Two wives behind him, and also all the girlfriends, the graduate students, the colleagues, the women at conferences—there were decades of competition there, and she was not his greatest, or smartest, or most beautiful love. Did she stop her movement, stop in the middle of a turn so that the fringes of her shawl whipped back on her, did she pause with that expression of pity and fear, did she still the ringing second with her hand because she knew she was his last?

Lydia watched the tall woman lean forward to kiss her father on his cheekbone, above his beard. She saw the woman's eyes close, her hand touching his other cheek to comfort him, one braid falling down her shoulder to dangle between them. She saw her father's eyes looking straight ahead of him, his arms, useless, reaching out to the woman. She saw his unblinking stare at this kiss. Then the woman gathered herself together, away from him, held the hem of her white dress and left the barn, whispering that she loved him.

Swift stepped slowly back, and ink poured into the creases of his face. "Ah," he said, so quietly that Lydia could hardly hear him. "No you don't."

Lydia watched her father as the bits of hay flew through the lamp-light. The old man rested one hand against a pillar of wood, staring out the back door where he must have seen that triangle of white fluttering into the weeds. There must have been a longer speech beforehand, when the lamp had first gone on and Lydia had been admiring the couple on the grass. It must have been a stirring speech, careful and loving, reaching back in time and taking lines he had given to Lydia's mother, when he and she were thirty, rewrapping them, presenting them with dusty hands to this young woman. His words were always miraculous to Lydia. She watched him staring out the door. Apparently, this once, it hadn't mattered what he said.

He turned and sat down on the hay, hiding the box inside his palm. Lydia grew aware of herself at last, her mind still hazy, aware that she stood only yards away from him in the gray darkness of the barn. There was a sound, and her father faced the loft; an owl was in there with them. How would Lydia ever turn and leave now? She could not be softer than an owl. Would things be better if he saw her there shivering in the doorway? Or would life sour in a second?

The wind blew, and Lydia felt the lipstick that mottled her body like a plover's egg. He was a great man to her. This man on the bale of old hay had held her on his shoulders in Golden Gate Park so she could see the buffalo. He had dangled her by her ankles over the grass many times before she grew too tall. And once he made her believe that he had invented chocolate. What would happen if he turned and saw her, knew that she had witnessed this scene in the barn? She felt the red lips all along her legs, her arms and neck, her cheeks, trembling in red pairs, and then before she could stop herself the lips were parting, coughing, gasping in the dusty air.

And even if he did hear her, would all of this—the girl, the long night, the whole family and life—would it go under *P*?

1977

near perihelion

How many other bodies besides these comets move in secret, never rising before the eyes of men?

—Seneca, *Natural Questions*

"You know, I never think about him."

They were on the beach, Kathy and Eli, just as before. A little older, their faces had fallen into the expressions people would always think of them as wearing—hers in grim amusement, his in perplexity—and they stood close enough to create a shadow between them, a coolness they could talk into. The Spivaks were slightly apart from everyone else, the crowd of scientists who had come to see the comet Swift, which had returned. It was found—"recovered," that was the phrase—at the last moment this past December by a team of Australians who, thinking they had found a major comet, threw a party for themselves until the CBAT informed them they had documented the return of the famous Comet Swift. Professor Swift himself called the Australians late that night, awakening them, thanking them, extending an invitation to his perihelion party, never hearing their sleepy tones of disappointment. He didn't care; he was already pulling strings at the NSF to raise money for yet another meteor investigation in the South Seas. A reunion with the comet. So here they were, the old crowd, some bald, some fat, most of them calmer and happier than before, with wives and teaching positions. It was a smaller crowd than twelve years ago; the ones who had failed or given up on science had not returned. These were the survivors.

"Who?" Eli asked her.

Kathy looked at him as if it were obvious, saying, "That little boy—we don't even know his name—the one who died. I never think about him."

No one thought about him. No one had mentioned the accident, though high above them they could still make out the crumbled part of the wall, how the cement was darker than that around it, despite more than a decade of blazing sun. The topic, somehow, had been banned from conversation. Maybe, in contrast to all the rationality of these scientists, it was a superstitious silence, or perhaps—and more likely—time had dulled that memory. The cry, so stark in their minds after the accident, had softened, faded behind more personal sorrows. The witnesses had to admit to themselves that they had never noticed the dark-eyed boy before he died, and that the grief (now more than a decade old) had never been over him, a clumsy foreign child. It had always been for themselves, so young then, learning that you could not tailor your hopes like a suit and expect them to fit forever.

Eli sipped his gin and tonic, smiling at a grad student whose name he didn't know. He said, "Well, you just thought about him now, so—"

"I wasn't done," Kathy said without expression, taking his glass away. "It was Jorgeson's wife—she came up to me and—first it was very strange—she said she'd missed seeing me around all these years, and missed how close we'd been. What did she mean? I'm not sure we ever talked." Kathy sipped the drink. They all had drinks, all twenty or so of them out there in the hot glare of the beach. The island ban on alcohol had been lifted five years before, after the old sultan died, buried in his gold slippers and cap.

Eli pointed at his wife, smiling. "In fact, you used to make fun of her and say she was a mail-order bride."

She stared, confused. "I never said that."

"You did." His look was insistent, then he wiped some sweat from his nose and said, "We'll ask Denise."

The name seemed to change the moment, as if stirred by a breeze. Kathy handed his drink back to him and looked around for one for herself, continuing, "Anyway, then she looked at me very dim-wittedly and said, 'I think about that boy every single day.' "

"Are we bad people? Are we selfish people?"

Kathy was shaking her head. "I never think about him."

Eli's voice changed, became louder now that he had something to say, an affectation he'd picked up from years of lecturing: "Well, I thought about him on the plane. I thought about how we'd all be talking about him and staring at the wall where he fell, and how children would be kept away from the parapet this time."

Kathy kept watching Swift and his daughter, now a teenager. "There are no children this time."

"Are we that old? What happened to all the children?" He felt Kathy take his hand.

"Maybe we shouldn't have come."

He kissed her forehead. "Let's not talk about that again. We'll see Denise and Adam."

The name again. Another shadow thrown briefly on the sand.

She turned for a moment, head sideways against the blast of sun. In silhouette, Kathy looked the same as ever to him. The triangular profile, the giant glasses and the ponytail. She said, "But isn't it ter-rible? I think we all wish it hadn't happened, but not because it was awful for the boy. Just that it makes things so awkward now."

"Kath . . ."

"It ruins our fun." She looked back at him, grinning, and she was older again, silver in her hair. He touched her face and she said something about needing the shade, and another drink, and the touch crumbled as she was off across the sand toward a set of palm trees. He saw, too, teenage Lydia standing near the bar, talking, fanning herself with a hat. He knew his wife well enough to realize her interest had, as always, turned elsewhere; she had to know how this particular strange girl had turned out. It was a reunion, after all.

They were in a different world again, this group of scientists. Not in space; in time. Twelve years before, they had stormed the beaches with their intelligence and pride, sure that the world would soon be theirs; now, however, they felt gray and tired and confused. In 1977, the country felt like a man recovering from a heart attack—the parties were over, the night terrors, and it was time to be quiet and kind. Nixon had been followed quickly by the bicentennial, girls marching through towns in red-white-and-blue high boots, and two presidents who vowed forgiveness: the draft dodgers were urged to come home, and even traitorous Tokyo Rose, a sixty-year-old woman now, was pardoned. Science was grand and awful again: a space shuttle that would fly between stars, a neutron bomb that promised a softer, more invisible death. The panic of youth had passed, but still these scientists felt tentative, as if they stood inside a giant ball that had been shaken over and over by a child. Dizzy, stumbling, they had at last found the door. But would they ever be the same?

Eli stood in the blazing white heat of the beach in this crowd of men and watched his wife make her way to the shade, eavesdropping on the red-haired girl. He watched her standing alone: dark and segmented like an ant's body, hips and breasts and the implied antenna touching the words she overheard, the view, some unknown thought. She read everything around her like a book. He tossed her an inquisitive glance, and she caught it in time to raise her eyebrows and let him know that everything was all right with her—the heat, the red-haired girl nearby, these dull old men and their hairy stars. She was only here for the day, on her way to a conference in Japan. She felt no need to mingle; among these men, her presence always faded against the sand—she would stand there, biting her lip, features dilated down to neutral—why did she dim herself like that? Or was she like those star clusters, hidden in constellations, that glimmer beautifully in the night sky until a car's headlights pass by and the eye, so frail, deletes the cluster in the wash of light?

He had loved Kathy in England. He'd run there to escape, and he had done it. He had found a few great postdoc positions that enabled him to work on his research on cometary nuclei, struggling for a faculty position, then finally settled for something slightly lower than he'd hoped. Eli felt bitter at the ease of positions in America, but he'd found a way to stay in London, and the transition was complete. They got a few letters from Denise, but Eli tore them up and never answered them, so they dwindled into yearly Christmas cards that made him smile to remember her at such a safe distance. Kathy, finally as comfortable in a place as Eli was, worked editing books for an independent press and helped a friend put out a poetry journal with an electric typewriter and a ditto machine they kept in their flat's kitchen. The hot smell of the machine kept them both content, feeling they had not sold their hard-won intellectual freedom unwisely—at least, at least there was bad English poetry around in sheaves of purple ink! And the foreignness of their lives in England never lost its appeal (although, after the fourth year, they had stopped finding the English "fascinating" and instead felt most of them were hidebound and homicidally obsessed with class), nor did the shops in London wear thin, nor the new funny accents they came across, nor the sight of ugly Americans stumbling through Piccadilly. They struggled together, made mistakes together, fought, and this at last was marriage. The time in England, difficult and impoverished as it was, would come to seem, later, a charmed and impossible phase, colored, like art from a lost empire, in simple platinum and blue.

Then in 1973, out of nowhere, he was offered a position in Los Angeles based on his research of cometary nuclei and, though the school was less impressive than the institutions his old classmates had found out of postdoc, Eli saw it as his last chance to move up in his career. Scientists get ranked so early on, and the English were not eager to give any American a step up, so if Eli wanted a career, he had to look west. He swallowed his pride and, in a move he would sometimes regret, he took the job. The Spivaks moved back to California, to a bungalow, and for a little while they were astonished at their old country, at the excesses and gaudy beauty of it, the prickly dryness of their western landscape, and they could notice already some of the hippie men and women turning back into the corn-fed cheerleaders and quarterbacks they once had been. Money, careers, apathy and hot tubs. They felt so changed, and it was wonderful to know that they had changed together, had an alliance against their strange homeland. Within a month, they got their first visit from Denise.

On seeing her in the doorway, trim in a yellow linen dress, a wooden necklace crossing her breasts, her neck beginning to cord with age, her eyebrows plucked quite high, Eli saw how fine she was, how totally fine and not lost at all. He also saw himself as she must have seen him, realized how bald and fat he had become in those eight years, and had the strangest feeling of relief—even more so when she showed him a picture of Adam and he saw how much handsomer the man had become in that time, fuller, more muscle and jaw than ever—and thought to himself, *Now we're safe, now there's no danger, we can be friends.* Immediately after it came into his head, he swallowed the thought, cracked it like ice between his teeth, and forgot it. They embraced, and then she and Kathy embraced, and it was all right.

He watched Kathy trudging back toward him through the sand, her face turned away. He saw the dark oval of sweat forming on the back of her shirt, under the ponytail with its old-fashioned leather barrette. He saw two silver hairs slipping from the knot, one straight and glittering, the other kinky, waving behind her now in the faint breeze. What an old, familiar sight. How strange to see it projected again onto the rough green head of that volcano, this panel of hot sky, those dragonflies knitting into an emerald near her hand. He felt a knot of worry.

"I couldn't hear anything. I'm going down to the huts." Kathy was beside him, shaking the sand from her shoes.

"Why? Denise will be here in a minute."

"Someone said Adam was sick and she was still in the huts. I want to go down to meet her."

He understood that she wanted to meet Denise alone. They all lived in California now, but Santa Cruz and L.A. were farther apart than it seemed when they were younger, and the kinds of private moments that Kathy loved couldn't happen over the phone, or with that child around, or that husband. He knew Kathy didn't want to see Denise in this crowd of men, this professional setting where the first comments were bound to be about Denise's university work and about her recent collaborations with Eli that had brought them both so much attention and jealousy. Eli knew how Kathy needed friends in private, how crowds dispersed her feelings.

"You're not going to be morbid and look for where the boy fell. . . ."

"I'm not going to be morbid."

It had been years since they discussed children; but once in a while this fascination of hers became apparent, glittered like an old coin in a muddy fountain, though he didn't dare to touch it. He let her fret and worry over others' children: kids on the street, Denise's son, this boy. If he touched it, that meant talking about it, and he felt the topic was too precariously balanced for any talking. He did not want children now, although twelve years before, on this same island, he had longed for her to be pregnant. Now, it seemed, their positions were reversed. She pined; he changed the topic. Eli had all kinds of clever diversions, funny conversation pieces about how children changed people, aged them in a weekend, how kids' awful tastes infiltrated their parents and ruined them forever. But these were just bits. He still loved children, but he knew how a child with Kathy would lead him further into a life that, already in the past year, had begun to look like a maze.

"Okay," Eli said. "Don't wander too long, I'm not going to see you for a while."

"You'll see me."

"But *really* see you. Don't fall asleep in the sun—come back for lunch."

"I'll come back for lunch," she said, but she wouldn't.

He watched her entering the shade of the jungle path, waving to the guards who seemed to be everywhere on this island. So recently back from England, she was beginning to have a life without him. As though returning to the States was like returning to her childhood room, looking around and remembering how she used to want things—quiet, separate, free—and beginning to put the old things back in their places. He did not mind it; he preferred it. All on her own, Kathy had saved him a great deal of trouble.

He went over to the group around Swift, gathered under a parasol, and began to talk to them about the comet. A few old jokes were made and the men laughed. Professor Swift seemed smaller, older and less patient than before, restless as he talked; he had quit cigarettes and alcohol and was still getting used to it. He wore a shirt patterned like graph paper and dotted with sweat, and he kept patting the breast pocket for a pack of cigarettes. Manday, in a white suit with the jacket thrown over his arm, rubbing the dark crescents under his eyes, had stepped forward slightly from the others, and just the tip of his nose escaped the parasol's violet shade, a sunlit knob. Beside him was a young man of about nineteen, whom Eli had not noticed before, but who now tapped Manday on the shoulder and whispered to him. It was Manday's beloved son, Ali. He was one of the youngest on the beach, handsome with a long, dark face and a body that wanted to move, his hands restlessly tapping his thighs, his head nodding. Manday whispered back and looked at his watch, then held his son's arm and kissed him on the mouth. Ali smiled and ran across the beach into the trees, released from his father's astronomy, which, in bright daylight, became mere theory and conjecture. Manday explained proudly that his son needed to study for his American college classes.

Young people, sons, daughters, everywhere on the beach. All of them shedding youth as quickly as they could, scrubbing it off like a stain. Eli thought it was a shame to bustle forward so impatiently, as if the doors might close before you made it to thirty, but then he remembered that he had felt that way ten years ago, in England, begging time to pass so he'd forget his indiscretions, so he'd learn to love his wife the way he had when they were younger. It was still a shame, but he couldn't blame them. Lydia, flirting with all the men. Ali, anxious to leave his family. He couldn't blame them.

Then the professors (for that's what they were now, all of them) began to talk to Eli in tones of excitement. Not about his career in L.A., which was almost beneath their notice, but about his amateur forays.

"I wish I had the time," one of them sighed, and Professor Swift kept slapping Eli's back as if they were at last colleagues now, the mentor and the chosen son.

"I hope you hit the jackpot," the old man said gruffly, coughing, and what he meant was that he hoped Eli found a comet like his, above them now, the Comet Swift. Because, on weekend nights now, Eli sat on a hillside with a small telescope and camera and searched for comets. He was a comet-hunter, a small hero to the group of stargazers who found themselves mired more and more in papers and committees. Eli, frustrated with his department, and with the encouragement of Kathy, had returned to boyhood romance in his free time, and had already found a minor comet with his partner. Thus all the congratulations. And who would have guessed it? His partner was on the island right now, in the trees, talking to his wife. His partner was Denise.

Jorgeson, bald now and sunburned, asked, "Now why did they put her name first? Periodic comet Lanham-Spivak. Why not Spivak-Lanham?"

"Alphabetical," Eli explained, remembering the night of its discovery.

Swift put his finger on the side of his nose. "You've been hoodwinked, son. You should put it in order of contribution."

Eli sighed. "Dr. Lanham gave the greatest contribution."

Someone made a dirty remark and Eli blushed, turning away, letting them have the rest of their conversation without him. It confused him, sometimes, to realize his old colleagues had got through the sixties unscathed, unenlightened, and were turning into the same leering, jokey professors they'd loathed back when they were BAD-grads. But scientists were somehow impermeable to society. Fashion could not affect them, nor etiquette, nor politics nor the passage of time. It was wonderful, and kept them separate, honest; it was hideous, as well. Eli looked toward the jungle, but Kathy hadn't returned. He noticed a figure above them all, on the overlook, but the relentless sun blinded his view. He sought the shadows and held on to a tree.

His collaboration with Denise had begun a year after his return to California. They saw each other very rarely, and usually in the company of her son and husband, that dull and likable football player to whom Eli had introduced her—introduced before he'd left for England, as a way to keep her happy. But hadn't she realized it? That he'd never meant for her to marry him? Usually Adam was around, so their conversations were placid, with child stories, minutia of the suburban life, Adam's store of WASPy jokes. But once, Denise had come down for business alone. Eli and Denise had sipped port together and finally talked about their favorite subject: the sky. How it always kept its word. There was something desperate in her that night which Eli had been yearning to see, hoping was not dead inside her, and he'd grabbed the chance. He talked about comet-hunting. He convinced her that it might bring the bloom back to her romance with the stars.

So it started. Every other Saturday, they drove from their respective cities to a midpoint near Tranquillity, a nothing town surrounded by pistachio and almond fields. The drive took each of them about three and a half hours, and they met in a diner and ate pancakes and drank coffee. Then he got into her car and they drove with their equipment partway up Ciervo Mountain. On a rocky overlook, she laid out the woolen blankets and arranged the folding chairs while he set up the sixteen-inch telescope and camera. Each imagined wild animals hooting and rustling, but they were never disturbed, not even by humans. Although they were here in an amateur capacity, they kept strict laboratory roles: Denise adjusted the telescope every six minutes to search the sky vertically, and Eli loaded the film, timed the aperture, and carefully preserved the images, which he developed the next day. He mailed the photographs to Denise and she studied them on her own that week. If they caught a comet on any night, therefore, they wouldn't know it for days. Here, under the stars, they were merely gathering data, so they could relax; the young professor could bring out his college bongos and play to the sound of the trees, and his friend could stand, listening, gazing up at that old familiar view.

It was far from Tranquillity, though, deep into their sixth month of searching, that Denise made the discovery that would lend them small immortality. They had decided to search the photographs using stereo imagery, an uncommon procedure at the time. Eli stacked the hundreds of images in order, mailed them to Denise, and she, sitting in her bathrobe while she heard her husband typing in the other room, would fit two photos into her stereomicroscope and peer within. It was something like the turn-of-the-century stereopticons—two sepia photos (usually of a dour mandarin in front of the Yangtze River) were placed side by side with a barrier between them, and the viewer looked through a glass that sent only one image to each eye. The optical effect, because of slight differences in the angle of the photographs, was three-dimensional, and the sepia mandarin appeared to float angrily in front of his muddy river. For the comet search, Denise would put a photographed square of sky on one side and another photo taken six minutes later on the other. When she looked through the eyepiece, anything exactly the same in both photos would stay flat, but any object that had moved in those six minutes would appear, like the mandarin, to float mysteriously above the other stars. This is exactly what Denise Lanham saw that afternoon in May.

"Adam! Call Eli!"

Eli flew to Berkeley to see what she thought she'd found. There, in the eyepiece, in a close shot of Scorpius near dawn, hovered a smudge of light—which was just how a still-distant comet would look. Eli brought out his edition of the *Uranometria* to confirm it was not a known star or a Messier object. There was nothing known in Scorpius. Denise searched her shelves for the *IAU Circular* for March, as well as the *Minor Planet Circular,* and she and Eli, dizzy from a lack of sleep and pale with hunger, put their shaking fingers to the long ephemerides for bright comets present in the skies, moving down the columns in search of one in Scorpius, nervous as snakebite victims searching for an antidote. But there was, again, nothing. They had discovered a new object in the sky. Yet the scientific method could not end there, so they spent another anxious and slightly drunken night out on the rocky overlook, focusing, this time, entirely on that square of Scorpius before dawn, when comets glow coldly near the sun.

"I want this comet," she told him forcefully as he loaded the film. She lay on the blanket with a bottle of wine.

"I know," he said.

She shook her head. "No, I mean I really do. Remember when we were grad students? And we all secretly wanted the Nobel Prize?"

He thought about it for a moment. She seemed so sure, so like she used to be in school. She frightened him again, the same way. "No, I never wanted that. Astronomers don't win Nobels...."

"But you did want it, you did," she said, sitting up and resting her hands on her knees. The only light was a red flashlight, which lay on the Messier catalog. "I know, you thought you had a chance. We all did. We thought it was just a matter of being smart and being lucky, that we were all young Hubbles and Halleys, but you learn it's not true. You don't just get smarter and smarter until finally you're a genius. Being a genius is something else entirely."

"I never thought I was a genius," he said, having at last a chance to tell her how he'd always felt about himself, but knowing she wouldn't hear it that way. She would just hear modesty.

"I thought I was," she admitted, smiling, touching her thick wool sweater. "But I'm not. It's all right, it's fine, I found out early on when I couldn't land a job and everyone else could. I'm a woman, I know, but a genius woman would have gotten a faculty position. I worked for the government, and the government lets you know you're no genius. So I gave up on that, but I wanted something else."

"I hope it wasn't money."

"I wanted an effect. An effect or an object. I wanted people to talk about calculating the 'Lanham effect' on a white dwarf, or the complex rotation of a 'Lanham object.' Maybe a 'Lanham force,' or a 'Lanham diagram' or—hell—even a 'Lanham tube.' Something named after me. And the funny thing is, even with Dr. Swift around all the time, I never thought I'd get a comet."

He paused, then asked, "Is that why you agreed to this?"

"Of course that's why. You can't just do all this science and die."

Then she stood up to readjust the telescope, and he recognized the stern, impressive tone in her voice. He had heard it before, standing in the San Francisco fog outside the doorway to her apartment.

It had been just this way, just this tone, with different words: "We don't need to have this conversation." Such focus, direction, control. He had always seen her as so fragile, but it wasn't true. She always got exactly what she wanted. And, of all things, instead of heartbreak, this new vision of her thrilled him. Denise would find this comet for him; she would save his career, and would not even expect to be thanked. There was no one like her.

Eli was careful but trembling in the Berkeley darkroom the next morning as he looked over the photographs they had taken, breathless in the red light as he saw the faint fuzzy spot appearing in the emulsion, this time teardropped with a tail. Then it was hurriedly lent to Denise in the next room. She panted, placing it in her stereomicroscope, turning the dials and he waited, pacing, holding his hands before him. After a minute or so, she stood up, and he could see she was weeping. She looked at him, then yelled for a telegram to be sent: *new comet in scorpius magnitude 8 stop 8 hours ut stop discoverers lanham comma spivak comma professionals in amateur capacity stop right ascension. . . .*

And here she was.

Stepping from the shadows of the jungle, in the sunglasses and the white straw hat that students now associated with her, bending a banana leaf out of her way, Denise appeared. She nodded and waved to people, so unlike the timid girl Eli had known in Campbell Hall, yet somehow still consciously awkward. She had done well, produced important papers despite her constraining governmental position. Her success showed in the scientists' response: They were nudging each other, ridiculing or admiring her, and she walked right through the group of them, using her gesturing hand like a machete to cut past the conversations they threatened to start. About her comet, her papers, her ideas. She spoke briefly with Swift and promised to come back. She made her way through the sunlight to Eli. Blue beads around her neck. Here she was.

Denise touched his arm and whispered, "Just give me a quick kiss, because your wife is on the overlook."

Automatically, he obeyed, feeling angry once more at the commands she'd always given to people, especially him, but his anger faded as he kissed each cheek. He let himself look up to the great white concrete parapet above them. It was Kathy up there, leaning over the edge, coiled within herself like a heavy knot, and she held something in her hand—a berry, a butterfly, a stone?

"I just saw her in the jungle," Denise said.

"She headed out to meet you. You're her best friend these days, you know."

Denise laughed, and whispered, "I want to talk about her. But people are listening, so we'll use a code name for her. We'll call her Bob." Then she began to talk in her loud, natural voice: "Bob doesn't seem very happy. . . ."

He was staring at this woman in her late thirties, that stiff trapezoidal nose high in the jungle air, its bump darkened with a broken capillary; he was listening to her talk in code about his wife; he was watching the circular gestures she made to append her words; and all he could think of was how it had begun again. She might change everything about herself over the years—the makeup overdone with blue around her eyes, her thick hair bleached, some lilac scent spreading as she waved her arms—but still the actual rare presence of her warmed him entirely. He carried on this coded conversation with her, but he felt that they were discussing something else—not their collaboration, because that no longer existed as others believed. In this last year, their record of the sky had turned back into romance, into that old affair as easy as a familiar room, so easy it hardly seemed illicit. They both leaned against a palm tree as they talked, and she lowered her hand slightly, rubbing against his. They were lovers now. A blanket on a hillside, a clear veil of stars—something else besides the comet had been recovered.

Kathy glanced down from the overlook. She could not see the beach—she faced the jungle and watched Lydia making her way down the cut path from the huts, headed toward a clearing where the Mandays had their home. Kathy took great pleasure in this, although she knew it was childish, watching a girl like a boat you'd set free down a creek. It was good, though, to see someone else who couldn't stand the crowd out on the beach. Women so rarely chose to be alone.

Kathy's greeting of Denise had been brief—they saw each other so often, of course. Denise had not brought her son, after all, and Adam lay feverish and miserable in the hut. No, it was probably best that no one visit him. Kathy could recognize some terrible happiness in Denise's voice, and she wanted to tell her, *It's all right, you can be glad you're on your own today,* but they didn't talk like that anymore. Denise was Eli's friend now. Afterward, Kathy had made her way up the long cut stairs to the overlook, curious to see the old place, since she'd be leaving so soon, before the count of meteors. She entered the spiral stairs, and emerged from the golden dome as if from the lip of a honey jar, realizing that she'd never seen this view in daytime. There was the place she'd sat twelve years before. And there was the wall where the boy had fallen. Would he have been nineteen now, twenty? She walked over to the edge and down below she saw Eli, standing alone and looking out to sea. It pleased her that he stood apart from the scientists, that he hadn't seized her absence as a time to plunge back into the world that upset him. The bundle of hatless men in the sun. The water glinting like a chandelier.

Then, to the east, she noticed Lydia making her way down the jungle path. She had thought about Lydia so often, remembering the few times she'd talked with her as a young girl. That subtle strangeness she'd found. Kathy no longer pulled at people's oddities during dinner parties; it had grown exhausting for her, and men and women seemed less open these days, palming their true eccentricities and offering feigned ones: yoga and mysticism and sex. They were all adults now, and closeness was something too difficult to bear. With friends, with strangers. The people around her had made life choices they took to be permanent; now, whether confident in or afraid of their choices, they no longer allowed any examination; she could learn no more about them than about characters after a book had ended. She rarely went to parties anymore, afraid to come across another sad, perfected person. But Lydia was young, and Kathy thought there still might be something free in this girl, unaltered, something to be learned. Also, Kathy had brought a gift with her to the island, especially for Lydia. She watched the girl's movements through the trees, wondering if she had the nerve to shout, call the girl up to the overlook, hand over what had been waiting twelve years in her pocket.

She had it by chance. Back in 1965, on the boat over from the mainland, Eli had slipped her a heavy camera and she'd taken it without questioning. She knew it was Denise's, but Denise was drunk at the time and didn't need it. Kathy had headed out to the bow to look at the island that was appearing on the horizon, holding the camera before her. She remembered someone shouting *Land ho!* and the little girl beside her saying that she couldn't see it, and that's when Kathy turned and took a picture—an angry child, her face red and squinting in the salt air, her hands thrown down to keep her dress from flying in the wind. Later, when others were sleeping in their huts, Kathy had wandered along the jungle paths until she found Professor Swift with Lydia again, the man washing his face in a tub and Lydia stark naked in the orchids, staring. Another picture. And on and on as the evening progressed, as they gathered in their stations on the overlook, all photos of Lydia, until Professor Swift told her to stop using the flash; it would ruin their eyes. Kathy gave the camera to him then and got it back the next morning, but in the flurry after the accident, those bleary-eyed days on the plane and alone in California, she apparently removed the roll of film and then forgot all about it. Denise got her camera back, but Eli's sudden decision to move to England made it hard to keep track of the small objects. Most random junk went into a box, in storage, and the roll of film went in there as well. She did not think of it again. Not until a few years after their return, when going through the box to find a book, did she recover the film. Kathy pulled it out, the rattling jar of plastic, knew instantly what it was, and stopped herself from developing it. She knew what was on it—prying shots of Lydia as a girl—and Kathy decided it wasn't for her to see first. The pictures had a painful innocence to them now that she didn't dare expose; they were a record of Lydia just before the accident. To see them, then hand them over—it would be an ambush, a trick. No, she would keep it for the reunion, for Lydia to see alone.

That's what Kathy held in her hand, which Eli had thought was a stone.

Kathy watched as the girl passed through a clearing, nodding her head at two women who sat smoking cigarettes. Lydia was moving toward the island's interior, skirting the summer palace on whose overlook Kathy stood. She seemed to be making her way to the beach, brushing her hair back vainly and ripping the leaves out of the way. Angry youth, or impatient youth. Then she disappeared behind a curve in the path, and Kathy replaced her form with the memory of her that day on the beach. Taking that face from the age of five to here, seventeen, was like watching the expansion of a crumpled tissue dropped in water—the unkinking of the hair, bringing it to this shine, the outward floating of her features, the long kite-shapes of her eyes, the rosy pimpled chin, Swift's upturned nose amid the faint pollen-scattering of freckles. It fascinated Kathy to consider what awful things the girl had got through to reach this age, and what she still might face.

She had thought of Denise this way, once, when they were young. The rich, heartless scientist too long ignored. But Denise was no longer that for her. The leave-taking long ago at the airport had been tense, interesting to Kathy, almost as if Denise could not bear to part with her and yet could not wait to drive home to her flat and begin new projects alone. And then no letters in England. No letters at all. Eli had not seemed surprised, but despite her eagerness for friendships to change, for people to change, it had broken Kathy's heart. After a year, she had to give her friend over for good as one of those characters in an Elizabethan play who enters brilliantly in the second act banquet scene, has all the best lines, then never returns again. Kathy missed her, though; she and Eli talked about her. They said they missed her confusion, how she seemed perpetually unhappy but, oddly, good-humored. How she worried endlessly yet took for granted that she would succeed. How she nervously rubbed her face so that her makeup disintegrated over the course of a dinner party (Eli's anecdote); how she beat the table when she argued and made the glasses ring (Kathy's). In England, Denise seemed very far away, and Kathy assumed she'd lost her.

Her disappearance was, however, the product of Kathy's own device. She and Eli had introduced her to the man who would become her husband—Adam—but Kathy hadn't realized that this would change anything. She had only meant to salve Denise's loneliness, and grabbed the closest thing at hand—an odd, bookish young man from the edge of their circle, an acquaintance, really—but, in the same way a quick fix on a table leg can hold for generations, that conventional Adam, also never made to be permanent, stayed. What could you say when it was love? How could you tell her that you'd never really meant for her to marry him?

Eight years passed. Christmas cards came, hilarious and weirdly upper-class things with a picture attached of a family Kathy could not imagine belonging to Denise. Was this the life she'd chosen? The smile seemed the same in each photo, and as the color processes improved over the years, her skin appeared to grow more natural and pink, her blouses more expensive. One year, the card came in the mail and Kathy laughed out loud to see that brain-heavy Denise had permed and frosted her hair into a kind of macaroon. She showed the photo to Eli, who simply repeated a dictum from his grandmother: *You can't judge anything you didn't pay for.* Oh what an awful world if that were true, she thought. And hadn't they paid in some way for that macaroon? Wasn't there an investment there— the Shabbat dinners, the sangria and fondue parties, the late nights, the neat package containing her future husband? Hadn't they given her all this so that she'd yield something better than her mother's life out in the foggy mansion, lunching at Neiman Marcus but buying, *bien sûr,* at Saks? Were these appalling cards to be the only dividend they'd ever see?

When Denise did finally reenter their lives, it was as Eli's friend alone. Kathy was not hurt this time; she understood that she was no longer crucial to her old friend's life, and had not been for some time. A husband, a son—it changes you. Denise had hardened into the place where she had fallen at thirty, and Kathy assumed that, like so many people, she couldn't bear the analysis. There were to be no more late-night talks on the carpet or sitting on the steps outside a party whispering and complaining. Eli was an easier friend, rarely petty or hurt by anything you said, content never to delve deeper than a discussion of ion clouds. Kathy understood that Denise was happy, and she gave her husband freely to those comet-hunting nights. But she ceased admiring the woman.

Soon enough, she came to see a different side of Denise, the one her husband loved. It was at a party in L.A. years after their return, when Eli was beginning to have difficulties with his department and came home depressed, that Kathy and Denise were standing in the warm night air together. It was not an astronomical gathering, which made it all the nicer because it meant they could all admire the moon without any comment about how it ruined the stars. It was a neighbor's backyard party, the weird seventies brand where all the men wore hemp bracelets and beads and all the women still came with their hair newly set. As the stars awoke, the two astronomers could point them out, delighting people as if they were all children, and had never noticed that Mars was red. Kathy remembered that the host came out with a pitcher of punch on a tray, full to the top with ice, and the hostess laughed and said, "Harry, you idiot! The ice'll melt and it'll spill all over everything!" Denise then flatly and innocently explained how it was a stupid thing to say, since ice, in contradiction to common sense, is more dense as a liquid: *Worry not, Harry; the ice will melt harmlessly.* The host and hostess stood stunned as oblivious Denise took a glass of offered punch, and Kathy saw that she was nothing like she'd thought she was. She had not become complacent or ordinary at all; these days, Denise merely said and did what she liked. And from Eli's ecstatic face, Kathy saw he had always known this. Why had she never seen it? Was this the reason—had Kathy always held her back, tamped her friend down like brown sugar in a measuring cup, and so Denise had to be free of her? Was this why she had written no letters?

Lydia had made it to the beach, was already past the spit. She had stripped to her bikini, clothes in a bundle under her arm, and walked awkwardly across the sand, picking up her legs like a sandpiper, re-arranging her hair against a hopeless breeze. Scandalous white girl in a green bikini. Seventeen years old and finally away from the crowd, away from her bullying father, the anger of his old age, away from the worthless handful of jerks down the beach. They couldn't see her—she was on the most desolate strip of beach, and only Kathy, leaning a little over the wall, could make out the girl stepping through the hot sand toward a clump of coconut trees. She could finally see what a girl might do if you just left her alone.

It was hard to have no friends. Nearing forty, with everyone around you stuck in their personal tar pits, complaining about the loud music these days, the clothes, the morals, and the death of the English language on the lips of the young—did they really believe the seventies were the end of the world? Couldn't they recognize all these phrases from their parents' mouths? They were simply grow-ing old. They had turned thirty-five and put a full stop on their lives. Where did this leave Kathy? Watching a girl who might grow up a little different.

Then a dark form came from the jungle, walking at an angle to meet the girl. Kathy could see Lydia still walking, not noticing, just fussing with her hair and with the bundle of clothes, looking out to sea. But Kathy could make it out: a man walking swiftly toward her, an island man. Shirtless, long pants, his arms hanging as he made his way. And then Lydia saw him. She froze, dropped her bundle, standing hands-on-hips in false bravado. Perhaps the man said some-thing as he approached, perhaps the girl yelled back; Kathy never knew. It was distant mime play for her, a dark form and a light one under the hot sun. The man drew next to Lydia. Kathy leaned over to see, inching for a view, terrified. Should she yell? They wouldn't hear. Should she call a guard? It was too late. Yes, now he was sound-lessly talking to her, his hand on the girl's shoulder. Then she saw: It was Ali, Dr. Manday's son. And also: Now Lydia's hand was on the back of his head; now they were kissing.

From there, Kathy let time move quickly. She leaned back from the wall as the distant figures kissed and groped like the teenagers they were, as he undid the bikini and the girl let it fall to the beach with the rest of her clothes. Kathy walked away from the view as the boy took the girl's hand and led her down a spit to an old stone hut. She turned from the sight now. This was some other kind of youth, some foreign land, and she no longer knew how to read it. An in-nocent girl on a beach, a dark man. And to think she had almost screamed. Maybe she was old, too. She went through the gilt entrance to the stairs, making her way down through the shadowed spiral, then down the cut stone steps, her hand against the wall. The night ferry was many hours away, but she might still pack. Rest on her bed, read her book. There would be dinner, talking with Eli and Denise. God, there was so much time to kill before she could leave.

When she reached the bottom of the stairs, she handed the film canister to the sultan's guard, telling him to give it to Dr. Swift's daughter. They had some trouble working this out. Dr. Swift, his daughter, Dr. Swift. Then the guard grinned and took the roll and Kathy was in the cool of the forest again. And she could not know it, she would never know it, but this comet would come around again before Lydia saw those pictures.

By four o'clock, you could see the comet in the sky. This day in March was the perfect time to view it; the comet had already passed out of the blinding halo of the sun, but still reflected the sun's light, making it bright and clear. A greater comet had come the year before, Comet Kahoutek, and astronomers had grown excited, proclaiming it to be the comet of the century. It had sizzled, though, and hopes were high for Periodic Comet Swift. The same thing had happened: Comet Swift was faint, a scribble in the daytime sky, possibly with two tails this time, but nothing like it should have been. Few on the island were watching; they were all chatting or sleeping now, or awake in the hot darkness of their huts.

One was watching: Dr. Swift, sneaking a bourbon at the abandoned bar. He was not supposed to drink or smoke, but who was there to stop him now? Where was the lady in white robes who would tsk-tsk at his weaknesses, grab the bottle from him, stub out the strong cigars? Who would be enraged by anything he did to himself now? No one. There was just this broad, hot beach in its glittering Tiffany case. So he looked up at his comet and it brought his burning mind to a furious boil. A wait of twelve years, only his third viewing, and such a disappointment. Even now, near perihelion, it hadn't ever blazed or smoked bright blue with ions. The professor had said nothing to anyone, but he had a private reason for his anger: He was ill. He considered the notion that this might be his last sight of his comet. At sixty-four, twelve years felt both too short and too long; that length of time, in the past, had seemed to move by so quickly, but now of course it seemed unreachable. His research was waning, he had fewer grad students and papers; life seemed to tire him. So this might be the last time, and the old man, dreaming of its fiery approach from Mars, had wanted housewives to gasp from their kitchen windows. He had wanted kings to shake in fear. He looked up from the fringed beach. A white scratch on the perfect sky.

Several hours later, the comet was even more visible. Dr. Manday lay asleep, but his wife sat wakeful by the window of their hut. She noticed the scratch in the blue above; her husband had told her where it would be, what it would look like, and she wasn't a fool. She'd seen it twice before herself; she remembered the day they'd found it, how Swift had burst in, yelling for the sultan; how they gathered in the little Japanese communication office to send that telegram. She remembered her drunken husband later that night, Dr. Swift in his open Hawaiian shirt, that giant awful man. She remembered with bitterness, too, the contents of their telegram: *comet discovered in centaurus by swift stop*. A *stop* where her husband's name should have been. A *stop* instead of a *manday*. She turned away from Comet Swift; it was a stolen jewel, and she would not gaze on it in awe, or admire it or consider what its appearance might now foretell.

The sun moved lower in the sky. Lydia sat at the bar, and this time the comet was plain to see above the water. She hardly noticed. It was her third gin and tonic, on top of a little pot Ali had given her, and she was glad to have planned it so well that none of the scientists would be around—they were all still having their stargazer naps, or reading their journals, or scribbling in their notebooks. It was just her and the bartender, a stout man who never asked her age and who happily put it all on her father's bill. She stared out at the high tide, at the ocean-gutted rocks, the perfect curve of a palm bending like an open hand, the poisonous gemlike corpse of a jellyfish on the wet sand. She was so different from everybody else. She and Ali. She'd guessed it for a long time, but the conversation she'd over-heard about the boy who fell from the overlook, this sick, secret anniversary—it had confirmed it; they were disposable. She, Ali, anyone who wasn't one of the scientists, the squares. She thought of Dr. Lanham's husband, Adam, and how she'd always liked him, ever since she'd met him in the barn; how he was sick today, but they didn't care. The journals, the notebooks. Hadn't she even seen Dr. Lanham walking on the beach with the Jewish guy? The bartender brought her another drink and she smiled. He smiled back. God, how was she going to hide the alcohol on her breath this time?

She was right: The scientists were asleep or studying. Most were only a few years into their teaching positions, still assistant professors with loads of low-level classes to teach, desperate for a few hours to finish their research. They still had hopes of greatness, those of them who had landed at major institutions; and those who had fallen lower—they still labored as though they might break free. Denise, in her signature glasses, was working with Dr. Swift's new calculator, an object as rare and valuable back then as a diamond. Eli edited a collaborative paper, nervously chewing the tip of his pen, Kathy asleep behind him. The others all busied themselves with figures of the sky before the sky itself appeared; they were young, as scientists go, their time eaten up by committees or, for those who had not made tenure, by a desperation too close to be ignored for sun or sand.

And all around them, so easy to forget in its maroon and pea-green undulation, lay the forest. Millions of trembling leaves, each with an insect sticking to the pale undersurface, sailors on rafts riding out the wind. The wind changed its mind. The leaves, with their castaways, bucked wildly in the forest. On the overlook, the sultan's old telescope creaked in its joints. The comet did not seem to move an inch.

Deep in the cluster of huts, surrounded on two sides by banana groves, a man lay moaning in his bed; he had hardly seen more than the beach since his arrival. Some bad beef stew the night before, a sensitive stomach, and he'd been attacked by beads of sweat like an army of ants. He was recovering now, alone, staring around the walls of his hut. It was Denise's husband, Adam, and he felt he just might lose his mind.

It was the cry that did it. He was coming off his fever, lying in the sweaty darkness, the late afternoon sun parting the curtains of the single window, and every time he tried to rest his eyes at last, he was awakened by a piercing, mysterious cry. Adam was the kind of man who couldn't ignore a sound like that, or any distraction—each night before they went to sleep, he carefully swept any dirt or crumbs out of the bed, and Denise always watched him, smiling, softly ridiculing his sensitivity by saying he was like a Poe character. He couldn't sleep with the sound, therefore, this cry piercing his heated brain. At first, deep in his fever, he had worried that it was a child fallen outside his hut, wounded, crying for its mother, and that he was the only one who could hear it, but soon the regularity of the cry made this impossible. No, it was no child. The noise, then the silent shadowed room, then the noise again. What was it? He was driven mad trying to figure out the source until a lucky gust of wind blew open the window and he could see, plain and calm, a large parrot hanging in a cage across the way. It seemed to turn and sneer at him before the wind died, the curtain fell, and he heard once again that maddening cry. He knew what made the sound, but it had not calmed him. Now Adam had to figure out what the parrot was saying: "*Help* it"? "*Hop* it"? "*Stop* it"? What had they taught it to say? He could not sleep. Normally, sleepless, he would try to think about his novel, move the characters around like a boy playing with toy soldiers, but he'd given up on those thoughts half a year ago. Instead, he lay there for hours in his fevered dreams, waiting for Denise to arrive.

Adam dreamed for a long time about the boy he had thought lay outside his window. This was not uncommon; he often found it hard to rid his mind of terrible images. He would walk down a street and see the sharp edge of a broken window, thinking, *I'll hurt myself on that,* and even though he never did, he saved the mental picture of his bleeding hand for hours. So he dreamed about the boy lying wounded, bitten by a serpent, and then about his own son, whom he missed terribly. His son Josh, a proud and creative boy whose talents his mother could not see. To Denise, the blond kid seemed wonderful but not exceptionally bright, no good at math, at science, only happy playing soccer or drawing. Adam felt that only he saw the boy's great confidence and charm, something Denise would never value. Then Adam dreamed of himself as a boy, as the sunlight suddenly entered his room like the angry husband of a lover. He remembered being in Connecticut at his grandparents' house in winter, before his family had moved to Hollywood, where he would spend the majority of his life. He was in Milford, Connecticut, in the backyard of the house, and in this dream both the house and the yard took on plantation-sized proportions—a brick mansion with a widow's walk, an impossibly unmowable lawn acres wide, striped and gilded with winter sun, yellow leaves floating in the crisp air. In reality, he knew it to be a suburban lot backing onto a stream. He made the stream into a brown flowing winter river, chinked with ice and black twigs, and in this memory he stood on a small cliff looking into a dark eddy in which twirled a soup can. Memory moved lightninglike to the next shocking moment, when he found himself in the icy stream, looking up toward the overhang where there was just blue sky. Adam was taken downstream, suffering, frozen, calling, but nobody came and he was sure he was going to die until, just as suddenly, he found himself clutching the dead arm of a tree branch. He pulled himself out and staggered, almost blind with fright, into the mud room where he changed his clothes and appeared in time for dinner. This was just after the war, and his disbelieving family still kept their windows blacked against attack, so he walked into a warm box of a room, sat down and ate. No one ever noticed that his being alive was the most amazing aspect of the meal.

The door opened and in came Denise, lifting him from his fever so that he tried to smile, feeling relieved. Bits of the dream still clung to the room, though, and for a few moments his wife seemed to wade through icy water, pushing cracked branches out of her way, moving forward to save him.

"You're back!" he said.

"You look better," she told him merrily, although she didn't approach. She took off her ridiculous white hat and put it on a post, then removed her sunglasses. Tall, all in thin white fabric, a weightless being near his bed. She walked across the room to open the curtains. The sunlight she let in cast a wavering lemon parallelogram across the mosquito netting, and it moved in the wind like something afloat. The parrot began its cry, and Adam sat up, overjoyed that he could share it with her.

"Listen!" he insisted. "Listen to that!"

She still looked out the window. "It's Manday's parrot."

Adam pounded the sheets like a child. He asked, "What's it saying? What do you think it's saying?"

They listened to the noise together and Denise leaned against the wall, considering. The broken capillary on her nose looked blue in the cool, dark room, almost a bruise where she had fallen.

"*Hopeless,*" she said at last, turning to look at him. So serious, so sure.

"Really?" he asked, shifting in the bed and feeling the stubble on his chin. "I don't think so, I think it's a little more like '*help it.*'"

"What would that mean? No, it's '*hopeless.*'"

Adam said, "It's been driving me crazy. It's all I think about."

Then, wanting to smooth the serious look from her face, he said, "Does this mean I'm in love?"

"Oh yes," he heard her sigh, coming toward him at last, smiling. "I always knew I'd lose you to a cockatoo." As his wife approached, she blocked the light a little more, so that he could make out less and less of her face in the shadow she created. He closed his eyes and felt her weight near him on the bed. He could hear her undoing the little knot he'd made in the netting, and the swish as the fabric fell behind her. Then a pause as she wiped back his hair. He tried to guess how cool her wrist would feel on his forehead when it came, to gauge his own temperature, and when it touched him, he was surprised to feel each bone and tendon of hers moving, like block and tackle under the skin, as she adjusted her hand. He opened his eyes, and there she was, his wife, shining with perspiration and the faint early glow of sunburn, wearing on her forehead her mother's crease of worry.

"I'm fine," he said, to make the crease go away. It irritated him when he saw Denise disappear inside herself, replaced by some ancestral woman who was efficient with sickness and death and impatient with sorrow. He could not fit this person into his wife, and at times he wondered whether perhaps everyone suffered a variable personality and inside any head lived a thousand starving understudies, waiting for the lead to break her leg.

"I'll tell you when you're fine," his wife said, breathing deep and looking at him, tapping her fingers on his arm. He saw the muscles moving in her wrist again as she did this. He felt he could see through her. "I talked to Josh long-distance."

"What did he say?"

She waited a moment to tell him, hands together on her lap. "He said you'd promised to bring back a butterfly with big turquoise dots on the wings."

Adam smiled. "He remembered that? I'll find one."

"Alive?"

"Whichever way they'll let it out. I'll sew it into the hem of my coat if I have to. Anything else?" But he knew she wasn't going to tell him anything else; she was jealous enough that Josh had thought first of his father, of some private wish which only Daddy, always magical Daddy, could perform. There was always some whispering when she left the room, some planning of the wonderful thing the two boys held in secret from her. Adam knew she heard them; he saw her face turning in the hall, lit blue by a Batman night-light.

Denise had her own secrets, is how he felt, though she would never call them "secrets," exactly; she kept them hidden to spare others. Her work, of course, which she dismissed modestly when people asked her, even though this silence made her even more mysterious in the candlelight of dinner, leaning over to scrape peas onto her fork. At first he thought she didn't know it, how people talked to him during drinks and said how wonderful, how smart and fascinating his wife was, and it made him proud that she cared so little about the effect she had on others; now, though, he suspected that Denise cultivated this religion. He knew this much of her secret life—that she longed to share it. But Adam knew he would not do.

Her father's death was treated the same way, and this time it was Denise and her mother together guarding the secret. The man had been dying for years, from smoking illnesses and cancers, though it was clear in Denise's last call to him that morning that this heart attack was different. There was an operation that would save him, but his heart was too weak for it, and what would it mean to "save" him, her father asked? He was a man who could admit no change in his routines; who, when he visited Adam and Denise down in Santa Cruz, insisted on parking in the same place each time, even if it meant sitting in the bay window, waiting for the space to open. He would die with no change also. Denise called her mother at the hospital that night as her father lay sleeping, and ten minutes after she'd hung up, the phone rang again and Adam watched his wife huddled in the chair they never sat in, weeping, the phone cord trickling from her hand onto the floor. She said nothing for the entire call, not "hello," not "I'm sorry, Mother," but absorbed it all into herself. Adam could only stand and watch and try to decipher the moment.

He had thought of Walter, her father, the stooped, skinny man with the hook nose and bulging eyes you see in WPA photos of workers (only, he was a rich man), with a mustache to hide his dwindled upper lip, and a small diamond in his lapel from some obscure association. His kind wife, his big house, his parking space. A good life forbidden to change—was that so terrible?

Denise and her mother wouldn't allow Josh to go to the funeral, so Adam didn't go either, but took his son up to the San Francisco Zoo, where they stood in the cold sea air, watching an elephant chained to a cement wall, as they swatted the seagulls away from their vinegar-soaked french fries. It wasn't that Grandpa Walter's death was a secret from children; it was a secret from the whole world. It was a club with two members in beautiful black dresses. This club, at their annual graveside meetings, would argue furiously over dull dead Walter, but it was only theirs to argue. Adam was not to say a word.

So why shouldn't Josh and his father smuggle butterflies in secret? They were really, of course, only smuggling them past Denise's own customs. More and more, Adam was hoarding the beautiful parts of his life away from her, bringing the treasures instead to his son. Was this a marital crime?

"Kathy's only staying today, did you know that?" she asked suddenly, standing up. He watched her eyes discover a banana leaf on the floor, and then, after she considered for a moment whether to pick it up or not, he saw her lean down and grab an edge. "Not even tonight."

"Maybe there's trouble in paradise."

She stood holding the leaf. "What?"

Adam laughed, trying to hold a conversation while he felt so ill. He was afraid he wasn't making sense or that, as always, he wasn't clever enough for her. He said, "The perfect Spivaks. Maybe she's off to have an affair."

She frowned. "You never liked her."

He was shocked, and tried to respond. "I knew her first, remember? I like her. I just don't understand her."

Denise dropped the leaf out the window and came to sit down on the bed again, saying, "Nobody does."

"You should, she's your best friend."

But this comment obviously upset her. "Why is everyone saying that?" she said, fussing with the mosquito netting. "She's not, I barely know her. Why do you say that?"

Adam tried to sit up. He reached for a glass of water, studying his wife. Yes, as always, she had some other secret, and he longed to know it. "What's going on?"

She seemed tired of this subject. He saw her eyes flicker to a journal on the table, a physics journal. She relented, explaining: "It's just that, you know how it is in some relationships, how one of them is a little more in love. Well, it's like that with friendships. Sometimes one of them thinks they're really close, closer than they are. And the other one doesn't feel that way."

"And Kathy thinks you're close."

She looked pained, as if he were forcing her to say things she didn't quite believe. In truth, he was weak, ill. He could barely sip the water. He was thinking of her words, how, in relationships, someone is a little more in love.

Denise's face was plain and thoughtful, obviously focused on an image of Kathy, perhaps of herself with Kathy at some moment in the past. She said, "She doesn't get very close to people, so with me she thinks it's special. But I'm used to being close, so it's not special anymore. Not that I don't love her. It's just something I realized one day."

"I think that's terrible. That's really sad."

The words came out before he knew it. Adam never said these kinds of things to her. His role was to amuse her, relieve her. He was afraid she would turn away now, kiss his forehead and leave him for hours again. Instead, her face almost brightened as she sat beside him, saying, "You can use it in your writing. It'll make you famous."

It always surprised and pleased him to hear her say this, to realize that she believed it. Her faith made her so pretty across the room. The thought had not even been on his mind, and he saw again that she believed, after all this time, the lie he'd given her: He was a genius writer. This was an old, old lie; he'd stung her with it in their first year together, in the false bohemia he'd shown her, in the romantic persona he'd created years before to attract girls. That's how he thought of it, as a sting, like the hymenoptera wasp painlessly keeping its victim still, stinging again and again if necessary, keeping it quiet for days while it readied its batch of hungry children. Denise knew nothing about writing, although he told her everything about his days, the torture of a bad line, the exhilaration when something finally came, something good, and then the quick return to gloom in front of the typewriter. These habits must have sounded just like work to her, as any purposeful struggle is, and she took it on easy faith. She listened with unskeptical eyes, two white buds, eager, happy to support him. But underneath, Adam wasn't happy. He knew it was a lie. He knew that writing, for him, was work in the way that the seduction of pretty women might be work; a struggle, of course, but purely selfish in the end. Purely to feed a compulsion. Only a bit more than bad habit.

Although her own work, despite all his prodding, remained a mystery, he understood the way she thought about her work. It was to feed her curiosity, the kind of curiosity that made her stop while Josh tossed his yo-yo badly toward the ground, stand in distant fascination as she watched the plastic object spin on its string, wobbling in an ugly way, until her son managed somehow to jerk it back and it came, a reluctant pet, halfway to his hand before dying in the air. "Do it again," she'd say, whispering to Adam something about the wobble—it had been the wobble she'd been watching this whole time! Then in she'd go, working out the calculations, showing that the wobble of a dish thrown in the air is exactly blah-blah-blah of its rotation (how had a yo-yo become a dish?). Her body shone like silver plate as she announced this to their blank faces. Her compulsion was her curiosity and this was a kind of love, he'd always thought. His desire didn't feel that way; he never shone like silver plate. He worked for approval, and fame, and because of some old fantasy about himself he'd invented in high school to impress the girls. He knew this truth about himself.

Adam's mind was already up for lease. Denise could not see it, but his precious writing notebook (one in a numbered series of blue composition books) was lying outside on the ground near Manday's house where he had flung it, under the parrot's window, lifting page by page in the hot wind as if the invisible jungle were thumbing through for a last look before devouring it. That part of his life was lost, and she could not feel it, still numb from his stinger's decade-old poison.

His father had been a failure, too. He had been a radio crooner in the fifties, the "Sinatra of New England," and it had been wonderful to turn on the big wooden box and hear his father's voice emerging, although it was always a little hard to believe, his father being such a prankster. He sang on the local *Liberty Soap Music Hour*, and his signature song was "I'm Forever Chasing Rainbows." That was when they lived in Connecticut, in the big house, near the swollen river that had almost drowned young Adam. One evening, while Adam was playing with his pet hamster, his mother leaned down, her starched skirt crackling, smelling of the mint she used to cover up the cigarettes, and whispered that they were moving. To Hollywood. He dropped the hamster and it ran away, lost for days behind the china cabinet. He had daydreamed about Hollywood at night in bed, the movie stars bringing him Jell-O in crystal cups, and here he had made it real. It scared him. The move was long and difficult on his parents, making the car ride silent as they crossed the hot states, but there was an unspoken hope for what was promised out there. Then the new house, the odd desert air. The huge pink refrigerator that made his mother laugh. The orange trees. Hearing his father coming home late at night, the murmurs of long talks and clinking ice in old-fashioneds. The movie when it came out—*Hurrah for Harriet!* with his father all black-and-white in a smoking jacket, spraying seltzer on a starlet—and the change to emptiness soon after. As if someone had come and taken all the furniture overnight. Within a year, his father was selling insurance door-to-door. That was 1955. They never spoke of his father's past as "Sinatra," and sometimes Adam thought it was one of his childish fantasies. A wooden radio, a bottle of white seltzer—dream objects. He learned then that failure was not a mallet; it was a trowel, smoothing and solidifying a life.

"I was thinking about the boy," Adam said, and from his wife's face he knew he wasn't making sense. "The boy who fell." The image had come from a long chain of fevered thought. "Were you all together?"

He saw her putting the thought in place: "Were we all ..."

"When it happened, were you all together?"

"Why does that matter?"

"About Kathy, why she's close to you. She was with you, right?"

She didn't answer; there was something more complicated about it than she could bother admitting, and she gave him her profile and faced the curtain with its bent square of light. The ceiling fan blew dust down on her through the shadows of the room. The wind blew open the curtain and the sun, a lion, reached its searching paw into the room.

"Come over here," he told her quietly, and she came, a little girl now, smiling and scuffling her old sandals on the worn floorboards, not knowing what to do with her hands and holding them close to her long skirt. Her eyes, those buds, had changed when he said this. She sat beside him on the bed, and with the tiniest gesture he had her lay her head on his sticky chest, on the hard bone between his muscles. He could feel her ear pressed between them, like a flower flattened in the pages of a book.

"I'm sorry you're so sick," she said, lying half off the bed as the sun threw its desperate shapes at them, fighting against the curtain.

"It's kind of fun," he said. He stared at the wall opposite the window, which was bare and hazy behind the netting.

"I wish Josh were here."

"Me too," he said and held his hand just above her hair, as if willing something to happen. His upraised arm made his chest muscles tense, and the back of her head raised with it. She stirred a little, noticing. He stroked her hair, stiff with spray. "I love you very much," he told her. He felt her fingers jerking, the old funny signal that she was falling asleep. He leaned his back against the wall and looked at her: the shine of her cheek, the moth-powder color of her eye makeup and this unexpected expression of relief in his arms. So often, he was afraid he wasn't enough for her, that she stayed with him out of duty.

But that couldn't be true—look at her, her face, how she believed in him—impossibly, stupidly, she did. He would fight for her; he would do anything to keep her, to make her happy. He would hurt people, lie, go to any lengths.

But look at us, Adam thought sadly as he stroked her hair. *Sitting in rooms, cracking our worries like nuts . . . and handing each other nothing but the shells.*

Some sights are only for the dark-adapted eye. An eye like Eli's or Denise's: shaded from the California sun, trained from years of stellar observation far from cities or suburbs, from radio towers or bright windows that might contract your pupil and ruin your vision. An eye shaped from childhood, when you sat in the backyard making out the stars as they appeared. It is the best practice for a dark-adapted eye: You watch the night's ether freezing above you, losing its blue, turning darker and more transparent until it reaches the exact shade of indigo at which the stars begin to show. First you will only spot one, usually Venus if it has risen, then begin to notice them one by one, floating up like bubbles from the bottom of a murky pond; only, you can never watch a star force its light through the atmosphere and appear—you can only see one that hasn't been there before. They make you feel foolish; once they are all out, firm and bright as though they have always been there, you wonder if it was simply your idiocy, your own faulty eyes that hadn't seen them. And in the end, of course, this is the truth of it.

And once your pupils are dilated, wide nets to catch those moths of light, you will begin to notice more than planets, more than stars and galaxies. More than satellites making their steady way across the constellations. More than meteors or comets. In the evening, such as now on the island, you will start to see a strange phenomenon rising in the west. At first it seems imaginary, a haze against the sky, hard to make out with all the stellar objects clamoring for attention, but as the night progresses you will see it is a faint disk. It is called the gegenschein, the counterglow. It will reach its peak at midnight, sitting high in the sky at the point exactly opposite the sun—because, some believe, what you are seeing are particles blown off Earth's atmosphere by the solar wind. The Sun is creating a stream of dust behind Earth. And some would say this stream we are staring into, this dusty gegenschein, is like nothing so much as a comet's tail.

The scientists on the island, gathering now atop the overlook, had all heard this theory. Eli, Denise, Swift, Manday, Jorgeson, the others—they had all read the crank reports about how comets were birthed in Jupiter, or how they were swarms of objects rather than dirty snowballs, or this one about Earth itself having a tail. Yet each had thought about it: Earth with a tail. Earth as a comet. Why not? It was just another object with a period around the Sun. The skeptical mind would say, "It has a much larger mass, an atmosphere," but who could prove some comet didn't have these as well? The idea struck, once again, at the heart of earthly arrogance. Here, if they waited until midnight, they could stare at Earth's tail burning away from the Sun, just as if they stood Jules Verne–like on a rocketing comet with its mist of gases flowing into space, no different from any other object. But the idea was too sad. It is said that Ernest Rutherford, on learning how much space there was inside an atom, was afraid to step out of bed onto the floor for fear he would fall through. Science has that kind of terror to it, and it might feel the same staring at the comets from a mere cosmic accomplice. Without our special place in it, the universe would seem to turn away from us, a bored lover, showing only its cold back scarred with comets. And what a poor comet our own Earth would make: a hunk of nickel and iron, caught in its unadventurous orbit, never turning outside the most common plane of movement.

Lights on the island were slowly being extinguished, and from the overlook, the scientists could see (much better than before, down on the beach) the town below slowly snuffing itself out, with only a few lights visible in the jungle or high in the tea plantation, even these lasting only half an hour longer before the sultan's decree of total darkness went into effect. The new sultan seemed just as helpful as his father, providing by law an untainted view, with all the locals going to bed in darkness. Despite the decree, however, a mist of lawless fireflies arose from the jungle, as if the star-mirroring surface of a lake lay down below, slowly filling, creeping to the high edge of their walls. Someone said that this would affect the meteor count, but the insects would depart long before the deep darkness of the morning when stars would shoot across the sky.

Eli was not on the overlook, however. He stood on the beach in his long sleeves, smelling of mosquito repellent, smoking a pipe. He was searching for a particular light. Not the stars, not the fireflies and not even the light from the departing boat, which carried his wife. That boat had left for the mainland half an hour ago, and its glow was already lost out on the darkened horizon amid all the other fixed and fluttering lights. He stood on the beach, past the spit, on the most desolate strip of luminous sand, beside a small stone building; he stood at the edge of the jungle, in a darkness so thick he could not tell one thing from another, searching while the waves rustled their pale skirts on the shore. What he searched for was a human glow: the bobbing stripe of a flashlight, eagerly approaching down the path. It would be Denise.

We have been here before. He thought this, smiling, just as anxious as he'd been the last time this comet came around. *We have been here before.* Waiting on the darkened twilight beach for this woman to arrive, trying not to think of what they were doing, trying not to think at all as the hot air blew in from the ocean and the insects swarmed around him, somehow gathering in the corners of his eyes. He felt the rare exhilaration of being very young, and he had not felt young in a while. Even earlier on the beach, as he stood with Denise under the tree, he had looked at his hand above hers on the trunk, and they did not seem the same age. His seemed paler, older, all wires and buttons, and he knew that he seemed older than her all over: the few sweaty curls on his bald head, his body growing cylindrical despite his jogs in the university woods, bruises taking a week to heal, and how his face seemed to have the black-and-white grain of an old photograph. Yes, a photograph of his father. Kathy recently said to him, *I can't look at these old pictures of you and think this is the same person.* So his own wife saw it, too. But this feeling, this waiting on the beach and wondering if his old friend would come, made time fold on itself. Those few nights after the boy's death, those stolen moments on this strip of beach. This feeling had come then, too, just the same. Young, saved, immortal. He would fight to keep this; it would be unfair, be the worst unfairness, if it, too, should grow old.

He had to keep his mind at bay. He could not think of Kathy innocently and coldly traveling toward Japan, of the good hours he had spent with her even today, in their hut, talking of literature. He could not think of anything but leaving her, because this was the rare moment when he could believe in such things calmly; it was the time for mentioning one's heart's desire. He could not think of the night, twelve years before, when he had stood at Denise's doorstep, wet with fog and desperately confused, begging her to right his upturned life. He could not think of how her face turned like a lock, spun irrecoverably closed in that thin space of the open door, stating *We don't need to have this conversation, we don't need to have this conversation* before she sent him away. He had not loved her then, not at all—he had only panicked in his marriage, and groped for some relief—but when Denise said those words, he saw how terrified of love she was. That strange, brilliant woman, terrified of love. And then it happened—the last thing he expected: He felt the possibility, alone with her on that plain doorstep, the possibility of their lives changing. They were young—it could be done—he might step into that hall and never leave. It would take only a few right words to convince them both of how life might go. At that moment, though, she shut the door. The light went off; the night air moved in. He stood for a while with his finger on the glowing doorbell, caressing it softly, hoping he had the nerve to press it again and see her face appear suddenly, tear-streaked now, certain of what would happen. The doorbell moved slightly under his finger. He could not do it. He fled to England.

So much time had passed, yet he still thought of those words: *We don't need to have this conversation.* He struggled for years to understand them, yet now he felt that he did; he knew, for instance, that he would do the same. If Denise hurt him, if she even threatened to hurt him, he knew he, too, would end things without a word: *We don't need to have this conversation.* Eli, at last, agreed with her about what needed to be said. He understood, and this was forgiveness. He was all forgiveness tonight. Tonight, just as he had been that time under the stars when, heady with their newfound comet (a child given their hyphenated name, as if from a modern marriage), she had touched his back as he stood there by the telescope. Put her palm against the bone of his right shoulder so that he had to turn, had to see her face alight with need. He forgave her then, though she had not asked for it. He forgave himself tonight. He forgave Kathy for not making him happy.

He searched the jungle. She was late; he felt a rip of fear at the thought she might not come. He couldn't see well in the darkness— what was that? It could be a fallen tree, or a rock, or a panther watching him from the leaves. There was no way to know. Was she coming? Of course. Yes, he would leave Kathy. It was simple; they had no children; they had few relatives to please, or friends, for that matter. If Denise asked him, he would leave his wife. If she asked him soon enough.

They would swim in the warm ocean tonight, he thought, growing happier by the minute, imagining the scene: Dropping their clothes on the sand, shouting and falling into the oncoming waves, treading the dark liquid as they laughed and remembered how this had all been before. Spitting salt water from his mouth. Her arms waving in the water, keeping afloat, her breasts almost visible in the starlight, and how she might turn over to swim a few laps along the shore. Her white legs in the water. This must be love, this, rather than the odd comfort his wife gave him. Surely love was beating time. Surely love was never dying.

Where was she? Oh, there—a light began to stab the jungle darkness, dipping and curving in a stream among the trees. It was her; she was coming. He could feel the warm waves already around his hips. What man could drown in any ocean tonight?

The blackness around them thickened like pudding, sending the fireflies away from their search for mates, back to the leaves or flowers where they dimly slept. Crunches came from the jungle, a scurrying panic of noises and then silence again. On the overlook, the scientists were arranging their chairs, their telescopic cameras set with rotating blades to capture a streaming meteoric tail. They laughed and sipped coffee, moving to their quadrants, calling "Time!" and "Time!" and "Time!"

Her stars would not be performing tonight. Kathy stood on the stern of the boat, and above her glowed a Southern Hemisphere sky filled with constellations she could not recognize. No Libra, no Orion. Their parts were being played tonight by rougher, tropical understudies: the Peacock, the Cross. Nothing that Eli had taught her. Nothing at all familiar.

From where she stood, the island was completely dark, invisible against the night sky. The lamps along its mountains, its volcano and the houses that edged the beach had been extinguished by the sultan's edict. So, from the departing boat, from Kathy's view, the island was gone. No lights, no fires, no radio towers blinking their red eyes above the mountain; only, if Kathy looked carefully, a rabbit-shaped place in the sky where the stars stopped. Even that absence grew less distinct as the boat moved away, and it would have taken an astronomer indeed to recognize the missing space. Yet Kathy stood on deck, a shawl around her shoulders, and watched what she assumed to be the island's retreat into the distance. She hadn't looked back at first, caught up in a novel she was reading in the fluorescence of the cabin, but it occurred to her that this was what people did. So she closed the novel, headed out to the stern where a young island man in a white shirt stood smoking a cigarette. The stars were everywhere, randomly, and the boat's wake was a pale ruffle in the blue dark.

"You are leaving?" Kathy heard beside her. It was the young local with the cigarette, who then noted in his island accent: "You are much sad." He had a wide, dark face, perhaps the widest she'd ever seen, and his upper lip rested high on his teeth in an unintended smile. She saw now that he wore a hemp necklace around his throat, set with shells, hiding a tattoo. Where he held his cigarette, his fingernails looked two inches long.

"No," Kathy said. "I'm not." She was suspicious; she knew that she wasn't pretty to a young man like him, so it interested her to think there might be another trick here. Kathy was nearing forty, her face overcome by her thick glasses, her wiry hair threaded with silver in its tight barrettes, fitting more and more the role of a librarian as time passed. She didn't care; her body was an old favorite dog-eared book from her childhood, and nothing but a passing fancy now.

He smiled and pointed his cigarette at her. "I think you are!"

"Maybe you're the one who's sad, is that true?" she asked, and he didn't say anything, but elegantly brought the cigarette to his mouth with those long, shining nails and, closing his eyes, inhaled. Then the young man turned and went inside and she was left alone with the receding waves.

Kathy unknotted her shawl and knotted it again, better. She did this without thinking, just as she looked out at the view-that-wasn't-there without any deeper consideration; her mind was often elsewhere. Having abandoned her old hobby of picking at people's minds, having discarded her voyeuristic curiosity about Lydia, she was left with only her private habits. She was the kind of woman who kept ideas for a long time in her head, the way some women, in brick apartments high above a city, keep many cats. These ideas were hidden from the world, from the rest of her life, but she found herself sometimes tending to them—at a dinner party, for instance, when others were talking about a recent movie, Kathy would bring one out to warm herself, stroke it under the table, feed it a little. Ideas like a fantasy about the perfect city, or how time functioned, how she could manage to fall from an airplane; silly, odd ideas she would never want to mention to anyone else. They would crawl over her while she was doing something important, dishes or something: *Oh, but what would it be like to fall above Barcelona?* And, of course, like pets, sometimes they felt more important than people.

The one about time was visiting her now, on the stern of this boat; it was leaning against her ankles and mewling. She remembered something from her last trip here: that the sultan's invisible island had never accepted the Gregorian calendar, that it was always thirteen days earlier there. That island was set back in time, a temporal hollow like a thumb's dent in a ball of dough, and as they approached the main island, they were approaching real time. Each wave passing under this boat, each wave rolling out of sight was, maybe, another second she had to pay back to the world. They were a quarter of the way to the big island, so that was three days lost. It made her smile a little. She stood here on the night of March fifteenth again, as she'd been seven days before, and time was doubling forward here. It amused her to think that there were two of her: one here, in a shawl, watching the boat's lights drown in the sea, and another time-lapsed Kathy in their house, sipping scotch with the neighbors, her left hand's fingers held loosely by Eli's. The other Kathy must now be listening to the woman's story of her youth in Denmark, nearing the point when the young woman would turn to clasp her lover's eyes and remark on when she met him. "We were such strangers," the woman would say to the other Kathy. Then Eli would hold Kathy's hand more tightly. "I know how you feel," he'd say, giving a broad smile across his face, blue-shadowed with a late-night beard. "And you come to know each other so well."

He'd look at Kathy and it would take a moment for her to tell him: "Yes."

It was all passing under the boat again for her, four times the speed of life. She was thinking what a funny thing it was to say, "And you come to know each other so well." They often said that, and they meant it. But what did they really mean? Just that each knew the *other* so well, all the while holding something small and secret to themselves, turning out their pockets for marital inspection but palming this trifle. Like Kathy's ideas, her pets in her brick apartment. She knew this had to be true, because of course she thought she knew him, too, better even than he did himself; but how can you *know* you know? Like a cosmological theory Eli might carefully explain to friends, there was no way to prove it true, and it didn't claim even to *be* true, only to fit what they saw. It could merely be proven false, by one odd color in a star, and down it came. So Kathy tried to have no illusions about her husband, since any moment her theory of him might fail; still, she couldn't shake the sense that she, above all people, knew him. Of course she knew Eli! And he, naturally, didn't know her at all.

The long-nailed boy was back, holding a triangular paper cup, through the translucent sides of which Kathy could make out a restless oblong of water. The boat suddenly rocked starboard, and they both hop-hopped to the side, automatically grabbing the railing. The young man had not spilt a drop. She commented on this, and he told her he was a dancer. He held up his beautiful nails, as if this explained something.

She tried to ask him about his dancing, and he told her a little—how he was raised even as a boy to be a dancer, and all the lessons he'd taken—but he kept lighting cigarettes and looking away. Kathy thought she understood this, or at least she placed on top of his silence her own, familiar silence: the wish to be done. Her undergraduate chemistry career, done, and now, after this last conference, her literary career, done. People with one passion never understood—people like Eli; or Denise, with her confused expressions; or even Denise's dull husband, Adam, scribbling in his notebook. They always thought she was disenchanted, restless, that she had made some mistake and was correcting it, but they didn't see. It was a new life. Were we really issued only one?

"Visiting the island?" she asked him at last. It turned out his name was Nasur.

He shook his head and the curls of his black hair, down to his ears, trembled. He exhaled his cigarette smoke and said, "No, I live there my whole life."

"So . . . hmm . . . maybe this is your first time away."

He looked at her, his wrists resting on the railing, hands dangling, smoke being pulled away by the wind. "First time for a person of my family," he told her, but again without emotion.

She said quietly, "You don't seem excited."

"My family asked me to go," he said, and then, seemingly embarrassed by this confession, he walked away to another part of the boat. Within a few minutes, he had returned, crumpling the little paper cup and standing again at the railing, wrists crossed, hands dangling.

She asked him, this time, about the shadow doctors she'd heard of on the island, and he nodded, smiling, telling of the time when he was a little boy with a fever and his mother brought him to a shadow doctor, and the man had stood him naked in front of a bright lantern (though now they used electric) and let his shadow fall clear and dark onto a white mat. The old, awkward, grasshopper-like man sewed and cut at the mat for an hour, at the shadow, of course, then sent the boy away. He was cured.

"I don't believe in it," he added. "But I remember."

Slowly, over the ride to the main island, with the minutes passing now beneath them rapidly, foaming in the wake as they watched, she had him tell her more about his family. Kathy did it carefully, as one would remove a tick. This was her old favorite hobby back again, a patient one, which now worked only on the very young. Nasur mentioned a few more times that his family had "asked him to go," and she could tell, through the repetition, that he really meant that they had sent him away. He had done something awful, and they had sent him away. Over the rest of the crossing, Kathy thought she guessed at what he'd done.

"You have beautiful nails," she said, smiling for the first time that night, keeping her lips tight over her teeth. "And necklace."

He leaned over, embarrassed again, staring at his nails. "I think in the world I need to cut them?"

She shook her head, saying, "No, keep them. They're beautiful. Girls will be envious. See," and here she held her hands out, plain and pale, "mine are chewed away." He did indeed look at her hands, interested, then showed her his own, shining in the light above them, each slightly brown, translucent, curved like a little sword.

One of those ideas was creeping over her just now, just as she held her hand against that of the young man: Eli would have an affair tonight. Perhaps that was why she had leaned uncharacteristically against the stern rail of a ship, pink shawl-fringe flapping, in this sentimental pose, searching the darkness for a sign of what she supposed. They had talked, theoretically with friends, about affairs and the foolishness of marriage, but she knew, although some couples had tried out alternatives, that for them it was just talk. Yet somehow she also knew he wanted one. Not even sex (though clearly all men wanted that, always), but some intellectually pleasing affair. Something in a rented garret in a major city—not L.A., but San Francisco. Kathy thought a man could have an affair so easily in San Francisco. An affair with Denise—because she had assumed for some years now that she and Eli had slept together back in '65 when they first watched this comet come around and the boy had died, on that wild trip to the island when they were young and nervous, when Denise clearly had such a crush on her husband. And he on her, of course, one of the blond goyim. She remembered how lovely they both had been in '65, and she recalled the breathtaking view from the overlook—the moonlight on the beach, and the fireflies. Who, at twenty-five, wouldn't succumb?

So perhaps thirty-seven wouldn't be so different. It worried her, made her afraid, but also somehow pleased her, to think that tan Denise and schlumpy Eli could have their steamy island moment once every twelve years, on the occasion of this comet's return. It was one of her pet ideas. To think of them each, guiltily, terribly, looking forward for *twelve years* to that evening when they would be left alone in one of those see-through huts. She was almost happy to give that to him, even if it was purely imaginary; to give him the shivering adolescent expectation, even more than the adultery itself; to give him a little something to look forward to. She didn't believe that they were lovers at home, during their comet-hunting on that hillside. That would have been too much. Kathy tortured herself with the idea for a while; here was one of her more fascinating, nastier pets: it bit.

She looked at Nasur, at his black curls, his left foot held sideways in memory of some dance, his girl's hands. She knew that she was right about him. It was more than shame, though, that sent him away from his island. She learned this as he began to tell her the truth about his life. Nasur, head low as he watched her, told her that after shaming his family, after some discovery down on a dark beach, they had not merely asked him to leave. His father and mother had sat him down one night alone and handed him a leather bag with all the family's fortune, weeping, begging him to go away.

"So I am very rich now," he told her, grinning, then cautiously, "Don't tell a person!"

"I won't tell anybody. You get a whole new life! It's kind of lucky," she said, seeing he would believe this easily. She wondered what it must have felt like in that hut, seeing the bag of coins weighed against your childhood, and what a young man like him would do with a fortune, how he could possibly approach the world. She wondered if he imagined what was in store for him, or if it still felt like an extension of his former life. Did he, like her, want that old life to be done?

"The first thing I do I buy a car," Nasur told her seriously. "A Cadillac."

What was it her husband had said when she got on the boat tonight? "I hope I'm doing the right thing." He had bent his long face down to hers, all eyebrows and shadows, and she had put her arms around his thick, comfortable body and held him and he had said, "I hope I'm doing the right thing." What was it he was doing? Letting her go on this trip away from him? Or was it something else she hadn't seen until now?

Nasur was nodding, his black curls shining, and he was still talking to her: "On the main island, with a Cadillac, a servant and . . ." Here he trailed off. "They give me . . . twenty thousand rupees in the bag," he said, raising his eyebrows like someone impressed with something you have told him. Then he spread his mouth in a grin, holding his long-nailed hands against his neck, closing his eyes, imagining it.

"How much is that?" she asked.

Nasur turned, as if just noticing her, and said: "Much. That is, I think, seven hundred dollars."

Seven hundred dollars. Kathy smiled and kept her face clear of emotion. She said nothing; she felt terrified of life. She thought, *I miss Eli, I want him here, I can't help this boy, I can't help him.* But time was moving too quickly; under the boat, away from her, like scarves ripped from her body. Plans were moving forward. A streamer passed over a star, and another—the meteor shower was beginning. Oh, they must be side by side now in their folding chairs, her husband and that woman, lying back to face the fires above them.

Perhaps the sight would be enough for her poor husband. The meteors were coming faster now, brilliant, a few sharp teeth of night's violet panther appearing as it paused, stretching its velveteen back, yawning for the public, quickly retreating into its black leaves. Below, head back in his chair, breath shuddering in his chest, he might pause and gasp at such a thing. He might. But the hand of a woman who does what she likes, one warm hand meeting a thigh, and a man's gaze is brought down even from the sight of falling stars. Oh, the heavens hardly matter.

Her hand trembling, Kathy begged a cigarette from the young man. There was nothing to be seen of the island now, and they smoked together from the stern, watching the stars come loose and drop into the sea.

1983

near aphelion

I feel rather at a disadvantage in speaking of comets to you; comets nowadays are not what they used to be.

—Arthur Stanley Eddington, 1909

Manday could not be forgiven.

Martin Swift slowly climbed the sandstone steps of the planetarium, lifting each leg stiffly like a traveler abroad making his astounded way through the mud. He had a cane, but it was no help at all, and neither, he believed, was his daughter Alice, who kept a firm grip on his left cane-arm, nor his granddaughter Benedicta, who pulled on his right middle finger. Swift felt that the two females made this trip up the steps much harder than it needed to be; it was the famous Three-Body Problem. This astronomical issue states that while the Newtonian calculation for one body in space is simple, and while that for two bodies interacting (such as Earth and the Moon) is only somewhat harder, the equation for three bodies and their differing gravities is so infinitely difficult that it can't be done. The math was the same for this left-hand woman in her pink college sweatshirt and fresh perm, this right-hand beribboned little girl proudly scuffing her "party" shoes, and the rough old mountain swaying in between. Any astronomer would have thrown down his mechanical pencil in despair. The way Professor Emeritus Martin Swift paraphrased it under his breath was, *We'll never get to the top of these fucking stairs.* And Manday could not be forgiven.

It was only ten steps, however, to the planetarium entrance, a beautiful dark square set in an enormous carved scallop, so that each visitor got to be a Venus skidding along the foam, surrounded on all sides by fanciful, engrossing and inaccurate portraits of the constellations of the zodiac. It was a wealthy neighborhood down on the flat, sandy marina of San Francisco, with views of the bridge and the Golden Gate and the lumpy green anatomy of Marin across the water. It was beautiful—a lake, swans, willows planted long ago in the twenties when it seemed they could build nothing wrong in this city, but now the houses here seemed wan and faded beneath the translucent day, rain-streaked, as if this part of town were the skylit back room of some museum, hung with glorious time-darkened masterpieces in need of restoration.

Swift was here because he had promised for years to take his granddaughter Benny to this place. Actually, he had promised Alice. The last five years had been full of promises to Alice, who, after years of therapy, had shed fifty pounds and returned to his life with a bag of issues to be worked out between them, like those stories of mailmen ringing doorbells and then dropping canvas sacks on old ladies' porches, sacks of undelivered love letters sent forty years before by their dead husbands in the war. He was forever rifling through Alice's bag, finding some new wrong to right, or some event that his daughter clearly misremembered. One particular note—*You were never there for us, Daddy*—twanged such a wire within him that almost every weekend he pulled himself out of his retired torpor to bring joy to his grandchild. His divorce from their mother, the ink on the papers dry now for fifteen years, felt to Martin Swift like a gambling debt that he would never stop repaying. That's marriage, he thought, that's being a father. Never trust a comet or a woman.

Martin Swift could not see the zodiacal friezes he was approaching at the planetarium entrance; he could not see mud-bellied swans stepping from the water; when his granddaughter let go of his finger and ran ahead to where a man sold piñatas and balloons, he quickly lost sight of her and simply knew, from his calculations, that she must be somewhere in that hazy cotton-candy nebula of color. Despite all the last-minute precautions of his sixties (the diet, the abstinence from smoke or drink), and his own indomitable will not to grow old, the diabetes that forever haunted his family had caught up with him as well—the Hound of the Baskervilles, he called it, as in "The fucking Hound has me by the throat today." Professor Emeritus Martin Swift would find himself standing in dark lecture halls, dizzy, unable to see anything of the slide projected on the screen, his mouth still reciting the lecture he had been giving for over forty years: *Note how the hot star in the center excites the interstellar dust and causes it to glow. . . .* The mind whirs on, the mind whirs on.

Old age had fallen on Martin Swift from the trees, when he had built the strongest fortifications against it on all sides. It was unfair; it was the most terrible unfairness of the century, because he *wasn't* old. He was only seventy! He was only seventy, with hair thick on his head, a fearsome singing voice, and the stomach (but not the chance) for ten whiskeys a night. He had ideas; he had plans to travel; he was a senior project designer of a European spacecraft which, in three years, would take photographs of Halley's Comet on its way around again. Photographs! Of Halley's Comet! He had done this! And yet now, bent over in a chair, he would sit in the meadow near his Sonoma farm and have his granddaughter point him north so he could describe the sky for her, Ursa Major, Cassiopeia, Serpens, because he could no longer see the stars himself. He suspected, sometimes, on those summer nights, he suspected that she pointed him the wrong way, or put him under cloudy skies, merely fascinated to see the old man perform his useless art beneath a dark, blank sky.

But Martin Swift, more than just growing weak and blind with his disease, had fallen into that invisible trap of age which he had always avoided so cautiously before. At seventy he believed the world to be proceeding strangely, badly, coldly. He no longer found anything good in what was new, in the tin, sickly music of the eighties, the candy-shop fashions, the politics that brought out the young communist in him once again: Reagan, MX missiles, Lebanon—it could hardly be believed. Sixty years after Emma Goldman, twenty after King, and Swift felt nothing had been accomplished in the world. The world no longer seemed about him: Martin Swift, who never used to look back for a moment, who used to be impossible to get a childhood story from, now openly longed for bygone days. And not just the days when he was still vibrant, still "with it," in the seventies or even the sixties. Martin Swift, struggling up the last step with a roar of triumph, fell into the past deeply, as a weary traveler might into a soft, white bed. He longed for the twenties, the thirties, pieces of that era. He had become a creature of the past.

"Benny, you hold your grandfather's hand," his daughter was saying. Swift watched the blurry interactions of the woman and the cashier, hearing children's voices dropping like coins all around him, and motherly whispers, and the crowlike barking of teenagers coming in a crowd behind him. Teenagers frightened Martin Swift a little, although he hid it, angry at himself. He felt his granddaughter's hand in his even as he heard her complain that his palm was hot.

"You'll live," he told her, turning to face the vague flower of his daughter's face. "Make them give me my ridiculous discount."

"And one senior."

"One senior astronomer!" he thundered, with no further explanation for the people who turned their heads. Martin Swift felt the little girl pulling him along toward deeper darkness. He was very fond of her, but he thought sometimes that little Benedicta treated him like a pet gorilla. "Where's Benedicta?" he teased, gazing around in blind mockery of himself.

"I'm here!"

"Where's Benedicta?"

"I'm here!" he heard her say, a little frightened, and he grabbed her roughly so she laughed. They were in the planetarium proper now, a huge, brightly lit room where the professor could make out at its center the machine that would produce the stars, that monstrous many-eyed insect, asleep and glistening.

Martin Swift wanted his granddaughter to ask him questions, plague him with her worries, her concerns as she found her little world growing unbelievable—he was waiting for the moment when tiny Benedicta with her froth of lemon hair and agate eyes would look at a dark fizzing soda and think, *What are those bubbles, why doesn't water bubble, why doesn't air bubble?* Grandpa Swift even had a simple, elegant answer for questions about the color of the sky, and he kept it ready in a soft box like a present of a ring. But Benedicta never asked. Not questions like those. She worried about her friends and why they couldn't come, or why Daddy had to leave or why she wasn't allowed to go running down to the water. Her face would fold over and darken, but never did he see it smooth and bend in curiosity. In fact, little Benedicta had almost a horror of the inner workings of things—she would recoil if her tape player were opened to replace a battery, and she regarded her father's dark basement workshop with its gray TV tubes, circuit boards and unwired transistors as an abattoir. Perhaps it would pass. Perhaps, though, his eldest daughter (her dreidel-shaped head turning a knowing facet toward him as she indicated the plush crimson seat where he was to sit) had poisoned little Benny against curiosity, against her father's decades-long armchair babbling. Hadn't even his younger daughter, Lydia, the one time she had flown over from New York for Thanksgiving— hadn't she, in the middle of a riveting discussion of nuclear power, thrown down her napkin in heart-rent despair to proclaim, *You're nothing, Daddy, but one of those intellectuals!* What did she mean, *those* intellectuals? Were there others she preferred? And if Alice felt the same, wanted her little girl to think like a picture book ("the stars are flowers in the sky!"), then why take her to a planetarium, a carved temple for the city-bound and curious? There was no understanding people, Martin Swift decided, settling onto his narrow cushion, ignoring the sticky armrest, grinning at a blurry child's face turned hind-to from the seat before him. People, Swift thought, like Indian gods, came at you every minute in a different form.

"Daddy," his elder daughter was asking him, leaning over little Benny, coming close because she knew her father's eyes, and tried to enter his sphere of vision when she talked to him, emerging now from the darkness as a gum-pink mouth and a chin knife-sharp from dieting, "Don't be shy. You shout out if they make a mistake. These recordings are probably ten years old."

Martin Swift laughed. "I hope they tell us Mars has jungles, like they used to. Ones that flourish when the ice caps melt. But I can't shout that out in a crowded room!" he added, teasing, putting on a crotchety old-movie voice: "*By God, man, it's a lie!*" He guffawed again at the image. "There'll be a panic!"

He saw Alice's smile wax in a crescent before she moved away into obscurity again, talking in a kind, girlish voice to her child. He liked Alice, certainly more now than when she'd been a sluggish, angry teenager escaping from her boarding school to run off with boys and scratch initials into her arm. Clearly she'd had some private vision at the age of twenty-four (perhaps a bad trip with that boyfriend whom she now called only Final Straw) that transformed her into this new woman: a careful mother, a good cook, a part-time administrator in an old age home (a job that terrified Martin Swift). Alice seemed happy at last, trim and comfortable in her jeans and sneakers, beautiful now in a practical way, and dewy and frost-blond as a Chablis. Martin Swift was grateful for the change, and liked her; yet somehow she irritated the hell out of him.

It was Lydia he missed. He would not have told anyone; he would not have let himself think it, but he missed her. He missed her as a little girl asleep on the overlook as his comet burned overhead and stars fell around her. He missed her as the devoted daughter who chose him over her mother, who went to trial and wept because she chose him. He missed the questions she asked, because in them she showed the same curiosity he'd had as a boy. Not exactly the same, of course, but in a different form—questions about color and living things. He did not know why she was gone. There were fights, and years of distant smiles and brief telephone calls, but mostly what he remembered was that line: *You're nothing, Daddy, but one of those intellectuals!* That laughable phrase stayed with him, ached inside him like flak from an old battle. He felt that some clue to their estrangement must lie in that angry statement, but it was beyond him. Wasn't she an intellectual? He didn't often think of it, but he wanted her near him. Instead Alice was near. It turns out that you don't end up with the people you really love; by definition, you end up with the ones who stay.

It's the price for having only daughters, Swift thought to himself, looking down at the next feminine generation beside him, clicking the heels of her shoes on a seat-back. *They're smarter, but sons are easier all around.* The teenage boys were shouting at some girls across the aisle from them, lobbing their voices over the crowd, outdoing each other, speaking harmless nonsense in a fight to appear brave and handsome. Swift heard them, pictured what they looked like and two painful thoughts attached to the moment like photos clipped to a line to dry. The first was of Lydia at that age, loud and argumentative, wearing a baseball cap, but he hastily put that image aside. The second took its place: Professor Emeritus Martin Swift, just yesterday while visiting his old office in a false search for important papers, had heard from the secretary that Manday's son Ali was dead.

The news had turned the old professor rigid in the office, standing with a misty can of soda and a pencil. The sincere sadness in the woman's voice, the tilt of her head and eyes when she said it, prefacing it all with a regret she had to be the one to tell him—it was all a challenge to his mind. Fate had brought this as a test, not for Manday, but for Martin Swift. Because of course the father couldn't be forgiven, no matter what. There had been a coup on the island, a year before; the sultan had been toppled, rebels had taken to the trees—all this Swift had already known. But little tawny Ali Manday dead. He had sat by him on that night, laughing as they caught the meteors together like bugs in a jar—yet it didn't matter. Manday couldn't be forgiven. Nothing could stir a friendship once entombed.

Three years before, the Central Bureau of Astronomical Telegrams had discussed, as a last item of a meeting, the name status of P/Swift, also known as comet 1953 d, 1953 II, 1965 III, 1977 II; also known as Comet Swift. Apparently, a petition had been brought to the bureau containing information regarding the 1953 discovery of that comet and the calculation of its period and return. The petition had been prepared by none other than retired Professor Hayam Manday, and it had been granted. P/Swift was forever dead; now in the skies, innocently burning, there would only be P/Swift-Manday. Martin Swift had found this out only through a clipping left anonymously on his desk, under an abstract paperweight. Swift had put on his thick lenses, lifted the heavy stone and read (marked by a red circle, like a tick bite) the bureau's cold correction and its author. Ah, he'd thought, you cannot keep your kids from dying.

The lights were dimming and Alice, as if to rebel again at last, began to talk excitedly to her father and to her little daughter, who both shushed her loudly. Then the darkness became complete, and a teenage boy shouted and others laughed; and then suddenly the insectoid creature in the center of the room began to move, an angry god, pulling itself upright and spinning its multifaceted eyes to view them all. And then, as a dull voice began to speak of ancient times, across the whole great hemisphere of their vision came artificially, like dear false hopes, the stars.

Lydia stood in the faint spring rain, unable to believe what she saw. Perhaps she noticed the advertisement because she had never walked so slowly down this street before, though it was her own ginkgo-lined neighborhood in New York, and she had scurried through it countless times. This time she was in no hurry. She had left her place half an hour earlier for a quick pack of cigarettes, returned through the building's broken front door, and reached her apartment to find her key didn't work. Lydia stood there jiggling and coaxing the lock as she'd learned to do in so many apartments, knowing, after years of sublets, that there was a certain English to every copied key, but she finally stood back with the key in her tight fist, vanquished. She was not getting into this apartment, and it wasn't because of any subtlety of the lock. With a smile, she realized that this was simply not her key. In her usual muddle, she must have grabbed one of her friends' extras she had lying around, and here she was, a woman near the end of the century, foolishly locked out. Lydia opened her palm and stared at the key, astounded. What a tiny object to have altered her day so entirely. What a dull comic device.

It was a hopeless situation. Lydia had no secret key hidden anywhere. She had never befriended her neighbors. She had no money except the change from the cigarettes: two quarters and a dime, which might get her either a cup of coffee or two phone calls if she managed to remember anyone's number, which she surely wouldn't. She did not have her father's mind for numbers; they flickered in black and white in the back of her brain whenever she tried to retrieve them, never to surface. The number of the boy she'd dated a month before, for instance, floated back there dimly—he might have an extra key, and would gladly help her—but her fading interest in him had made the number fade, so that only four wan digits remained. She knew it began with a five: five-three-two? It was hopeless—not that she had money for more than two phone calls anyway. And no umbrella against the rain, since she had left dressed only in sweats. No shoes—only slippers. No pockets. No tokens. No watch.

And this was going to be the day for her own work! This was going to be the day for art! She stood in that hallway, clenching the key in her fist, feeling the mouse-bite of its teeth, marveling at how life was turning out. It was always this way, always a joke. Great things—friends, trips, jobs—materialized for her out of the blue sky, unbidden, but whenever she longed for something, worked for it, no matter how minor and everyday, the world failed her. She would send a dress to the cleaners and the place would burn down. She would set a plate on a counter and the steampipe's rattle would send it crashing to the floor. Some simple thing was wrong with her—she was a typewriter with a sticking key; she was a sorceress with a stutter.

But she had her art. Something to beg time for, something frustrating and thrilling all her own—a canvas and a photograph pinned to the wall beside it. Her tubes of paint. The idea, still forming, of what might happen there. Something her father would never understand.

What was there to do now? Plan some calls, find someone with an extra key. But surely the key in her hand wasn't an office key; it had to be to someone's apartment. And certainly someone who lived close by—what else would be the point of an extra key? So it was Kelly's, or Angela's, or her mother's. Well, Lydia decided, turning in the hallway to descend the stairs, she might as well try them one by one. As she stepped outside into the rain, the day lost all its urgency and desperation; it seemed to widen before her. She lit her first cigarette: What a wonderful, unlucky pleasure.

It must have been her slow, pointless walk back down the street that made her notice the ad. Or her bored mind, which, having given up on her work, her calls, finally lay open to other interests. It could even have been something as simple as the bright pink-toned paper of the ad itself, or the slant of light through the clouds, or the awning of the travel agency which offered some protection from the rain which, Lydia realized, she would be suffering all day in slippers. But, looking back, Lydia would see herself at brokenhearted twenty-three and would believe it was deeper—that her future self had reached its bony arm through time, grabbed her young head and twisted it to look in the right place.

The ad itself was merely a photocopy taped to the inside of the agency window, an offer for the kind of tropical package tour that Lydia and her friends never could have afforded, nor would have desired. Five days, four nights in a hut in a remote island paradise. Seafood buffets, the traditional rice dance, snorkeling, drinks with the general. And then a photo of a set of palm trees on a beach, in the background a ruined building on a spit. There was no mistaking it— it was Bukit, the island of the comet.

Lydia found it hard to breathe. What had existed as a kingdom of mystery to her—a hot, dry place that seemed almost a figment of her imagination in her early youth, and then a sultry warren in her cynical adolescence—was now no mystery at all. It had become obvious, bourgeois; perhaps it had always been that and she'd never seen it. Her anger built without direction—she had turned into the kind of young woman whose emotions came strongly and then went nowhere, spreading like a slow flood before retreating. Lydia didn't know where to aim her fury—whether at herself, for her own naïveté, for taking those two sunny weeks of her life for granted—or at time, whose tide seemed to approach while her back was turned, soaking her childhood sandcastles until they lost their shapes and crumbled. Her mother, her father, her island. All gone, or changed. But it was easiest of all to be angry at the man mentioned in the insipid invitation to "drinks with the general." She had heard about him, about the changes on the island that had surely invited this ad, and, finally, she had heard about the death of Ali Manday.

It was during what the newspapers called a "bloodless coup." What that meant, Lydia believed, was that the sultan had not been killed. When the army entered the overlook where the potbellied sultan lay sunbathing, his mistress by his side, he must have felt the coolness of their shadows over him and known it was over: the centuries of his family's rule, the despotism, the riches, the benevolent changes he himself had made to undo clerical law. Oil gleaming on his dark skin, he must have decided that if he could keep the palace, he would give them the island. Perhaps it felt something like relief—a family relic stolen, gone forever, nothing to worry over now. Half the island's men were not as pleased; the military rule would mean a right-wing kind of freedom that many of the pro-American boys were unwilling to swallow. Virtuous, wrongheaded, it was hard to say. But there were protests, some strict, unwise decisions on the general's part, and one night Ali found himself in the wrong place and got a bullet in his gut. His friends took him home, choking with blood, where his mother cleaned his face and wounds, wailing, and watched him die. It made no newspapers.

Lydia looked at the picture again. The beach, those palm trees, the stone house on the spit. Only six years before, she had made love to tawny Ali Manday in that building. "You're so beautiful," the teenage boy had whispered, grinning, eyes closed, at his good fortune, breathing heavily into her neck, "You're so beautiful." The rough feel of the reed mat on her back, the cool air the stone had trapped for them, the light coming through the keyhole in the shape of a chess piece. A few afternoons of rough sex, that was all, and now he was dead. Sweet Ali Manday. The beach, the trees, the house—what seemed most awful was that these things would live on so heartlessly, unchanged in this picture, betraying Lydia and Ali. The trees would not break in despair and rot away; the stones would not sigh and collapse. Some rich businessman and woman, in swimwear from a catalog, would walk hand in hand and believe they were the first to see that palm, that sand, that stone, that color in the sky. *Nothing is yours,* Lydia thought angrily, *not any landscape or painting or word you speak. Nothing will remember you.*

The island was still on her mind as she stumbled in her damp slippers, ignoring the lights at the intersections as she swore over the fate of Ali Manday and that spit of sand. People passed and she did not see them; storefronts blinked with lights but she did not notice; Lydia had even forgotten that she wore only sweats in the chill air, though she clutched the mysterious key tightly in her hand. She had not changed in all this time—her mind still sent her body forward like a torpedo while she dove deeper into her thoughts. She practiced a conversation with the general while two taxis on Seventh Avenue screeched and swerved around her. She was the same as the little girl who cut through a field of wet grass without noticing the green stains on her socks or the nests she crushed underfoot. A ghost passing through a wall. It was not mere dreaminess—it had never been that—rather, she looked like a scientist working out a formula. Lydia would have hated that, knowing she looked anything like her father.

They were very different people, now. It had come, of course, in both of them, with age. Swift had grown increasingly difficult, nervous from all the habits he had been forced to quit, weary from his research and terrified that his reputation would crack somehow. He tried to stay young, though, and this was the worst for Lydia because, while he was holding on to a younger version of himself, she was trashing everything about her youth, and could not stand it when he would appear in the basement with beer for her friends. Or his round, hairy body in the hot tub as he passed around a joint. It was the usual teenage hatred, but in Lydia it burned bright—she considered her life possessed by this demon, and she longed for an exorcism. It came in the strangest form: the return of her mother.

Altered, faded, sad, but free of madness, her mother began to call and invite Lydia and her sister Alice out for lunches, trying to undo those terrifying evenings they had spent while in her custody, the nights alone, or worse, when she woke them to hold them to her. Alice, already deep in college with a boyfriend, rejected her mother's attempts, but Lydia readily accepted them. She did this because she'd been so young when her mother went mad, and therefore kept all her memories cloudy at the edges, still hopeful. But she also went because these meetings infuriated her father. Half an hour before she was to leave, Swift would begin to stomp around the house, shouting, almost weeping. Lydia felt such a conquest when she stepped out the door and drove away to seek her mother's dimmed presence.

None of these events really tore the two of them apart. There was no particular scene, no one terrible phrase that shattered their affection. Instead, Lydia knew she and her father had grown distant in the way the stars grow distant—because of time's simple expansion— and even this metaphor made Lydia wince. Her last few visits with him in Berkeley had produced no fights nor raised any deep issues, but each conversation frustrated her. For her, the main frustration revealed itself as her father's too-literal mind. On a walk along a high hill, she would point out to the bay, saying how it looked like crumpled tinfoil, hoping to impress him with this line she'd heard in a play; but the old man always frowned, shook his head, saying that was nonsense. The bay was exactly what it was. Tinfoil? Lydia so often described life in these metaphors and vagaries, but Swift would not accept them; he wanted to know how it *really* was, and Lydia did not understand what he meant. They would see a movie, and as they exited the theater, she would talk about the characters with whom she identified. "Identify?" he frequently asked, stopping in the lobby. "You think you're like those people?" She tried to explain how her life seemed similar in some way or another. "But they're *French!*" he'd insist, throwing out his arms. She showed her life to him in moments and impressions, but he could not see it. And she could not paint it any other way. Nowadays she was less worried by this blindness. They simply never spoke.

But Lydia did know what day this was. The ad had reminded her, but she would not have forgotten. It was a day taught sternly to her in her youth: the aphelion of Comet Swift. No, she remembered, not Comet Swift. It was now called Comet Swift-Manday. Everything was changing this way.

She lit her second cigarette. She was close to Kelly's now, just two blocks away. The rain had increased and Lydia stuck close to the awnings, hiding the burning end of her cigarette in her hand. The rusty odor which had permeated the morning was gone, and even the usual scent of bread and garbage in her neighborhood had been flattened by the rain. All the windows in the Village were closing one by one against the downpour, and to Lydia the city seemed to curl into itself. The streets looked emptier, and the water which had previously drained away now stood deep and unmoving at every corner. People stopped at the intersections, working up the nerve to jump the puddles, and one such man lifted his head to look at Lydia. She did not see him at first; she felt his eyes on her skin, and turned in his direction to look: a handsome young man in an old-fashioned hat and coat, earrings in both ears, staring at her in the private way people do when they don't expect you to notice. But she had noticed, and she felt surprise. That long bluish face staring out of the dim city. She felt as if the rain had cleared a space for her on the sidewalk, and she stood dry and bare for a moment before his eyes.

As soon as the young man realized she saw him, he turned away. He held his hat and leaped across the puddle; his coat flew out; he landed flat-footed and stumbled, glancing back to see if she'd noticed, then continued on down the street. She realized she was soaked through, from her sweats down to her slippers. She saw herself as pale, fat, drowned—what had he seen to make him turn? She ran for cover in a phone booth, holding herself and feeling the water in her clothes. It was funny; the boy had changed her slightly. Until she saw him, she hadn't felt lonely all day.

She used her first quarter to call her mother. When her home phone rang ten times, she hung up and tried the office instead. Her mother had returned to her old career as a scientific artist on the staff of a magazine. Because of her Ph.D. in botany, she specialized in leaves and cells, but often took on the tougher jobs: microscopic creatures, viral interactions, cutaways of the human heart. "The trick," her mother told her, as she had when Lydia was a little girl, "is knowing what details to leave out." She had repeated this advice because Lydia now worked at the same magazine; she was calling her own office number.

"It's Lydia, is my mom there?"

"I don't know." It was Lucas, the young gay man who worked as their receptionist. Lydia wasted a lot of time talking to him, especially about her love life, but he didn't quite feel like a friend. Good advice, clever stories; but nothing deeper ever evolved. Perhaps he wasn't very smart. It killed her to reject someone for that old reason. Lucas told her, "She was here, about half an hour ago, I'll see."

"Hurry, I'm in a phone booth."

It wasn't quite a phone booth; more a clear plastic alcove off the street. She leaned against the plastic as she waited and listened to the rain on the street, constant and soft, hushing the city like a baby. The young man who'd turned to look at her was nowhere to be seen; he had not returned to talk, to ask her name. Of course not, of course not. She noticed a cheap trinket shop across from her, and a series of plastic pictures displayed outside the window, beaded with water. They were tacky portraits of Jesus touching his heart, but she discovered that when you turned your head, the face changed to Mary's. Jesus, Mary, then back again. She remembered pictures that did something like this from Cracker Jack boxes. While she waited for her mother to answer, hoping her quarter wouldn't run out, Lydia swayed her head from side to side and watched the portraits change. Jesus, Mary, Jesus, Mary. Surely this meant something dear to someone.

"They say she's here, but no one can seem to find her."

"Fuck."

"Can she call you?"

"I'm fucking locked out of my place, Lucas. I'm in slippers here out on the street, and I've got—oh, Jesus, forty-five cents or something."

"Why don't you come here? I'll loan you money."

"It's raining. That's like an hour's walk in the rain. I'm in fucking slippers."

"Call back in half an hour. I think she'll be here."

"If she's not, that's my last quarter."

"It's an interesting situation. What do you do in New York all day if you've got no money?"

"Play chess in Washington Square."

"Call in half an hour or so. If she shows up, I'll make her stay."

"Thanks, Lucas."

She hung up and headed toward her friend's house once again. What a strangely ordinary conversation, she thought. A young woman in a panic, trying to reach her mother at the office. The kind of call that must happen every day, to all kinds of people. How strange—as if it were her real mother. As if that woman had been there all the time these last ten years, criticizing how she dressed and acted, worrying over her bad choices, weeping when she moved to college. A mother to call in a crisis. A dull, average mother instead of this old botanist with a gardening hat and a medical history— this relic from her distant youth transported, nearly whole, into the present. Time was not meant to work like this. We are not meant to skip.

Lydia turned the corner of Charles Street. By now, her dyed-red hair was wet through and through. She squeezed it and it dripped down her back. There was something thoroughly satisfying about being completely soaked; there was no further harm the day could do. At the doorway to her friend's building, she pulled out the key—if it was the one, it should open the outside door as well. She thought of the warm room upstairs, the cat meowing, the half-eaten breakfast on Kelly's kitchen table, the couch with its afghan thrown over it. She tried the key. It fit neatly but refused to turn. Another few minutes of wriggling and coaxing and Lydia gave up, leaning against the door. Not this lock, not Kelly's lock after all.

She lit her third cigarette. What *does* one do in New York with no money, no hat, no shoes?

Gravity is a disease, the woman thought to herself. She sat on a bench in a Roman square where market stalls were arranged in rows, their plastic canopies flapping in the early evening wind. Her son was beside her, chattering on about the marketplace and the dinner they hoped to buy there. Salami, he insisted, salami and mozzarella and big crusty bread. This was a woman whom Lydia had mostly forgotten, remembering her only as an intermittent character from her past made up of three pictures—an add-a-bead necklace, an anatomy book with transparencies of the body and a friendly black cat. That was all that remained. The woman, in expensive slacks and a short haircut that looked nothing like her old self, nodded to her thirteen-year-old son as he rubbed his crew cut and shouted his hunger. Girls drove by on Vespas, men whistled, pigeons left in a flock from beside her, circled and landed again where they had begun. The woman watched their flight and this made her think of gravity. It was Denise, far from her home, having lost the love of two men in a short span of years.

Gravity is a disease, she considered again. She was to give a lecture to a freshman class here in Rome, and so she was taking mental notes on one of her own lectures. Something that would translate well. Denise had chosen this one about gravity. The idea infuriated her young astronomers, and it was a silly argument, but she enjoyed playing with them, testing what they assumed to be true. "We take it as a primal force," she would tell them, "but maybe we're just studying an aberration." A disease. You catch it from everything around you—things pull at you and stretch you out, tugging at the path you planned until you bend back like a willow branch to where you began. Everything is grabbing at everything; even beams of light, infected by the planets and the stars, loop crazily in space like those doves, until we cannot quite know what we see, whether gravity's virus has contaminated even the spread of stars above us. No, it has, she considered; we know it has. The moon pulls at the ocean and the tides go in and out. The earth pulls at the moon and traps it like a pale maiden in a high tower. Even a comet cannot shoot with shivering light through a galaxy—the planets spread infection and the comet is drawn in, stricken, spiraling or ellipsing around a center in a skewed, pointless orbit until some other greater planet crooks its finger and the comet comes running. Everything is pulling at everything; no one gets through untouched. "And we can do nothing about it," Denise would remark to her classes with open palms. "We observe the victims. We take notes on the plague."

An unusual thought to come to her on this sabbatical in Rome, but it pleased her like any idea before sleep. "And if it is a plague," the lecture continued in her mind, "what would be the cure?"

A yellow wind-up bird went clattering above them, its plastic wings flapping frantically as it gained height, then began to glide and drop, moving more like a bat than a sparrow with its dipping, random shuffle through the air before it hit the stone of the square and, after a few hopeless bursts of its wings, skidded to a stop. Two boys in jackets came running, one with a shining key in his hand, the secret to the bird's movement. They took the object gently in their hands and began to wind again.

"They're going to close soon," her son said forcefully. He was talking about the market stalls, which she was afraid of approaching.

She sighed dramatically, wanting to amuse him. "We'd better get this over with."

"I'll do it, you know. I'll totally do it."

Denise shook her head, saying, "But, you know, I'm the mother. I'm supposed to be in charge and buy dinner, but . . . God, those ladies are so intimidating. . . ."

"I'll do it," Josh repeated, touching his chest. He was serious. "I took Spanish. That's like Italian."

"Go do it, then," she said, trying not to laugh at his intensity. She brought her purse onto her lap. "Just point and give them the money. Here. Here, give them a really big bill, and that way you always have given them enough. So, salami . . ."

He rolled his eyes. "Mom, I know. Salami, mozzarella and bread."

"Grazie."

Her son, Josh, running toward the stalls, some of which were already closing, her wonderful son. There was an arrogance about him that should have irritated her, but she felt overjoyed; perhaps she recognized it in herself. And not just herself at that age, at nervous, fantastic thirteen, but still in herself. She loved it, for instance, when he said what he just had—"I know"—because she knew it as a ploy. He would stand holding a lemonade at a party, grinning, crew cut stippled with sun, hand-on-stocky-hip like an espresso pot, and when you told him, "Apparently there's a total eclipse tomorrow over Europe," he'd keep his steady grin, letting his drink melt, and say "Oh, I know." His mother loved it when he said it, and not because she liked him to be arrogant, but because it was so obvious that he *didn't know*. It made her want to laugh, and she egged him on with sly trick comments like "You know, they found out two male movie stars are actually women" or "Turns out Nancy Reagan once voted Communist," and there Josh would go in his almost-bored voice: "Oh, I know." It was a terrible habit, but it pleased her to no end.

The bird went through the air again, this time less successfully. It barely cleared the head of an old woman in black, who stood up and shouted at the boys for a long time. They seemed to take her very seriously. Josh stood under a canopy talking to another woman in black, and he pointed and gestured and bent over to hear her words. He was buying dinner, happily taking on a language he didn't know. His bravery always astounded Denise; neither she nor her husband was brave in any way. In fact, she knew very few people who were brave. Kathy, perhaps. And, in his way, also Eli.

She lost Eli nearly five years ago. It happened a few months after the most recent trip to the island, after half a dozen or so midnight visits to that hillside near Tranquillity, wrapped together in a quilt to search for comets in the early morning sky. Denise had no glimmer of doubt, either on the island or during those nights. In fact, she felt that those evenings on the island, with Kathy gone and Adam sick and fevered in his hut, had changed their affair. It had gone from something quick and simple, a pleasant nostalgia and weakness, into an affection that threatened their other lives. And Eli, Eli had been the one begging her to stay. She remembered lying on the old reed mat, Eli whispering in her ear about the great mistakes they had made in their lives. "There isn't enough time to keep going like this," he told her softly. "We're too old now." His face was desperate and loving in the dim light of that stone hut, the same expression he had worn years before in the doorway of her flat, hoping to change her mind, as if this conversation took up exactly where that one left off. As if no one had hurt anyone or loved anybody else. And time had softened him, his mind as well as his body, taken away the rough anger of his idealism and the tension in his muscles. She rubbed the furry roundness of his belly. "I'm going to leave Kathy," he whispered, staring at her in the darkness.

"No you're not."

"And you're going to leave Adam."

This time she didn't say anything, and they did not speak of it again. He smiled and lay down beside her, because there seemed to be an implicit understanding that he was right, it was true, this was what they were both going to do. Not as if Eli were telling her his decision, but as if he had caught some cloudy glimpse of the future in the bat-grimed darkness of the ceiling: he would leave Kathy; she would leave Adam. She felt him take her hand, and she stared out the window. Had he seen her flinch?

This was too much for her. The hot room, this old friend, the returning comet—everything in the past had got tangled up somehow. She had a bout of anger at herself; she had not thought it through this far, and yet Eli's hope was surely the obvious future. Surely this was what she had wanted, yes? Why she started all this on that chill evening when she touched his shoulder? Denise had noticed the uncertainty in his eyes that night, felt hope staggering noisily in his chest, yet she had made it happen. A kiss on a comet night, and a hastily whispered promise to be kind. Had she meant it? Wait, wait, she kept thinking as the waves shifted on the sand outside the hut, I haven't thought this through. When she started this, a year before, it was for different reasons: a loneliness that both of them could recognize, a memory of what it felt like to be young. That old crush, that old affair—he was an accomplice, a co-conspirator in the plot to kidnap time. They would trap it and raise it as their own. They would make a little life inside of life. But this, Eli's clear and awful vision of the future—how could he expect it, for someone to throw off her old life for something just as difficult, as unsure? She squeezed his hand and smiled through her doubt.

Their next two comet hunts were beautiful: cold; the gegenschein, that disapproving eye, glimmering overhead; the two of them wrapped in her family quilt as they waited to adjust the telescope, whispering in the wilderness for no reason except the excitement of having to whisper. This still excited her, and having Eli to talk to, his wandering mind flashing with ideas. Eli seemed to have become more amorous, which annoyed her, since she hadn't begun all this just for sex, just for clouds of breath on a chill mountain; he also became rougher, biting her, and she wondered if he were trying to get her caught, leaving red marks that she would later have to explain to Adam as "fleas in that old blanket." Denise thought it was funny that they even searched for comets anymore on those evenings. The hunts were just an excuse to be together, discuss science and their lives, and they could easily have lied and met in a bed-and-breakfast on the coast, sitting in a hot tub and watching the surf pummel the shore. She told this to Eli as they were packing the equipment at dawn, and he shrugged.

"It would feel different," he said, folding the telescope into its case. "Ordinary."

"But why even come up here? Isn't it funny?"

"Maybe we're bad liars. Bad liars always stay as close to the truth as possible."

She remembered giving a sly smile and saying, "Oh, but I'm a very good liar," and how he laughed and kissed her.

There was something in his face as he came back from kissing her—something of the old Eli, that distractable, exciting man leaning in her office door when they were very young—that made her pause and watch him as he loaded up the car. Denise thought for a moment she might do it; she might tear her easy life to bits for him; she might do the thing that would please him most. Back home, many hours later, she had already forgotten that feeling, caught up in her papers and the still light of her house at dusk.

On the third hunt, though, Eli seemed different. He wouldn't eat his pancakes at the diner before their drive up the mountain, and when they arrived at the viewpoint, he brought out two plastic folding chairs that they hadn't used since the beginning; they usually huddled together. He set them up quietly and brought out his pad and his red flashlight. It was typical for them to begin with work, with choosing a section of the sky to examine, discussing technique and variation and timing, but he scribbled and mumbled to himself instead of consulting her. She tried to ask him about his work on ion tails, but he smiled and tapped his pad, sending her away. It went on this way into the morning, the two of them in their separate chairs, wrapped in blankets, his ballpoint pen clicking and scratching in the darkness. And then, without turning to her, without lifting his pen, he said he couldn't do these hunts anymore. His research had gained attention, and he didn't have the time. He lied to her in profile. She knew it was a lie and, a little later, when she grew angry and confronted him, he sighed and talked about the impossibility of their lives together, which she knew was another lie. He gave her a story about Kathy's fragility, and one about Denise's own child, and Adam, and they were every one of them lies. Like the myth of a man buried in a pile of stones, each bearing the name of a god, so Denise was up to her chin in a cairn of gracious lies. Stones tossed her way: he was doing this for her; he was considering the future; he was thinking of their careers.

"You don't believe that," she finally said, shaking with confusion. "None of it. I know you don't believe it."

"I do. It's true, Denise."

"Why are you doing this?"

"We're too old for it," Eli said so wearily that she almost believed him. "Too fucking old."

And as they silently packed their belongings into the car for the last time, she thought of how she should have known it would be this way. He was not like Adam; he would not cling forever, but would drop her with barely a word. She noticed the angry relief of his face in the early dawn; there was something else in his mind that she would never know. The hollow falseness of the occasion struck her, the cruelty, and with a shock she remembered Carlos. She thought: *We have been here before.*

Denise drove them down the mountain again, and the hour's drive was wordless, filled with the noise of the bumpy road and of their own jostling equipment. She felt Eli burning with silence beside her, and with a shock she realized that her hands wanted to send the car over the mountain, wreck everything, hurt them both, force them to share something again. *What is this?* she wondered. She slowed down and steadied her grip. The tires crackled on the road, and stones clanked against the underside of the car. *What is this?* She could see a plume of black smoke rising from the forest, some farmer burning his leaves, no doubt. She watched it rise and disappear into the air. So many wasted hours, lit recklessly, burned into smoke like this, gone. Hours at the telescope searching for a comet, in the hut avoiding Eli's touch, in her marriage bed listening to her husband's chatter, in the hallways of the school arguing a theory—a hundred thousand wasted hours. She had always thought there would be time enough— that you could lead a certain life and then, when it faded, exchange it for the one you'd always longed for—but time was over. It was burnt to ashes now. Here he sat beside her, brushing his leg against hers at every bump. Here he was. There was an hour when she could have taken his face in her hands and told him she would do his heart's desire. But that hour had past long ago. Ashes. He sat beside her silently, and when they reached the bottom, he stepped out of the car, waved and drove away. She understood she had never been here before, not with Carlos, not with Adam. *What is this?* Not friendship, not comfort. Too late, she understood this was the love you're supposed to fight for.

Josh was back with the food, running toward her in his shorts. He acted like her—the look of pride on his face now was hers, completely hers; it was her gift to him—but he did not look like her. He looked just like his father.

"Here you go!"

"Fantastic. I'm starving—what took you so long?"

"Mom! It was tough, she tried to give me something else, then the . . ." Josh gave a staccato account of the interaction, and Denise tried not to smile. He never understood when she was kidding, but he would eventually, and she would miss it, this innocence that he tried to pass off as experience.

On the way back to the hotel room, Josh reminded her to call his father, who had a right to hear how things were going. *Adam,* she thought, *oh, I forgot.* He'd offered her so little after she returned from Tranquillity; it was suddenly so obvious. Adam was moody and irritable, but lacked genius as an excuse; he merely built a life out of reasonable hopes, a solid life that might steady him and his son, and Denise was to be part of that forever. She couldn't, but she didn't blame him for expecting it. For now, Denise simply wanted her husband to fade from her life without anger, a harmless local ghost whose manifestations would come quietly and sadly to her, glowing in a corner of her dark bedroom, talking the way he used to when she loved him.

Lydia remembered Adam. She thought of that older man as she sat in a plastic chair inside a copy shop on Seventh Avenue. She had found shelter from the rain. Memories of the island were floating through her head, and Lydia remembered Adam far better than she did Denise. He had meant something to her. Adam was different from all the scientists she had known when she was growing up in the department, in that youth she had spent playing in the offices with discarded vacuum tubes and lenses. He had treated the child like a child. Oddly, she had needed that—not condescension, but a patience and humor which none of the guffawing astronomers seemed to possess. Adam talked with her quietly, carefully; he made her feel safe. If she had never seen him again after her youth, she would still have remembered him fondly as that blond halo of hair in the barn, looking up at her with a grin as he petted her dog. But she had seen him again. She saw him when she was seventeen, six years ago on the island, at around midnight below the overlook when he emerged, stumbling in his fever, to find her smoking on the beach.

She sat indoors as she thought of this, eating a slice of pizza. Her luck had changed immediately after leaving her friend's doorway; there, crunched in the space under the mailboxes and protected by the rain, was a baseball cap. Wearing a cap lessened the rain's irritation by about half; the cold drops on her scalp had hurt and depressed her, but now she merely felt the chill moistness of her clothes. Things were looking up. At the next place, her friend Angela's, her key didn't work either, but now, with this cap, the day had lost its misery. She had some wild ideas about begging for money or jumping a turnstile, but it seemed too wet for people to stop for her on the sidewalk, and she actually got as far as the inside of a subway station, slippers in her hand, before deciding this was idiotic and she would surely get caught. So Lydia walked back to the surface, thinking of trying the key at her mother's apartment, when she happened upon a party. A grand-opening party at a copy shop, with free copies and pizza. It was fairly empty except for an eager manager and a cheapskate art student hogging a machine to copy his portfolio. She sat down with her pizza and smiled at the manager, who seemed willing to let her wait out the rain.

And the thought of Adam came to her. She recalled Adam's voice in the darkness of the beach, six years before, and how it had startled her. "Can I have a toke?" she heard, and it jolted her out of her contemplation of the midnight ocean. Here was the man in a T-shirt and jeans, sitting beside her with a pleasant, distant expression. The sand must have silenced his approach. She passed him the joint, and only a little while into their conversation did she realize he was the same man she'd seen in the barn as a child, Dr. Lanham's husband. Then she understood that he was sick, feverish in the cooler night air, floating in the same haze she was in. That made it easier to talk, and to sit saying nothing as the fireflies winked out one by one.

"You're a writer, Mr. Lanham?"

"Adam," he corrected her. "I'm a writer."

"I want to be a writer."

"No you don't," he said seriously. "And I'm not really a writer anyway. Mostly I'm a liar. I tell a lot of lies, Lydia."

"So do I."

It was hard to think of herself back then without laughing. She thought he was handsome—she thought every man was handsome when she was seventeen, and she flirted heavily with boys in school, with Ali on the island, thinking that if she could trick them into adoring her she would have won some prize. What was the prize? The memory of the adoration itself. She hoarded these memories, spending them on herself when she felt worthless and alone. But she didn't usually sleep with these men and boys: It was enough to know they wanted to sleep with her. It was enough, in a crowded bus, fully clothed, to feel a college boy's hand on her thigh, squeezing, his eyes blank with desire. She would catch the look and feel it inside her— the coin of his passion clanking on her heart's metal floor.

So it was enough that night with Dr. Lanham's husband on the beach. To talk about her boyfriends and her dalliance with Ali that very afternoon. He seemed interested, amused, but she could tell he asked more questions than a married man should. About how she met these men, about the beach, about the little stone hut out on the spit. She wished she could show him, she said suggestively, puffing the last of the pot, but someone else was in the hut right now. She had just come from there. Two white people were having sex in there.

"Who? Who is it?" he asked. Something had gone wrong with his smile.

She told him she didn't know. Two of the scientists, she assumed, a chubby white guy and a blonde. Some married couple trying to relight the spark, and at the word "spark" she flicked her lighter and smiled. "Time to go skinny-dipping!" she announced.

It was enough to see his face melt like wax as she stripped off her bikini. Married men were so complicated, and she wasn't even going to seduce him; she had just wanted to know that perhaps she could. The story about the people in the hut seemed to have changed him, and she was afraid he'd gone cold, but then suddenly he was lifting his shirt over his head. Off went the shoes, the pants, and he stood there looking a little dazed and sad, fat around his middle and his balls hanging low from the island heat. That moment was enough. After their swim, which was colder than she'd expected of the South China Sea, she put her clothes back on and said goodbye. Adam stood there, stoned, sick, confused, holding his shirt over his half-hard penis. "Yes, you should go," he said seriously.

"I'm supposed to be counting meteors," young Lydia explained with a sly grin, pulling back her wet hair. She had enjoyed his desire when they were swimming, but now his numb look had dulled her pleasure. His body looked so old to her now, all hair and muscle that had turned to fat. She felt faintly disgusted.

"You shouldn't do this, Lydia."

"What do you mean?"

Adam stood shaking his head, looking down the beach to where a clump of coconut trees cut off the view. "You know. Neither should I . . . oh, Jesus. . . ."

"Don't be so square, Adam," she said, laughing, holding her sandals in one hand. She used her usual lines: "It's just skinny-dipping. It's just bodies."

"True," he said. Adam was still half-naked, troubled, one hand to his head. Then he looked up at her with an expression of concern: "But not for you, I don't think."

Lydia sighed and turned away, saying, "I've gotta go. Good night."

She was off into the deeper darkness of the path, her feet feeling the sharp end of twigs in the sand, when she heard him shout to her "I'm sorry!" and she was more perplexed than ever. He was sorry, when he should have been ashamed or angry. Why sorry? Lydia was unsure of what had happened, and of what she had won this time.

In the copy shop she felt a wave of shame for her old self. She put down the pizza and let out an angry sigh, making the art student turn his head in concern. Lydia rarely did this—tortured herself with how she had acted in the past. There was no reliving and undoing the events, yet once in a while they still felt very real to her, very much in the present. She wanted to go back and speak to each different girl she'd been—the heartbroken twenty-year-old artist, the cocky adolescent slut, the lonely stupid child—and give them a good talking-to. Lydia did not feel as though they were part of her, but rather that these former selves were the team that had built her; and, like a monster ashamed of its creation, she wanted to confront her makers. She knew, though, that even if she could, she would not have had the nerve—they would have stood before her, shaking, merely children.

Lydia used the manager's phone to call her office once again. Lucas said that her mother still had not arrived. He suggested taking a cab, saying that he would pay for it, but Lydia found herself turning him down and hanging up the phone. The manager grinned at her under his mustache, starting a chat about the rain. He was still in midsentence when she left the store and headed up Seventh Avenue. She lit her fifth cigarette.

Here is how it happened:

Eli got a call one Saturday afternoon while Kathy was off at a violin lesson. This was a new fascination of hers, since she had learned the violin as a child but, through lack of money and her own adolescent stubbornness, had given it up too early. Her forties brought her a kind of mission: to eradicate regret. The violin lessons were part of this—as were plans for closer contact with her sisters, with other details of her past that she was saving from the trash and reestablishing in her life. Kathy had just left and would be gone for hours, so Eli sat peacefully alone in the house, aware that he would soon leave this place, noticing the canisters of flour and sugar that soon, if he so chose, would no longer be his. Or they might be his and Denise's. He could rearrange it all. This was 1978, five years before.

The call came.

"Eli, it's Adam. I'm actually in town and wondered if you wanted to get lunch."

"Well," Eli said. "I've had lunch, and there's some work I've been doing. . . ." This reaction wasn't unreasonable, since the Lanhams came down to L.A. often enough, and so meeting up wasn't essential. Eli thought he could shrug it off this time.

But Adam would not let him go: "We need to have lunch. I need to talk to you."

They met at a Jewish deli that made heart-shaped cookies filled with chocolate. Adam was already there when Eli arrived, and he looked very much the part of a writer: polo shirt, rumpled tweed jacket, thick sunglasses and a dazed, uneasy look. He never looked like this; he usually dressed carefully, like a younger man, and while Eli had often thought he looked foolish, this disheveled look was worse. Adam seemed as though he had not slept for many nights. They shook hands, sat down, ordered coffee and a sandwich for Adam, and then the man said what he had come all this way to say.

"Denise is having an affair."

Eli tried very hard not to change his face, and not to appear to be trying so hard. He breathed very deeply in order to appear serene, yet he had panicked at the last word. He could imagine Adam finding out about the affair—he could even imagine Adam's fear and desperation—but the man was so passive and shy. Eli would have expected poison in his coffee before this kind of confrontation. So Eli sat perfectly still while he thought of what to do next.

Adam took a weary sip of his coffee, staring and telling him, "I know, Eli. I know all about it."

All Eli could think of was to ask a question: "Did Denise say something?"

"No," Adam said, dismissing that as impossible. Yet it had occurred to Eli that Denise might treat her love affairs as methodically as her experiments. Adam shook his head. "No, of course not, but now it's so obvious. I found letters."

"Letters?" Eli asked. This made no sense; there had been no letters. "I don't understand."

"It's that old boyfriend. She's been seeing Carlos."

Eli laughed. It came too loudly, out of relief, out of vanished fear, out of the giddy sensation of deep memory shooting suddenly to the surface of the brain. There was so much to worry about, so many sharp objects in that dark drawer in which Adam was rummaging, that it seemed ridiculous to have come up with Carlos. Eli laughed so loudly that Adam looked concerned, sad and almost angry. Eli swallowed the laugh and tried to calm himself. He had escaped disaster, and he had to hide it. He apologized, twice, patting Adam's hand.

He said, "Oh no—God—Adam, there's no way! It's . . . I can't tell you . . . listen, I met the guy." Eli still knew to form his words very carefully, acting the role of a friend giving abstract advice instead of a man with intimate knowledge. "I met him, and I remember, and there's no way. Carlos? He was an idiot. She didn't give a shit about him. And that was, what, fifteen years ago?"

Adam would not accept this humorous attitude. Something in him seemed to bristle with anger. He said, "Thirteen. I asked her."

"You confronted her?"

"Of course not," he said, this time bitterly. "But you're wrong, Eli.

I know it sounds stupid. Like she wouldn't be that stupid. But it's more than letters."

Eli smiled, waved the idea away. "Your hunch."

"No, I saw them together."

It took a moment for Eli to realize what had been said. It was ludicrous—he had been with Denise two weekends before, on that hillside under a quilt, whispering together.

"I don't believe it."

Adam told him a story about how he had followed her one night and seen them together going into a movie theater, laughing like adolescents. He had bought a ticket for himself and entered after the movie began, listening for her voice, finding the two of them near the side of the theater, huddled close together. He sat two rows behind and watched them kiss and pet—his wife, nearly forty, and this handsome, ludicrous man from her past—until, after half an hour, he could take no more and left. When she returned home, Denise claimed she had been at the office, looking over Eli's photographs from their comet hunt. There was no doubt.

"I don't believe it."

"But I do. I was there. Eli, you're my friend—what do I do now?"

But Eli had nothing to say. It seemed as though someone had taken the sun's lamp and flipped it over, shedding some harsh new light on the images that he thought he knew by heart: that night when the boy fell from the overlook, his time in England, the chill midnight of the comet hunt when she touched his shoulder, the humid evening on the island and all the other nights since then. He did not want to talk to Adam anymore, confront his guilt, comfort the man he'd wronged. He wanted to sit alone and rifle through her looks and phrases. He wanted to test each day scientifically, dip it into strong solutions that would reveal its composition, as if the days were beakered powders sitting by the dozens on a rack. He needed time to do this; he no longer wanted to be here. Somewhere far away a store alarm went off and rang dimly through his thoughts.

Adam rambled on: "If it's just sex, I don't care. That's all right with me. But I don't want to lose her."

"Of course you don't," Eli said automatically.

"I've . . . I've had my own, you know . . . it's not like I'm per-fect. . . ."

Eli looked up, briefly distracted from his log of days. Adam's own affairs! It had never occurred to him; nor to Denise, he supposed. But yes, Adam in a motel room with a student, a young poetess with suede boots and fluffy hair, Adam approaching her tentatively in the dark room, lit only by the louvered glare of streetlamps. Adam's own desires, Adam's own mistakes. He wished he had known this before.

The image passed, though, and it was replaced with a similar scene of Denise and Carlos, and in Eli's mind his rival stood unaged, still twenty-seven or so, grinning like a young married man. Denise and Carlos. It was absurd, but not impossible. She had been so silent on the island, making no promises. He began to feel for doubt in his chest, like a patient searching for a tumor, and there it was: the hidden sense that Denise wasn't sure about him. A few weeks before, on a comet hunt, she had even told him how good she was at lying. "Oh, but I'm a very good liar," she'd said. The ridiculous idea was growing, second by second, into a possibility. Denise and Carlos. Eli tried to phrase his questions well.

"You really think she's going to leave you for Carlos?"

Adam stared intently, asking, "Do *you* think so? Do you think she'd leave me?"

"Maybe I should talk with her."

But Adam would not let him. He insisted that this was his prob-lem, his marriage; and he wanted, he supposed, simply to tell some-one who would understand, who remembered Carlos and what he'd meant to her once. "She's so logical," Adam said, "but I think that makes people . . . I don't know . . . so sentimental somehow. It's weird, you know? But he was the one. He was the first. It made a great difference in her life, I guess."

Eli paid for lunch. He had the waitress bring them the famous cookies and for the first time Adam showed a little pleasure, closing his eyes and licking at the chocolate. It almost seemed to Eli that the funny man had forgotten—he could be so easily transported while Eli, his tongue numb, turned the conversation over and over in his head like a child's puzzle, finding in its many sides new horrors.

It began there. The snap of some tiny electric spark that started the whole heavy machinery moving counterclockwise in his chest. It would take days for Eli to understand what Denise's rumpled husband had told him over lunch. Only a week later, he would have it confirmed—by an unwitting Kathy, of all people—that indeed Denise had run into Carlos three months ago, on the street, and had mentioned him happily a few times. After two weeks, doubts would solidify, silently, still without evidence, into unscientific certainty as he lay awake in anger, deciding whether to say something or to simply let her go. Then a month would pass, and by that time, with another comet hunt approaching on the weekend, Eli would be changed, chill and resolute. He would sit in his plastic chair at dawn and bury his lover in stones. *We don't need to have this conversation,* he would repeat to himself that night, somehow satisfied. *We don't need to have this conversation.*

Eli sat in the deli after Adam left. The distant store alarm rang rhythmically in his head, endlessly turning. His heart was slowing down, gently, pedaling to the stop where it rested for a moment. Then it began to spin in the other direction. The terror and freshness of that moment had a beauty to it. Not often in a life can one point to a scene and shiver, remembering all the ways things might have gone. Eli put the cookie in his pocket and stood up to leave. His mind could not shake the alarm, not for hours and hours, and he was still filled with doubt and worry over how his heart had turned. This was five years ago, though; by 1983, it was all over and done.

Four and a half million miles away, the dark, icy shard of debris was falling slowly away from them all, on a curve toward a globular star cluster, but slowing every minute, shifting by degrees to imitate, though tilted far below them, the orbits of the planets. The planets were hundreds of millions of miles farther still, just discs of light, eggs hidden in the deep black field. No constellation was visible; the stars had been thrown into the junk drawer and pulled out again tangled, glittering, and nothing made a sound as the rock rotated opposite the sun. Dust came in a haze from its surface. It began a slow freefall again, but this side of its orbit became stretched out by Jupiter's nearby mass, like the pulled string of a bass, so that its approach became erratic. This was not a unique moment. Millions of other stones and icy balls also were falling through space, also hissing near the sun, also becoming cold flares. This was happening everywhere.

If you turned Earth in your hand, you could see the hemisphere of darkness rotating behind the movement of the Sun. Turn it, and you could see the lights of New York City coming on, one by one, in the late afternoon, and Lydia sipping a beer. She had found the place where her ex-boyfriend tended bar, and, after debating the wisdom of this choice, squeezed the rain from her hair and walked in to see him washing glasses. He loaned her dry clothes, set the jukebox to a favorite song of hers, bought her a beer and, over the course of an hour, quietly tried to win her back. Lydia let him do this. She watched him be in love with her; but all the time she knew it wasn't in her heart to give him what he wanted. So he talked, full of hope, and she sadly listened.

Turn the globe further, and Italy was far behind the line of darkness. Denise and her son had just finished dinner. Josh had told a story about the museum he had just visited, a boy he'd met, and an experiment with static electricity. His mother listened to him happily, trying not to touch his hair where it glowed in the light of the kitchen, trying not to take his hand and keep him here beside her. Then he left to get ready for bed.

Gravity is a disease, she wrote on the legal pad before her. Josh was off in the bathroom, and she could hear the rhythmic sound of him brushing his teeth, a restless sound, a bird fussing at its nest. In two days, he would be gone, back to California to live again with his father. She was never going back there, not to his father. Denise had decided a month before that she would buy a house of her own—her old family wealth could bring that freedom—and start a new, simple life without Adam. He already knew it; he had sensed it and asked, before she left for Italy, when she was coming back. "In August," she'd said, perplexed, "you know." But they both had known what he really meant. Adam in the doorway, bald and handsome, one hand touching the sill above him, a man stretched as far as he could go. A meaningful phrase, a meaningful look, and she wondered if this was it, if this was Adam fighting to keep her.

You catch it from everything around you. She wrote this on the thin blue line beneath her first words. These were notes; this was an outline of the lecture she would give tomorrow. Denise was as careful a speaker as she was a scientist; her notes were exact, extensive, but loose enough to leave room for a natural voice, free enough to let her look out at her students and persuade them. Here, she just wrote down the phrases she wanted to make sure to say: *Everything is grabbing at everything.* From the bathroom came a loud series of gargling noises, and Denise put her hand to her mouth, stifling a laugh. These walrus sounds, a silence, then a definitive spit. Her son loved to make a production.

At dinner, he had told her a story about the science museum. Wheezing from a cold that had suddenly come upon him, staring at her bleary-eyed with his minor illness, he related his encounter with the static electricity exhibit, where a dashing young instructor had touched a charged metal ball and talked in Italian as his hair stood on end. Then, apparently, the handsome man had grabbed a nearby German tourist, a terrified blonde, and kissed her straight on the mouth. Her long hair, as Josh put it, flew straight up "like in a horror movie" (though Denise could not imagine any movie like this). The tourist had not expected the kiss, Josh claimed, but took part in it willingly while this crowd of schoolboys stared and giggled, astonished and, Denise guessed, aroused. Why else had Josh mentioned it? What else would he have been thinking of? And yet there was something else to the story. He was not telling it all, and she would never find him out.

Perhaps, Denise wondered as she heard him splashing around in his pond, he had shown the exhibit to another girl today. Perhaps another blonde, a twelve-year-old in pigtails, had asked in careful

English how it worked and, seeing the empty room, the charged ball glowing there like the bald head of knowledge, he had shown her. Perhaps brave Josh had done what Denise never dreamed of in her youth—put his hand to the metal, feeling the little hairs on his head springing up, and kissed the girl tenderly (or puckering, she supposed, not knowing how to do it), while her own pigtails rose like pale wings above her head. It was improbable; but what seemed likely, with this vision in her head, was that Denise's son had surely touched and kissed a girl by now. If not today, with the imaginary electrocuted girl, then surely before. He seemed so sure, fighting through his sickness to tell the story, spitting and singing to himself in the bathroom just now, more sure than she had ever been as a child. That's all there was to it; he was getting to know love.

She approved, but from a great distance. His life was a foreign movie, and she watched in puzzlement, trying to catch the subtitles while the action moved on without her, squinting at the unfamiliar motives, nothing like her own life. Because where had she been at twelve, at thirteen? Out on the porch with two cardboard tubes, two lenses and a roll of tape. Trying to construct a telescope from instructions she'd found in a library book. The tube bent severely, and she couldn't fix the lenses right, but the memory wasn't unpleasant: squatting on the cold tile and peering through the tube at the stars, the moon, fly-casting her line across the sky, hoping some planet would bite the hook and leap into her eye. Two sweaters and a coat, her mother yelling from the kitchen. The numb feeling of her cold nose. There was a vivid passion to it—could she convince herself that this was anything like love? No, it was just childhood's fever still unbroken.

His life would be different. It should be, it must. What was the point, otherwise? Her son would break a heart or have his broken within the next year or so, and she would silently rejoice. To see him woeful as he hangs up the phone, chewing on his gum and stomping up the stairs—it would mean he would be fine. Like measles, love was the kind of thing you had to catch in youth, dispel, so that it would not leap upon you in old age and kill you. So that you would not sit in some damned flat in Italy, she thought. So that you would not mark a postcard with scrawled equations, calculating the perihelion of an ill-named comet you once found with a lover on a hillside. So that you would not bend the equations to suit your hopes—that it will return in time to win him back, to take the chance you botched before—as you sit begging with the numbers like a penitent. Josh's life would be different.

Denise turned back to her notes, breathing deeply and closing her eyes to give her body little breaks, little sips of sleep. *But gravity has a cure,* she wrote, and then stared at the ink, shining there on the yellow page until it dried. These were her notes: It has a cure. There are two moments that we know of when the universe is free of gravity, when it matters so little that it is barely worth the calculation. The first is at the beginning of the universe, say in the first one hundred millionth of a second, when all matter is jammed together into a speck and, next to the other great forces at work, gravity is insignificant. And then also at the end (as she believed), when matter will converge into that single point again and gravity will not matter. The cure rests at the beginning and the end.

These were her notes. She thought of what they meant to her. She thought of Adam again—she was trying so hard not to think of him, but he came to her, and she thought of the morning she left to come to Rome. They both had known, since that moment in the doorway, that she would not be coming back. Denise had even packed all her clothes in boxes in the basement, saying it was for space, and Adam had not said a word. Strangely, though, that last morning had been quiet and serene. They had awakened slowly to the radio, listening to the news. They had made love and then showered together. And then she had gone to the closet and put on the one dress still hanging there. She had kissed her husband without a word and gotten into the cab. He did not come out into the driveway to watch her leave, nor could she see him standing at the picture window watching; she assumed he went on with his day, also, arranging his notes, calling Josh, writing a plot in his head in which she had not left him. Denise did not think of it as leaving him; she considered herself to have lost him. And Kathy. No struggle could regain them. And Eli.

She never learned why he left her; in all those years, Eli kept a friendly silence on the subject, seeing her at conferences, the few times she was in L.A. Just as she had treated him a decade before. So Denise sat at her pad of paper, listening to her son's watery noises in the other room, puzzling over how love had buried itself so quietly. Her husband never mentioned the affair with Carlos. Eli never mentioned it, as Adam knew he wouldn't. And she never thought of that reason herself—because it wasn't true.

She had never swooned into the past's waiting arms; she had never necked in a movie theater with her husband glaring behind her; none of it ever happened.

If she had been there at the restaurant five years ago with her husband and her lover, she would have been furious. She would have grabbed Eli's shoulders and shaken him, yelling, *It's not true! Don't you see it?* And Eli should have seen it, if Adam's careful words had not been axe-strokes on his spine. He should have noticed the man's bitter glare across a breakfast table. He should have recognized the wooden characters in this tale of Denise and the long-lost lover, the unlikely setting, the flimsy motive—the work of a minor novelist desperate to keep his wife.

"Goodnight, Mom."

That was years ago. Denise heard her son and, without turning, pictured handsome long-nosed Josh in the doorway, hand on hip, brown from all yesterday in the sun, burned on his nose and cheeks. His hair would be mussed; his mouth would be hanging open lazily with an unuttered vowel; his eyes would stretch their gray-blue wings impatiently.

Before turning, Denise carefully wrote her final line: *The cure for gravity is time.*

Adam looked up from his book as if he had been struck by a stone. What made him think of it? Not of Denise packing her bags, or of his triumph over Eli at the café. Not those obvious ghosts. He thought of teenage Lydia, standing on a beach to dry her hair, utterly naked under the stars.

He sat on a folding chair in a Bay Area bookstore, signing copies of his book. It was a novel, what Adam called his "great novel of no importance," and he wasn't signing copies for fans; he was signing the store's stock, moving through a stack of hardcovers with the assistance of a bored employee. Then he stopped, pen touching the page, as that memory of Lydia came to him.

It was after their swim and before she left him to go into the jungle. She stood there so young and beautiful, leaning sideways to let her hair drip down, darkening the sand. Adam remembered how she stared at him, and how he knew what this stare meant. He was a teacher; he had seen these stares from young women, had acted on them more than once. But this time was different. Lydia leaning sideways, body glowing in the moonless evening, nipples hardened from the cool breeze. The reddish pubic hair. The stare of longing. He felt his head burning with his sickness and the pot he'd smoked; he should have been in quarantine. But he felt aroused; a moment more, and he would not have been able to stop it.

The bitter doubts about his wife were true. When Lydia told him about the scientists making love out on the spit, hope had finally broken in him. Denise and Eli. It felt as though he'd found his marriage just now on the beach, a gold chain half-buried in the sand, something his wife had long since discarded. Now, in this memory, he held its broken clasp between his fingers. He could drop it, too, right here, back into the sand where it belonged. It would merely be an act of gravity then. He could step forward a few feet and take the towel from Lydia, kiss her, give her the simple thing she wanted. Wasn't this what the moment asked of him? To give the girl what she wanted. He never could do that for Denise; what she wanted from him was too complex—change, variation, genius—no, he couldn't give it. But this girl, twisting her hair onto the beach, staring at him with desire—it was much simpler. What he did now could make so many people happy: Lydia would feel like a conqueror, Eli and Denise could live guiltlessly together, and only he and Kathy would be left alone. It was simple. The balance of happiness fell heavily on one side. The seawater dripped from Lydia's hair, traveling down her arm, down her naked body to the wet sand. People could be happy.

But your duty, Adam reminded himself in the present as he shook the memory from him, is not to make them happy. Your duty is to save your life.

The pen had leaked onto the page, making a black circle a half an inch in diameter. The employee had noticed, annoyed, and Adam tried to smile and sign and move on: *Adam G. Lanham, Adam G. Lanham.* But it came to him again: Lydia, leaning sideways, wringing out her hair. The seconds ticking, passing; the moment passing. The girl, impatient, picking up her clothes to leave. And then backward again, back to Lydia twisting her hair under the comet, staring with desire. He was aroused again, in the present, and Adam thought it was funny he'd be stuck there. His mind, a slide projector, stuck on a random image: not at the scene of Denise's leaving, or of his cruel episode with Eli, but deeper in the past, on the beach with a girl of seventeen. A moment his wife would never guess as being crucial. The choice you didn't make. A hard choice, the wrong choice. Because wasn't he still left with this? Signing stock in a small bookstore, aroused by a girl who was grown by now; a lonely, loveless man. He was no friend to love, he felt, not after what he'd done. So—was this the life he'd fought to save?

Lydia could hardly believe it: The key fit in the lock.

It was late, four o'clock by now, and the sidewalks had been filling ever since the rain had stopped. She'd stayed at the bar with Max far longer than she expected; but with the warmth of the room, the free beer and food, the comfort of this man playing all his tricks to win her back, it was hard to leave. People began to come into the bar— some regulars, some groups of blond women nervously looking the place over and almost leaving—but Max always dealt with them quickly and came back to talk to her. She told him about her father and his lost comet and the sad half-birthday today represented. She told him about the island and her foggy memory of a boy's fall to his death, almost twenty years before. Max leaned his elbow on the bar and rested his chin in his hand—a classic pose from a sculpture—and for that hour or so she regretted that she didn't love him. It seemed like such a waste that she'd be heartbroken over her most recent boyfriend, and here was a decent man, a rare moment, yet she couldn't feel it. There should be a scene here, she thought, with a silent stare across the bar, a drinking bet, a quiet dance under the neon sculpture while Tom Waits growled on the jukebox. But we don't pick them, she thought as she watched him talking. You love them or you don't, and there's not much you can do about it. So Lydia drank her beer, enjoyed the time, and when Max leaned too close and began to whisper in her ear, she smiled. She kissed his cheek and walked away. She felt bad that Max had played it all wrong that afternoon—it was not the time to state one's heart's desire.

Lydia had made her way through the crowds to the one address she had left. Perhaps it wasn't a spare key after all, she considered. Perhaps it was some old key left from a former apartment, a former office or a former car. A key from her college dorm—that women's college that her father always ridiculed, snidely telling people it lay on the "famous Lesbionic River"—or something even older. A former house. The farm back in Sonoma, which she had not seen in nearly a decade, or a key to the barn out back where her old doll must still lie hidden in the hay. The key could be a useless relic, knowing only itself where it belonged. So when Lydia stood at that apartment house on Grove, the smells of a soul-food restaurant next door coming through a vent, she had no expectations. She slipped the key in out of duty. And it fit, caught, and turned. The front door opened and the scent of ammonia floated toward her. She stared at the brass object in her hand. All this time, she had been holding the key to her mother's door.

Lydia had been in her mother's apartment building before, but there was something different about walking up the stairs and knowing her mother wasn't there, knowing she was about to enter an empty place. There would be the couch she'd imagined, and the cat. There would be something to drink in the fridge and a dusty bottle of wine in a high cabinet. The late sun now appearing would flow from the wide windows and, filtered by the blinds and palms set in its way, would crosshatch the floor in an etching of light. This once, though, she would be alone. Lydia felt an excitement building in her, one she recognized as childish, something brought over from her girlhood like a rare orchid brought over on a steamer from the South. There would be filing cabinets unlocked, with records going back thirty years or more. Perhaps even a file marked *Lydia*. Dental records, school reports, complaints from teachers and principals. There would be hatboxes, perhaps, which Lydia would open to discover were stuffed with the letters she had sent her mother in the institution, the unanswered letters. Carefully ordered by date, each ripped neatly at the top—by a younger version of her mother, a woman who, even on pills in some therapeutic-pink room, might have taken her sharp thumbnail, slit the envelope's creamy throat, and blown into the wound to make it gape. On the shelves, there would be photo albums posing as books. Perhaps containing pictures she had never seen, photos of them all together in the sixties—young, jolly father, beautiful mother with her thick eyeglasses, caterpillar Alice, and baby Lydia held in everybody's arms. Photos of some vacation which came to Lydia only in sparks of memory—a cabin with yellow jackets, herself being bathed in a water pail, Alice with an inner tube—now shown in true scale. Photos of the island.

She was at the first landing where the small incinerator door, now welded shut, still bore the words TO BURN. She was excited to enter her mother's place alone, without permission, and she hadn't decided whether she would do it—whether she would rifle through her mother's old things, the objects and mementos the woman had obsessively collected over the years (the botanist's nostalgia). Lydia had, of course, already gone through the medicine cabinets while her mother was there, poking through the pills to make sure her mother wasn't taking something dire and, slowly counting through them, also making sure she took enough. She'd seen the pills, and the gun up in the pantry, and the dollar bills wrapped in foil in the freezer. Those were all the hidden pieces of her mother's mind, and she had seen them. They were no longer crucial—she had accepted her mother's madness long ago, and even preferred its present safely frozen form. What Lydia sought, instead, were the pieces of herself. The ones that, in any ordinary family, would have been brought through the years intact. Instead, Lydia felt like the housewife who, coming across a shard of china, saves it in a drawer on the off chance that one day she will find the rest of the dish.

She was on the second landing—her mother's floor. A spiny display of dried flowers, dusty and a decade old, sat in the window like a time-stopped explosion. Ah yes, the flowers in her mother's room, they would be there, too, she thought as she approached the door. The fresh flowers, the branches of blooming fruit trees, the bowls of seed pods rattling angrily when you disturbed them. The artifacts of her botany, and also those from her other religions. Lydia always forgot about them—they were not part of the old mother. The Buddhist portraits and beads and mystical books—they always surprised Lydia, who was brought up by a father who insisted religion was a hoax. Her mother, back then, had agreed. Scientists sought the meaning of the universe, too, she'd told her daughter. They sought it in the distant stars and how they burned, in contemplating the reality of time, in the pattern revealed when you brushed nail polish on the underside of a begonia leaf (something she once did with Lydia, to show her the little breathing holes there). "But we don't claim to know," the woman had said, touching Lydia's hair. "Religions will give you an answer, but who wants just any answer? It's all right to say you don't know, Lydia. Smart people say it all the time. Try saying it. Do you know why we're alive?"

Lydia, so young, had been upset by this lesson. "I don't know," she told her mother, fearful, knowing that in any other case her parents would have grown frustrated by such an answer.

But her mother smiled that afternoon, holding her daughter's little hand. "I don't know, either," she had admitted. "Maybe nobody knows. Maybe you're the one who's going to find out."

Not me, Lydia had thought. One thing is for sure, it won't be stupid me.

But twenty years later, her mother could no longer accept not knowing. Suddenly, with old age approaching, she had to know. She had to believe in something, and it simply turned out to be Buddhism. And like so many other dissonances in her family life, Lydia accepted this change by refusing to talk about it.

She was at the door. She put her key in the deadbolt lock and, after catching for a moment, it turned. The same with the doorknob. She walked in and the room was nothing like she'd pictured it.

"Mom?"

The blinds were drawn—there was no glowing cat-scratch of light cast on the floor. Instead, a dead brown darkness. The dining room table was piled with books, and clothes lay strewn in the order her mother had removed them—stockings, skirt, blouse, bra—but arranged, by accident, so that they re-created another flattened woman on the floor. There was the smell of garbage, and only later would Lydia realize that it was the flowers she had pictured so vividly— garlic flowers, sitting in a vase of murky green water. The bedroom door was closed. As Lydia walked in, she saw containers of food out on the kitchen sink, a folder of sheet music spread out on the linoleum, and, oddly, a phone neatly unplugged, wrapped up in its cord and set atop the refrigerator. The room contained the muggy disaster of a fishtank left untended.

"Mom?"

Somehow she got the impression that her mother was there. The woman's current project—sketches of the human eye and nasolacrimal apparatus—lay stacked on her desk, and one drawing sat squarely alone, half-inked on thick paper. On it, Lydia noticed, were her mother's reading glasses. By chance, they rested on the drawing so that each lens contained a small human eye, capped with a tear duct and ribboned with muscles, staring into the room. Lydia got the sense that something was unfinished here, that a calm rainy morning had been interrupted and hastily abandoned. She stepped quickly over the clothes and turned the knob to the bedroom door, forcing herself into a cool, breezy room where her mother lay motionless on the bed.

At first, Lydia thought she was dead. The woman lay on top of the sheets, legs together and hair spread out white on the pillow. For a moment, the thought of death came partly from the surprise of seeing her mother so old—Lydia still had an image of the woman from her youth, thin with a tight auburn bun, lowering branches to show her the leaves. She half expected that same mother to appear in this apartment, yet this older woman was always here. That was part of the shock—the oldness of her, the corpselike repose that seemed to come to her more naturally year after year. Lydia rushed to her side, but then stopped, because her mother was clearly alive. She saw the slow breaths, and the dried marks of tears running in a delta through her makeup. Her hands, also, were not relaxed; she held them palms together against her forehead, a folded butterfly. She was not dead; her mother was praying.

"Just a moment, sweetie," she said quietly.

Lydia stood and waited as her mother lay there motionless. She felt so angry to have come all this way, to have wandered through a hopeless day in search of her mother, calling at work, calling even here only to find the woman fallen apart once again, tear-streaked, sewing her body tight with prayer. A moment, she had to wait a moment, and Lydia considered not waiting this time, not laying her hands on this woman in pity and whispering that she loved her. She considered shifting her slippers in the dust of the floor and leaving. Walking back out into the locked-tight world she'd left. Maybe to find Max down at the bar, maybe to drink enough beer to feel as though she loved him. She might end up sleeping behind the bar tonight (not the first time) or, more probably, in Max's cramped room, where the bass of a late-night club downstairs pounded like an angry neighbor on the floorboards. She might do something she would never recall, if she did this, this not-waiting.

Or she could talk. She could snap her mother's spirit just by re-counting her day. The sort of thing her mother often wanted to hear, when she was well, when she sat carefully combed and dressed, with a cup of tea in one hand, a matching saucer in the other. But what could she say about a day lost in the rain? About her father and his comet? About the vague memory of a boy falling from a cliff? About that other boy her mother had never met, that grinning Ali Manday who was dead?

Her mother opened her eyes just then. "Things sort of fell apart. . . ." she began.

Lydia stroked the woman's forehead and she fell silent, expressionless. *The trick,* she'd been told as a child, *is knowing what details to leave out.* There was so much to say. But it was not the time to state one's heart's desire. It was the time to notice one silver hair waving in the breeze, reaching vainly into the air above the woman's face. It was time to take the hair in her hand and tuck it behind her mother's ear. It was the time to study the faint shadow her mother's hands cast along her body, falling to the bedspread and floating again here on Lydia's arm. There were these small farewells.

Lydia hushed her mother wordlessly. She stood up and closed the open window, then turned to the apartment and began to pick up the mess.

The lights came up in ash-blond simulation of the dawn. Martin Swift awoke, trembled a little in fear and then pretended to his granddaughter (who was talking to him about a doll of hers) that he'd been listening all along: "Yes, that's nice, she's very pretty," he grunted vaguely as he blinked in the bright theater lights and the clouds of color moving all around him.

Outside, it was unexpectedly dark and chilly. They came out from the gaping scalloped mouth as from a tunnel of love, all three holding hands, and felt the moist air groping them and pushing the warmth from their shoulders like a robe. Alice leaned down to button Benny's coat. Martin Swift tried to walk to the steps, but his body seemed to disapprove of every move he made; he would lift his leg and feel an ache echoing through the muscles. His hands, as usual, were numb and stiff and useless as paws but still he shook them, as a boy might shake a broken radio, hoping that all the frayed wires and broken tubes would, by chance, fall back into their proper places. The scientist in him knew that the probability was low, but Martin Swift was only human, and so he still thought, like a child, *perhaps. . . .*

"Daddy, Benny wanted to ask you something," Alice said. He could see her, coiled down like a mainspring at her daughter's waist, pushing the large buttons through the cloth. He could see the smear of pink and gold of her face, and he could make out the effort of her smile. She was whispering to her daughter: "Ask Grandpa, honey."

But the little girl was turned sideways, watching something in the distance that Martin Swift couldn't see. A parade or something, a busload of clowns, surely something bright and red to catch her eye on this soft woolen afternoon; he could even hear something like music coming from far away, perhaps a band.

"Honey, honey, ask Grandpa...."

But little Benedicta was twisted in fascination, her neck taut as a lapdog's pulling at a leash, stubbornly sniffing a nondescript thornbush. There was music. Martin Swift quieted his body and looked out toward the streets, and it was like looking at a stall of cheap flowers: soft and bright, varied in color but otherwise all the same. He tried to squint, to reach into those bunches and pull out the striped lily his granddaughter saw. He loved that she stood there watching a distant avenue, thinking she saw something she adored. He loved that she lived in her own world, quietly, alone; it made it seem as if this little girl—frail and silly in the red crocheted hat her mother was pulling over her head—as if she might be like another.

"Honey!" Alice pulled her daughter out of that reverie; the music was gone, anyway. Swift had never found that flower.

Benny looked up, still dazed with recent memory, one hand rubbing her cheek. "Is the moon a star?" she asked.

Children gave you foolish hope; they were a set of random pictures, Swift considered, like the tea leaves in the bottom of a cup, in whose jumble any adult could find a compelling prophecy. And yet you had to depend on this hope, on this brief possible sign, to defend your utter love for them. Children spilled these crumpled hopes from their pockets, unawares, and we, the adults, were forever bending to pick up what we saw as treasures. Little Benny could be a scientist now: She could be anything now that she had asked this question. Martin Swift was overjoyed. "That is a wonderful question," he said, putting out his hand for her to take, ignoring the unnerving numbness when she held his middle finger. "The stars—you know this, right?—are all suns, like our sun."

"They're on fire."

"Exactly. They light up like a lightbulb, and you know how at night? At night, when we're walking around after a party? You can see a woman in a white dress better than a woman in a black dress, right?" The girl nodded. "And yet the woman doesn't have lightbulbs on her dress, does she? She isn't a light. She's *reflecting* light, like a mirror. And the moon is like a woman in a white dress at a nighttime party, you see?"

The girl stared at him, smiling. He looked over at Alice, unbending now and watching him, her face trained on him carefully. Yes, uncoiling like a mainspring, that was exactly it; surely Alice saw herself that way, working her spine into a tension that could make the world move in her direction, cause the people in it to spin like counterweights within her watch. Helpful Alice. It was a setup, the question about the moon. He should have guessed that sweet Benedicta didn't care, didn't think the moon needed an explanation any more than her mother did, or her grandfather. For her, the world was easy and good. She sat in her red hat, staring at an invisible parade. So his daughter Alice was giving him sweet lies. This would be love?

Martin Swift felt tired. He looked away from them and sat down on the step, and it was cold and rough like sandstone. He let his hands rest on his legs and breathed slowly, letting the blurry crowd pass, watching the heads float by like balloons in the misty air. *What's the name of that poet I was thinking of?* He was a distant cratered moon, breathing the people in, breathing them out, causing a tide out here in the pool of the concrete park. It was better sitting down; still, he found it hard to think. There was a terror in these moments, when the thoughts he had taken for granted all his life, had picked wild and untended everywhere, became suddenly dry and rare, hard to find and withering easily, blooming whole only in a forcing jar. There was the terror of loneliness. *The diameter of the coma is equal to one-fourth the interval in seconds times the cosine of the comet's declination. . . .* The mind should have no winter. The spiders in his eyes should never be allowed to crawl inside his skull, spinning their dusty webs there. He had to protect his mind somehow, like those Iberian cities that, defending against Roman attack, burned the palaces around them to save the stone tower of the library. *What is that poet?* His fingers rubbed his forehead slowly, trying to get in. The mind should have no winter.

"Daddy, you need your shot. Benny, you sit next to Grandpa and hold his hand. Daddy, it'll just be a second. . . ."

Manday could not be forgiven. It was the half-birthday of the comet that Martin Swift had discovered that hot afternoon in that island hut, staring at the floating image of a blur, exactly thirty years ago on this day. He remembered Manday's face, so young with the island astronomer's first try at that ridiculous mustache, as Martin ran into his house and joyously demanded that he find the sultan and a telegraph. The man had been eating a bowl of rice, and his fork hovered in the air like a silver dragonfly. He was frozen in what Martin took as joy, as love. Manday's wife stood behind him with her long hair down, young and beautiful, wearing a Western apron over her sarong, solemnly staring, slowly wiping a plate with her checked cloth. That parrot hung silently in a bamboo cage. The room was dark and smelled of earth, but threads of the brightest sunlight came through on all sides, under the uneven boards near the floor, through chinks in the walls, the thatched roof of the house: Light seemed to be falling around them like hay in a barn. It was the anniversary of that moment today, and where was Hayam Manday? Where was his old friend with that astounded expression today?

It was easy to imagine: Far away in that same house. The same wife, grown stout and gray. The same parrot chattering in some foreign language as it picked the green dull feathers from its back. The same dishes, and tables; perhaps the walls, though, had been plugged with cloth to block the light. Manday, who was younger than Martin Swift, still might look older. He would be eating the same rice from the same bowl; he would have chosen the wrong life out there, life on that wretched island instead of his professorship across the bay, his students, his research. He had given that up, and yet . . . yet he insisted on appealing to the CBAT. Perhaps there was a cake there at the table, instead, celebrating the half-birthday of Comet Swift-Manday. Who could ever understand him? You meet a man, you speak with him three or four times, and from those points (like those of a comet hurtling toward the sun) you should be able to chart the whole rest of his orbit. His personality should be clear; the mathematics were complex, but not profound. And yet, eventually, the damned data for this man would swerve and never fit again—maddening! These people—Lydia, Manday, his old wife, all of them—what was one to do?

Alice was at his side, pressing his finger into the little white box, feeding it a little blood. The box was always hungry at this hour. He watched her performing her nursely duties, talking the whole time (although he couldn't quite hear it) in tones to reassure him, and she was close enough for him to see the round bump on the ridge of her nose, the careful blue mascara, the one holy bead of sweat caught in the downy hair between her eyebrows. Alice held the box to the light, frowning and nodding and talking wordlessly. Then she brought out the little tin kit with the needle and he turned away. Benedicta was on the other side of him, holding his finger tight as if he might float off into the soft sky. *I might, my dear, I might.* He could hear her short, wet breaths, and he could smell the powdery odor of her hair that he had memorized just as he had memorized the eclipses of the coming year. He knew the shape of her at a distance—a triangular blob running with two arms straight out at the sides. He knew the shape of her up close—face round and pointed as an acorn, always a shimmer under her nose. But this time he could see so little of Alice in there; he rummaged in Benny's features and found only the pollen freckles, the thimble nose, the plump chewed lower lip that belonged to Lydia.

The needle slid into the crook of his arm. If only Lydia were here, five years old again, beside him. Before she learned that he was nothing but an intellectual. Back when she was his out on the overlook of the island, sleeping under his warm coat on the stone, beneath his own bright star. A mist of red hair beside him that he could stroke as the stars fell from the sky, and her tiny voice talking in her sleep, and the frown of dreaming on her face. She was still here, though—

she was in Benny sitting beside him holding his finger and breathing with a whistle through her nose. He sat and held each feature in his hand; perhaps they were all in here: Ali, Lydia, his wives, the boy who fell, his best friend Manday. Perhaps he hadn't lost them at all. Perhaps, after long enough, time would return the things it borrowed.

1990

near perihelion

One might, one might, but time will not relent.

—Wallace Stevens

The British man had never seen the Pacific before—and there it was, spread out in miles of pounded metal, gleaming in the midday sun among the groves of eucalyptus. He sped happily down this road in the Headlands, and to his left the waters of the Golden Gate ran under the famous bridge in bars of sun and crashed against the cliffs outside his window so that he could reach a hand out and feel the cool pointillism of the air. The city lay across the water, visible in his rearview mirror. He later said that this was what he had come for, this view, this drive down from the battery to Point Diablo jutting out there into the water. It was 1988, a few months before the Loma Prieta earthquake, so all these old roads were still firm and good, begging you to speed on them. The sound of surf and birds and rustling trees, the view tugging you forward, the wind grabbing at your hair. The British man felt a kind of freedom, a weightlessness as the road descended, turning beside the cliffs. The sun was too bright—he squinted, smiling—and eucalyptus trees blocked the scent of every other thing with their medicinal odor. He later told the police that those trees blocked the stop sign as well, the one placed at the entrance to the road from the abandoned military barracks. Now he was rushing toward the trees, though, taking the curves more quickly than he would have back home on the wet roads outside London, and it occurred to him that he'd seen this road before. Was it an advertisement on TV? A car like his, hugging the curves amid the brush and salt spray, in just this brilliant light? His brain flashed for only one second with a vision of another car—small, white, a face turned in terror—and then everything stopped. He found himself thrown forward into the sunlight, blood stinging his eyes and staining the deflated airbag before him. Heaps of broken glass lay everywhere—in his hair, his lap, across his arms—and the sunlight, changing with the leaves overhead, moved across him like a living thing. Birds sang, and the eucalyptus shuddered in the breeze; no other sound came. How much time had passed? He looked up, shaking off the glass, and saw through the hanging remnant of the windshield, as through a break in the clouds, that other car. Wedged against a tree, crumpled along the driver's side. But, most terrifying of all, he saw what looked like a woman's face staring at him from the broken window, staring motionlessly, twisted, wrong, one trickle of blood coiled in a question mark around her lip. She stared at his car for three whole hours before the police were able to pry her body from the wreckage.

The earthquake came half a year later: waves of angry earth toppling overpasses and bridges on one unseasonably hot day, setting the richest areas of the city on fire, killing. That intersection in the grove of eucalyptus, that square of asphalt facing the beautiful ocean, split into pieces and crumbled. The blood and oil had long since washed away, but the tremor erased the scars of tire tracks and embedded glass, and what was left was repaved, undone, forgotten. And once again came the comet.

Manday had expected a coffin. They always had a coffin—Westerners needed their lacquer and their wood, a few brass handles on the thing so it more closely resembled the door to some great mansion. That was the idea, wasn't it? A mansion, glowing grandly in its copse of clouds, and this the door? Ridiculous—*knock-knock, who's*

there? Just awful death. One might as well attach a doorbell to the lid
and have it done with. Manday had sat through many Western ser-
vices in his one black suit, dutifully fanning himself in the California
sun as they mechanically lowered another shining box into the rocky
soil. Fake grass always lined the grave, a hymn was always sung, a
hawk always turned overhead, and then it was either egg salad or
whiskey and, in any case, a long forgetfulness. That was the strangest
part, the forgetting; as if those gathered around the grave in their
new black lace were weeping not over the end of this person, or his
passage, but over his strange misfortune. Yes, their grief always had
this touch of disbelief, surprise. *Awful death*—because this would
never happen to them, of course, they thought as they ate their dev-
iled eggs—*they* were never going to die.

Manday had seen his former students go down like this, wrapped
in American flags, a battered helmet set at the head of the grave. He
had seen colleagues and their wives and children, people he barely
knew, but the one funeral that might have mattered had gone on
without him. Swift, a month before, his heart failing him in bed, old
Swift. The telegram arrived both too late and too early—late enough
that, with two days before the memorial, he clearly was not expected
to make the complex and expensive plans necessary to airlift himself
from his island to California, but early enough that, if he really felt
unraveled, despairing, he could still make it. Yet he had not gone.
He had not even arranged an international call to give his regrets.
He simply had sent a card, and the family's response a few weeks
later gave a kind description of the service: school chapel, a crowd
of international scientists, a quartet of grad students singing the periodic table set to Gilbert and Sullivan. Manday imagined the same
old American grave, the same set of relatives looking annoyed. The
smallest taper of religion set alight. With Ali, of course, it had been
different but, of course, the same.

Manday had expected a coffin, so when he saw Lydia arriving on
the early boat with nothing but a suitcase and a bag, he assumed the
body was coming on the next boat. He had pictured four men in
sarongs lifting a cedar crate onto their shoulders as the young woman
directed with her handkerchief. Yet she assured him this was all, and

then, because he had to pry, she opened her bag, lifted out a box and showed him the aluminum urn that lay within. Ashes—of course, that was how they did things these days. Manday's efficient mind immediately appreciated the idea, admired the savings in space and expense and peace of mind, preferring it to the island's own culture of raised tombs on rocky beds. Why, you could compress the ashes into a lozenge, and keep it gold-plated around your neck! How elegant and simple, Manday thought, and then it hit him—the full understanding that it was his best friend in there. Old growling Swift, his paranoid brilliance stoppered forever now, an evil genie in a bottle.

They stood on the overlook in the gray afternoon: Manday under a parasol, sipping an orange fizz, and Lydia over at the edge, looking out at the ruffles of the overcast sky and the clear broad plane of water. The bright light kept her in silhouette to the old man, and he could see so little of the girl he remembered giving cotton candy to. She was pregnant. Manday could not think of them as girls when they were pregnant. No, they had passed into some other class. Like his own wife: no more smiles, no more beauty; a switch from tending to the present, to him, toward the future. Some child in her belly. He watched Lydia place a hand on her stomach. He knew what that felt like; he remembered touching his own wife's stomach, feeling the hardness of a foot against her soft skin. Beside her, resting on the wall, sat Swift's urn, ready to be emptied once the other guests arrived. How could she know what this felt like for him? The angry, aching loss of that old friend, but also the unspeakable: the triumph of outliving another man.

He had made it to the end of another decade, or nearly to the end. And yet it seemed to Hayam Manday that very little had happened in the world. Mostly, from his vantage point, he watched how the iron grip of Bukit's government was loosening, how General Malak had become President Malak, how people were forgetting the coup and the few boys killed in that demonstration, an accident, a little blood to feed the growing county. Elsewhere, he read about the space shuttles in America—he'd known about the plans, of course, but here it was, happening without him. Women walking in space (an idea that scandalized his wife, as if it were the height of immodesty), the secret shuttle launches that Manday objected to, and then the disaster in 1986 that seemed likely to close down space exploration for good. The newspaper made him cry only three times in that span of years: when he saw that the physicist Richard Feynman had died, when he read that a fire had destroyed the L.A. Central Library and 800,000 books, and when he saw a photograph of Comet Halley taken by the spacecraft Giotto before it was damaged by dust. A boulder darker than coal, shooting reddish jets of light behind it. Some fingertip of God. Otherwise, the world passed by like a serial TV show whose crucial episodes he had missed: jets exploding, terrorists and their demands, presidents and prime ministers rising and falling, scandals, AIDS, earthquakes in California. He had left to forget, and so he allowed himself to forget.

But he could not ignore Swift's death. Worse, it only reminded him that there was double grief to bear: Another telegram had come a year before, another hurried announcement of a death. A car accident in California. Manday had felt fury as he read it, shaking his head and making the tears fly from his lashes. Death should come only for the old! Only for men like Swift, like him! Death: the cheat, the cheat. Was it what the shadow doctors always claimed: the comet's fault? Dripping poison down below, into each unblinking eye?

Today, Manday stood beside the golden dome in full command of the day. He was anxious for the other old scientists to arrive, because he had so much to do. So much planning, fussing, arranging and greeting—because though Swift's ashes might be tossed into the island wind, this was, after all, Manday's great day now. His comet had been recovered—albeit unnervingly late, putting this event off by a year, a bad sign—and this was the perihelion party.

"Wash them again!" Manday insisted to a bartender who had come up the stairs behind him. The boy, tall and sullen with a faint mustache, held two spotted glasses before him. His shoulders bent wearily under his white jacket, and the beads of sweat on his forehead gleamed more clearly than the glasses.

"There is no more hot water," the boy whispered to Manday.

Manday stared, furious, turning the one glass over and over in his hand. Spots, spots—it was not right, it was not right. "No hot water?" he asked, something taut as a wire in his voice.

"It is used up from washing."

"Then boil some!" Manday commanded. Lydia turned to listen, both hands on her belly now, and birds went by in a flock behind her head. The boy just stood there, uncomprehending. The old man, nearly seventy, motioned to include the island, caught in its time lag. He educated: "That's what we used to do, we used to boil the water for the white people. We used to boil it to wash our white shirts for temple. In the . . . in the war we boiled water to sterilize the blades, the bandages, everything . . . and the Jap laundry, the prisoners did it, we'd set up cauldrons on that very beach. . . . It doesn't matter. It doesn't matter. Just do these again."

"The ones with spots?"

Manday looked at him curiously, almost smiling. "No," he said slowly. Then he saw Lydia, her inquiring face, and he lowered his tone. He swatted as if at a mosquito, whispering: "All of them! All of them!"

It was very important for Manday that things be perfect for this occasion. The bar must be all white and crystal; there must be a bower of shade made from green woven bamboo in which the guests could rest; the local women must stop hunting the endangered lizards for their aphrodesiacal tails, at least for the weekend; and the hummingbirds with their poison-red throats must be released, quietly, to seek out the glass tubes of nectar in the garden. He had a vision of how it would be different from all the other times they had viewed this comet. Manday had realized long ago that the appeal of his island was not really in its spectacular view of one solitary meteor shower shed by a comet; only a few Australian amateurs might come to see that now, and only as part of their vacations. No—Manday understood, as Martin Swift never could have, that the island had an allure of geological nostalgia. There was no bomb-testing near here, no hunting, no overfishing or pollution or industry. To the Western world, his island was pure, and so it gained a deeper level of paradise. An island thirteen days in the past, so far from the main island that no insect could survive the flight; the place had its own kinds of insects, glinting as they darted, vicious emeralds, through the jungle. New brands of science had arisen—environmentalism, ecology—and Manday had merely to advertise in a few places, call some reporters, direct their attention to his birthplace. Manday spoke with the president, announced a global conference and found himself at the center of a wild adoration. He looked to the overcast sky; he would give his comet its due at last.

He could not think, as he sent the sad bartender away, about the cauldrons he had pushed onto the beach forty-eight years before. Building a fire while in shackles—a young man of twenty-two, angry at the world—waiting for the women to pour in the fresh water, the soap, and then churning the uniforms for what seemed like hours until they lost their jungle stink. The women lay the clothes out on leaves on the beach, military trousers and jackets and green-red caps, each with its red sun on a white field, drying and bleaching in the daylight. The heat of the fire, the heat of the sun. How the prisoners fainted, tried to drink the boiling laundry water, how they were whipped or ridiculed as the sultan himself sat in his stony white tower, silent. The women in the village, yelling. The return to that cell on the spit, hungry, watching that chesspiece of light thrown at his eye.

"No, give the running water to the women," he insisted to a girl who had arrived after the bartender, showing him the room bookings at the huts, the lower palace, and the new hotel on the unfashionable side of the beach. "Women want running water, yes, Lydia?"

"I don't care," she said, turning back to the view.

The girl sputtered: "But the huts have the garden. . . ."

"They want running water more than gardens. Redo it. And give Dr. Spivak a ceiling fan, he is an important person."

He could not think of his son Ali at the moment, or how, if he lifted his eyes, he might see the broad red back of his wife making her way around the volcano, carrying the basket of flowers and the jug of oil for the noon anointing, nor, off in the distance, how the raised tombs looked like plain white teeth among the vines and trees. And there was another woman he could have seen, coming to anoint another grave marker, on the beach, for her son dead now twenty-five years on this night. The boy who fell; his mother had come every year, with the shooting stars, to mourn him. But Manday could not think of death, nor of the old man compressed into an urn, nor of a high cliff north of San Francisco, two cars embracing beneath a eucalyptus grove, and the woman buried now in a posh cemetery beside her parents.

"Tell the president everything is going perfectly."

The girl departed, bowing. He saw two men walking along the path, surely some scientists arriving for this small ceremony. And then he recognized them: Jorgeson, Spivak. Such stout and healthy middle-aged men now, chatting as he used to with Swift on this very path, walking slowly to the palace. Spivak, rubbing his chin carefully and looking distractedly at a bird-of-paradise flowering gloriously beside them as they stepped from the shade of the palms. He had come after all. Suddenly, from within the golden dome of the stairway, came Manday's grandson, walking toward him across the stones, carefully carrying Manday's old parrot in its cage. The boy's tongue showed between his lips: the look of concentration. The parrot, pale, disheveled, turned one eye to its master and cried "Salaam! Salaam!" as the little boy smiled and looked up to his grandfather at last. Manday motioned to the boy and grinned. He could see Lydia watching him; he didn't care. "Do you see it?" he asked happily, pointing out to sea. Voices rang within the stairway's nautilus.

On the water was the boat carrying the journalists, approaching from over the horizon. A little top hat floating on that pale meniscus. It was still a half hour or so away, but Manday could not keep from staring at it, feeling in his body the shivering, awkward hope of castaways. The day would be his; the comet would be his; it would all be worth it. The years of captivity in the stone hut, the decades of study and smiling and bowing in America, the years stolen from his family, from his sons, from Ali, the rough arrival back here on the island. The life as a scientist floating on a raft of unimportant papers, the phone calls that came from that blind man in Berkeley, begging to have his comet back before he died, the love and distaste that

Manday felt around him. It would all be worth it. They were coming to honor him at last.

"Dad, don't lift that. Let Henry get it."

"Henry's not here," Adam said.

Josh held the box against his hip, pointing at his father. These were his things, his belongings wrestled from his canceled college life and carted across the bay to San Francisco where, under the watchful eye of his father, he might thrive again. Adam looked at his son: nineteen, but so commanding, so in control. "He'll get it later. You bring the lamp," Josh said, then went inside the house.

Adam put his box down, on which was written *Books A–J,* and turned to the thrift-store desk lamp beside him. "Just the lamp?" he asked, then looked around at the piles of heavy things his son would never let him carry. "Why am I even here?"

Josh was back, sweating heavily. "It'll be over really soon, Dad. I don't have much to move."

"Well, I'll take you to dinner in a little bit. Decide where you want to go."

"I don't care."

"We should explore. It's your new neighborhood."

"I have time, Dad."

That was true enough, Adam thought, but how did the boy know it? Wasn't it the quality of youth to be impatient, to stretch out in time and yet, paradoxically, to feel that there was not one moment to be wasted, as if the hours spent asleep or alone would be counted against you in hell? But Josh seemed in no hurry, wiping the sweat from his head and then replacing his baseball cap, breathing heavily and lifting the very box he had forbidden his father: *Books A–J.* He had a nineteen-year-old son who alphabetized his books. The very soul of patience and order. And yet despite all his maturity he was still so young, and made mistakes, like this one. Not just the Christmas vacation surprise where Josh assembled a turkey-and-stuffing sandwich and announced he was taking the next semester off to pull himself together, to look at his life, but this mistake happening right now. This pile of broken furniture and boxes hauled into a Victorian flat. Josh had taken time off from college for this—of course to deal with his mother's death, but obviously also for this—in order to move in with his boyfriend: Henry, the owner of the flat, a man of twenty-six. It was a mistake, the kind of mistake a parent can't tell the kid about until it's long over. The kind of mistake you worry about at night as you sleep alone, picturing your son sitting in a room of older men with wineglasses, your son wanly smiling and trying to seem bright as they all snicker. Hard to take, hard to take. We'll see, Adam thought. He looked at a long crack in the entrance's mosaic; one good sign, at least, that it had survived two earthquakes.

Josh lifted the box from under his father's arm, and Adam noticed that he'd been wrong about the alphabetizing. *Books A–J*, yes. But it wasn't Josh's handwriting after all; it was Denise's. Not Josh's books, but theirs—his and Denise's—from their last move to the city. A borrowed box. Yes, that seemed more right, he thought as Josh went inside again, appearing a moment later in the room above. His mother had been an alphabetizer for sure.

"When's Henry coming home?" Adam yelled when Josh reappeared.

The boy stood in the doorway, looking around at the boxes on the sidewalk, the empty truck parked across the street. Not much stuff in the life of a nineteen-year-old, even this one. Josh, hands on hips, a handsome boy.

"He usually gets out of work at seven."

"So we have time for dinner."

Josh smiled and stood there. So much of Denise in him, in his dusty reddened skin, the shape of his nose and the color of his eyes. A handsome boy; not stunning, but the kind of boy, Adam supposed, a man of twenty-six would cherish. There was something missing, though, of the cockiness Josh had as a youth, the brazen confidence and imagination. Something had hurt him a little, and Adam could only guess that it was love. What else could it be? He could only hope it wasn't Henry, that it was some other man whom Adam hadn't heard of. Surely there were some of those; Josh never confided in his father, certainly about these things, and Adam would not have known what to say in any case. A man breaking another man's heart—what advice did he have for that? He merely hoped that this Henry was a good man, a kind and unclever man, the sort of man you settle for. That he loved Josh a little more than he was loved back.

"Does Henry keep beer in the fridge?" he asked, walking toward the door.

Josh stepped out of his way with a cynical expression. "No," he said. "But I do."

"Good. I need one," Adam said, walking inside.

"And one for me!" he heard Josh shouting. But Adam didn't go straight to the refrigerator. This was his first time in the flat alone, the first without Josh leading him from room to room explaining their functions ("and this is the bedroom" had been his favorite, gesturing to the clean white comforter as both father and son turned the same shade of red); like a child dressed up for company, the tour had been sweet and unconvincing. Something was not being said, but what more could be hidden? Two men in a Victorian flat: one teenage Josh and one much older Henry Wong, the son of a disgraced city planner—could there possibly be more to the story? He pictured the two of them that morning before his visit—Henry in his suit and tie and Josh in sweats—working quickly, taking photos off the walls and stuffing them into a filing cabinet. Adam opened the filing cabinet: nothing but files. He imagined them turning book spines inward on the bookshelf, thinking he wouldn't notice; books that might point to some other portion of their lives. He pulled out the misordered books he found: old college literary theory, novels (not his own). In the medicine cabinet, just antibiotics and eye cream. In the refrigerator, just beer, leftovers, and half an onion swelling with moisture on the cold shelf. He took two beers and popped the caps. He sipped his beer, relieved.

"Hey, do I get a beer?"

Josh was standing in the kitchen, watching him.

"Here," Adam said, handing it over. "And here's to your new place. Here's to you and Henry."

Josh clinked bottles with him without a word and swallowed his beer greedily. Then he looked at his father with such precision that it made the older man shiver. It occurred to Adam that he might have this all wrong: What if their roles had been switched while he wasn't looking? Then Josh would be the careful, worrying one, searching for a clue to heartache. And his father would be the irresponsible one, the headstrong man making bad choices, keeping old secrets. Maybe Josh thought his own life was fine, stable, with his youth and this new love to steer him, but that his father's might topple at any moment. A lonely widower in San Francisco. A man who'd lied and fought to save his wife, and then could not even save her.

"You think Mom would like Henry?" Josh asked at last.

"Why do you ask that?" Adam heard himself giving this careful, parental answer.

His son looked at him as if it were obvious. He said, "I wonder all the time what she'd think. I hated it, how she always had opinions about what I did. It's not like I miss that. But I guess I was so used to knowing."

"I never learned to figure out what she'd like or wouldn't."

"You think she'd disapprove."

Yes, Adam thought. *Of course she would. Of course she'd want you to pick your life so carefully, because of how it sticks to you.* But he said, "No, of course she'd love him."

Adam looked over at a picture on the kitchen table: Josh and Henry at the beach, grinning. It was a photograph like this that had first made Adam understand about his son: on the wall of his college dorm, in a nice frame, just a photo of Josh and a friend. Some young man he didn't know, tall and blond, standing beside his son. Nothing overt. But something about their smiles, something about the expense to which Josh had gone for that frame, its careful placement, had made everything quite clear.

But his son was speaking: "I know what I'm doing, Dad."

"I never said you didn't," Adam said.

"I love him, Dad."

Oh, that isn't what I want to hear, Adam thought as he smiled. He patted his son's hand, looking at his face, which was so pained and unsure. *It turns out that doesn't matter at all.*

He thought briefly of Denise, as Josh must have been doing. It happened all the time—whenever he threw away her junk mail, or used her old shampoo or answered the phone and realized it would never be her. The image that came to him was not one of the stock images he kept of Denise—posed for his memory in the kitchen, in the shower, in the bedroom smiling—this one was of her arriving wearily from Rome through that airport gate. The tired expression and blond-streaked hair all out of place, the odd Italian jacket, the overstuffed purse weighing down one shoulder. She came out of the gate and he saw her, not knowing whether he should hug her, and then he rushed forward anyway and held her and she whispered in his ear, *I'm coming back, Adam.* Not that she *was* back, but that she was *coming* back; she was still on her way. She slept for days after that. The image was of Denise at the gate, so exhausted and unpretty and old, longing to fall into his arms. Not love, not passion. Just the sense to know that he was all she had. It was the most he could ask for.

After Rome they had only three years together. Had he known, he would have quit his stalled novel and taken her around the world, indulged her with presents of gold and diamonds, fed her dangerous foods and filled her up with wine. He would have talked her into sex in a minaret over Istanbul, no birth control, just the two of them the way they'd been as young people back in Berkeley. A passionate gamble, little chances taken again. Rather than hold her close and hoard her, he would have pushed her out of airplanes, screaming happily; made her swim with sharks; run with her across a war-torn nation— he would have taken every risk because why not? What worse thing could happen than what was already going to happen? Of course he had not known. So, instead, he trapped her at home as much as he could; he kept her safe, watching TV while their son was off at college. She would fall asleep on the couch with her mouth open, and he would lead her into bed. Years passed like this.

Then the call, the police. He had been in his office, struggling over a new novel long overdue at the publisher, and the phone's light began to blink. A phone for the deaf, something he had purchased to keep himself undistracted, but it didn't help at all; he always watched it as it blinked, made its silent plea. This time, a rare time, he picked it up. A torrent of information, carefully given to him in a list. It was easy to take as a list: first an accident, then trapped inside the car, and no not alive, and you can identify her here or at the morgue. He took it all very calmly, packing his papers and getting his car from the lot, driving through traffic to the Headlands road and even taking note of the view from the Golden Gate Bridge. A hawk hovering in the hot blue. Because it wasn't true, of course. Even when he saw her on the hill, it wasn't true; on that beautiful high point with the trees all touching his shoulders, patting him with every breeze that blew. The men had just laid her out on a plaid blanket on an incline of grass, her arms and legs outstretched not in the way a person would lie, but in the way a child would draw a person. A hand bent the wrong way. The men were very proud of their effort, the hours wrenching her from the car, the careful way they had arranged her broken body before taking her to the ambulance. They presented his wife, and stood in a row, looking at him as if he should applaud. He smiled and felt bizarre. Denise, wearing her new jewelry of broken glass, the gleaming strands of hair caught on her lips, and a tree of blood on her forehead. What he felt upon seeing her was rage—and not at some abstract Fate, not at the neglectful sun which moved, unstopping, in the sky, but at her. At his wife and this new betrayal. The thoughtless dead.

Adam was sitting at the kitchen table, caught in a box of gray light, with his son staring at him again. Both of their beers were empty. Yes, his son was the worrier and he was the one on the edge.

"Let's go," he said, and Josh's face lit up as it had when he was a little boy.

They were quickly up and outside, dizzy from the beer, breathing in the city air, colder now that the fog had settled. Adam was wearing one of Henry's coats, brown wool, expensive, wonderful to feel. Josh was beside him, walking quietly with a little smile. Such a bad life?

"That café down there," Josh said, pointing down the block where Adam could see only an empty metal chair on the sidewalk. "Henry was in there in the earthquake."

"Really?"

"There's a crack in the asphalt—look, see, here."

"There's a lot of those."

"He said he was reading and he fell over. Not from the quake—from the surprise. Henry's a little jumpy."

Adam had been sleeping that morning of the quake, heard a crash, then run into the living room to see all the awful crystal figurines, ones Denise's mother gave them years ago, falling to the floor. A poltergeist seemed to be picking them up, one by one, and dropping each of them with a tiny shattering. Adam was living alone in the house by then, and felt a particular joy at the violence of that day. Then he had called Eli. He didn't know why; Adam was always calling Eli those days, trying to get him to chat, emote, anything. He had phoned him to tell him that an earthquake had happened but not to worry. Some of Denise's crystal had broken, that's all. Eli was silent on the other line.

Josh was still talking. "I think we were all a little jumpy. I hit my head on a lamp."

The calls to Eli had grown important to Adam, ever since the day of her death when he found himself phoning the poor man from the scene of the accident. Adam had stood on that hillside looking at her body, enraged by his wife's departure, by this eviction from his own life, and grabbed a police phone from a car. He got Eli on the line and that was when he felt it—as he heard Eli's soft *hello*—felt what had happened to him. Adam began to sob, telling his wife's old lover everything, every gruesome detail that he saw—her earlobes darkened with blood, her eyelids and jaw so stiff—wishing Eli could be there to embrace him. Eli would understand. Eli would hold him and whisper the kinds of words Denise would have offered, comforting words, lovers' words, because Adam felt somehow that he and Eli were the

closest thing to lovers; that now, with her gone, they were left together. Yet Eli had said nothing for a long time, until, before hanging
up the phone, simply: "Thank you for telling me."

"You want to eat there?" Adam asked.

"What, here?" Josh said, concerned. They had reached the café,
which Josh mentioned had suffered only two broken plates in the
earthquake. "Crepes or something?" The door was propped open, a
dog leashed to a rail outside. Within, two women sat sipping coffee.

Adam said, "Crepes sound good." He was trying to be flexible, to
be anything for his son.

But he thought once again of what he'd done wrong. Perhaps he
shouldn't have packed up her equipment, her charts and textbooks
and terrifying logs of stars. Perhaps he shouldn't have given so many
away to colleagues, or sold the rest, keeping only a few beautiful
drawings for himself and Josh. Perhaps he should have done what
he'd longed to do: buried it all with her. The way King Tut had
been buried with his ships, his chariots and dogs, and three hundred
servants for all the tasks he needed done in hell. If King Tut was to
have tasks, Adam thought, then Denise would as well: to view the
stars from the other side of the firmament, to look down on that
etched globe of light. Or no, he thought; it would be an Egyptian
hell, where the sky is a goddess. The sky is Nut spread naked above
the earth, and so Denise would sit above her in a sling. An exalted
servant, Denise would pick the stars, those burrs, from the goddess's
weary back.

"No," Josh said after a moment. "If you're paying, I want Thai."

"There's Thai in this neighborhood?"

Josh laughed. "Isn't there always Thai?"

"I want to tell you something, Josh," he said, stopping in the street.

"What?" Josh's young face wore a blue veil of shadow from the
awning, and a breeze brought in particles of fog that caught in his
hair, on his lashes, a net of little beads spread over his worried face.

"I want to tell you," he repeated, surprised by himself, and then
Adam gave his son the story of his marriage. It made no mention of
Carlos or Eli or the lie told before a heart-shaped cookie could be

eaten. It made no mention of the rage on a cliff near a broken body. This was the version he wanted Josh to keep, the permanent version, the final draft to be published in his son's mind. The story his son would tell Henry, maybe years from now, as they lay together in their own kind of marriage bed. This story began with the dinner party at the Spivaks, seeing his wife across the room in a zigzag dress. Her distracted heart, and how he won her. The struggles of her career, and his, their early poverty in Berkeley set against the splendor of the wedding her parents threw. And Josh's birth, and the new house in Santa Cruz. . . . Josh looked interested but confused under the awning, sure these were details he already knew by heart, simply by being there himself, but Adam pressed on as their stomachs grumbled and the air dropped shawls of mist onto their shoulders. He told him details so he could imagine it, picture this life as real. He knew he was falling into the role of fathers, who will surprise you, oddly, by saying things like this so that their boys will love them.

But he also wanted Josh to know it would be good, his son's own life. Like a lunatic, or a man in love, he went rifling through the drawers of his memory, picking out anything of value and handing it to his bewildered son—"She begged me to quit smoking, and would hit me with a wooden spoon if she smelled cigarettes on me!"; "I used to sit beside her at the telescopes, midnight, two in the morning, and hand her doughnuts"—piling old heirlooms in the poor boy's arms because he wanted to give him the best. Not the truth, but the best. The best of his life, of his wife, of himself; the best lies, the important ones. So that he would finally see that fathers, meekly turning over steaks on grills, talking nonsense about money or grabbing their guts in front of mirrors, could be the walking cemeteries of old loves—just as Josh himself was. Just as this day was, with Josh stepping into a life with Henry Wong like a child stepping into a stranger's car.

When he was done, Adam stood there panting, feeling excited and alive.

But his son simply looked at him, hands thrust firmly into his pockets, leaning against a wall and examining his father from the long distance of their years. "Dad, I know," he said. A look of pain and amusement, a little love. "I know." Around them, the fog, that flock of doves, fluttered in the failing twilight.

Eli had learned of his life's mistake on the lip of a volcano. It was back in 1986 on a visit with his old colleague Jorgeson to the Mauna Kea observatories, as they stood on the crater struggling to breathe in the chill, thin air. It was just after the space shuttle had exploded, and scientific programs everywhere could feel the congressional finger on the switch, waiting for a word of funding, poised to close them down. So Eli and Jorgeson had come as experts to promote this project, and morning mists spread below them, filling with the sun's faint ginger light and hiding the northern volcano, Mauna Loa. They had sipped their coffee on that morning, talking of the Keck domes to be built in the next decade; and of Swift, who was merely ill then; and of Kathy, of Denise. Then Eli, he didn't know why, asked the ugly Swede about Carlos. It struck him, as the blond astronomer turned and blinked, that he had been here before. A different view, twenty years before, with Denise urging him to pry this same information from this same odd man. Eli had felt a nervous shiver as two distant pieces of his life touched, stuck briefly, and parted.

"Carlos?" Jorgeson repeated on that cold morning three years ago, wrinkling his soft face in concentration.

"Your friend Carlos. The handsome one."

Then the man's face settled: "Oh, you mean the military man. Did you know him? I haven't heard from him since he was reassigned to Africa, I think. Back in the seventies. Is he okay?"

Eli shivered again. "Africa?"

"He's been there for years. Never coming back. That's right—he wrote me a letter in 1973 and I think I never replied. I always forget whose turn it is. People are so touchy." Then Jorgeson, turning his back on the breathtaking view, pointed to the ground. "Ten-meter lenses! How will they do it? It dazzles me, Spivak, absolutely...."

Carlos in Africa, for years—the idea was still falling, as from a great distance, from Jorgeson's chapped lips into Eli's mind. Falling, turning, growing larger, forming a shadow on his eye as he looked up, unable to move, unready for the blow. Not in her bed—in *Africa*. And Adam, sitting in that L.A. restaurant, smiling as he licked the chocolate from his heart-shaped cookie. It seemed so improbable—conventional Adam, stuck in the concrete nouns of his novels, play-acting for Eli's benefit and building his little lie—how could it be true? Such a fragile lie, as well. One broken so easily, such as now, here, with this man. Carlos, the old lover whose face had burned in Eli's mind so many sleepless mornings, driving him to destroy his affections—he had been in Africa all along. There was no man in a movie theater kissing sweet Denise. No letters hidden in coat pockets, no whispered calls. He saw Adam and that chocolate-smeared smile again. What a punch line to the whole affair. *Africa. For years.*

And he understood, as Jorgeson rattled on about hexagonal mirror sections, that the lie was not so fragile after all. Adam had never depended on his own performance. He could never have hoped to be such an actor; in hindsight, even those sighs and expressions of fear that had seemed so convincing looked flimsy, amateurish. It occurred to Eli that the poor man must have been fighting down an urge to bare his teeth at Eli. Instead, those silly sighs. That chocolate smile. But of course what made the lie so strong was not its content, nor its likelihood, nor its presentation. It was Eli himself. He saw that. It was Eli's own stubborn pride. The anger flashing in his skull, singeing every doubt. It amazed him most of all that Adam had known all about that and with a few easy sentences had twisted Eli's heart, like the cartoon barrel of a gun, to shoot itself.

Then there was Denise. The clouds were burning off, revealing the steep slope of the volcano and there, glittering beyond, the silver rind of the sea. There was Denise as he saw her just at this time of the morning, five years before with another mountain view—from Tranquillity, searching for a comet. There was Denise's face as he told her it was all over, the look of something ruined by the rain, and her eyes in the car as she drove him down the mountain: two clenched fists. It had felt so gratifying to sit beside her and feel her hatred—it was the same brand he had felt. Eli had passed on that disease. He knew what it felt like to search for a word to save things; he knew what it felt like to know there was no word. All there in her eyes, locked tight, all there in her shaking hand on the gear shift. He knew she longed for him to take the hand in his. An inch away, an inch. And he would not do it. No, it occurred to him as he stood on the volcano looking back, you do not become a monster with a little lie, like Adam's. You become a monster in the inch that might save someone, the inch you will not move.

He tried to think of what to do. Five years had passed: five years of minimal contact, friendly conversations at conferences and dinner parties, each day numbed like a tooth and then extracted. He could have spent those days with Denise—but he couldn't run to her and tell her that. It's what he knew he was supposed to do at a moment like this, grab the oversize military phone and make them contact Dr. Lanham in Santa Cruz, put her on a plane to Hawaii, lift her in a helicopter to this high observatory where, an oxygen mask held to her face, she would step onto the lava rocks and make a simple sign of forgiveness. Offer her mask for him to breathe. A man and a woman, forty-six by then, ready to begin what should have started half a lifetime ago. He could have done it if he wanted; he could have shut Jorgeson up and run to the observatory office. Eli stood there watching the twin volcano, Mauna Loa, appear from the mists. This wasn't quite what he wanted; things were more complex. Time was passing, flowing quietly, taking everything with it. So much had changed.

Denise was still married; maybe it was best to say she had returned to marriage, had spent a lonely sabbatical on the Tiber watching the mechanical birds in the piazzas, and finally come back to Adam and Josh, unpacked her boxes in the basement, and begun at last the life she'd promised him. Why shouldn't she? After all, Adam was the man who fought for her. It had always seemed so sad to Eli that she'd be left with Adam, that dull athlete, that meager partner for her life; but on the volcano Eli no longer saw it that way. You can either look around and long for the people who have left you, he thought, or you can forget them; you can turn to face the ones who stayed. There was something to be said for staying. And at middle age, why would Denise ever choose a different life? An old one that had always failed before? That would be the choice of a gambling woman, and Denise, for all he loved her, was never anything like that.

He did still love her. It was horrible, it was the first thing he felt, the thought that he loved her. Not in the way he first had, not in the dumb excess of youth when he ignored his marriage, whispered so many promises in that hut out on the spit, when he ran to her doorway in the fog to try to wreck their lives for this small chance. When he stood with his finger on the doorbell, unable to make it ring. This time was different; this was a young man and an older one listening to the same piece of music. The first is astounded that such a thing exists, that no one has ever played it for him before; he wants to stand up and shout his passion to the orchestra. The second is just surprised to hear it again, one he had sadly forgotten, and he's listening carefully now for that rapturous second movement, just where the violins descend. It made Eli want to lie down on the lava rocks and sleep away the past five years. He struggled for breath in this airless place and saw his past rewritten, saw a woman set right. And he felt that whatever might come, he at least still had this. A page of that music. Such a different sensation from when he was young—but the same love, the same.

Yet his life had changed, also, and in ways that left him, oddly, no more free than Denise. All his choices had been based on the idea that he had to come up with something else to long for. Not that silly, obvious affair with a blond girl, but something real. A few months after the last comet search, he sat down with Kathy and told her everything that had happened, and she simply stared at him, face stained with red, and said "I know" with such finality and despair that he realized of course she'd known, of course she had. Kathy had simply expected his longing to be kept hidden, like a photographic plate, meant only for a special room of one's mind. Now that he'd shown it to her, now that he'd turned the light at last onto his broken heart, it was ruined. They could no longer have this life.

So they had separated and, at last, divorced. Though the legal tangles were complex, and she was bitter and unyielding in taking her share, it upset Eli to realize that they really had so little to split up. A house, furniture, the silver, gardening tools, and books. No children, of course. And the things that mattered to him—his job, his private life inside his mind—she could not touch, and had never touched. He had always thought they were attached in some great, parasitic way that would allow no separation; but in the end he felt they were simply two great ships, lashed together to wait out the high waves of an ocean storm. It was simply a chore, and no terrible one, to cut the ropes at dawn.

He had his apartment in Hollywood, and Hector, the dog he'd bought five years before and which Kathy had never cared for, never even called by name. He was the interim chair of his department and things were looking good. And, after a few years of dating, he found a girlfriend, Penny, a thin and big-eyed Jewish girl from Baltimore who taught high school botany. A little cynical, but a bit younger and therefore impressionable, adoring even if she didn't know it. When he was out of town, she took Hector on walks. They had begun to own things together: season tickets to the Dodgers, two paintings (one at his place, one at hers), a plate-filled picnic basket kept in the trunk of her car. The ship-lashing process had begun; marriage was obviously coming within the year. Soon they would own rings together, and furniture, and maybe even still a child. Did he dare to upset the world he'd made without Denise? Could this be, perhaps, the way things were supposed to turn out?

No, he decided, as Jorgeson chattered on about lenses and computers, as the stark sunlight came through the mist like a pail of water thrown into a basin. No—and yet this isn't like any other kind of risk. Even if he called Denise, even if he wanted that, even if she forgave him—it was difficult to see what might come then. You chance everything, ruin everything once again, wreck it all and still you aren't left with a fortune. Still you're only left with love; another risk, just as great, just as awful. It couldn't be done. At twenty, of course; what was there to lose at twenty? Thirty, perhaps. Not forty. Not fifty. And yet—he couldn't simply do nothing. He could not stand on the edge of the dormant volcano, realizing his terrible mistake, and not move to correct it. Not with this feeling come alive inside him again, eating him. Eli stood breathing heavily and thought of what should be done. Not just to make the most people happy; that was impossible. He only wanted to be able to live with himself. And, gradually, as the light filled the valley on that morning back in 1986, he knew exactly what to do.

For young Josh, in San Francisco, it was beginning. His dad had left, said his quiet goodbyes, and any minute now, Henry's shadow would appear on that curtain—the window curtain of the front door. It would fall across the pleats, a jagged profile. Then Josh would hear the scratch of the key, the unseen mechanism of the lock. And then of course the door would open, and then of course it would be Henry Wong himself—first with his blank face, the face of a man clearing his mind of the working day, looking around, and then, when he saw Josh there in the room with all his boxes piled around him like a pharaoh with his treasures, a second lock would turn in the doorway.

It was how Josh imagined it. He stared at the door, a man making a tough decision, but still very much a boy in his hopes, his expectations of how things might turn out. He had been raised to believe that great things would come to him, and he had never questioned it. They did, they always did. His father had driven off up the hill, and the sun was setting, and Josh was here, where he had waited so long to be: staring at this plain white paint, the stiff pleats of a small curtain, the first truly shut door of his life.

Only the young could understand. A room, a hall, a life forever spent in bathrooms yelling "just a minute, jeez!" and nighttimes endured, the first part, listening to the clink of ice in your parents' drinks as they came upstairs, letting the dog into your room to wake you with a tongue smelling of leftovers, or the second part, pretending to sleep while your roommate turns the crackling pages of a book, or hums to his music, or masturbates with a mournful rustle of the sheets. A truly shut door. As a guitar, restrung to replace the taut and brittle old strings, relaxes into warmer music, so Josh could feel, sitting in the chair and staring at that shut door, the nerves of his spine falling into their new places. Any minute the door would open onto a new life.

He turned on music, rock music, the kind of stuff that Henry raised an eyebrow to but tolerated. He turned it up loud and beat his head to the rhythm, all the while watching the door, and he opened another beer. He needed loud music, and booze, because this was all too much for silence, and because he was really so teenagerly, still, feeling the raucousness beginning in his heart and not being careful with it, not holding his palm against his chest and feeling the frantic beat there, listening quietly, but wanting it to spill out everywhere, loud and boisterous. Henry could not understand it when young Josh woke up in the morning—there! right there, in their bed!—and started to bounce naked on the mattress. When he sat next to Henry in a movie theater, staring at him, whispering that he wanted to become so small that he could crawl into his ear and live there. When he turned on every radio in the house when "their song"—or so Josh called it, since it was playing when they met at a party—was on the air. Another raised eyebrow from quiet Henry Wong, another bemused kiss as he watched the scene. But surely it was what Henry loved about him. The boy's belief that he, Josh Lanham, the alchemist, the genius, had invented love itself.

He did not believe his parents had ever felt this. How could it be true? He had seen all the photos—he had pored over albums and boxes with his mother just the year before she died, talking about all those characters from their past. He'd seen the picture of them both when they were first dating: a dinner party with the Spivaks, and all of them sitting around a card table in his mother's old efficiency in Berkeley. His parents had to sit on the bed, and the Spivaks sat in folding chairs; and though they grinned with heady youth, and though a bottle of wine sat empty on the table, still their expressions looked so weary, and their clothes seemed as if they'd be coarse and uncomfortable in any era; and there was something yellowed and dusty about the photograph, as if the world had been covered in a cloud back then. Yet there they were, very much in love, and in the background, a door. The first truly shut door of his mother's life. Josh did not believe it. You should be able to see love; like those

Russian aura photos, it should spot and distort the negative and give the lover a dark glow. But he couldn't see it there, in anyone. Some people walked by on the street; Josh could hear their laughter over the music, and for a moment he wanted to be them. He wanted to be people passing on the street, looking up at a frothy Victorian house with one light on, music coming loudly through an open window and the shadow of a boy running around, arranging things, putting things away, singing along. He wanted to feel their jealousy. He wanted to be jealous of himself. He took another swig of beer.

They had never done this, his parents. They had never gone on a date to the Sutro Baths and walked along the ruins of that turn-of-the-century bathing parlor—a set of rocky foundations against the pounding ocean, wind-bashed junipers, a Roman setting—or visited the Musée Méchanique with Henry Wong and watched as he put a quarter in an antique fortune-telling machine—a typewriter moving to invisible hands—and would not let Josh read his printed destiny. All the old penny machines, the Plantation, the Opium Den, the Gold Rush, with wildly spinning dolls in age-tattered clothes, and how this man beside him—square-faced, a birthmark on his nose, lips always apart as if he were about to speak—stared at Josh in a manner so different from the college boys. Not mere desire, not loneliness. He grabbed Josh's hand and took him outside into the sun again, onto the wide concrete patio crumbled by the earthquake. They stepped into a little building, the Camera Obscura, and it was so unreal, utterly dark except for the ocean pounding blue and white on a giant horizontal disk. Henry kept staring, and Josh, nervous for once, stupidly explained the lenses, boring them both (damn his mother for telling him!). His heart was a bagpipe, wheezing, and when Henry took his hand and kissed him, Josh thought it might be the last thing he would ever do—he might die, and this optical hut would be his tomb.

"As long as it holds with the laws of physics," Josh's mother once told him, paraphrasing the inventor of the electric motor, Michael Faraday, "nothing is too wonderful to be true."

She had been speaking of scientific theories. It was years ago, during their time together in Italy, when they sat on a tiny balcony, two metal chairs crammed in there, eating salami whose skin he unwound in long, translucent strips. His mother, a little drunk, had joked about being asked to join the Academy, and how all scientists secretly hope for it, the way writers hope for the Nobel, silently, just a little. The National Academy of Sciences, she told him happily. Well nothing is too wonderful to be true. But Josh took its meaning for himself. *Something terrible has happened,* his father told him years later on the phone, but Josh had not been able to hear it over the stereo in his dorm room, and his father repeated: *I said something terrible.* After the call, after the shock and the burial where rich relatives appeared with excited faces and his father threw a melodramatic rose onto the coffin, Josh understood that his mother had been speaking of the future from that balcony, a future she would never see, of course, with him here in this room, waiting for his lover's shadow to appear at the door. Knowing nothing at all of love, she had still meant this.

No one missed her like he did. His mind tricked him to forget she was gone, and this was easy to do, because she had already faded from his mind these last few years. The crises of college, the constant revelations—they had nothing to do with her; she dwindled to a voice over the phone, a cook at holidays. If you had asked him, a year ago, what his life was like, he would have described everything to you, each bright detail and fumbled affair, everything except her. She did not count; she was something other than life. That made her doubly lost. Missing her was not an obvious grief, like his father's, but a curse. And when he thought of her, it wasn't as she'd been before her death, as a fiftyish woman who dyed the gray out of her hair, but as she'd been years ago in Rome, when both their lives seemed about to change.

It was the one time he told her everything. Back when he was too young for love, thirteen, terrified to be without her on the streets but also overjoyed. He was thrilled to have stories to give her about the things she never saw: the boats, the men fighting in the streets, the girls on mopeds. He came back each day to tell her, there on the balcony, and he felt her warm gaze searching his face for some sign. Who knew what she saw there? He felt that gaze when he told her about the friends he'd made, the girl who sold him a paper flower, the science museum. The handsome Italian man who had placed his hand on a metal sphere, kissed a girl and made her hair stand on end. That had made his mother smile a little, chewing on her salami. But the gaze made him leave something out, something he wasn't sure he could tell her. How they had all stood in a line in front of the static electricity machine, each waiting his or her turn; and the man leaned down to touch them, one by one. The man had kissed the women on the cheek, touched the men on the forehead, and when Josh finally stood there and had that grinning man look into his eyes so unwaveringly, press his warm hand to the boy's face, he wasn't sure if it was truly science that caused each hair on his body to stand on end.

Henry was late. Josh felt a little tipsy already. The beer with his dad, another at their brief dinner, now this one. He took another swig. The sun was setting, streetlamps were coming on, and as the curtains leaked their light into the room, Josh stood and waited for the next song to start. No, love was not what they'd shown him. Not the fine accumulation of affection. Not the sediment of the heart. It was something that put you in grave danger and, like Josh's own as he sat once again to stare at the door, it lay spring-loaded in your chest.

"Dr. Spivak! Dr. Jorgeson!"

Eli had not even stepped from the humid, echoing chamber of the dome before Dr. Manday, in a linen suit, his broad form eclipsing half the visible sun, approached with arms wide open. A little boy ran after him with a parasol, struggling to keep his grandfather's forehead in the shade. The man seemed so overjoyed, so immense with pride, that Eli could hardly believe this was a man of seventy. Yet, as the old professor grew closer and grasped Eli's hand, and then Jorgeson's, Eli quickly recognized the signs of age: twelve years before, Dr. Manday had seemed so healthy next to half-blind Swift, but here his body seemed muted, appearing to stumble against his grandson,

and his white hair, which used to be so carefully combed and bril-
liantined, now lay spidery and thin. Still, he shook their hands vig-
orously, grinning. A parrot squawked from its cage, and feathers
floated in the air.

"So glad you could come! So glad you could come!" the old
man said.

Jorgeson spoke first: "I always said I'd come back. Didn't I always
say that? And of course, yes, well, after all ... unlike the two of you
... I don't have my name on a comet."

False modesty, Eli knew, because, out of all of them, he was the
one who had achieved Denise's old dream: He had his name on
something. He was famous, with his "Jorgeson effect," and could
afford these awkward efforts at humility. Eli, hot in the direct sunlight
now and feeling pain all down his back, leaned against the wall.

But Manday frowned. He lifted a finger. "This morning, we are
here for Professor Swift."

"Of course," Jorgeson said, lowering his chin to his chest.

"It is a time for remembrance," the old man said again.

"Yes."

"For more than one scientist," Manday added, looking over at Eli
and lifting his eyebrows. Eli realized, suddenly, that the man meant
Denise, and he found himself stiffening.

"I noticed reporters" was all that Eli could say. They had run into
a few on the boat, Australian science writers who seemed absurdly
happy with this assignment, not having heard, perhaps, about the
mosquitoes.

Manday switched emotions abruptly, clapping his hands. "Oh yes!
Dr. Swift's comet is a celebrity, you know."

Eli tried to smile. "And so are you, as you should be."

"No no." The old man bowed. A member of Eli's thesis commit-
tee, who had thrown decades of science away for this life. Eli wondered if he should tell him, if Dr. Manday would appreciate the
humor of knowing that his former student, now Dr. Spivak, had been
a frightened and desperate young man once. That he had trimmed a
set of data once, twenty-five years ago, for a presentation that led to
a paper with Swift's name attached, and Manday's approval. A career

founded on a youthful lie, and that no consequences ever came of it. Here was science. Yes, Manday would enjoy that; perhaps Eli would tell him later, under the falling stars. He watched the grandson as he approached, handing the parasol to Dr. Manday before he took off again toward the cage.

Jorgeson spoke up: "I was interviewed!" And then, seeing his humility act was suffering, he shrugged and fell into a nervous monologue about the corrosive effects of fame on science.

Oh dear God, Eli thought, *we have been here before.* Once again, he was letting Jorgeson babble about some scientific minutiae with that expression of vacant pleasure while Eli, sunk inside himself, sighed over some loss. As he had three years before on Mauna Kea. As he had twenty-five years before, on that evening when Denise made Eli ask about her lover. Young brokenhearted Denise; then Denise far away; then Denise in her grave. The overlook, the volcano, the overlook again—three points in time, all exactly the same: chatter flowing around one stony regret. This was it, Eli decided as Jorgeson's eyes bulged with enthusiasm, his skin blushing from the heat, his voice ringing off the stone; this was the loop of his life.

Eli's hand hurt suddenly, and he lifted it to discover, all along the wall, a line of red ants on patrol, an angry thread wriggling along the cement, glowing as if spun from fire. Eli lifted his arm and the creatures were there, as well, having climbed onto him in the spirit of reconnaissance. Now they wandered aimlessly, a little gleaming galaxy of them, among the hairs and moles on his skin. He wiped them off briskly. He felt a bite, two bites. Down on the floor, he saw, they had survived the fall and were moving crazily again toward his feet. He stamped them dead.

Manday's grandson now returned with the cage, which he carried like a heavy pail, and feathers spilled from the sides and scattered along the stones.

Jorgeson, apparently pleased with his own voice, felt the urge to comment: "Your bird doesn't look too good."

Manday laughed and leaned down to the cage. When he did this, the parrot fluffed its chest and clucked loudly at him. The old man stood up again, saying, "You know how long I have had him? Forty years. He is forty years old. His name is Rama, isn't it?" he asked the parrot.

"Salaam, Rama!" said the bird, watching Eli with one eye.

"And you know what?" Manday said. "After all that time away from him, maybe twenty years, I come back and . . . he's decided he's in love with me. Aren't you, Rama?"

"Salaam, Rama!"

Manday touched his eyeglasses and looked weary. Then he smiled at Eli. "He's in love with me. He wants me to be his mate. The veterinarian told us. He cannot stand to be away from me, he plucks the very feathers from his back when I leave the room, you see. Parrots do that, old parrots do that. They go a little mad you see; there is actually an asylum here on the island just for parrots. Old parrots. But Rama is harmless. He just wants to nest with me, don't you? Hadi carries him around so he can be with me." Manday patted his grandson's head. "I don't want to break poor Rama's heart."

Manday leaned down again and the bird puffed and gave that clucking sound. "Yes," the old man said quietly, holding out a finger for the bird to bite. "I love you, too."

An image came to Eli's mind of something else, something he tried to keep far away and so he worked to erase it. He looked again over the edge to the calm bay and noticed that the water's reflection was full of clouds. They undulated in the waves as far as the eye could see—they looked like billowy creatures lingering just beneath the surface. Wave after wave they huddled, dull and gray, watching. Eli stood still as the others talked; he was fascinated by the water's effect. It easily cleared his mind. Then the sun arrived and the creatures seemed to scatter, dazzled, diving below, until moments later when it left and they appeared again, that flock of clouds, that school of eyes.

It was so far to come for just a comet, a hatful of falling stars which, with the full moon up tonight, none of them would be able to see until just before dawn. So far for just a funeral, or even a reunion. In fact, before yesterday, Eli had not planned to attend. He'd received the invitation in the mail—a ludicrous thing Manday had sent to everyone, engraved and formal, as if he were handing his comet off to a new husband—and Eli did not consider it for an instant. A gathering of old men, war heroes, bragging of the stars and nebulae of their youth—certainly not. But chance had landed him in Hawaii the week before, on another visit to Mauna Kea (using its new submillimeter-wavelength telescope), and he stood in that same breathless spot as he had in 1986 when he realized how badly he'd been cheated, when he plotted the next crucial curve of his life. And this time he had looked at that same ginger light, that same shy volcano being stripped of mist, and knew he should go. For her, somehow. So he extended his stay, bought a ticket for a flight, and slept against the window for the few hours of sunrise before the clumsy landing awakened him and he was rumbling on the landing strip of the main island, young boys running alongside his window, grinning and shouting.

So Eli stood apart from the growing crowd of astronomers. He had not come here to see them, and he faced away, out toward the beach. A flash of red caught his eye—there on the rocks, the figure of a woman walking away down a path. In and out of the palm shade. He could not know that it was the mother of that boy who fell, returning with bottles of oil and spices in a basket on her head, having just anointed her son's grave. Yet for some reason he thought of a grave. On a hill. Eli watched her careful walk and, because one must always pretend something in the face of death, he fell into a fantasy of his own.

He imagined he had come here on a nervous mission. He imagined the plane ride, the landing, the run to catch the boat over to the island, all of them with the same frenzy as the ants struggling along the wall, the same desperate purpose, and that here he was, breathless from his jog up the stairs, waiting to see if she would come. Denise. He let himself imagine this. He spent those years after Mauna Kea working himself into her life again—this was the true part— putting himself beside her as a friend, as a good friend, pressing no notes into her hands and whispering nothing into her ears, just being there again. That was the plan he'd made at the volcano's lip: to be slow and kind. She took it well, letting him make a speech at her son's birthday party and then sitting with him on the back porch, sipping lemonade, while Adam and the boys went to a movie; but she would not relax. Still, he thought of it as retraining an animal you'd hurt; you sit beside it and let it glare at you with luminous eyes; you touch its fur while it bares a few back teeth, and after years, he thought, it would come again when you called it, jump into your lap and sleep again. So he sipped his lemonade beside Denise. His plan was never to seduce her back; he did not know himself what he desired. But unless he got them back to where they started, as friends and comet-hunters, he would never know. He would never reach the day he longed for—the one when he would finally explain to her what he'd done—and examine Denise's face for some sign of what might happen next.

That day came the very last time he saw her. Years had passed, and they now talked about science with some of the old excitement; and if the nervous joy of their youthful friendship was gone, the arguments in the hallways, the joking on the boat, it was replaced by something calm and silent that was good as well. He decided that she had forgiven him, and when he came up to give a speech at Berkeley (crowds of nervous BADgrads twitching in the audience), he called Denise and got her to spend the day with him alone. He took her to see an old fort looking out on the ocean, a poured block of concrete with rusted iron semicircles on the cliffside showing where the machine guns used to pivot in preparation for the Japanese attack that never came. Grass had overgrown it all now, and they walked on the mounded earth, on a path bordered by wild ice plant blooming with pink jagged flowers. The cold wind rushed up from the water and, caught on the hilltop, dropped its spray onto the pair. She held her hat to her head with one hand, talking about their comet.

It was to return in five years, and Denise had already been making preparations: assembling grad students, arranging telescope time in Australia. They chatted about the next apparition of their comet, knowing of course that it might not happen, knowing that it was the most common thing in the world for comets to miss their mark and disappear.

"Maybe there's an associated meteor shower," she said.

He knew it was ludicrous; all the known showers had already been linked with their comets. But she was enjoying the thought as they walked along, and he indulged her.

"We could have a party like Swift," he said.

She nodded, stopping, hand on hat, to look at the ocean. Somewhere out there was an island dedicated to birds, but it was invisible that day.

He went on: "A comet party for us. That'd be fun."

"Come on," she said. "Were they ever fun?"

It felt like the moment then. I'll tell, he thought, and when I see her eyes, I'll know what I want to do. Take her hand and kiss her, or reach for a phone and ask poor Penny to marry me. He started to talk, but the sound of the ocean beat his words down to the grass. Later, he thought, when things are quieter. Denise pointed out toward a long strip of foam in the ocean. He thought she said something about a whale, but he couldn't hear her. He just watched her take off her hat, using it to gesture. Her freed hair exploded in the wind.

He had another chance on the drive home. They were sitting in a tunnel, mired in traffic, with a half-moon view of the Golden Gate before them. Denise was fixing her hair. She had thrown the hat into the backseat, and it sat there like a punished child while the mother took her own hair and pulled it back into its old waves, revealing, as she lifted and coaxed, how it had already unblonded at the roots. Such a fuss and perfection. Yet she'd grown beautiful; she'd learned how to do it. It took Denise nearly fifty years to learn true vanity, but here it was; and if she was older now, with lines around her eyes and that sag beneath her chin, she was lovelier than ever.

This was the moment. Here, at the height of his affection for her. Eli knew he should force it out, he should will his body to do what it refused to do years before: touch Denise's hand there on the gearshift. That smooth pale hand resting on the knob, shivering with the engine. Just tell her, test her, and move her, for this third and final time, out of their constant double orbit. There, her hand, choked by a bracelet, one nail tapping on the plastic. Will yourself to touch it. Just as, twenty-five years before, he had stood with a finger resting

236 · Andrew Sean Greer

on her doorbell, grazing the surface, Eli sat now watching her tapping on that gearshift, five more taps and he would tell her. He waited, watching, counting in the silence of the car.

"I need to tell you. I was misinformed, and I was quick to hate you," he began, but someone up ahead began to honk, filling the tunnel, and then another, and then everyone was honking and letting the echoes gather around the concrete walls in a cloud of noise. Even Denise was doing it, laughing, pressing on the horn to the consternation of the women in the car next to her.

"What?" she asked, distracted. The horns kept going.

"You need to listen."

"I am!" she shouted.

So he shouted back, feeling his words were echoing, too, careening along the walls of the tunnel with all the cacophony, and this gave him the bravery to press on, not knowing if she really heard him, not willing to repeat it now, but simply saying it. And as his own speech died down, the horns began to fade as well, and traffic began to move, so that they slid in silence out of the tunnel and into a creeping fog. They stayed in silence for the next hour. They passed along the wharfside freeway into the shroud of the city's fog, across the Bay Bridge and various tunnels and overpasses, more traffic, and out into the sun of the East Bay again. Denise said nothing, and since he had only asked that she listen to him, he could not bear to press for anything more. Had she heard him? At stoplights, or in traffic, her fingernail kept tapping against the gearshift. That was the only sound. Patient, he did not ask her to give him even the slightest sign, and so they drove on with just that persistent tapping; this, later, was what he could never forgive himself for.

In Berkeley, where his car sat ticketed outside the astronomy building, she let him go with a slight two-fingered wave. The way she looked at him, though—she had heard him. There was something in her eyes that promised more, later, if he would wait, and he took this for what it seemed and smiled and waved and watched her drive away. It seemed like all he could do: stand there, waiting for her to think it through. Later, he would learn how life would go. Her car rounded a green hill where students lay in the sun. The rear window flashed with sunlight and was gone. This was the last.

His fantasy, today at the wall, continued as if life had never happened. It erased her death. It erased her silence. Instead, it produced a different kind of day, still in a tunnel, with cold air, horns blasting like migrating geese. This time, though, she said something; she made a promise, a pact with him: If either of them wanted to have back what Eli had thrown away, they would arrive on this island, on this day, and stand beside this golden dome where they'd first touched hands. He had built this fantasy over the course of a year, so it was full of detail and drama. They would arrive here. That would be the sign.

So Eli, leaning now against the wall to give his weary back a moment's rest, pretended he had made his own decision, left Penny with his dog back in L.A., flown here in an impatient rush of love to stand and look out at the path a woman would have to take to reach the old palace. The path that curved behind a grove of sealing-wax palms. A bird-of-paradise bloomed miraculously just at the grove's edge, and he imagined he was a man staring desperately, hoping for the sight of a woman's leg stepping past that bright origami blossom. Her hair would gleam with gold lacquer in that square of sun just now appearing; she would walk quickly, her face covered in sweat, because she would be a reckless woman. Possibly mistaken, years too late. She would appear from the shadow of the palms, looking everywhere for him, then catching his eye up here at the wall. A foot stepping from the shadow. It would be now—or wait . . . yes now. The trees moved softly in a breeze. Or now.

Eli watched, blinking. The square of sun moved along the path and faded as it reached a clump of dry grass; the bird-of-paradise stood unmoving as a sentinel, and the palms tilted quietly in a solemn row, the breeze lowering the fans of their leaves to show bright red stems. Birds came from within the grove, singing, and flew in a long parabola up into the sky, whose clouds were breaking up and drifting. He watched and smiled and pretended—innocently, just to hold his heart—that it had happened. That any of it, from the admission of mistakes, to the pact, to this very day—that any of it had happened. Just for a few peaceful minutes. There was a whole lifetime to understand the truth, so it did no harm to have this, just the possibility of a gold foot stepping from the shade. The sun returned in long, broad stripes. The birds flew back into the bower. It would be now.

"Dr. Spivak?"

He turned, seeing a few yards away the form of a woman with her hair held back in barrettes. She waved, and for a breathless moment he saw Kathy.

Eli knew in an instant that he was wrong. How could he have been so mistaken? A pregnant woman in her thirties—when had Kathy ever looked like this? Yet he'd felt the strangest pull of sorrow at that picture. His young wife the way she might have looked if things had gone differently. The woman approached, holding an envelope of some sort across her belly.

"It's me," she said cautiously. "It's Lydia. Dr. Swift's daughter."

"Lydia, oh . . . of course I know who you are. My God." He looked her over. He felt a little gulp of time's fleet passage.

Lydia was now beside him at the wall, and she had a look of concern. Lines around her eyes, he noticed, and something firm in her face. She had cocked her body, one hand on the wall, one hand on her hip, looking at him with worry before she smiled and said, "Sorry—you were thinking."

He looked back at the palms. Those garish red stems in all the green. Two scientists were coming along the path, gray-bearded and sweating as they talked, batting against the bird-of-paradise with their khakis. Eli turned his back to the view. "It's all right."

"I don't know if you remember me. . . ." she began.

He laughed. "I'm surprised you remember *me!*"

"Well," Lydia said, rolling her eyes, and it occurred to him that maybe, as a young girl, she'd had a crush on him. But when had they spent any time together?

"You look wonderful," he said, knowing this was dull; but she accepted it.

She winced. "Well, I feel gross."

They talked for a little while, and mostly, because of the old assumption that the younger person has the more interesting life, Eli asked her questions, which she answered honestly. She told him she was moving from New York, would be living at Swift's old farm while she had the child, maybe teaching art again when things settled down, and he got the impression that there was a sadness here—surely something to do with the baby's father, whom she did not mention. But he also detected something women of his own generation did not show so readily: a determination, coupled with quick flashes of anger, that he recognized from her girlhood, from her teenage years. He remembered seeing her at the island bar, clearly underage, and drinking and smoking without a care. What an amazing girl—and here she was, a woman. If only Kathy were here, he thought; she would have loved this. Even if it meant being near her ex-husband, even if it meant another nauseating trip out to this island, she might have come if she'd known Lydia would be here, so complete, so undiminished by the years. This particular girl, this young stargazer, the only one his ex-wife ever cared about.

Eventually, Lydia paused and changed the topic. Obviously, she felt close enough to him now—either through their years of association or simply their mutual estrangement from the crowd of bespectacled scientists—to ask him something that concerned her. It was, he saw, what she had been wanting to ask for some time: "Dr. Spivak. Do you remember the boy?"

"Sorry?"

"Do you remember the boy who fell?"

Eli felt the relief of a switch in memory, back to something very old, something he well understood. He said, "I thought you were there. I remember you playing with a monkey or something. . . ."

"I was five; I don't remember it. Isn't that too bad?"

He found himself laughing. "Not really."

Lydia frowned, moving and crossing her arms high on her chest, over her belly. The air was hot and yellow around her and she squinted even in the diffuse light. She said, "I just wanted to ask. My dad never talked about it. I don't think he was upset, I think he was over it. Bored by the topic."

"That sounds like him."

She leaned back. "Did the boy trip? I don't know why I'm so curious. It's just so weird, don't you think? A boy died. And then you all have these reunions." When she first began, he thought there was something angry in her voice, something peevish, but it died away by the end of her sentence and he thought he must have imagined it. There was always something disagreeable about begging someone to provide your own memory.

"I wasn't really watching very closely. I was over there," he said, pointing to the southern corner of the stone floor. He saw himself in a folding chair, looking up at the blackest sky he'd ever seen, the stars rising like ashes from a fire. "I'd been talking to Manday's wife. She was a beautiful woman. Then there was a shout, I turned"—he did this, turning his stout body to face the yellowed break in the wall—"and it had all already happened. I remember your dad and the sultan standing there holding the telescope." He gestured to where the telescope still stood, that old killer, now rusted firm and pointed permanently out to sea. "Everybody rushed to the wall. It was crazy, now that I think about it, everybody running. I stood here... no...."

Eli moved along the wall, feeling its rough surface, until he found the place. Lydia followed, arms still crossed. Glancing below, he noticed that a group of palms had grown in the last twenty-five years, and that two huts sat in their shade where once the view was only of the beach. Why hadn't he noticed this twelve years ago? "I stood here. We looked down and women were running everywhere. Some torches, I think. You couldn't see anything."

"What did you do?"

Eli had not noticed the change because, twelve years before, he'd been down on the beach, in the darkness, down on the strip of sand waiting for the bobbing movement of a flashlight.

"What?" he asked, turning to meet her gaze.

"Did you run downstairs? Did you find a doctor?"

He shook his head, confused. It was so hot here, with the sun breaking through, and he wished he'd brought his hat. "We could see him down there, on the rocks; his neck was broken."

"You couldn't see anything. You said it."

"We could see him."

"Did any of you try to help him?" she asked, her voice pitched higher, her face drawing closer to his. "Even try?"

"Lydia, he was dead."

She stood there with her arms crossed, looking at the yellowed bit of wall, then at Eli. The auburn hair, round face and puffy lips that hadn't seemed like they ever would be beautiful—and yet here they were, at thirty, lovely. He could see so many of her girlish gestures showing through this woman's body, despite her grown-up anger; he could see the nervous fluttering of fingers, the fingers of a little girl revealed briefly like the red stems of the sealing-wax palms. He could see her father, as well, in her face, which hardened before him.

She asked, "The next night, did you grieve? Or did you just count meteors?"

He could only smile. There was nothing to say to this: the interrogation of a woman who merely wanted to remember an important moment, remember how her father stood next to the whispering sultan and silenced them all, told them all what to do. Send some away on boats; keep others—Eli, Denise, little Lydia—to lie out another two nights under the stars. The show must go on. Perhaps a bad choice, considering—a cold, scientific one—but so long ago. Eli understood her anger. He knew how, at a death, you want to hate the dead a little.

"We went to the funeral. Your father paid for a grave marker; the son's family couldn't afford it," he told her, and she softened immediately. "Bronze, down there on the beach. And at night we counted meteors."

"Where was I?" she asked.

This was the real question. He saw it in her plain freckled face, in the hand she held now to her belly. Perhaps she wanted to clear things up, clean them, stack all the memories carefully in the cupboard because all that was over. The first half of her life. Now there was the lover whom Lydia carefully didn't mention, the father who wasn't around, and so this child, and her art and her teaching. It was the time for a long look at the past, as if it were a view you've come quite a distance to see, and then you pivot on one foot, face the other way. He admired her for it. It was something he could never do.

"You stayed on the island with us," he told her.

"What about that night?"

Eli shifted his weight to save his back. He told her, "With my wife. She picked you up and held you."

Lydia smiled as if she almost remembered. She kept her hand on her belly—was she transmitting this to her child? Then, tilting her head, she asked a strange question, "Did you take pictures of us that night?"

"What?" he said, shifting again. "No. . . . Pictures?"

"Photographs."

He squinted and shook his head, seeking out the stability of the wall again. "No. I was here, looking down." And then he realized he'd lied to her; those nights after the boy's death, he hadn't counted meteors. Eli, twenty-five, dazed by catastrophe, had been down in that stone hut with Denise, curing his troubles with his body.

Hard to believe. His youth had been like that, so quick and hurtful and ecstatic. Eli looked back and wondered if he'd been in control at all, or if the words from his mouth, the movements of his arms and legs, had all happened too quickly, went on somehow without him. As though youth were a drug that wore off too slowly, left you in a parking lot some early morning wondering what happened. The young woman standing before him would never have guessed he'd felt that, too; that her generation did not invent it. He could not have explained to her how his life moved from standing on the beach and waving to the departing boat, the one taking his new wife away, to a silent moment in the leaves one afternoon when he was slipping off Denise's bra. Time moved more quickly then—or no, that wasn't it. Time was so slow, he remembered, it felt so warm and slow. Slow, lazy time. It was his body that was quick. Now, with this aching back and a nap that had to be taken each day at four, he could hold himself back so easily. But then, at twenty-five, he'd been a puppy pulling at a leash. Gnawing at a leash. Always breaking free.

He almost wished he could tell her. What it felt like to have seen a boy's head cracked like a melon on those rocks below—the sharp sting of poison. He thought of an island plant Manday had told him about, the devil's nettle, whose pricking leaves brought on fever in men but whose antidote, luckily, could be found in the dark berries of the tattoo bush that always grew beside it. So it had been with him. A sting of terror, and then nearby an antidote: a hand reaching for his. He wished he could tell Lydia what he knew she could never believe—that it didn't go away, ever, the gaudiness of youth. It just became smaller, a gilt room in your mind. But it did not ever go away.

Lydia was holding something out to him. An envelope, the one he'd seen her resting against her belly. Apparently, her anger had quickly passed; she was onto something new.

"I wanted you to see this. I thought you should see this," she said, gripping the envelope stiffly against the wind. She didn't open it, but let him read the shaky lettering: KATHY'S PHOTOS. "I found them in my dad's stuff," Lydia said. "Do you know what that means?"

"Yes," he said, touching the envelope with one finger. "I think so, I think I remember she . . . Kathy, my wife . . . she took some pictures. She wanted you to have them. . . . You never got them?"

"So she's the one who took them?"

"I don't remember what they were. She never developed them. But she held on to them for some reason. Maybe privacy." He looked up and saw Lydia's eyes blinking in confusion. He said, "You didn't know my wife, she was always hard to understand."

She sighed and handed them to him, saying, "My dad got them somehow. They're old pictures, but he developed them and some came out. He never showed them to me—it's strange. It's strange, because mostly they're pictures of me. But you'll see."

He took the envelope and slid the flap open. The pictures came in a clump onto his hand, stuck together slightly from the heat, a gleaming stack of mirrors.

"They're out of order," she said. He felt her leaning forward, watching his reaction.

The first ones were of Lydia. Very young, a little girl, standing on the painted wooden deck of a boat, inside a coil of ropes. Her red hair was blown sideways, tangled, brimming with captured light, and as she held down the bottom of her dress with two stiff arms, she had the expression of a street kid, a tough girl squinting in the sunlight and unhappy to have her picture taken. Behind her, there was the pale sky fading at the horizon and the faint smudge of the island, this one, appearing in a whitish haze. The people around her, against the railing, were pointing, and their clothes and hairdos were the only markers of the sixties. Otherwise, with the time-fogged print, the starkness of her look, it could have been any time in the century. He looked up at the present Lydia and saw it—the same careful look as she watched him. Eli unstuck the photo and looked at the next.

A few more of her on the boat, and some of her walking away. Then a new setting: Lydia in the sun-spotted jungle, standing in a tin pail with soap all over her naked body. A fat man (presumably her father) leaned out of the edge, but Lydia was focused directly on the camera. She had a vine of orchids in her hand, dry and brownish near the bottom; it seemed she had just grabbed them from the bush. A bee seemed to be exiting one of the flowers (or it could have been a drop of water, or an error in the old film), but the girl didn't notice. She was smiling. It was a smile of astonishment, something like the previous frown: I don't know why I'm here, but I'll be fine. A few more of these pictures, with middle-aged Swift moving in and out of the frame. Eli wondered why Kathy had taken these, and when? Had he been sleeping in their hut? Had she crept away from her husband's bed? And then, below, a darker set of photos entirely.

That night, the meteor hunt. Lydia, her hair in pigtails, wrapped in a shawl and looking at a local woman who had a rhesus monkey on a leash. Kathy had caught the monkey with its mouth wide open as if it were singing. Everything was washed with cold light, people looked shocked, and the sky seemed utterly dark. Then one of Lydia smiling, with the wall and a red-haired boy in the background. Then Lydia asleep on her father's lap, with the professor, as he held a piece of chocolate in his fingers like a pawn, looking enraged at the camera's forbidden flash.

And then Lydia screaming. A crowd behind her, turned all directions, slacks and sarongs and high-heeled shoes, with a few faces looking straight at the camera. Chairs were overturned, coffee mugs spilled, and Lydia's face was ugly and red and mangled with fright. And then Lydia in Kathy's arms. Eli looked carefully at this one— Kathy as a young woman, with shining black hair and a skinny face and arms. He had never realized there was something so stylish about her, and not just the sixties-ness of the moment, but the layers and patterns of her clothes that now looked effortlessly beautiful. Had he ever thought of her that way? She held Lydia gently to her and, with the little girl still screaming fitfully at the camera, reaching one paw toward the photographer, Kathy's lips were pressed against her cheek.

"Who took these?" he asked.

"I . . ." she began. "I can't tell for sure."

"Why would someone take these? With the boy dead?"

But Lydia just crossed her arms and shook her head.

He didn't care. He was glad to have these pictures. Here was another one, closer now: Kathy's eyes closed under her glasses, her neck stretched to reach the girl, and Eli could almost hear Lydia's terrible cry, feel that struggling body through more than two decades of time. His wife, at twenty-four, kissing a child. Yes—it made no sense, after everything—but he felt the itch of love. He lifted the photograph to reveal the next.

These were out of order; daylight filled this scene. He felt the muscles of his back tighten, the tug of a bellpull. It was Denise.

He thought of the call. It came in the afternoon. It was a beautiful December day in 1988, and Eli had already moved to his new Hollywood apartment, sitting on the couch with Penny watching a baseball game on tape. She was a fan, and the incongruity of this fragile and pretty woman shouting at the screen comforted him, let him think there were more mysteries to her than he suspected, ones worth pursuing. Penny sighed in disappointment at the screen, and then the phone rang. Eli paused the tape on an image of some fans in the stadium, standing and yelling, and he picked up the phone. It was Adam. A low voice of endless words. Eli sat there and listened to the details. It was a long call, and all the while Eli just kept staring at the screen, at that blurry, frozen image of two women in the stands waving their banners: a tall blonde, overweight, delighted by something that had just happened, and a woman beside her, a red-head, flag held sideways, seemingly unsure of how to feel. Eyes turned down, a look of doubt, an image he would never forget. "Thank you for telling me," he said at last, hung up the phone and stared at the frozen women while Penny asked him, over and over, what had happened. In a minute, the tape automatically unpaused and the raucous game began again; the woman landed on the ground, clapping, and the camera switched to focus on the sweating pitcher. Tied, bottom of the ninth, two bases loaded. They watched until their team lost, an outcome they had already known, and then Eli turned and said at last that his best friend was dead.

And here she was. In his hand, in a photo from the past, one he'd taken of her, in fact. He remembered it. On the boat over to the island in 1965, a few sips from her flask of bourbon with the guards looking on, the shadows from the gulls passing over the canopy, over her face shining with sweat. Very young, both of them. Talking about Carlos, Kathy, his worries back then that seemed so innocent now— whether his wife was happy, or would have children with him. As if Denise had ever really cared. She was so focused on the stars, on her fame that wouldn't ever come. She had taken off her hat and let her hair fall in sticky waves. He hadn't loved her then—it was hard to look back and imagine himself so hollowed and yet happy—but Denise stared at him in that moment on the boat, fanning herself with the hat, and he'd tried not to smile at her harmless crush.

"I've had too much to drink!" she had said, holding that long look.

He remembered leaning against the railing, amused at this rich girl. He had asked, "You think it's a good idea to be drunk so early?"

"Yes. I do."

"Good," he had told her. "So do I." And, with her yelling in protestation, he had taken the picture. This one in his hand. He remembered it perfectly.

And yet, the actual image did not quite fit. Denise was young here, of course, but much younger than he'd made her in his mind's eye, with such unlined skin and a long face, a clumsy expression before she learned how to control these things, the surprised face of a girl.

But he was shocked to see it. She looked so plain. Eyebrows plucked severely, gray eyes slightly bulging in her profile, especially in this joyful shout, a flat forehead and a stiff hairdo crushed by her hat and loosening messily in the heat and sea air—the kind of girl you see and hope the best for, but don't love. Why had he remembered her as something else, someone so carefree and beautiful? Gold swirls of hair and jewel eyes and a sharp, clever face gleaming under the powder? The dark and muddy print put her out of context, made her seem like a young woman dressed up for the prom—the prim blouse and skirt, the hat—when back then all this had seemed so natural. But he couldn't blame it on the print. It was simpler than that. She was not pretty.

He did not want there to be pictures of such things. They ruined the past, flattened it in all dimensions. Why couldn't he have kept her beautiful? Because it wasn't true. The picture showed it. And the sense that she'd been funny and mysterious and brilliant as all hell couldn't be felt on that glossy square—now she was no one even to look at twice. Would there be photographs of them together in the hut as well? Of the perfect body he remembered, wet and stuck with sand? And of the night of the comet hunt when she touched his shoulder? And even of Denise at nearly fifty, staring out to sea with her hat in her hand, her explosion of hair? *You were wrong,* the pictures would admonish, *there was nothing there to love.*

He began to hate the dead a little, too. A young, plain girl from San Francisco shouting on a boat. An older woman on a hilltop, letting her dyed-blond hair fly out in a nebula. Unfinished, unsaid. He was to blame, of course, but she was also. She had grown beautiful without him. She had been happy with her son. She had sat in a car, wordless, and not fought for them. And of course now, being dead, she had the last word, and it was nothing.

"That was Dr. Lanham, right?" Lydia asked.

"Yes."

She laughed. "It's hard to think of her so young."

"You know, actually, it's hard to think of her so old."

Lydia paused. "That's interesting," she said.

"Well."

"And that was you," she said, showing him the next one, and it was.

But different. Different from the last one. Yes, Eli gaunt and clean-shaven, with a crew cut, his eyes warped by thick glasses as he wrote with his red pen in a little book. A novel of some kind. He noticed a painful-looking pimple on the corner of his mouth—he'd forgotten that, but the sensation returned to him—and the absurdity of his clothes: woolen pants, a button-up shirt (sweated through) and a tie (folded in his pocket). Those old glasses, that shy grin. But what made him gasp here, even more than at the old photo of Denise, was not just the sense of himself—of all of them, his wife, these scientists here—so very young, so ignorant of what would come, but simply the way the photo had been taken. A shot of a young Jewish man caught in a private act: writing in a book. A quiet photo, composed in a way that made him seem much handsomer and smarter than he'd really been, a generous photo; and at the bottom edge, to the left, he could see the wind-lifted edge of a skirt. Her skirt—Denise's—as she took the picture. Because for Eli it was really a picture of her, more so than the last one—of the skirt and angle and the light that implied her, and her busy mind, and how she looked upon this young man with a schoolgirl's crush.

He took it all back, his petty rant against the dead. He saw himself through Denise's eyes and it was happening again—the moments when he couldn't grasp it, how things had gone, when his mind suffered some eclipse of the spirit—he had to leave. Eli dropped the photos in Lydia's hand and walked away. The other scientists were approaching, muttering and laughing, and he went in the other direction, to the edge of the wall. Always here, to the edge of this wall.

"Are you okay, Dr. Spivak?" the young woman was asking. He said nothing. She would understand, when she was older, how you cannot look directly at the sun.

I should have come here, he thought. An island thirteen days in the past, a place to tear the seams out of time and sew it back correctly. *I should have come here that day.* The day of her death. Rather than sit with Penny in the TV-flickering room, letting it all fall wordlessly into the past, he should have rushed out of the house, driven to the airport in a frenzy, flown across the Pacific to arrive here the next day, to step onto the hot sand of a place where she was not yet dead. Thirteen days until she died, thirteen days to prepare himself. To sip cocktails and think of her calling to her son or arguing with Adam or reading a book, ordinary and still alive. Days would pass. To swim and nap and have her still alive. And then the day would have come at last: Eli, standing in the shallow ocean water off the spit, staring east to where the future would arrive, when Denise would be torn from his life again. A few moments of still ocean. A gull crossing the sky. Then it would have come, in waves like light, to cover him.

The line of ants was here before him, yards and yards of braid upon the wall. Eli put his finger down and let them crawl over it— an odd feeling, a trickle, like drops of blood. He thought of the photograph again, the ruffled edge of skirt. Of Adam's mournful voice over the phone, giving a crazed and terrible description of her body on the hill: her pale neck blooming with a purple bruise, the stale blood, the wreath of broken glass. There it was, the awful image, the drop of poison convulsing in his throat. He leaned against the wall, covering his wet eyes with his thick fingers, and let his mind heave.

Out there, past all the asteroids and planets, halfway to the nearest star, to a point in space where the sun was dimmed to just a subtle fleck of light, another mass of ice and rock was moving. Moments before, it had been still. The light from everywhere was equal, cold, and all around were gathered icebergs of similar giant size; there were more of these objects in this part of space than there were stars in the Milky Way. From their great frozen distance, they circled the sun in a halo; this was the Oort Cloud, that auditorium of ice, that house of comets. A star passed close by, disturbing them. Then another; and then a final star that tipped one comet off the shelf, sending it slowly toward the sun. It fell, turning slothfully through the darkness, growing ever warmer so that eventually, in a million years or so, the ices would begin to sublime from its surface, causing the wisps of a tail; and in a few million more, that tail would paint a broad white stripe across the earth's sky. This has been happening for longer than we can imagine.

Our comet lay once more in the open sky, blazing, a dozen or so astronomical units away from the sun, which it had once again looped during this apparition. The bright sun blocked it from view on the island, and tonight the rising full moon would outshine it as well, drawing all attention like a celebrity arriving at a party; but still the comet wobbled on its dust-strewn ellipse as if all the world were watching it. It was dark, most of its ices gone into space long ago; it was one of the darkest objects in the universe. Occasionally, gases jetted from its interior, but they did not change its orbit; that had already been done, years before, by Jupiter's great presence. Warped and altered, unpredictable yet again, heading toward the outer solar system; a swarm of dust falling through cold space.

And thousands of miles away, on an even more eccentric orbit, a similar object was approaching on its own loop, a comet whose last apparition was in 1974, discovered by two astronomers on a mountaintop in California. Two comets with hyphenated names, two cousins floating through the ether. And not even the scientists below, at countless observatories across Australia and America and the world, pouring numbers into their equations like grains into sand-clocks, not even they could tell you where those objects were headed, where they would be in a year, or when the time might come, a lonely hour, when they'd be lost to greater gravities than ours.

Kathy felt two shadows on her. They came from some men who stood outside the window; shadows, even in the gray light of the muddled evening, falling across her table like a scolding. She was wishing these two would pass; wishing the sun would come out full again, although the fog had clearly settled in for good; wishing the woman beside her, reading now, were someone she could trust enough to tell the truth to. But was there anyone for that, really? Anyone who could even audition for the role?

She was in San Francisco to visit her college friend Rita, the one now reading, and she kept telling herself that she would call Adam. She would call him so they could talk or, rather, so Kathy could at last have a crack at that strange man. So blond and right, so all-American, as handsome as an extra in a football movie—which was not to say stunning, but acceptable anywhere, at any barbecue. But she was convinced he was crazier than anyone she knew. That old hobby of hers had returned, picking at minds—what Rita called her "cocktail vampirism"—and she could hardly resist. After all, she knew what Adam had done to Eli and Denise.

Eli had told her, of course, in that terrible conversation before their divorce, but she herself had known about it, in her way, for years. Kathy guessed it in the moment that Eli, freshly paranoid from that breakfast with Adam in L.A., suddenly turned to her one night, magazine lowered in a glossy V, to ask if Denise had seen Carlos recently. A stern and careful look on his face. Kathy knew exactly what that meant; there was a thrill to it, knowing her husband was in terror of something, and that she herself was in terror. Something great and awful was rising in their lives. "Oh yes," she lied to him. "Yes, they've become good friends, I think." She heard herself say the lie, and that also delighted her—her lips were thinking faster than she could, acting without her. Her husband's expression did not sink or weaken; it stiffened like meringue. That's how she knew he had some idea, and that now, with what she'd said, it could not be dis-believed.

So they were accomplices, she and Adam. Criminals together. And yet, in the end, she had not called him. There was still time, but Kathy knew, sitting there with her book and friend, that she was not going to call him. Could she really tell him what she'd done to aid him? There seemed to be no point now. After all, nobody had gotten what they wanted.

"What are you reading?" Rita asked her, looking at her now. An old friend, kind and good with long hippyish blond hair gone gray behind her ears, skin lined from years in the sun, smart and unaware of how a fifty-year-old woman was supposed to look. The kind of friend who could sit with Kathy in a coffee shop and read a book. Long silences, polite pauses like this one, chances to return to the life she led inside her mind. A good woman; and while no great replacement for Denise, the same quality, the same kind of friend.

Kathy smiled and put down her book. The cover was a cheap painting, B-movie style. "Not what you might expect," she said.

Rita leaned back, interested. "I don't expect anything in particular, Kathy, not from you."

"It's a book about scientists."

"Any good?"

Kathy paused. She wondered how she looked to Rita, if she had aged so thoroughly, her hair short and gray, her clothing out of style by a decade now, her glasses by even more; if she had changed so much as to be a disappointment. Not the brainy, solitary girl in woolen slacks and a beret passing under the bell tower with a book in her hand. Not the quiet one in class who simply shook her head angrily until the professor called on her. Or could it be that she had aged but stayed exactly the same? Ridiculously, stubbornly the same like this longhaired woman before her? She surprised herself by finding this was what she wanted: nose in her books, to have sidestepped time. But now she had lost track of the conversation.

"Sorry, I was thinking."

"Any good?" Rita asked again.

Kathy tapped the cover. "Kind of the wrong question."

Rita sighed, clearly a little tired of Kathy's old games, but still intrigued, still friends with her for just this reason. "Well, are you enjoying it?"

Kathy looked at her and considered what to say. There was a story to tell, but Kathy wasn't the kind of person who told stories or gave any background to her life. Her actions came with no context to explain them, but she had no need for explanation; she had no wish for other people to understand her, and the idea that understanding her might make them love her more—this was a strange idea, a strange motive, a bad one. Love didn't come from understanding, did it? Love came from nothing. That was the whole point of love.

But something made her smile through chapped lips. Perhaps the men stepping from the window, their shadows removing themselves from her body, taking with them the odd murmurs of their conversation. A clean canvas of light thrown on the table, ready for her to paint it.

"It's called *The Search*," she said quietly, showing the cover to Rita, who leaned over to touch it with bitten nails. Two men in white lab coats, a red-haired buxom dame in a tight yellow dress and, of all things, pearls. "It's from the thirties. About scientists."

"Sexy scientists."

"Eli's owned it for years. Since we met. It's one of his favorites and he always wanted me to read it when we were first married." Her friend looked up and watched her. "I made him read Virginia Woolf, and I pretended I read this. I didn't. I hate books that are 'about' things. Race. War. But I picked it up recently."

"You were missing him?"

She was, but Kathy would never tell that to a soul. Longing was not a public act for her, and absence was simply that: an empty space, nothing to speak of. And, if she were to be honest, she was doing fine alone. Kathy was happy by herself. When she was a young woman, being alone had never been an option; but here, near the end of the century, it had been chosen for her and she discovered, like someone who has stepped into the wrong movie theater only to find herself transfixed, that she liked it. You did not really have to cook. You did not have to clean. You could read endlessly, stay up late reading and wake up Sunday morning with nothing ahead but a hundred cups of coffee and a million words in print. There was, of course, the debris of loneliness spread everywhere. But it was bearable. She did not long for a man in her life, after all; she only missed her husband.

Not that he had understood her. A number of women, somehow discovering Kathy's divorce at a party or a meeting, held her hand and told her that they knew her sorrow: they, too, could never find another man to understand them. It seemed to Kathy such a bizarre comment. Understand you? How was that possible? Even if it were, even if you had found a man who understood your every whim and quirk and mood, could you really blame the poor fellow for moving on? Simply to stanch his boredom? But Kathy also knew that these were a different sort of woman from herself, the kind who, while much younger than she was, having come of age under Nixon or Johnson, still somehow kept refrigerated within their chests the frosty ideals of much earlier decades. Eisenhower. Truman. Kathy had trouble finding women like herself—thus her renewed friendship with this old college gal—or even people like herself. There was no longer, of course, the old argumentative Eli to provoke. That was gone. And another: Denise.

That terrible call in the afternoon, some relative she didn't know who drew a picture of a car crumpled against the rocks, the confetti of glass, a pale forehead stained with a tree of blood. Hang up with a rattle, and it's too clear: Despite it all, there never was any friend who got so close.

But she said nothing of this to Rita. She changed the subject to her book again, saying, "I picked it up because it's a particular day today. There's a comet that returns every twelve years, and a meteor shower that happens tonight. I'm old and I've gotten sentimental."

"I don't think so."

She picked up the book and looked at it. "I don't know how I got it. I know he loaned it to Denise for years." Her old friend grimaced, because she knew all about Denise. Kathy had not confided; she had simply dropped information over time. "But somehow it ended up in our house again, and somehow it ended up with me. I don't know why he didn't take it."

"Probably because of her."

Kathy put the book down. A waitress refilled their coffees from a green-lipped decanter. She continued: "So I started reading it, and it isn't terrible. It's kind of interesting and antique. All about the glory and frustration of science. I'm sure it would be very comforting to a young astronomer, like those books they give adolescents about puberty, to reassure them. Everything that you're going through is normal, that sort of thing. A quick read, amusing, a little drama. And then I came across a page. It happened yesterday."

Here Kathy took the book from the table and opened it near the middle. She pressed it flat with the palm of her hand and the old paperback spine gave a little crack, settling into place. The smell of the old binding came into the air between them. She presented it to Rita. There, at the top right-hand corner of the page, was a sentence written in red ink.

"It's Eli's handwriting," Kathy explained, still smiling. "Denise must have read it."

It curved around the text and down the edge of the paper in a question mark, in ink that spotted and bled into the cheap paper. Kathy was shocked to feel it coming over her again, the deep chill of reading this for the first time yesterday, what she took to be some secret code passed between her husband and his now-dead lover. That bad, boyish cursive she recognized so well:

I knew you would read this, and I wanted to tell you what I never could say somehow . . . that you're my life's great love.

Kathy watched her friend's reaction, a look of pity that she wanted to shake free from the woman's face, shatter like a mask. She recalled sitting in her apartment in L.A. just the day before, sitting in the chair and staring at this page. *Everything*, she had thought with horror then. *Everything is haunted.*

"Look at the bottom," she said quietly. Kathy herself had not noticed this at first. She had put the book down on her chest with the strangest feeling of sorrow because, as always with her, she loved to watch her own reactions. Part of her stayed in that chair, and part of her moved to a seat across the room where she watched the body stiffening as it stopped the sobs from coming, the glasses removed and held out in one shaking hand, the teeth clenched so tightly that the bones of the jaw, on either side of her face, appeared beneath the skin. She knew books often held these extraliterary objects—pressed flowers, bent photographs, dollars used as bookmarks—but she had never before come across anything more than an old receipt. Here, however, she could touch Eli's old note, and it was surprising how—though she had known about his indifference to her, though she had felt it, had heard him all but tell her—it had never been real until now. Ideas were changeable, but this was not. Her old husband— with this short phrase, with the prick of each letter, he had tattooed his feelings on time's rough skin and now it could not ever be removed. In a way, Kathy enjoyed the image: time, tanned and burly, covered with these foolish admissions that people would come to regret, flexing a muscle to make some dead love dance. Eli had made so many bad mistakes. It was only hours later that Kathy, her forehead wringing with anger, found herself in that chair once again, bent over, paging through the book to find that curve of fiery letters, and noticed, there near the bottom, a figure made nearly indecipherable by the bleeding of the ink: *3-65.*

"It's a date?" Rita asked, blinking to make out the numbers.

Kathy's expression didn't change, but she pulled the book from her friend's fingers and shut it, holding it flat against the tabletop. "March of 1965. We were very young. We were on a boat then, headed toward an island."

"He wrote it for her twenty-five years ago. I don't understand."

Kathy looked out the window. The fog sat overhead in heaps, like snow. "It took me a moment. It's funny, his 'life's great love.' He didn't write that for her at all," she said. Kathy stood up to go to the ladies' room and crumpled her napkin onto the table. It unfolded like a poppy. She felt her expression weakening, so she looked away from her friend for a moment while she composed herself. She did not cry in front of people, not even Rita, and especially not over something that had happened so long ago. She turned back to her friend with a calm appearance under her glasses.

"It was for me," she said. "For me."

It was time to spread the ashes.

"Shall we begin?" Dr. Manday said, and Lydia couldn't believe the callousness of this old man. First to steal her father's star. Then to bring reporters to record it all. Then to look at his watch, smile, and shove the urn over the edge.

And there was Dr. Spivak, bundled against the wall, a round and bald man in a too-hot jacket sweating through the day, his hand outstretched as red ants marched across his fingers, jostling each other as they climbed over the mark where he'd once worn a ring. He had noticed it on her, as well, that empty left hand. It was strange to think of him without Mrs. Spivak at his side, but so much time had passed, and she supposed he was happy. A new woman, he'd told her, and a new ring on that finger soon. What was the name, the fiancée he mentioned? Some girlish name. Jenny?

Some of the men began to introduce themselves. She tried to be polite, smiling and shaking hands and nodding, listening to the little stories they told about when they'd seen her at a party, dancing, or read to her when she was too little to sit out all night under the stars. She had been beautiful, then, they told her, a little wild and distracted but adorable. And they repeated, these men, how much her father loved her. She watched them telling her this. They were the same. The same as she remembered: brilliant, careless men playing at conversation the way a drunk would play at darts, tossing the right phrases at you but somehow, absently, not quite hitting it right. They could smile like this and insult you or confuse you, and yet, how could you blame them? They did not know what they were doing. Mumbling through their gray mustaches, glaring through thick glasses and gesticulating with their broad fingers stained with ink or (she noticed this on two of them) penned with calculations above the thumb. Lydia loved these men and their odd jokes, their clever ideas, the way they reminded her of her father. But were they really "friends" the way she knew friends? Did they call each other up late at night, weeping? Did this tall one here, Jorgeson, did he fly out to surprise this one on his birthday, this one with the ridiculous sideburns? Or were they in love? Jorgeson and the man with sideburns, having their decades-long homosexual affair. Lydia began to laugh.

"See, I told you she'd get the joke. It isn't obscure," the man with sideburns told another.

The other man shrugged and said something about Schwartzchild radii.

Dr. Manday gathered them together with his hands, saying, "How do you want us to do this, Lydia?"

His eyes were on her, and she could tell that there was a specific way he would do it, if she would just smile and gesture to him. Dr. Manday looked as if he'd thought carefully about how to dispose of his best friend's ashes, had drawn diagrams at his kitchen table, shown them to his wife, grinned with satisfaction at their elegance. She could give a gesture, just a simple one, and he would set his whole plan in motion. After all, he had choreographed everything else about the weekend. She had seen him going over the glasses, spot by spot.

"I think we should each say something about my father," she told him, leaning against the wall and resting her hand on her pregnant belly. "And then I'll cast the ashes." She could tell that Manday was not entirely pleased and that he was about to speak, so she added, "I'd like to do that part myself."

"But perhaps we all," the man said despite her statement, "we all could . . ." and here he made a cupping gesture.

"Let her do it herself." It was Dr. Spivak, returned from the wall. He was sucking on his finger; it was red and swollen. An ant bite? Manday grinned. "But some of you have come so far. . . ."

Spivak cut him off with a shake of his head, still sucking on that finger. The wind picked up and blew a curtain of sea air onto the overlook, fresh and bitter. Lydia could see the men lift their heads to let it cool their necks. She closed her eyes.

The heat made her so tired, more tired than she was used to. In New York, she'd stood all day waitressing at different restaurants, running to galleries to coax them with her slides, standing in grade school art rooms and demonstrating some ridiculous project (always with wax or paper plates) in the intense blaze of a New York summer; but here, even at five months, she was fanning herself in any heat, unable to stand for more than an hour, even in running shoes. The whole pregnancy, in fact, felt like a long descent into herself—especially since the father, a musician and waiter, an old boyfriend who had returned for just three months of exceptional but unworkable romance, was not around. It wasn't that he left her; in fact, he had asked her to marry him. They were in the bar where they'd spent so much of their youth in New York, and he had plucked the cherry from her Shirley Temple, tied it into a knot inside his mouth, and placed it on the napkin where, bleeding in a pinkish nebula, it formed a heart, arrow and all. Then he asked her to marry him. She considered, and thought of how she'd loved him when she was so young, in this very bar, standing on this sticky floor. No, she'd said. You need, you need to go away for a long time.

Lydia soon regretted it, but only because it was so hard to be alone and pregnant. Her friends were there, of course, and her mother tried to help by giving advice and making medicinal teas that Lydia refused to drink, since the smell of them nauseated her and because, secretly, she thought they might be potions—a "Rosemary" paranoia—something to make her lose the baby. Ridiculous, but her mother looked so witchy with white hair and that crazy smile. And she knew her— Lydia had seen her wandering in the snow with a martini—she knew that you could not exactly trust this woman with your life. She stuck to bottled water.

And her mother couldn't help with the physical effort of her body. That became clearest on the afternoon when Lydia got the flu, standing in front of those fifth graders and explaining how to make scrimshaw (wax, again, trying to use up the school's overordered supply) and beginning to feel so hot and angry. She had to sit down on the floor. Little girls gathered around her and begged to bring her water. Those next three days spent in bed were the hardest: calling her obstetrician to see what flu medicines she could take, worrying over how it would affect the baby, missing her old boyfriend. He would have stood over the bed and patted her forehead with a cloth. He would have whispered of an easy future. But she'd sent him away.

Lydia told them, "I need to sit. Is there a chair?"

Manday gave an imperious thrust of his arm into the air and a teenager, all in hot black cotton, came running with a chair. The boy scraped it underneath her so forcefully that she found herself losing her balance and falling onto it. The parasol was passed from Manday to Eli Spivak, who held it over her head, a kind eclipse. She felt mildly annoyed at all this attention. It was the fuss of men who didn't know what to do, who were confused and were trying to hide it, a bustle of embarrassment.

"Dr. Manday," she said once she was seated, "maybe you should start."

He stood silent for a moment, the grin still on his face. His grandson stood beside him, clutching his linen pant leg, and the parrot made a fuss back at the staircase. He looked like he might not forgive her for something. "Yes, yes," he said. "Yes, yes, of course."

He turned to the group of men, his bald head exposed now to the sun and sweating, the white hairs lifting from it like heat waves from a boulder. He began what Lydia assumed to be a prepared speech: "Dr. Swift was my best friend. We met in Berkeley in 1949. And Martin was very crazy, and when I first met him he was . . . do you still say this . . . roaring drunk. . . ."

She looked up through the shadow at Dr. Spivak. A thick but good-looking older man, with a red scar on his cheek and unkempt hair growing in a fuzz over his ears. A three-hilled forehead shining in the sun, the forehead of a careful thinker and, her mother would say, the forehead of a jealous man. Manday was still speaking, but Lydia didn't listen. What was it she'd read? That only the jealous man knows perfect love. He knows his own love, and he knows that love perfected in the rival he imagines. What a funny thing to come to her, now, of all times. It was hard to see Dr. Spivak as a jealous or a passionate man. The lines falling from his eyes, his firm mouth as he listened. Whatever had made him ill from those photos had passed. Yes, she thought as Manday went into an anecdote, he was a man who controlled himself.

". . . I remember, I think, I remember Martin my first time at the telescope. I had not slept well the night before because of . . . of a letter from my wife, if you must know . . . and I would nod off and he would hit me! Hit me with the back of a book!"

What had those pictures meant to him? She couldn't guess. Maybe, like her father, a wish to hang on to youth, a longing not to grow old and distant from the world, not to be simply a moon, her father always said, slowly falling out of orbit. As Dr. Manday talked, Lydia stole another look at the pictures. She slipped them from the envelope and felt their sticky edges with her fingers. She flipped past the ones of the old people, the ones that had made Dr. Spivak cry. Those meant nothing to her; instead, she searched for herself. Little Lydia, pouting on the boat, naked in the forest, on that dark overlook playing with the monkey. All taken by Kathy Spivak, who had not come to this reunion, a woman whom she always remembered looking at her, wherever she was—a party, a meeting—looking at her from the shade of a tree, or from a window. It never worried Lydia, not even the time when she noticed Kathy Spivak watching her from this very overlook, following her path through the jungle to where she was supposed to meet Ali Manday. She had always found it comforting. Kathy Spivak, a worried soul watching over her. A kind of mute ghost in her life.

But there were also the pictures Kathy did not take, the ones Dr. Spivak had asked about. She had wondered about these herself, upon seeing them a few months before, after going through her father's things with her sister. Alice had come with a box of her own to store what she desired, and she had ready-made arguments for why she deserved the TV, the silver, the files. Poor strange terrified Alice. But it was fine; Lydia was moving to the farm for her pregnancy. Alice had suggested it, in fact, so Lydia let her take what she wanted. It was pure luck, really, that she found it first: this envelope marked KATHY'S PHOTOS. She had pulled it from the box, puzzled, and then sighed loudly when she saw the first picture and felt the past threading through her. But very quickly she noticed the strange thing. The last three, the ones with Kathy in them, were taken by someone else. That meant the boy had just fallen over the edge, the cries were already coming from below near his broken body, the crowd was swarming to the wall—and someone had grabbed the camera. Someone had turned away from that and toward Lydia, fixing her on film. The face mangled with fright, a frozen cry. Why would someone do that?

Behind her, Alice began to ask about some charts and papers, some scribbles on pink construction paper of a comet, and that's when Lydia choked on her breath, laughing despite herself. It had been her father.

He had taken those and then more as Kathy lifted her up in her arms and kissed her—picture after picture of his little girl at a milestone in her life: the first touch of death. First steps, first words, and this. It must have been laid out logically, just this way, in his mind.

Lydia could so easily see her father, at forty, with his great belly and beard, announcing the death to those gathered in the crowd. He would have seen his little girl standing alone out on the parapet and, noticing a camera abandoned in the panic, he would have considered this a moment not to be missed. It was the same mind that stayed out night after night in search of an irregular comet, some string of fiery beads pulsing against the sky, the mind that knew when to click the shutter. "Take the data now," he had told his eager students over the decades, "and analyze it later." So why not catch your daughter with shock-white eyes? Instead of running to hold her, instead of whispering that life is frightening but fine, why not fix her image on an emulsion?

We were all for study, Lydia had sighed to herself as she looked at the photos from that box, her sister chattering beside her. *All of us, simply for study.* But she didn't think of this with bitterness, the way she might have a few years earlier, back when she wasn't talking to her father, when she considered him a kind but slightly inhuman old man, an antique book with gilt letters and a raised spine. She knew that what he'd felt for her was very simple. The long walks, the pompous speeches, the sad phone messages, the notes filed under *P*, the photos of her wild sorrow—he must have thought that this was love.

"And before I end," Manday went on, wiping his forehead, "I would like each of you to add a little something, a little memory you have of our dear professor. . . ."

The parasol began to flap overhead and the men began to speak, tell their old stories of Swift, re-creating younger versions of him that she couldn't recognize. Lydia tried to pull herself out of memory; while so much of her had changed in the lap of years, she was still a woman who had little interest in the past. In the way that, as a girl, Lydia had acted only in the clear plain of the present, so now, even with a past worth thinking on, and a host of possible regrets, she tried not to linger over an old error or consider how a lost love might have gone differently. Even at night, when she closed her eyes and thoughts played on that screen there, that drive-in movie, even when some sudden image of the past came to her—her mother very kind and sane, her sister getting stoned, some party, some man—she watched it with impatience, as if it were the barely tolerable second feature of her thoughts. She was trying to shake the past from her, but the images wouldn't fall away this time: the boy dropping from the cliff, Kathy's face, and, most prominently now, her father's dead body.

Perhaps Lydia focused on the body because she never saw it. He was cremated immediately, according to his wishes, and the memorial service, which she forced her mother to attend with her, was somehow empty without the body present. Fascinating, of course—three grad students sang a nerdy song, scientists gave speeches, old girlfriends appeared and glared territorially, two of his old communist friends gave sad and rousing speeches about his contribution to the revolution—but, without the body, it felt like an event without a context, like Christmas in the trenches, or a birthday message left on a machine: make-do, and something neither real nor right. "This is ridiculous," her mother had said, wrapped in a garish shawl. "This isn't like him at all." Lydia agreed. So, also according to her father's wishes, but against Alice's, Lydia had arranged this event. This spreading of her father's ashes beneath his (she had always thought of it as his) recovered comet.

"Almost a father to me," Jorgeson was saying now, shading his eyes with a flat palm, "he taught me everything I know about mass spectrometry. . . ."

And while it was obvious to think of him now, with Manday eliciting a few words from each of the gathered men, telling their anecdotes of her father's drunken midnights at the telescopes, or his many women, or his cursing in front of presidents, Lydia had never really seen her father that way, and so was unmoved. It was his broken body that fascinated her. The one that lifted her by the legs so she could watch the fireworks upside down. The one that took those pictures, stomped in fury at her when she was a teenager, and stood as silent as a monument in his old age. She had held his dead body, of course. In the plane, on the way over, crunched in the window seat with her father's urn upon her lap. That was what Lydia thought about as the men gave their memories; not a picture of her father at all—she had catalogued them all the day he died, nearly all the expressions she had never understood—but an image of his carbonized self neatly and heavily contained on her lap for those twelve hours. Being bored and lonely and longing to start some conversation with the ridiculous: a corpse.

Manday was ending his speech with gestures to the heavens: "A scientist who rose from what you call your Great Depression into a place in your university, and a good man, a discoverer and a friend. . . ." A strange way to talk about her father—a bowdlerized version, a life story with the terror taken out—but just the way he would have wanted it. That he grew too blind to read about Halley's Comet, that he made phone calls to all his enemies there at the end, that his life narrowed toward his death, it was so obvious. It needed no saying. Better with just these few brief statements of fact. Yes, she thought, describe him like a star. His ascension, his angle of declination, his magnitude and variability. It isn't how we thought of him, but in the end it's how he thought of us.

". . . and now I wondered if our little memorial could . . . excuse me for this Lydia, I hope it is all right. . . ."

Lydia put the photos away and came out of her head. Dr. Manday had put his mustached face into the violet shadow of the parasol and was looking at her. His eyes were asking a question she hadn't heard.

He continued, "I hope it is all right. Maybe it could, it could also be for one of our students, Dr. Denise Lanham."

"Of course," she said. She instantly felt that she had never liked Dr. Lanham—those funny glasses and hats, the bony nose and superior attitude—but she caught herself and felt ashamed. The woman was dead. How awful to remember her so badly, but those old feelings of distaste were just relics from her adolescence, mammals in the ice, left over from a time when Denise could steal the light from any room and she, Lydia, was left pouting in a corner, unable to understand a woman like that. So different from her mother, a woman who had fought to work in science and won. She felt the baby moving inside her, slipping its legs from whatever too-awkward position.

Dr. Manday turned to the others, out into the sunlight, saying, "There is a rotten irony. Two great . . . great astronomers, and here we are without them. Myself and you, Eli, attached to their comets, Swift-Manday, Lanham-Spivak"—and here Dr. Spivak grinned unhappily—"and that is all we have of them. But, you see, it is . . . they were both friends of mine, as well. I knew Martin was going to die. We all knew, and it was so terrible. But a year ago was Denise. I just wanted to mention Denise."

No one said anything for a moment. The wind lay motionless, as if the sky had shut its shell, enclosing them in mother-of-pearl. A bee began to walk along the parasol, attracted by the flower painted there, and it cast an enormous shadow on Lydia's face, crawling along her cheek in its vain search for nectar, its giant wings shivering across her lips.

Then Manday began to speak, and some others, telling stories of Denise Lanham as a young scientist. Lydia considered that if she'd met the woman now, she might have liked her. Then she noticed something: the parasol above her was quivering. She saw the dark bee struggling, shaken off and, as it fell, stepping its way back into the sky. She looked down from the shade, following the bamboo pole, and noticed that where he held the parasol, Dr. Spivak's hairy fingers were trembling.

"So let us remember her, as we spread the ashes of an old friend. Beneath his Comet Swift," Manday continued humbly, giving the name back at the one moment when it no longer mattered. "Denise and Martin clashed, yes, you know, at times. . . . He was not very modern about women in science. Never trust a comet or a woman, he used to say. . . ."

The wind picked up, pulled at the parasol, and Lydia watched Dr. Spivak's fingers tighten, not shaking now, but firm as the bamboo he held. She heard the paper of the parasol rustling in its struggle, and sun flashed into her eyes until the breeze died down. She felt sure that people, older ones especially, kept sorrows bottled inside them that you'd never guess. Maybe some young girl would look at her, one day, think her life so lovely, and not believe she'd ever felt the kick of a baby she wasn't sure of, sent away a man who loved her, or seen her powdered father sitting on a wall, ants crawling on his aluminum coffin.

"Dr. Manday!" a shout came from the dome. The professor turned and was informed by a shocked-looking teenager that the boat had arrived, the boat from the mainland with journalists from around the hemisphere. The president was greeting them at the dock. Cocktails were prepared. Manday waved the boy away and smiled at Lydia. Yes, it was time to be done.

They said their last words. The sun appeared through the last remaining haze like a disk of pressed powder, and the rest of the clouds burned off, a promise that there would indeed be a meteor party tonight, and most of the men here would later paw through the dark sky (as Swift himself had often put it) "like dogs searching for buried bones." The men stood on the overlook, though, staring stiffly out to sea, their ties being pulled by the breeze and their lashes blinking against the cloud of dust and sand emerging from the beach below. Dr. Spivak pulled at the placket of his shirt with a forefinger and thumb, unsticking it from his chest and letting the breeze cool him. The old telescope creaked in its skin of rust and Manday's grandson, happy that something was happening at last, ran to it and shook off some of the oxidized flakes in his eagerness to point the device out to the ocean. Manday clicked his tongue and the boy came glumly back.

"Did you want to say something, Lydia?" the old man asked. He was clearly pleased with his speech, with how he'd managed to get this done the way he'd planned after all, with the grieving daughter properly silent and seated under a parasol (although, she knew, quite improperly pregnant) and the men passing around the pipe of memory.

"No, nothing," she said and then, moving to stand up, added, "I'd like to do it now." It took the men a moment to understand what she meant, and then they arrived to assist her. Dr. Spivak moved the parasol aside and two of the men offered her their right hands. Grabbing both palms, she pulled herself out of the chair, belly-first, and made her way to the urn.

It was covered with ants. She brushed them off, suffering a few bites that felt like lit matches held against her skin. Below, the fallen ants, in a rage, were inciting the others, and a clump of them reached skywards for her fingers. She lifted the lid and set it on the wall for them to devour.

She waited for the wind. He was in here, her father, in those ashes already trying to blow away in the jungle breeze, nothing like ash from a campfire or a grate, she noticed, but something finer, whiter, more appropriate for what was to be done. He was in here somewhere. Then she saw an errant ant, a blazing red survivor, caught inside the urn and trekking its way across the desert that was her father. A stumble on the dunes, like an old, bad joke. Well, he would go down with the old man, poor fellow. She reached in and got a handful that included the ant, lifted it up and she could see his antenna turning as it noticed the shift in its world. She felt the ashes falling through her fingers, and with a flick of her wrist she sent them into the air.

"Bye, Dad," she said.

A puff of smoke falling into the distance. She scooped again, enjoying the feel of the smooth and weightless substance on her fingers; he was in there. That whole great body that could block any sun, that mind of numbers and facts and coarse jokes, abridged here into a powder. She threw him over the edge. Another puff, and another, a smoke signal out on the old parapet that might have meant anything until the wind changed and the ashes were pulled down onto the beach below. A few larger flakes, ones that had not made it through the sieve or whatever they used at the crematory, floated mothlike in the island air. The sun broke through its veils and hit the water with a crash of light. She heard the old men shuffling behind her, murmuring and watching and, perhaps, saying their own goodbyes. Because this was the end of him.

"Goodbye."

Handful after handful, sowing the air with her father until she was at the bottom of the urn and, weeping quietly now, she upturned what was left into her hand where it made too small a pile. She held her cupped palm over the edge and let her fingers melt and there, the ashes, blown up by a new hot wind, flooded over her shoulder to the crowd of scientists at the wall who shouted in muffled surprise. Lydia felt the ashes sticking to her tears.

She looked out at the plain, bright water. "Oh, Dad."

Kathy sat up, listening. She looked around the café, but the voice she'd heard couldn't belong to anybody here. Just students and old intellectuals like herself and Rita, who had traded books with her— *The Search* for *Nightwood*—and now sat reading happily through bifocals, sipping at a cold café au lait. Perhaps it had been a trick of the ear, or a woman passing on the street with a randomly similar voice, but for a moment, Kathy had felt sound bend the present like a needle pressing through thick leather: first deforming it, then piercing it in just one point, then withdrawing. It was an unpleasant sensation.

"Excuse me," she said. Rita looked up. One of the few friends she had left, and Kathy knew this, and knew you could not "make" more the way people spoke of it. Kathy stood up and gave one of her rare smiles. "I'm going to use the phone." Rita nodded.

Kathy pushed some chairs aside to get to the doorway, where the pay phone hung on the wall. Something was happening to her; she could not explain it, but it had to do with the voice she'd heard, and the note bleeding in the book. She needed to be alone. This wasn't unusual for Kathy, even now, to flee company in order to attend to her mind, and over the years she had worked out sly ways of folding up a little privacy within even the most crowded of rooms. There were balconies, staircases, bathrooms. One could exit to a little-used hallway and stare at the art until some helpful soul came across you and broke the spell. In the café, Kathy calmly used another trick of hers. She leaned against the wall and held the receiver to her ear. It was warm from some recent caller. Bees hummed across the wire and she was alone.

She felt life working backward. The note, that moment on the boat in 1965 when Eli had scribbled so lovingly as he squinted in the sun, she remembered the moment for perhaps the first time ever. Before, when she thought back on that spring day when they were all so young, she thought of the boy who would die later that night; recently, she had begun to search the day for clues of the love affair that grew and died with her hardly noticing. A smile by Denise, a shared sip of bourbon, a tilt of the boat and how they were thrown together, laughing, as Kathy stood by the edge among the coils of rope and watched. But the note—suddenly she remembered. Yes, he had been writing in a book. The shadows of seagulls overhead, passing through the canopy, onto him, the scraps of lemon light across his body as he leaned against the railing and wrote in his cheap paperback. The look of serenity on his young face, the smile at the corner of his mouth—and to think, if she had never read his inked phrase, the smile would never have returned to her. It would have been lost. And the knowledge that she, just the thought of her, had caused it. His life's great love.

Because the way she remembered it was that he gave no sign of love. His eyes glowed when she first undressed for him, and hope thudded behind his lashes when he asked her to marry him, but after that she never thought of him as the man who loved her. He was the man who knew her best, and then he was the man who left her. As a young woman, she was the one who watched him while he worked or thought; she was the one who looked up from her book to catch the light gleaming off his forehead, and felt a horse begin to run in her heart. She never believed that he loved her the same way, especially after the evening when he sat her down and told her everything, but she was wrong. Once, he had loved her. And she had even been there, watching, at that very moment, and it wasn't quite that she'd missed it; she had seen it and forgotten. How funny for things to work backward like this, she thought. For the future to seem so inevitable, for the past to keeping changing form.

The receiver began to talk to her in a recorded voice. She pressed her finger to the cradle's metal tongue and the peaceful hum returned. Alone again. But what Kathy longed for now was not to be alone, but to be back there again, on that boat, with the gulls turning overhead. With the lines erased from their faces, the pains from their backs, and their minds freed from knowing how things would go. To not know that. She thought of the boy she'd met years ago now, a tall dancer with long fingernails, a boy who almost believed in shadow doctors, who had never left his island and, thrown out by shame, took his family fortune to greet the world outside. Thirteen years had passed—what ever happened to him? Kathy could guess. You can't pretend a fortune in the mind will change so easily to gold. A boy like that, alone in Borneo or China: He would be dead by now.

But she remembered his face on the boat that night. Their own faces as they hurried across the South China Sea. No boy fallen from a cliff, no stars streaking across the sky, no lovers made or unmade, all of them simply eager for life to begin. The first sight of that island, Lydia shouting that she could not see it, and Kathy pointing it out for her: a rabbit-shaped clump of green on the horizon. Eli smiling nearby. In his hand, a book with a note fresh in its margin. To be there again.

Kathy held the receiver tight to her ear, tossed a quarter in the slot, and heard the silence and then a mechanical catch. She fished the wrinkled paper from her pocket and dialed the number. A few rings, an expectant hello.

"Yes, Adam?"

Josh sat watching the curtain on the door. Periodically he saw, with each passing car, the shadow of the front gate cast upon the fabric, a set of pointed lines, and it floated against the movement of the headlights, a dark hand waving at the window, until the car was gone and what remained was that pleated canvas glowing from the streetlight. The cold beer bottle was nestled in his lap and he rocked back and forth, singing to the radio. He was drunk, worried; it would happen any minute; Henry would appear any minute; where was he? Giddy from the beer and music, young Josh saw his life as a page of music—he had not been listening, but here were all the struggling chords in order, penned down, and here came this very moment. It had all been building to this; it all depended on this moment. This moment had come first, and the rest trailed before it in a bee-swarm of notes. Something great or terrible could happen now.

Where was Henry? He could feel a pain, a bite in his stomach, the tick of doubt settling there, and he looked around, wondering what he would do if it all went wrong. Call his dad? Move his stuff back, find a job, talk his way back into college? He had made no plans for it; he had bet everything on a lover doing as he promised. The stars will fall on this day, yes, on this one—but what if the sky stood fixed and dark? Another bite inside him.

He thought of his mother again. On that balcony, smiling. He wished he'd told her, then, at thirteen, what it felt like to have that man touching his forehead. Josh now believed she would have held his young hand; she would have understood. Something great rising within you. Something to change your life. He thought, looking back, that he'd seen it once in her. They had gone on one of their long walks where he chattered confidently about the day, giving his impressions, hiding his fears, and they stopped once for ices and once more at a fountain so he could take off his shoes and step inside. She unbuttoned her leather coat and sat on a park bench. It was overcast, calming the shadows and bringing out the age-old stains of the statues and buildings around them, and it was a little noisy because this was the hour for children to be moved about by old women. Josh stepped into the fountain and felt the coins on the bottoms of his feet. Foreign coins, of all shapes, against his skin. He looked back to see if she was watching him, but she had changed. On the bench, his mother stared straight ahead but blankly, absently. Something in her was moving away, and she disappeared for a long time as the water grew cold around his shins, and it frightened him to think, for the first time, there might be something inside her that he'd never guessed. He did not move to break her spell. Young Josh stood in the water and watched his mother sitting there, hands limp on her lap with her purse, face still and shadowless under the Italian clouds. In a moment, she would smile at him and yell, "Get your shoes, time to go,"-and he would leap out of the water, glad to have her back, but that unmoving face was what he would remember. A woman staring at the past, yes, but it was only years later that he recognized it in full: a woman taking a long last look.

Josh was pulled out of memory by a noise. A sound in the doorway, possibly one of the other tenants, someone opening a mailbox, but then there it was: a key grinding in the lock. And there: the elongated profile of Henry's face against the curtain. Josh stood up from his rocking chair and it banged against the wall. The door opened with the shout of his name. His mother knew, somehow—but how?—that nothing was too wonderful to be true.

Eli walked away from them. The old professor's ashes were floating everywhere now, and Eli brushed them from his sleeves, his hair, as he gently clucked to the parrot, which sat silent in its cage. It chewed a dull green feather and watched warily as he passed. He could hear the parasol clattering around where he had dropped it, and he imagined it caught by the wind, rolling around and around, a bamboo compass. The parrot made a sound and Eli looked back, but it just stared at him again with that feather in its beak, the snow of ashes falling faintly around it. He turned and entered the golden dome of the stairs.

It was too much. The day was accumulating in his head in small details—the comet, the ants, the photographs, the bird-of-paradise on the path below—and he wanted to clear them away and start again. The darkness of the stairway did him good; the sound of the others abated here, and just his steps rang out against the walls. Windows appeared at every landing, giving a blazing view of the tea plantations and the spit, and then he was into the darkness again and the damp, clean odor of the stone.

Now he was out into the humid shadow of the jungle. The path lay there before him, nothing more than dry gold grass flattened by passing feet, shining where it left the trees and went into the sunlight, but it crunched satisfyingly under his shoes. A few yards away stood that same grove of sealing-wax palms he'd seen before, bending in the breeze, flashing their gaudy stems among the leaves. He stood and rested. The grass smelled dry and good against the muggy scent of the jungle. For one last time, he let himself pretend things had gone differently. That quantum physics was correct, and all the ways that life can go—it goes there. Not time as a woman, picking up our choices one by one, but as the wind, which touches everything at once. A pact, a sandal stepping from the shade, now.

He heard a rustle in the leaves before him. Two birds flew out of the shadows and landed on a vine, trying to find footing before they looped again into the sky. He watched them as they crossed one particular point of blue. Where the comet lay. It couldn't be seen in daylight, but he of course knew where it would be: just there, beside that cloud. Not far off, but invisible, and moving away. He knew the fate that nobody on the overlook would speak of; he had noted the late arrival, done the calculations, and seen the obvious. It would not return. It was headed on a parabola out of this system forever. The last of Comet Swift-Manday, and of his own, Lanham-Spivak, which he knew now was lost as well.

The shooting stars, though, would return. Every year, on this day, as always, Earth would continue to turn through that trail of dust, and so the meteors would continue as well. But not forever. With no comet to replenish it, the meteor shower would begin to fade. Gradually, there would be fewer falling stars each year, until the day arrived when they were all in their graves—Manday, Eli, Lydia, all of them—and some boy might look up on this night, from this overlook, and notice nothing but the bright, still stars. *The sky,* Eli thought as he watched the hidden comet, *even that forgets.*

A breeze cooled his face and he looked down, staring at the bower of the palms. A few dead flowers had broken loose from a vine and fallen into the wind, sailing a little ways down the path before settling into the weeds where dragonflies rushed and halted in the sun. The jungle was still now; just an orchid smell, and the scent of mud and rotting. He waited, watching the blue trembling shade before him. Parrots jabbered in the trees. It would be now.